HOWLS FROM HELL

A HORROR ANTHOLOGY

PRAISE FOR HOWLS FROM HELL

"Quality horror by true believers—who can write. What more can you ask for?"

—Stephen Graham Jones, *New York Times* bestselling author of *The Only Good Indians*

"No two stories are alike in this carefully curated anthology—a chorus of fresh voices unafraid to search the depths of hell for the darkest horror and gouge it onto the page."

—Laurel Hightower, author of *Crossroads*

"An anthology for horror devotees by horror devotees, *Howls From Hell* first pays homage to horror's venerable tropes, then blows them away."

—J.D. Horn, *Wall Street Journal* bestselling author of *The King of Bones and Ashes*

"*Howls From Hell* gifts us with sixteen imaginative nightmares from some of the freshest voices emerging in horror and dark fiction. The stories in this collection are fierce and delightfully wicked. I'm certain we're going to be reading a lot from these writers for years to come."

—Cynthia Pelayo, two-time Bram Stoker Award-nominated poet and author

Copyright © 2021 by HOWL Society Press

All rights reserved. No part of this book may be reproduced in any manner without the express written consent of the publisher, except in the case of brief excerpts in critical reviews or articles. All inquiries should be addressed to bark@howlsociety.com.

Editing by HOWL Society
Formatting by Alex Wolfgang
Cover art by P.L. McMillan
Cover design by Molly Collins
Foreword illustration by Joe Radkins

Visit our website at howlsociety.com

CONTENTS

Foreword by Grady Hendrix	ix
1. A Casual Encounter by Quinn Fern	1
2. The Pigeon Lied by J.W. Donley	7
3. Manufactured God by P.L. McMillan	32
4. Red Punch Buggy by B.O.B. Jenkin	54
5. She's Taken Away by Shane Hawk	64
6. Suspended in Light by Alex Wolfgang	72
7. Gooseberry Bramble by Solomon Forse	104
8. Clement & Sons by Joe Radkins	114
9. Possess and Serve by Christopher O'Halloran	128
10. Duplicitous Wings by Amanda Nevada DeMel	174
11. It Gets in Your Eyes by Joseph Andre Thomas	187
12. Red and the Beast by Thea Maeve	204
13. The Intruder by Justin Faull	227
14. Sprout by M. David Clarkson	234
15. Junco Creek by S.E. Denton	250
16. A Fistful of Murder by Lindsey Ragsdale	277
Acknowledgments	291
About the Horror-Obsessed Writing and Literature Society	293
End Page	295

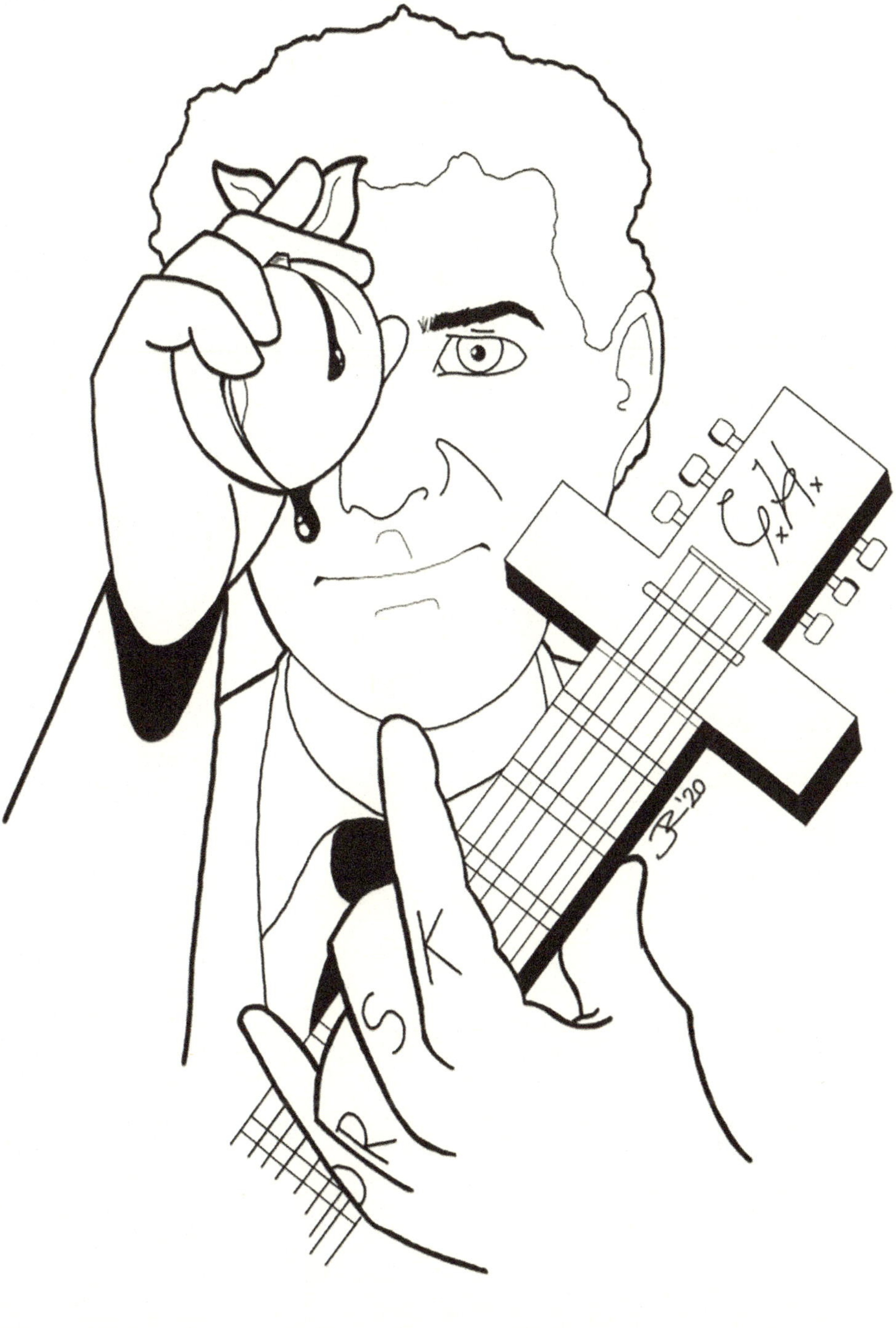

FOREWORD

GRADY HENDRIX

Whenever we slept over at Matt Gibson's house, we always played the game. His house was rickety and wooden, perpetually leaning to one side, surrounded by tacked-on porches, and sunrooms, and sheds with a small forest crammed into any remaining gaps. As soon as we arrived, someone would make popcorn, or find apples, or grab bread, and we'd pour outside into the late afternoon, a squad of 11-year-old boys, disappearing into the bushes and under the house, spilling out across the street, climbing the big magnolia that grew through the sidewalk, ready to play the game.

We called it "Rehash" and it was tag, except whoever got dubbed the Rehash Monster ran after you with a mouthful of food, chewed it into mush, and instead of tagging you, they spit a gob into their hand and pegged it at you as hard as they could. Apples weren't so bad, bread was nasty, popcorn was the worst.

Being disgusting was the point. No one wanted to wash regurgitated popcorn out of their hair and so when you rounded a corner and ran smack into the Rehash Monster your adrenaline legitimately spiked. When you found a hiding place only to realize it was also a dead end and the Rehash Monster was closing in behind you, your panic and terror were real. Who wanted a mushy blob of chewed-up hamburger bun splashed across their face?

We'd play as soon as we arrived and play again later that night, and between the daytime and nighttime game we watched horror movies. We watched *Evil Dead II: Dead By Dawn* and thought it was hilarious, then we made the mistake of watching *Evil Dead* thinking it would be funny, too. We watched *Re-Animator* and *Dawn of the Dead*. We watched *The Texas Chainsaw Massacre* and *The Hitcher*. And so we discovered horror movies the way everyone does: in a pack, at a slumber party, with our friends.

After high school, we headed off into the world and when we got lonely we watched the same movies all over again for comfort, and sometimes someone saw us do it, and that's how we made a new set of friends. Horror sparks questions: *Fast zombies or slow? Fulci or Argento? Name a good Stephen King book from the '90s?* Questions start conversations. Conversations let us know who our people are.

We don't have to agree. Someone makes an argument for *The New York Ripper* as a feminist manifesto, or claims that Joyce Carol Oates is the only American horror writer who matters and I may not agree with them, but I'll listen, because it's part of the running argument we're all engaged in, the one that started before we were born and will go on long after we die: the horror argument. Outsiders aren't welcome, because it's a family argument.

Of course, to go from being an outsider to being part of the family, all you have to do is care. You have to care that someone hasn't read Shirley Jackson so now you have to buy them a copy of *We Have Always Lived in the Castle*. You have to care that they've never seen *Martyrs* so now you have to show it to them. You have to care that you've never seen a Korean horror movie, or read a translation of a Japanese horror manga, or heard of this anthology of South African horror stories, but this person you just met at a party is going to give you a copy and you're going to read it because you care. You care because you're family.

Horror is always about families, sometimes biological, as in V.C. Andrews, but mostly found. Poppy Z. Brite and Anne Rice made their careers writing about outsiders banding together to form ad hoc families that watched out for, and sometimes murdered, each other, just like real families. Every band of scrappy humans standing down a zombie apocalypse, every group of parapsychologists investigating a haunted house, every motley gang of vampire hunters or creepy flock of vampires form a family.

The stories in this book were written by a branch of this family tree. The HOWL Society are a 1000-strong bunch of horror pirates sailing the Discord seas who grew out of a once-defunct subreddit, r/horrorlit, that I stumbled across back in 2011. At the time, r/horrorlit had about 300 subscribers which seemed a shame, so I started posting content, blowing on those few sparks, trying to build a fire that would last. We had some AMAs and slowly crept up to a few thousand subscribers, and they all gathered more fuel for the fire, and it became a massive blaze. I checked the stats last week: 185,000 subscribers.

That's a big family.

There are writers in this family, and readers, there are people who start arguments, and people looking for the name of that book that made them pee their pants in fourth grade. We're there for all kinds of different reasons, with all kinds of different attitudes, but we all care. We care that the end of *Haute Tension* doesn't make any sense, and that Norman Bates is fat in the book of *Psycho* and maybe Hitchcock should have cast a fat actor, and whether or not found footage is over, and which is the best horror novel set in colonial America. We care an unhealthy amount.

We care about each other's birthdays, and bad days, and the size of our to-be-read piles, and I can't tell you how many times I've stood at a con with members of this family while someone without social skills dominated the conversation and when they walked away everyone else shrugged and simply said, "It's cool to see them. They don't have a lot of friends." And in that moment we were that person's friends, just for that moment we were their family.

We all love horror so we all know the one thing we have in common: we're all going to die, *memento mori*, etc. What will live on after us is the argument.

Whether we're huddled around a crackling campfire after the electricity runs out and civilization collapses, or whether we're gathered around a warm VCR in a room full of kids who've just washed chewed-up popcorn out of their hair, whether it's by email, or snail mail, or subreddit, or the dark screens of Discord, the argument will always go on. We're just here to keep the flames alive and pass them down the line. We do it in books, and stories, and opinions, and hot takes, and anthologies like this one. As long as there are people who care about horror, the argument will outlive us all.

A CASUAL ENCOUNTER

QUINN FERN

xxxman_eaterxxx: looking for a good time with a bad boy ;P
ProfCunnilingus69: Watch out, she'll chew you up! Ha ha! ;-) Hello there, lovely lady. Your photo is breathtaking! I think I can provide what you're looking for, as long as you don't mind a more "refined" gentleman.
xxxman_eaterxxx: afternoon professor. how much pussy did u have to eat to get a doctorate?
ProfCunnilingus69: Ha ha! Beautiful AND funny!

I ROLLED MY EYES. Old dudes always have the corniest lines. They're easy catches, though—almost guaranteed. Younger men want to call all the shots, and women of any age are much too wary, so I tend to stick to the older guys. I'd had a few no-shows in my day, but not nearly as many as you'd think. They were so desperate to break the mind-numbing monotony of their middle-aged, middle-class lives. Maybe it was the relentless grind of work and kids and a sexless marriage, or maybe the crushing loneliness of a second or third divorce. They told the same old stories, but I always listened with a sympathetic little pout on my face.

🐾

xxxman_eaterxxx: lol ur sweet :)
ProfCunnilingus69: I'll bet you taste pretty sweet, yourself. ;-)
xxxman_eaterxxx: why don't u come find out?

🐾

WE AGREED to meet at a motel in two hours. It was my go-to place —a mildewing dump, but cheap, and the staff had the wonderful ability of taking notice of absolutely nothing their clientele got up to, so long as the rooms stayed intact. That hadn't been a problem for me in a long time. I'd learned to be very neat.

I got to the room a few minutes early and tossed my sundress over the back of a chair with fraying, faded blue cushions, revealing the silky black slip I wore underneath. Above the lace-trimmed neckline, there was a deep, vertical groove in my skin that began just below the dip between my clavicles. I'd hidden it in my photos with practiced poses—torso turned and arms angled forward, pushing my breasts together in such a way as to disguise it within the shadow between them. Not that a little thing like that would be enough to scare away desperate men on skeevy forums.

I looked over at the door when three quick knocks sounded over the drip and clank of the air conditioner. Right on time. I put on a sexy smirk as I crossed the room and opened the door.

"Professor," I cooed, leaning against the door jamb.

"Wow," he said, watery eyes blinking at me from behind his wire frame glasses. His hair, a nearly translucent strawberry blond, was combed ineffectually over a receding hairline.

"You're even prettier than your picture."

"You like it?" I said, running a hand over my satin hip.

"Oh, it's g-gorgeous," he stammered. "I mean, I'm sure anything would look amazing on you."

I giggled and bit my lip. I touched a finger to the knot of his paisley-patterned tie. A *tie*! What a nerd. A prominent Adam's apple bobbed in his throat as I trailed my finger down his chest. He laughed nervously.

"Come on in, Professor."

I closed my hand around the tie and pulled him over the threshold. He muttered a surprised "Oh!" as he stepped inside. I shut and locked the door behind him. He stood there, fiddling with his tie.

"You're new to this, aren't you?" I asked, sliding my hand down his arm as I stepped in front of him.

"Am I that obvious?" He laughed again. I took his hand in mine and lifted it, rubbing my thumb over his bare ring finger.

"Not married, though."

"Oh, no," he said quickly. "Not anymore."

"I see."

"Yeah," he said. "It's hard to start over, at my age. It gets . . . lonely."

"Well, you don't have to be lonely tonight."

I stepped forward and placed my hands lightly on his skinny biceps. He was a bit leaner than I liked them, but I was hungry for whatever I could get.

"So," he said, clearing his throat. "Do you—is this something you do often? You're so beautiful. I just . . . I'm surprised I'm your type."

I shrugged.

"I enjoy the company of older men." I lowered my voice, as if revealing a secret. "Must be daddy issues."

He chuckled. "It's, um, Ron, by the way. My name."

"Ron," I said, and then told him the truth, since it didn't really matter, one way or the other. "I'm Amy."

"Pretty name," he said, hesitantly placing his hands on my waist. I stepped a little closer to him, letting my breath play against his neck. There was a small nick from a hurried shave, just beginning to scab.

"Are you really a professor, Ron?"

"I am, actually. World history."

"Mmm," I purred. I tapped the side of his glasses. "I could've guessed. You have the look."

He took the glasses off and tossed them onto the seat of the chair that held my dress. His defenses fell as his arousal heightened, breath deepening and eyes becoming heavy as they traveled over my body. His hands slid up my sides, less hesitant than before. Wordlessly, I lifted my arms, and he followed my lead, pulling the slip over my head. I was naked underneath, and he looked at me with a hunger of his own. His eyes narrowed with curiosity as they traced the line that bisected my torso from chest to groin.

"Your turn," I said, reaching to undo the buttons on his shirt as he removed his tie. When we were both undressed, he cupped a hand around my breast and then, with the other, touched the deep, scar-like mark.

"What happened here?" he asked. I looked down, as if I didn't know exactly what he was talking about.

"This?" I asked, placing my hand alongside his. I shrugged. "I was born with it."

"Oh, I'm sorry," he said. "I hope I didn't offend you."

"Not at all." I draped my arms over his shoulders and caressed the back of his neck. "Hmm. You really are sweet, aren't you?"

He must've heard the little pang of regret in my voice. I held no moral qualms about what I did, having needs like everyone else, but it was more fun when I could be sure they deserved it.

He lifted his eyebrows.

"Is that a bad thing?"

"No," I said. "Just a shame."

The line he'd been tracing with a gentle fingertip opened with the soft, wet sound of parting lips. He flinched and tried to pull away, but my hands clasped tight around the back of his head, nails digging into the scalp beneath his thinning hair.

He opened his mouth to scream when he saw the teeth, but I yanked him toward me, and there was time only for a startled gulp before his face disappeared into the carnassial cavity that had just split the front of my body.

One of a thousand teeth slid into an eye socket, and I slurped at the jelly inside with one of a hundred tongues. I wrapped myself around him, sinking into him like the mouthful of ribeye on the end of that cheating businessman's fork last week.

His muffled shrieks and agonal thrashing vibrated against my spine. The deep, unreachable tickle made me gasp and giggle. His hands fluttered against me, too lost in his pain to strike with any real strength or precision. When his skull split inside me with a hollow melon thud, they dropped limply to his sides.

I was able to savor the rest of him. I chewed slowly, shredding meat and cracking bones. I allowed the flavor of each part to linger—butter-soft marrow and viscous vitreous. Sour bile and copper blood.

I barely spilled a drop.

I sank onto the bed with a sated sigh when I was finished, smiling with one mouth while the other closed.

A loud, drunken laugh from the other side of the thin walls woke me a few hours later. Still groggy from my meal, I stumbled to the bathroom and showered, washing away the scant remnants of the professor—some strands of hair clinging to a smear of dried blood on my torso.

Once dressed, I did a final inspection of the room and used a handful of toilet paper to wipe the few drops of blood that had fallen to the fake wood grain of the laminate floor. I left with the professor's glasses and clothes balled up in my purse. I would toss them in the dumpster on my way out.

At the bottom of the stairs leading to the parking lot, two men kissed furiously beneath a glaring yellow light. I felt a sudden gurgling in my gut as I approached them.

I belched. One of the men stopped to look at me, a curl of hair tumbling over a black-smudged eye, and I laughed, pressing a hand to my mouth.

"Excuse me," I said. The man's twisted frown went slack as he noticed the vertical line above the low scoop of my dress, a noticeable shadow in the harsh light. He smiled crookedly and turned as I passed, just enough for me to see his chest, visible above the deep V of his shirt.

There was a line there, in the skin, beneath the sparse curls of his chest hair. I returned his smile.

"Bon appétit," I said as I walked away.

QUINN FERN LIVES NEAR BIRMINGHAM, Alabama, with her beloved dog and two cats. She has a BA in English literature and is a lifelong lover of reading, writing, and all things horror. She can be found on Twitter @QuinnFernAuthor.

Illustration by Joe Radkins.

THE PIGEON LIED

J.W. DONLEY

All I wanted was a hat. That damned pigeon promised me a stupendous hat—one better than my dad's. A demon crafted that old bowler from the leather of someone damned to Hell for apathy and adorned it with a black harpy feather. Such a fine hat signifies the support of the infernal house of Azazel, General of Pandemonium's Armies. There were only three such hats in the Seattle area. My father gained respect because of it, and he always made sure I knew it was his and not mine. Never would be mine neither. That bastard.

I should've known better when the pigeon wouldn't tell me which house he represented.

"Pay no mind," the pigeon said in a tiny *Goodfellas* voice. "You'll get what you're after. You just gotta kill this guy first. That's all. Easy-peasy."

The possessed bird then shit on the ground and flew away, leaving me to my new assignment. I finished the final bite of my microwaved gas-station burrito before starting the search for Hank Havoline, my mark.

It wasn't long before I found him. They called him Hank the Hole, as I later learned. I knew nothing about the guy at the time. When I spotted him, he was gorging himself at some Chinese buffet in the industrial district. Huge dude. Six hundred pounds, easy. The mousy manager running the place didn't lift a finger when I pulled a knife and slit Hank's throat ear to ear, ending his reign of terror on the chicken fried rice and seafood casserole. The corners of the manager's pointed mustache lifted in a slight smile; I swear he was fighting the urge to cheer when I brought Hank down.

"Give me a five-minute start, then you can call the Five-O," I told the manager as I wiped my knife on a tacky, red velvet curtain hanging near the front door. I flipped the sign to CLOSED on my way out. I didn't need some excitable soccer mom stepping in and going into a hissy panic before I got away.

This whole Hell-adjacent underground thing goes way back—even before the ancient Sumerians. Those must've been some interesting times before Yahweh took over upstairs. Since then, all other *worthy* entities have fought over everything outside the Pearly Gates. Us humans—the lesser playthings of said entities—infected the world like rampant lice, leaving very little room in the mortal plane. So, all the other powers—gods, demons, whatever you want to call them—fight for control of the only remaining space: Hell.

I haven't been there myself, but I've had a few buddies go down for one reason or another. My friend Bubz went down as a mule six or seven times before he ran out of luck.

A semi-powerful demon from one of the minor infernal houses—he never told me which one—had hired him to filch some totem from a higher house of Pandemonium in exchange for a token hat of representation. The Twinkle Twins ended up getting ahold of him. These aren't your run-of-the-mill demons. They're the most feared and elite tormentors in the underworld, and they work for Lord Baal himself. No one really knows why they're called the Twinkle Twins. Not many survive to describe their appearance. There are rumors that the air around them has a glittery effervescence, as if it's breaking down in their presence.

They fed Bubz to a swarm of bile imps after working him over. I've seen one of those disgusting, diminutive filth-demons in person outside a sewage plant east of Jersey. Poor Bubz. What a shitty way to go. Too bad he didn't get the hat ahead of time; it may have afforded him a touch of protection.

The best, most lusted-after Hell-hat was a fez made from the hollowed-out skull of a bucket-headed demon only found in the hunting grounds owned by Pandemonium's ruling power: House Baal. They painted the bone with the blood of a sacrificed lamb and hot glued a decorative tassel to the top.

There is only one of these beauties on the mortal plane. Lyle Wayworth, the mayor of Seattle, guards it well.

I once knew a guy who tried to steal it. Over the next year, pieces of him were found all over Seattle, from White Center to Lynnwood. A couple toes and his head haven't turned up yet. I hear the bookies are still taking bets on where they might pop up.

My dad, Boss Robb, is a bookie for the bulk of bets with souls on the line in the Seattle area. That's how he built his status—helping the willing to damn themselves.

Me? I was nothing, a nobody trying to find a way to make a name for myself. I've always been good at sneaking into places and stealing things. Over the years, my name slowly shifted from Junior to Little Robber Robb, or Rob-Robb for short. Even when I raked in major bank after pilfering the only known copy of *The Demonicus Grammatica* in the U.S., Dad said nothing. His poker buddies laughed me out of the house. "Oh, look, Rob-Robb did something. Daddy, look what I did!" Those smug assholes, they'll get what's comin' to 'em.

On my walk home, after offing Hank Havoline, I daydreamed of the different possible hats coming my way. I knew it wouldn't be an Azazel. But an Asmodian rib-boned top hat? That would really be something. People would respect me then. At least people who mattered. Especially if it was one with human rib bones and not one of them pig-rib knockoffs.

It was well after dark by the time I made it back to my ground-floor apartment next to the railyards. I stopped at the door. I could hear my television blasting some spaghetti-western shootout on the other side. I didn't leave it on when I'd left that morning. I readied my knife.

I opened the door only slightly, trying to keep it from creaking and announcing my arrival to any possible murderous fuckers inside.

The stench hit me first. It was like the taste of orange juice after toothpaste mixed with a tinge of burnt hair. Brimstone. Had to be brimstone. Dad always told me the smell was different for everyone. It's supposed to be a preview of the little room waiting for you down in Hell. The real shocker came when I opened the door to find Hank the Hole mowing through my supply of potato chips.

He sat on my couch in nothing but a pair of dingy tighty-whities, leaving none of his hairy corpulence to the imagination. He shoved handfuls of chips into a toothy maw freshly formed in the wound I'd inflicted across his throat an hour before. Sheets of blood in various states of coagulation covered his hairy belly. His thin-lipped human mouth remained closed. Light from the old black-and-white TV illuminated the room in a way that only made the blood—still drooling from his slit throat—more vivid. That damned bird didn't tell me Hank was a fucking demon! I promptly leaned over and retched up the gas station burrito I'd had for lunch. The brimstone odor easily overpowered any trace of vomit.

"Little Robber Robb, we need to have a conversation," The Queen's English rasped from Hank's open bloody throat. "You're lucky I know your father. He's a greedy shit, but I like him. I've a cornucopia of jagged cleavers and rusted corkscrews waiting for him down in Hell." A tongue slithered free, hanging from Hank's opened throat like a raw New York strip steak. It flapped between rows of oversized shark teeth, moistening the ragged edges of his throat-lips with fresh blood. "Do come in. Have a seat. This is your home after all."

I wanted to resist. I wanted to turn and beat pavement. I was fine with never seeing any of my stuff again. I could always get more. But demons have powers, and one of them is influence. Hank had dosed his command with a considerable amount. There was nothing I could do but let my legs carry me into my apartment.

I plopped myself down in the beat-up recliner next to the couch. I felt the fake leather upholstery strain as I sunk into the worn cushion.

"Let's get down to business, Mr. Robb. I'm assuming you did not know who I was when you so rudely interrupted my dinner. Also, since I'm fond of your father and do not wish to upset House Azazel, I won't rip you limb from limb. Instead, I will give you a chance to explain your folly, then we will go from there. Please begin." The couch frame popped and groaned as Hank leaned back, waiting for me to speak.

"Well . . ." I fully expected to become an original Jackson Pollock splattered across my walls.

Hank sat up and glared in disappointment. "Spit it out, boy! I don't have time for your sniveling bullshit."

I jumped from sputtering idiot to pleading idiot.

"Oh god! Please don't kill me. It was this pigeon . . ." Hank raised a finger to his throat as if in thought. I continued, "He told me to do it."

I was ready to confess anything that would save my ass. My mind was reeling but still digging for some juicy sin to divulge. Demons get off on that shit. I stole a gold watch from some cancer-patient teen on his make-a-wish trip to the Space Needle a few weeks back. Nah, not horrid enough. I dropped bricks off an overpass bridge with Bubz when we were sixteen. We sent at least one car careening off the freeway and into a ditch. No real carnage. No blood or anything.

"Damn it, boy! What pigeon?"

"I don't know. He wouldn't tell me his name, or what infernal house he represented. He promised me a hat. One better than my dad's."

"Keep talking."

"That's it. That's all I know. He wanted me to kill you."

"So, you followed the instructions of a pigeon possessed by who-the-fuck-knows for a hat of which you know nothing about? What would Daddy think?"

"Not much," I let out a defeated breath. "He doesn't give two shits what I do."

Hank went quiet for a moment. Somehow his throat wound expressed pity.

"Well, fuck him, then. I have an idea who this pigeon may be." He paused to shove another wad of chips into his throat-maw. "Tell you what, you do this little thing for me, I let you live. And, I'll throw in a hat from my house. The House of the Fly is no power to trifle with."

The House of the Fly! I'd heard of them but hadn't come across anyone with a hat signifying that great Hell-house. Most infernal-assassin work is their doing. No one sees them, only the aftermath.

"Your daddy will piss blood if he sees that hat on you." Hank's gut bounced as a boisterous laugh boomed from his chip-filled throat.

I added my own uncomfortable laugh to Hank's guttural guffaw.

"Piss blood!" Hank said again.

Restating his hilarity further fueled his full-bodied laughter. Chip crumbs loosened from his shark teeth and sprayed over his belly.

I continued to laugh with him as my hands numbed from a white-knuckled grip on the armrests of my shitty recliner.

Finally, Hank's laughter subsided, a cue to halt my own.

"I haven't looked forward to something so much since I convinced Jenny to write her damned book to kick off the anti-vaxxers! The Horsemen and I still get a kick out of the reemergence of smallpox."

"Uh ... funny stuff."

The mood was changing for the better. Less tense. Less murdery. I no longer feared my immediate ruin.

"Ah. Good times." Hank leaned forward. He closed his toothy new throat-maw and opened his human mouth. From this came a prissy voice—in contrast to his guttural demon voice, "That pigeon? Most likely Squeak, of House Lilter. Thinks he's hot shit ever since Baal himself granted him a small duchy near the headwaters of the River Styx. He's been overstepping his social position as of late, and with the big election coming up 'down under,' he's looking to make some sort of power play."

The novelty of having a bleeding demon in tighty-whities on my couch was wearing off. I didn't give a shit about politics, not even the politics of Hell. I said, "What's all this got to do with me?"

"What's this got to do with you!? Everything, at the moment. Do shut up and listen, will you? Or I'll renege on our arrangement and paint your walls crimson!" Hank shuddered in annoyance before continuing, "I want you to aid me in reminding Squeak of his place. The little pip only has a handful of supplicants. Bloody hell, his altar piece is stolen from a defunct squirrel cult. You bring me the altar piece from his pathetic shrine, and I'll let you live. The leader of his tiny cult works at the furniture warehouse store down in Renton. I'm sure you'll find the shrine somewhere nearby."

I wasn't surprised by this revelation. There's all kinds of weird shit in that part of town.

"Get it to me by midnight tomorrow and I won't dine on your viscera. That's the deal. Got it?"

"Yes?"

"Good. See you soon Little Rob-Robb." Hank lifted a hand and snapped his fingers. His body disappeared in a burst of blue flame, leaving behind a charred depression in the couch.

I SHOULD'VE TAKEN it all more seriously. My double encounter with Hank Havoline had left me exhausted. After dragging the fouled couch out to the curb, I fell into bed and didn't stir again until noon the next day. The sound of someone hauling away that damned couch woke me from a dreamless sleep.

After the memory of Hank in his skivvies assaulted my thoughts, I decided to skip breakfast. I grabbed my messenger bag and left in search of a bus to take me toward Renton and the Cult of Squeak.

The busses were fairly sparse between the industrial district and Renton. Usually, I have to avoid a few due to rival factions. Officially, I'm not a member of any faction; many of them actively hate me. I've stolen priceless relics and tomes from most. The young Paimon faction beat the shit out of me last month at a bus stop near Gas Works Park. I'd stolen their prized golden camel medallion. I melted it down and sold the gold across every obscure market I could find. My rent is now paid through next year. I had enough left over to cover the medical bills from the beating—plus a stockpile of codeine.

I spotted a few younger members of the local Asmodian faction toward the front of the bus, but they didn't recognize me. They like to show off the stupid Goetic tattoo on their left wrists —a little too close to outright outing the whole Hell-adjacent culture.

The ride was uneventful. The wheels seemed to find every pothole in the city as I went through my bag, making sure I was prepared for whatever trouble came my way. Everything seemed in order: a couple switch blades, some brass knuckles with inverted crosses etched into the nubs, and my ultimate get-outta-anything card—the Treasure Troll. This particular Troll doll had glittery purple hair, matted with dried-out bubble gum.

Queen Regina, the baddest voodoo priestess of New Orleans, had put a curse on this thing. Here's how it went down: Once there was a teenage girl on a school trip to the French Quarter. This girl made the mistake of laughing at Queen Regina, who was asleep on a park bench beneath a blanket of shopping bags. The Queen spotted the brat's bright-haired Troll doll clipped to the back of her school bag and uttered a foul curse.

The following Christmas, after throwing a hissy fit about not getting a purple Discman, the girl began to tear the hair out of the Troll doll. She explosively combusted into meaty bits all over the affluent family's Christmas tree.

The doll eventually made it to my hands, still very much cursed even though it had already finished off its target. I was assured by the infernal shaman I'd bought it from that it had become a massive curse grenade.

I'D NEVER BEEN to Über Furniture Warehouse, but I had no trouble finding it. The parking lot is massive, taking up at least five city blocks. Even with this vast plane of pavement, there still isn't enough parking for all of these yuppies hungry for basic build-it-yourself furniture. To help with this, there is a parking garage at each of the four corners of the property, like guard towers standing watch over a domain of minimalist decor.

In search of Squeak's shrine, I entered the store and left the flow of corralled consumers. I took a shortcut to the cafeteria. Yes. You heard me. There is a fucking cafeteria in the furniture store, and it's famous for its schnitzel. Like I said, I'd never been to the place, but everyone knows about the schnitzel. Über Furniture itself isn't under the auspices of any specific Hell-house, but the meat supplier is controlled by the House of Gluttony, led by a demon named Barnaby the Voracious. The schnitzel is straight-up Soylent Green.

I didn't want any human schnitzel, but surely they would have an untainted bag of chips. What can I say? I really like chips, and Hank ate all of mine.

The cafeteria wasn't busy—too early for the lunch rush. Only a handful of homeless populated the tables, enjoying the shelter from the sun before being run off by management to make room for paying patrons.

I grabbed a bag of Lays and slipped into the bedroom department. I kept my eyes peeled for anyone who looked like a cult leader. They have a bit of a pompous look to them. Even the leader of the minuscule Cult of Squeak had to be completely full of himself.

I slunk to the side amidst the Bobby Bookcases and the Ocho Ottomans. It was a good spot, next to a tall display of bowling ball bags—another odd product for a furniture store. The salty chips were a welcome relief to my empty stomach as distracted shoppers moved past me along the winding path through staged furniture displays.

Across the aisle a couple employees in blue vests slipped out from behind a hanging cloth poster of a woman far too happy about her bedroom set. An odd place for a door, even if it was for employees only. Compared to all the other employees and shoppers, these were, by far, the biggest contenders for cultists. One had long, unwashed hair and wore a braided gold chain draped from his neck. Much too flashy for a warehouse worker. The other guy? He looked like my cousin Reynold. He had to be involved in some weirdo cult, that's the only way to get *that* skeezy-looking—short and bald with only a few strands of hair greased to his scalp and freaky, bugged-out eyes. There was a good chance he wasn't human. But I've seen fuckers more strange that still managed to be human.

I couldn't hear their whispers and, since I can't read lips, I waited. I wanted to see what was on the other side of the poster.

The bug-eyed guy looked over a couple times. I figured he'd seen me. I continued my charade of lounging next to the bookcases and munching chips. He seemed to buy the act and walked off, continuing his conversation with Mr. Gold-Chains.

I waited until they were out of sight before I made my move. After depositing the empty chip bag in a nearby trashcan and a quick check to make sure no one was watching, I slipped behind the large hanging poster. Fluorescent light filtered through the unnerving advertisement, illuminating a beige door with an aluminum knob.

I jimmied the door open. The showroom lights illuminated the downward steps. I pulled out my flip phone and turned on the LED flashlight before clicking the door shut behind me.

As I descended lower and lower, the stairs began to curve to the left tighter and tighter. The materials transitioned from steel and drywall to carved and set stones. I was deeper than any basement had any right to be, even for Seattle and its notorious buried streets.

A red glow and murmurs of conversation crept up from below. I slowed and softened my steps so as not to alert anyone. The murmurs became two distinct voices. One was nasally and suited for radio and sounded like someone from the local news. The other was a familiar New York accent.

I turned off my light and stopped descending once I could discern what they were saying.

"You said this would all go unnoticed. Why the fuck did you go and poke Hank the Hole?" said the radio voice. "I should torch your sorry excuse for an altar, you little pipsqueak!"

"Just wait a minute, Mr. Mayor." It was Mayor Wayworth! And the other voice definitely sounded like Squeak. "I've got this under control. Here's how it is. Now that Hank is all in a frenzy, all eyes are on him, and I'm sure he devoured the no-name fucker I sent to poke him. No way to track this back to you."

It was Squeak!

I wanted to run down there and stomp the life out of that fucking pigeon. He sent me on a goddamned suicide mission!

"I don't like it," said Mayor Wayworth. "If this turns south for me, I'm dragging your lousy name down with me. You hear me?"

I resumed inching my way down the steps. If I wasn't able to kill him, I wanted to at least see Squeak get scolded. Even if it wouldn't be as enjoyable as spreading his bird brains across the stone floor.

"Are you threatening me? The guys will love this. Some mortal threatening me. That's golden!" said Squeak.

"Some mortal? I fucking control Seattle *and* its votes in the next infernal election. I alone decide who remains on the throne in Pandemonium. Try and fuck with me and see how fast your impish ass is thrown in the bile-ducts of the fifth circle."

This was getting good. I figured while they continued their dick-measuring contest, maybe I could slip in and grab the altar piece. I finally reached the bottom of the stairwell. It stopped at a small stone archway, an entrance into an infernal chapel, with a skull carved into the keystone.

If you've never seen one of these chapels, imagine some churchy room like you'd find in the unused halls of a hospital or on the Vegas strip, but with less Jesus and more bloody depictions of demons and sacrifice. Between the pulpit and me were thirteen rows of wooden pews. A fresco of a pigeon wreathed in flame towered above the pulpit. I could only see the mayor, his back to me and wearing his priceless Baal-house fez. The bone was painted a deep blood red, and the tassel hot glued to the top was glorious!

I couldn't see Squeak.

I slipped into the chapel and ducked behind the back pews. Slowly, I snuck toward them, row by row.

"I don't want to hear another pip of this. If one more thing turns sour—if I fucking wake up with as much as a canker sore—the deal is off! I don't want to squander another million dollars to counter some curse. I'll turn you in to Lord Baal myself if it comes to that!"

I was halfway to the altar when the mayor stepped to one side, exposing the altarpiece. In this case it was a badly taxidermied squirrel standing upright and wearing a tiny Seahawks helmet, probably scavenged from a dashboard bobblehead. Hopefully the squirrel-demon cult upgraded when that piece of shit was stolen.

"Chill, Mr. Mayor." Squeak spoke from the dead squirrel, a red glow pulsing in the squirrel's eye sockets to the rhythm of his enunciations.

I guess the little shit had lost contact with the bird he'd possessed and now inhabited the altarpiece.

I slowly worked my way to the right, staying in the shadows.

"You keep your end of the bargain and I'll keep hounds off

your tail," Squeak continued. "Plus, you can't back out, not unless you want to lose a few fingers. You've got good lawyers—surely they filled you in on the escape clause noted on page 283."

"Fine. I'll lay low in my office until this blows over," said the mayor, turning his back to squirrel-Squeak. "When this is all finished, I'll be ready for some real rest. I'm so tired of all of this. Once you wrest control of Pandemonium, none of you assholes will ever see me again."

For a brief moment I thought he'd spotted me. It must've been too dark on that side of the congregational seating. He gazed straight through me, looking like a glorious idiot in that bloody fez. The tacky tassel flopped like a flaccid penis.

"That's what you think . . ." Squeak whispered.

"Excuse me?"

"Oh! Surely you know," said Squeak as I continued to slip closer and closer to the front, ducking beside the pews. "Your soul is already accounted for. It went to auction a few years back. There is a pissed-off demon who paid a shit ton of souls for you. And, from what I hear, he's building a whole carnival of pain dedicated to your eternal torture."

I wanted the fez. Not for me, no. But Hank would surely reward me for such a prize. Nearby was an alcove with an icon painting. A brass candelabra illuminated an image of Charles Manson holding a hand in the anti-benediction, known in the common vernacular as the middle finger. Quietly, I snuffed the flames and removed the candles.

"That so?" The mayor nested his chin in the crook of his thumb, mocking the little demon. "I've got my ways."

This guy really thought he had a way to avoid Hell? I was rooting for him and almost felt bad about walloping him in the back of the head. The impact sent the fez flying.

"Rob-Robb!? Hank should've fucking swallowed you whole!" squirrel-Squeak said in a panic, unable to move his taxidermied body as I stood over the mayor, still holding the candelabra.

"Well," I said, "he didn't."

I picked up the squirrel-Squeak altarpiece and promptly

tripped over the mayor's limp hand. I fumbled the dead squirrel twice before it fell from my grasp and fell into the fires of a sacrificial brazier.

It felt wonderful watching the dry fur burst into flame as the old bones exploded within, until I realized that I'd just burned Hank's prize. My joy quickly soured in the pit of my stomach.

"What have you done?" screamed Squeak as his current corporeal form burned away.

I was supposed to bring the altarpiece back to Hank, and surely the mayor's henchmen would find Mayor Wayworth lying here at some point. Soon after, they would be hot on my trail.

So, I snatched the fez and hauled ass up the stairs. I grabbed one of the bowling ball bags just outside the mattress department and threw in the fez. I paid for the bag then started to ponder how I would find Hank before Wayworth's hired help found me with the most prized possession of the Hell-adjacent criminal underground; not the intended target, but I hoped it would appease Hank and keep him from eviscerating me on sight.

I KNEW Hank would find me by midnight. The real question was where to go in the meantime to dodge all of Wayworth's goons? I avoided major streets and slunk along alleyways, working my way northwest back toward the industrial district, varying my path as I went. I even backtracked a few times, hoping that it would confuse any Hellhounds under Mayor Wayworth's employ.

After swiping some loser's Mariners cap, I headed for the large crowds of Westgate Mall. I knew I stood out among the twentysomethings crowding the area, but there was a small chance the sheer onslaught of people would hide me.

Inside, I slipped into some tacky novelty store and grabbed a pair of plastic glasses, as well as a fake beard and mustache. Not convincing, but it was better than nothing.

Back in the mall corridor I spotted a couple of over-pumped men in too-tight suits prowling the food court. Definitely

Wayworth's goons. A slight red glow escaped around the edges of their Ray-Bans. Hellhounds, not normal goons. The reek of dog breath wafted across the food court. I did my best to avoid catching their attention and merged with the crowds, passing lingerie and chocolate shops.

I made my way out of the temple of economy and into the connected parking garage. It was well lit with bright sodium lights like beacons, leaving no corner shadowed, and seemed empty of all but concrete pillars and a handful of cars. I thought I was in the clear and started looking for a nondescript vehicle to hot-wire. But then I smelled brimstone again.

"Little Rob-Robb!" A gravelly voice reverberated the air in a way which irritated every one of my hair follicles. "You've got something of ours."

I jerked my head around in a panic, trying to find the source of the demonic voice. I was still alone near a couple cars: a shiny yellow Yugo to the left and a rusty green Gremlin directly ahead. The demon materialized next to the Gremlin.

"Hand the fez over, and I'll kill you quick."

Bucky—yeah, this fucker's name was Bucky—was a nasty piece of work. Instead of arms he had bundles of coat hangers and barbed wire jammed into festering wounds where his shoulders should have been. His head, what was left of it, was human, as was the rest of his body. His brain—exposed and only held in place by gravity—looked like unset jello ready to fall from tipping Tupperware.

"Nah. I think I'll hang onto it. Thanks," I said, turning from the demon.

I started walking, ready for a cloud of pestilence or a barrage of hooked barbed wire to come at me at any moment.

Instead, I stopped in my tracks when I heard crumpling metal and shattering glass. I turned and saw the demon pushing and pulling at invisible ropes and clay with his wired appendages. What had been the rusty green Gremlin now crunched and shifted. It grew into something new, something gargantuan. Slowly, the amorphous, metal mass formed into a humanoid shape. A flame sparked within the head, bringing a fiery glow to what would be a face, like a snarling possum with black smoke rolling from its eyes, nostrils, and ears. A mouth glistened with shards of windshield-glass teeth.

"I did warn you," the demon said, "but I'm glad I get to play before you die. It's been so long since I've set one of my pets to work on the mortal plane. 'Such sights to see' and all that shit."

Bucky moved toward me and tripped. His jello-brain then fell out and slapped onto the concrete.

The Gremlin-beast froze. This was my chance to start a getaway.

The Hellfire-fueled Gremlin-beast started sprinting after me. I did have a trick up my sleeve, but it was only a one-time deal. A last resort. But it was all I had.

Bucky retrieved his brain and shoved it back into place as I reached into my pocket and pulled out the Troll doll. I picked up speed running down the ramp to the next level, bowling ball bag in one hand, the cursed Troll in the other. I lifted the Troll's hair to my mouth, gripped the crunchy bubble gum-matted hair in my teeth and pulled down, scalping the doll. I turned and heaved the naked, and now hairless, thing at my oncoming doom.

My heart stopped. In what felt like slow motion, the Troll doll arced through the air between the Gremlin-beast and me. At half arc I could see a glint of confusion in the Gremlin-beast's eyes, a strangely human emotion for a face so inhuman. I squeezed the handle of the bowling ball case and clenched my butt cheeks, preparing for whatever fucked-up surprise was about to unfold.

The plastic toy bounced off of a scrap of sheet metal jutting from the side of the Gremlin-beast's head with a slight plink. Both the beast and I let out a sigh.

Then it happened.

Like from a starfish's stomach, a large sack unfurled from the tiny toy. A maniacal grin spread across the Troll doll's face. The meaty stomach continued to unfold, larger and larger, until it was big enough to envelop the Gremlin-beast. I smiled as the Gremlin-beast's confusion transitioned to terror. Behind the beast, Bucky stood frozen in fear, barbed-wire arms and hands held at the sides of his face in shock, nicking the soft tissue of his exposed brain.

The Gremlin-beast wailed metal-on-metal screams as the top of its head crunched into the stomach. The Treasure Troll then sucked in the esophagus tube like a limp spaghetti noodle before every bit of meaty matter folded and disappeared into its mouth. It then fell to the ground, landing on its two tiny feet. It twisted its tiny plastic neck and looked at both me and Bucky before preparing for its next attack. Bucky must've had a moment of clarity, because he turned tail and hauled ass out of the garage and back into the mall.

The toy didn't give chase but turned back to me, smiling. As a final farewell, it tipped a pretend hat before it opened a flaming chasm and jumped in, never to save my ass again.

The normality of uncomfortable silence returned to the parking garage, leaving me standing alone with the prized fez, still tucked away in the bowling ball bag. My heart was still slowing when I heard a car driving up from a lower level. Relief washed over me when the nondescript sedan drove by, filled with a nuclear family who paid me little mind. It was time to leave before Bucky regained his balls or some other Wayworth goon tracked me down.

I WAS careful working my way out of the mall. The bank clock across the street displayed the time in bold diodes: 8:38 PM. The sun dipped behind the urban forest to the west, and the parking lot lamps were beginning to flicker. I needed to find Hank or get somewhere he could find me, and fast. I decided to hightail it to the Chinese buffet where we first met and lay low. Plus, I was starving. All I'd eaten that day was a bag of chips.

Keeping my eyes peeled, I made my way unnoticed along the sidewalks from Westgate Mall to the strip of restaurants in the industrial district.

I entered the buffet and found a booth, tucking the bowling

ball bag between me and the wall, wary of the handful of patrons picking at plates of greasy buffet food. Any of them could've been possessed by some demon under the employ of Squeak or Mayor Wayworth, but I didn't care. If those folks were after me, they would've already made their move. I was more worried about the ones passing by the large window overlooking my table.

The mousy manager came over, "What can I get you to—"

I pulled the beard down so he could see my face. His voice lodged in his throat, eyes widening in terror.

"—um, drink?"

"Hi," I said. The strands of plasticized hair caught in my teeth as I spoke. "Water is fine, thanks."

The manager walked away and busied himself at the front desk, seemingly avoiding eye contact.

I tore the facial hair away and left it on the table before going to load up on noodles and fried pork at the buffet—bowling ball bag in hand.

Back at my table, I returned the bag to its spot between me and the wall. A glass of ice water sat on the table in a puddle of its own condensation. Around the restaurant, a couple of truckers and a family kept tabs on me while they pretended to carry on with their meals.

Each time the little bell at the front announced a new customer my sphincter clenched—that is, until Hank the Hole entered in all of his corpulent glory, fit as a double bass, no open wound across his throat. Just another morbidly obese statistic.

He looked like a fat-cat businessman with his tailored coal-black suit and the stump of a cigar clenched in a corner of his mouth. I stood without thinking, grabbed the bowling ball bag, and hugged it to my chest.

Hank, a devious smile crossing his face, waggled a hand at the manager in greeting as he passed the host station.

"Fuck this!" the manager screeched before he abandoned his post and left his establishment to whatever was about to go down.

Hank turned to the patrons and subjected them all to the same smarmy smile, and said primly, "Ladies and gentlemen, I'm afraid this establishment is now closed for the evening. Kindly get the fuck out."

Hank then stared straight at me, unwavering with his discomforting smile.

No one budged.

"I said *get out!*"

Hank's throat then split open, revealing a ragged maw, overcrowded with rows upon rows of shark teeth. Blood dribbled down his neck, and he spoke in his much wetter voice, which rumbled and reverberated the air, vibrating everyone down to their bones. Most of the adults in the room, other than myself, screamed and ran for the exit. Strangely, the little boy and girl from the family table remained seated, quietly eating their stacks of pancakes.

Once the restaurant was mostly clear—only Hank, the two children, and I remained—Hank reverted back to his prim British self. Blood had ruined his well-fitted suit, but at least his nightmare-maw of a throat was closed.

"Little Rob-Robb. We have unfinished business. First, please join me in welcoming the Twinkle Twins, Lord Baal's most esteemed emissaries, to this fine eatery. Lord Baal has interest in these proceedings."

I nearly shit my pants then and there. These two looked like a couple of kids eating pancakes. A slight outline of glittering aura clung to their forms as they continued their meal while ignoring everything else.

"You've managed to cause a real kerfuffle," continued Hank before grabbing one of those sugar-coated fried dough balls from a patron's abandoned plate. "Yes, a very real kerfuffle, indeed. I'd say that you are most probably completely fucked," he said between petite bites. "Oh well, it seems things are well out of my hands now that the Twins are here. Please tell me the altar piece is in that bag. Give me this one thing before I leave you to your fate."

"Oh God. Uh—" I stammered. I wondered what Mayor Wayworth had said about me, and to whom. "I sorta burned it.

But—"

Hank's throat ripped open, and his reality-rumbling voice filled all space in the restaurant. "What?" Blood spattered from the ragged wound. The Twins continued eating their pancakes.

Hank stomped toward me shaking dust bunnies free from the ceiling fans.

"But I got something else," I said. "Mayor Wayworth was there talking to Squeak and—"

"Do be quiet! What's in the bag, then? I hope it's good, or else I might convince the Twins to let me tinsel the buffet with your intestines before they drag you to Hell." He stopped only a few booths away, a confused look across his throat and face. "Did you say Wayworth was talking to Squeak? Oh, that's *juicy*." The last words caused the concrete beneath the building to quake. The Twinkle Twins stopped eating, their forks frozen halfway between plate and mouth. "What do you have in that bag?" said Hank from his kinder, posh mouth, his throat still open in awe.

At that moment, I could have squeezed coal into diamonds between my ass cheeks.

Hank looked over to the Twins. A silent conversation, which I was not privy to, flowed among the three of them. The Twins nodded to Hank, and he replied with a nod of his own. I wanted to nod and feel involved in deciding my fate but didn't dare. I'd heard that the Twins like to disembowel folks with their teeth if annoyed.

The Twins turned and smiled at me in a smooth, synchronized motion before evaporating in a puff of smoke.

Hank returned his attention to me, both mouths smiling. "Let's see it then."

My glutes relaxed to a much more comfortable orange-juicing pressure. I set the case on the table next to my overloaded buffet plate and opened it like a giant oyster to get at a prized pearl. Hank approached, reverently. I lifted the heavy bone fez from within. In my head, I heard trumpets and an angelic chorus as I held it out to him.

"That is lovely." Hank spoke each word deliberately with his polished voice, making the moment feel even more regal. "Not what I sent you to retrieve, but lovely, nonetheless." Hank inspected me in silence. "I may let you live after all."

My whole body relaxed, every muscle went from taut and strained to slack as I fell, involuntarily, back into the seat.

It was then that a squad of mercenaries in cheap rental tuxedos burst into the dining room from both the front entrance and the kitchen. They formed a defensive barrier around Hank and me before rushing forward in a highly trained martial assault. I watched in confusion as Hank made short work of the spiffed-up goons. Definitely not Squeak's guys—too highly trained. Squeak could never afford such a crew.

"Mmm," moaned Hank. "This should be fun."

Hank was nimbler than any morbidly obese man ought to be, but he wasn't a man. He shoved me into my booth. I clapped the bowling ball bag shut and hugged it in my lap, watching the carnage rise in intensity around me.

The goons were large men, but still, they stood no chance against Hank the Hole. Like an unfurled bloody flower, inhuman appendages sprang from beneath his finely pressed suit edges and burst the ivory buttons and stitching. Some of these appendages were large like monstrous squid tentacles, others were small feelers, searching for targets the larger arms could grab. Hank was a mass of living spaghetti flinging gore in all directions, blindly ripping men limb from limb. I could only imagine how the carnage looked from outside the restaurant, blood and viscera splashing up against the insides of the windows.

The first man to charge Hank and me screamed in pain as one muscular tentacle grabbed him around the shoulders and another gripped him around the calves. The gristle and sinew popped and gave way as Hank stretched him farther and farther, finally surpassing the breaking point of flesh. The man's screams transitioned from shrieks, to gurgles, to nothing as he pulled apart. The two halves sprayed gore in all directions but somehow missed my plate of noodles and fried pork.

Hank's remaining arms, tendrils, mouths, whatever, dispensed their own destruction to the multitudes who dared continue their failed onslaught. He cackled in murderous glee from both his demonic and British mouths. A hell of a moment, if only I'd had some chips. Everything's better with a bag of chips.

"Okay, that's enough!" a shrill voice cut through the din.

The surviving goons stopped their attack and retreated to the walls and toward the exits, getting as far away from Hank as possible. A pigeon strutted between the crowd of over-polished black dress shoes, like a hot-shit rooster. "Dammit! That's enough! Hank, you're a reasonable demon. I'm sure we can come to an agreement."

"Ah. Squeak! You interrupted my evening exercise. Oh, do keep these tasty morsels coming. It's been a long time since I've had a real workout," said Hank, reabsorbing all of his projected tendrils and returning to his rotund human form, his suit undamaged and impeccable. "I rather enjoyed that. But, I think there's someone downstairs who would like a word with you."

Squeak lifted his wings in indignation. "I don't know what you're talking about. Who wants to talk to me? I'm here to pick up my property. That fucker there," he said, pointing at me with a wing, "stole something from my chapel, and I want it back."

"Oh, he stole *something*. He stole something from your conspirator. The Twinkle Twins are off to bring him in."

I was enjoying the show. It was wonderful to watch the will drain from that possessed pigeon body as I crunched through a fortune cookie.

Hank continued. "You and Mayor Wayworth will make a fine couple down in the bile pits. But I'm a gentleman. If Little Rob-Robb is ready to testify in audience with Lord Baal, we can cut this bit of butchery short." Hank turned to me. "What do you think? Ready for a little trip down under?"

Squeak turned on his little pigeon feet and started bolting for the door, attempting to take flight, but failing to lift off the blood-strewn floor. "Open the door, peons! Let me outta here!"

"You've always been a craven shit," said Hank. He then switched to his rumbling demon voice dosed with ample influence.

His throat freshly torn open, blood running out over his crowded shark teeth, he gurgled, "Bar the door!"

All of the surviving goons, now under Hank's sway, moved to block Squeak from escaping. Even the men bleeding out on the floor and missing their lower halves pulled themselves across the abattoir, their viscera dragging behind as they tried to comply with Hank's order.

Squeak flapped his wings in a final attempt to escape, when one of the mercenaries grabbed him.

"No! You can't do this!" Squeak screamed and squirmed.

I giggled as I cleaned the last bits of pork fried rice from my plate.

"Oh, I wouldn't laugh, Little Rob-Robb. I'm still sore about not getting my prize," Hank said in his prim British voice.

I clammed up and watched as the goons handed Squeak over to Hank.

"Thank you kindly." He then turned to address the room and switched back to his demon voice dosed with enough influence to turn the Pope into an orphanage arsonist. "I am done with you."

The remaining mercenaries still standing—about twelve of them total—pulled their pistols and blew out the backs of their own skulls, adding their blood, corpses, and gray matter to the already gore-flooded restaurant.

Hank again closed his horrible throat-mouth. "What a mess. This should confound the local authorities for a while."

Squeak continued his futile squirming. "Fuck your mothers! Fuck your fathers! Fuck your mother's fathers! Fuck all of you!"

"That's enough of that."

Hank thumped the pigeon with a middle finger, knocking the bird out. He plopped the rag-doll bird in his jacket pocket. "Pack up the fez and come along."

As I stood, Hank clapped his hands. This triggered the bones of the massacred to liberate themselves from the dismembered bodies littering the floor. They clicked and clacked, stacking themselves to form a bloody bone arch between us and the buffet. A human skull slotted itself in the top as the keystone. A slight puff of a fiery breeze—carrying the stench of burnt hair in combination with the taste of orange juice and toothpaste—tussled my sleeves.

A thin, filmy blackness with the sheen of Hellfire spanned the gateway. With the bowling ball bag gripped in my white knuckles, I followed Hank through the portal. We descended from the mortal plane to the citadel at the center of Pandemonium. There we attended Squeak's trial before Lord Baal.

THE TRIAL? You want to hear about the trial? Well, nothing surprising happened. The mayor got away. That poor fucker is freezing his nuts off doing hard labor at a monastery in northern Scandinavia, living on caribou and beans.

I fared well. Hank took all of the credit, saying he sent me as a mole to uncover Squeak's plot with the mayor. Hank decided to let me live, but only if he could call in a favor at a later date. Of course I agreed. You can't say no to a demon of his stature.

Lord Baal offered me the mayor's fez, but I declined. Owning that hat is dangerous.

Instead, Hank gifted me with the hat of his house, even though I'd failed to retrieve the altarpiece, as requested. It was perfect—a green-and-yellow John Deere hat with a Budweiser bottle cap bent over the edge of the bill.

Lord Baal also offered me a couple other boons, which I did not turn down.

First, he put me in charge of Dad's bookie business. I don't do any of the work; I've got underlings for that.

Oh, and my second boon? Hank the Hole acted as a personal escort for Dad and his card-playing buds to my personal toothpaste, orange juice, and burnt-hair room in Hell for a weekend. Since then, Old Boss Robb has left town. I think he's working as a mule for the mafia back east.

Best of all? No one calls me Little Rob-Robb anymore—except for Hank, because he's an asshole. They all call me Boss

Robb, and they all tremble before me as I walk the criminal underground wearing my John Deere cap from The House of Flies.

🐾

J.W. DONLEY, or Joe, was raised in Oklahoma and currently lives with his wife and son in the Pacific Northwest where the foothills of the Cascade Mountain range meet the Salish Sea. He enjoys writing in the weird, horror, and fantasy genres. Growing up he loved reading R. L. Stine's *Goosebumps* books as well as classics like Frank Herbert's *Dune* and J.R.R. Tolkien's *Lord of the Rings*. In college he discovered Stephen King's *Dark Tower* series, which in turn led him to King's short stories and later to books like Mark Danielewski's *House of Leaves* and authors like Clive Barker and Laird Barron. Joe's short story "Gustav Floats" appears in *Dim Shores Presents: Volume 2*, published in 2020. When he isn't writing or reading, Joe enjoys landscape photography, hiking, and fiddling with his fountain pens. You can find him on Twitter as @JWDonley and on his website (JWDonley.com).

Illustration by P.L. McMillan

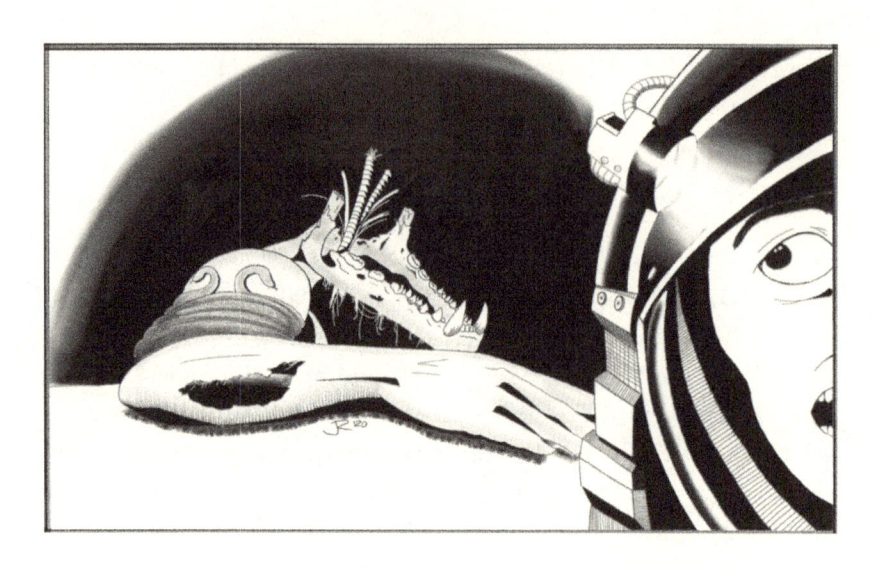

MANUFACTURED GOD

P.L. MCMILLAN

"6.14.497 A.C. This is Professor Gabriela Richmond beginning audio log for the Neo-Cairo region excavation. We have landed at the entrance of the drill site, which is near the northeast corner of what remains of the city limits. The tunnel descends sharply into the bedrock at a five percent grade. To recap, the underground structure was initially discovered by First Officer Maxwell Hart's team during a standard surface scan. Speculation leans toward a tectonic shift bringing the location within range of scanners."

Gab clicked off her tablet and slipped it into her pocket. She surveyed the jagged, broken land that spread before her under an ash-laden sky. From the archive, she had learned that Egypt had once been a place of shifting sands, oases, and endless blue skies. After the tectonic seizures of the Calamity laid waste to the Earth, most cities were reduced to skeletal husks as the bedrock beneath jutted up in thick, shattered cliffs and the once dormant super-volcanoes erupted in a hellish symphony around the world.

The resulting chaos had been as thorough as it had been unexpected. All human life fled. All animal and plant life perished.

Now the Earth was an echoing orb of howling winds, stormy skies, acid rain, and dead seas.

Gab's three students, handpicked from the Advanced Pre-Calamity Anthropology class she taught, had already descended into the complex and waited for her in the first room. Gab was loath to go down into the depths. She had heard reports of crews from the other stations risking subterranean missions, but it was a general consensus on Space Station 18 that all visits should be above ground only. However, this expedition was a once-in-a-lifetime opportunity to take three of her most talented students to an unexplored site, where they—and she—could make their futures by possibly discovering something new.

Her assistant, Lee Renford, nudged her shoulder playfully. Around them, the winds screamed through shattered buildings, around rusted cars, and over hulking rubble.

"Come on, Gab, let's get this over with. I'm still of the opinion that it will be nothing but junk down there, a verified dump of Pre-Calamity garbage," Renford said.

"Hey, we still get paid either way!" she replied, her heart kicking up a notch with excitement.

The entrance was located in a deep fissure between looming concrete mounds, the remnants of Pre-Calamity structures—stores or restaurants based on the vague outlines.

From surface level, the eight-meter-tall tunnel sharply descended, its walls burnt by the intense heat of the drilling laser, which had cooked the sand into brilliant, iridescent glass. Stepping into the threshold, Gab's foot displaced sand, sending it tumbling down the severe slope. As she reached up and switched on her headlamp, Renford gave a theatrical bow, indicating Gab should go first. She couldn't help but smile.

"Let's get this over with," she said and took her first step into the darkness.

The temperatures dropped as Gab crept down the slippery slope, wondering what the air would smell like beyond her mask.

Wondered what history would taste like—burnt stone maybe, dust, sand, age. Something thick, grainy, and lingering. Her breathing echoed back at her as her light illuminated the strange ribbing the laser had created as it had melted the earth.

In her chest, Gab's heart thundered with an unfamiliar excitement. The last new site on Earth was discovered over twenty-five years ago, when Gab was a student herself. Last time, a bunker was found in the area of Earth once known as the United States, in the state of Utah. Gab wasn't chosen to go, and that resentment still burned like acid in her memories, especially since the team had found seven dusty human remains and a multitude of Pre-Calamity artifacts, including several intact books.

Now it was her chance. Her moment.

The tunnel continued downward, the air grew cold and clammy. Gab shuddered but also relished the dramatic change in temperature. On the space station, the climate was controlled. You never shivered or needed to bundle up. It was an experience, something to cherish, this temperature pushing against her boundaries of comfort.

For a while, their boots scraping against the tunnel floor were the only sounds. Then the tunnel bottomed out and widened. It was here that the drill had pierced the side of the structure, allowing Gab and her team access to the site. Renford and Gab stopped at the threshold, their lights casting strange shadows across the walls. Gab sucked in a breath of bottled air. She could feel her hands growing sweaty in her gloves, feel them trembling. Needing his strength, Gab looked at Renford.

"This is it," he said, and she smiled.

He took her gloved hand in his and, together, they stepped into the structure, into the past.

Once inside, they found themselves in a tall room with walls built from cyclopean blocks of limestone and basalt, engraved with hieroglyphics. These images depicted people bowing to towering humanoids with animal heads. Framing these bas-reliefs were hieroglyphics telling a story that Gab could not decipher with her limited knowledge of Pre-Calamity languages.

"This stuff," Renford said, breaking the quiet, "is all so weird. Is this something the ancient Earth people liked?"

"From the reports, it looks like this is prehistoric," Gab replied. "I'd estimate it to be over six thousand years old based on the sample the previous team collected. It's fascinating really. How did the primitive humans build something like this?"

"I still don't understand why Commander Mason thinks there might be something of use down here. If it's really so old, there'll be nothing but dust." Her assistant yawned.

Gab let go of his hand to step closer to one of the walls, her boots crunching sand that hadn't been disturbed in kiloyears, and examined a scene depicting a cat-headed figure directing humans to dig. She turned to the only door in the room, where she heard the sound of distant voices, and led Lee into a narrow hallway, at the end of which shone a hazy yellow light.

Gab followed it into a medium-sized antechamber hewn into the rock, where her three students were waiting for her—Wayne Berry, Ardal Mendoza, and Carla Sloane. They had set up a small floor light, which sat in the corner of the chamber. It was battery-powered, and each unit held eight hours of light.

"Everyone ready?" Gab asked.

"Are we going to find dead bodies down here? Cause I'm not okay with that," Mendoza said, his voice muffled by his helmet.

"I can't believe we get to see something the previous generations never found," Sloane said.

"Everyone, stay alert. I want us to be thorough, but most importantly, careful," Gab continued as she took the lead.

Opposite the entrance hallway was another aperture, leading deeper. Gab stood on the threshold, and her light revealed a primitive staircase that twisted sharply to the right out of view. The steps were nearly nonexistent, worn smooth by the feet of thousands of Pre-Calamity humans and covered by a treacherous layer of sand. Keeping a hand on the wall, Gab focused on her feet and the floor beneath as she crept downward. It soon became evident that the staircase had been carved in a tight spiral, and as she descended farther and farther, she felt like she was riding on a drill straight into the heart of the Earth.

"Shit, I'm gonna be sick," Mendoza called from the back.

"Just focus on my back and not on the walls or floor," Sloane replied with no sympathy.

"Gonna puke on you!" he said in a sing-song voice.

"Make sure you remove your mask first, else you'll be breathing in your own breakfast," Gab called back to them, feeling a little dizzy herself.

As a distraction, she ran a gloved hand over the stone, relishing the sense of stability it gave her. Down this staircase, there were more hieroglyphics and iconography. She felt the raised edges under her fingers. Stopping, she looked up along the walls. Behind her, the others had stopped as well, due to Berry pausing in front of a large bas-relief revealing another beast-headed man sitting on a great throne. Gab didn't like the way it looked; it had the profile of a feral canine with a long, hungry snout and severely pointed ears like blades. Still, she couldn't help but be fascinated, even drawn to it. There was something mesmerizing about its depiction, its features, its malevolent intelligence.

Berry held his tablet up to the wall and scanned the image. He studied the tablet's response as it pinged a search back up the shipboard databases.

"Apparently this is an ancient god that was once worshipped in Egypt. Anubis: God of Death. You can recognize him by the jackal's head."

Berry caressed the foot of the giant in such a revering way that Gab shivered.

"Let's move on," she said.

The others resumed their journey again after her. Gab checked her watch obsessively, tracking the time and their depth. She'd read the reports of teams that died underground in their own investigations—victims of sloppy mistakes or earthquakes—and she refused to be remembered alongside the other failures.

The spiral staircase took them down two hundred meters before it bottomed out onto a large landing. This landing had neither railings nor walls, seeming to float in an ocean of darkness. Gab cast her light back and forth, revealing nothing. The way the sounds echoed led Gab to believe she was standing in an enormous room. Unnerved, she descended another set of stairs that ran along the wall and dumped her and her team onto the floor of this much larger chamber, which was so tall its ceiling was lost to the shadows.

Berry and Mendoza dropped their bags and each pulled out a lamp. Berry set his by the stairs while Mendoza crept farther into the room, albeit hesitantly. His headlamp revealed thick columns lining both sides before the room ended in a tall archway. It was here that Mendoza set his lamp and turned it on. Gab pulled out her tablet, started her recording again.

"We have descended just over two hundred meters and are now standing in another chamber. So far, no evidence of anything we can collect for study. This place is mainly dust and drawings." She ended her recording, putting her tablet away. "See anything, Mendoza?"

"Just a hallway. It goes on in both directions," he replied, a hand on the side of the archway as he peered one way then the other.

Berry cast the light from his headlamp over the walls, illuminating the story chiseled in the stone. He pulled out his expensive Vulpes IX camera—a piece of equipment that was higher quality than those supplied by the SS18's university—and the flashes lit up the cavern in brilliant, blinding snapshots. Despite the fact he had ignored her instructions to use university-supplied gear, Gab couldn't help but appreciate his fervor. He wasn't her favorite student. In fact, she might even say he was her least. He always interrupted during her lectures, arguing her points, but he had top marks, and she'd had no reason not to bring him.

"Mendoza, take Sloane and explore the right corridor. Lee and I will take the left. Make sure to put down the radio repeaters and report back in three hours. I want a lot of leeway when it comes to these battery-powered lights. Berry, do your thing."

"It's so strange. It almost looks like these show—" Berry started.

"Let's go, Lee," Gab said and led the way through the tall archway.

The passage banked down, and Gab's light revealed more engravings: detailed and grotesque closeups of bare-chested men and women with the heads of cats, crocodiles, and birds. Seeing these visages flash into view from the darkness made Gab shudder. Yet she feasted her eyes on this primitive art, relishing in its complexity and passion.

"What kind of crazy ideas did these people have?" Renford said, averting his eyes.

"It is eerie, isn't it? The art is beautiful in its own way though," she replied, touching the fingertips of her right hand against a stern-looking bird head.

"If you say so."

The walls pulled back, and the tunnel opened out onto a narrow catwalk spanning a vast void. Columns ran the length of the catwalk on both sides. Each featured a large jackal head carved from basalt mounted at face level, and each of these heads snarled with its own feral expression. As her headlamp flicked over the heads, the light caused the faces to move, sneering and laughing in turn.

"Watch your step now!" Renford laughed, but Gab detected a slight quiver of fear in his voice.

She wanted to study the faces more but forced herself to look forward, to the edge of her light, keeping her eyes on the catwalk. Heel to toe, heel to toe, she inched over the catwalk—edged on both sides by an absolute darkness that rivaled space. When she stepped into the next room, Gab let out a sigh of relief. Then she almost jumped out of her skin when her short-wave comms crackled.

"Prof? Sloane here. We found some living quarters, but everything else this way has collapsed. We brought the few artifacts we found back for Berry to document. Want us to join you now?"

"Yeah, be careful though. The tunnel opens on a catwalk that connects to the room where we are now. We'll wait for you here," Gab replied.

Renford set down her last light, but the chamber was so large that the vast darkness swallowed its beam. This time she didn't jump when her comms went off again.

"Berry touching base. Really interesting stuff up here. I've cataloged most of it. Anything your way?"

Gab rolled her eyes.

"Yeah there's some intricate but creepy carvings. Mind your step on the catwalk though."

"Careful, boss. Berry might catch on that you don't like him," Renford said.

Gab stretched her arms over her head to rid herself of the shivers crawling over them.

"I'm sure he's used to being disliked, considering." Readjusting her head lamp, Gab crept deeper into the darkness, watching the ground for any drop-offs.

She was concentrating so hard on the floor that she didn't see the metal counter before she knocked her hip against the corner of it, sending bright pain radiating through her torso. Gripping the edge of the counter, she sucked in a breath.

"You okay, Gab?"

She ran her hand over the smooth surface, casting up a thick cloud of dust.

"Did . . . did the ancient humans have this type of metalworking? This seems advanced," she said.

Renford joined her.

"I don't think so. Honestly, based on when this structure was built, the Egyptian people were primitive. They did build the pyramids, which were a marvel at the time, but nothing like this. What do you think it's for?"

"Holy shit," she said, running her fingers over a set of buttons embedded into the surface. "It's a keyboard!"

Each key was marked with a hieroglyph. She passed farther down the counter and found another, and another, yet no monitors or wires, no visible power sources or power buttons.

"Are we sure this is as ancient as we were told?" Renford asked.

Gab made it to the end of the counter and found a smaller, solitary station next to a massive doorway. This station lacked a keyboard like the others and instead was host to four small, unmarked buttons and three dials.

She knew better, she really did, but Gab reached out and tapped the button closest to her.

Nothing.

Feeling slightly reassured, she tapped the next.

Nothing.

She tapped the third.

The ground shivered and dust fell from above as something began to hum deeper underground. The air grew ripe with the smell of ozone, and all the tiny hairs on her body rose as electricity filled the air.

"Earthquake!" Renford hissed, appearing beside her and gripping her arm.

Things steadied, and they stood together, nerves sparking as they waited for something worse. From above them came a buzz, and the room was flooded with artificial light radiating from filament-thin tubing embedded in the stone ceiling. Behind them rose a short chorus of screams. Gab tapped her comms to relay a team-wide message.

"My bad," she said and couldn't help but chuckle a bit.

Renford returned to the counter nearest them. The keyboards were now lit from beneath with a sharp green light; more astounding was the fact that holographic screens had appeared above each one, projected from some unseen source. Renford tapped a button at random, and the screen flickered from green to white. There was a symbol in the middle—a half circle with two bars of unequal length descending from the flat bottom. Beneath it was a flashing bar.

"I think this is for a password," her second-in-command said.

"Well, this is pretty damn awesome," said Mendoza as he stepped in the room, Sloane on his heels.

"If we can somehow get this tech back to the ship, it will be highly valuable," Gab said. "This is something astounding."

The team became complete when Berry joined them, his eyes lighting up.

"I thought those Anubis heads would be the most significant find down here but this . . . this is something else entirely," he breathed, his hands clutching his camera greedily.

"Our tests must have been wrong. No way this is from six thousand years ago," Renford said.

"The tests weren't wrong. I've been carbon-dating the cloth scraps and pottery fragments Sloane found, everything checks out," Berry replied, moving to a keyboard and tapping a button.

"Then how do you explain this?" Renford asked.

Gab pulled up a database of hieroglyphics, placing her tablet next to a different keyboard.

"I think the evidence points to one clear fact," she said. "This facility wasn't built by ancient humans at all. Even the hieroglyphics down here are different. More sophisticated than the versions used by the ancient Egyptians. However, I think I can match them pretty well using this lexicon."

"So, what, aliens did it?" Mendoza said with a laugh.

"If that were true, we would have records," Sloane said. "There's no way we wouldn't know that we had been visited by extraterrestrials."

The others stared at the professor. She matched a symbol from the database on her tablet to one on the keyboard and tapped it. Her work was slow but steady.

"We have records of the Egyptian religion involving humanoid beings with the heads of animals." She tapped another button and the screen flashed green. "We know Egyptians managed to build incredible structures that lasted centuries until the Calamity. Did any of you even take time to look at the stories told on these walls? There have been legends of intervention with the ancient human races, technologies that evolved far past what was logical for human progress of the time. This could be evidence for that."

The login screen disappeared and revealed a complicated mess of symbols, cryptic diagrams, and graphs changing in real time.

"You figured out the password?" Renford hurried to Gab's side, his hand sliding around her waist.

"Simple with all the death-god imagery everywhere. I tried 'Anubis' first, but if it hadn't worked, I would have made my way through all the Egyptian gods hoping for the best."

"Is this something you think you can dismantle so we can bring it back to the ship?" Berry asked.

"Tough to say, honestly. There are no visible seams or screws on this. I can try my laser cutter. Hopefully I don't end up damaging the inner contents," she said, staring at the screen, hypnotized.

"What story was on the walls?" Sloane asked.

"An oblong shape descends from the sky as humans look on from below," Berry said, flicking through the photos on his camera's holoscreen. "Then animal-headed beings mingle with the humans, and the humans fall down in worship. The jackal-headed one appears most often, and in one scene, seems to be working in some kind of lab."

"What's in this room?" Mendoza was standing next to the large doorway at the other side of the room, opposite to the doorway that led back to the catwalk.

"We haven't gone in yet. The revelation of cosmic visitors was a bit distracting," Gab replied drily.

Curiosity, an irresistible pull, drew the five explorers to the large door. Beyond was complete darkness. As one, side by side, they stepped through the mammoth threshold. Overhead came the telltale buzz of the lights as they clicked on, creeping along the tubes towards the back, revealing the contents of the massive room in segments. Nearest to them were three large constructs of tubes, wires, metal, and coils—generators. Beyond that was a space of flooring that soon became splashed with color as towering holographic screens came to life, displaying schematics and anatomy diagrams.

Last to be lit was the body of a giant, lying on its back. Sloane let out a shrill shriek. Gab's breath caught in her throat as her skin became clammy and her hair stood on end.

The giant filled the majority of the room and, if she had to guess, exceeded well over two hundred meters in height. It had the body of a well-muscled man—though void of any genitalia—but, where a head should be, only the bottom jaw of an animal remained—a jaw the size of a small cargo ship. It was coated in a sleek black fur and rimmed with a thin ebony lip, from which jutted fearsome fangs. Gurgling softly, fat tubing ran from the giant's flank, feeding back to the three generators.

"Just what the hell is that thing?" Sloane hissed.

Gab swallowed down the lump of fear in her throat, forcing herself to move forward, though her heart quickened in her chest.

"Is it—was it alive?" she asked, pausing long enough to kneel and place a hand on one of the large tubes that connected the giant to the generators.

It wasn't warm, it wasn't humming. She prayed that meant the power sources were inactive.

Berry moved to examine where the giant's head should have been. Despite her overall feeling of dread, Gab joined him. She didn't like being so close to it, even if it did seem to be dead. Looming over her, the jaw was a crude mockery of what the inside of a mouth should look like. Instead of fleshy folds, it teemed with barbs and lacked a tongue. At the back, approximately where a throat would be, a massive tangle of tubes spewed out onto the floor.

"Is this going to be on our exam?" Mendoza asked, his voice squeaking.

While the majority of the tubing was a pale fleshy color, several were black and swollen. Berry moved forward and, before Gab could tell him to stop, he grabbed the edge of the tube closest to him and gave it a tug.

"It's rubbery. I don't think it's wholly organic. Nothing natural would have lasted this long without rotting," he said as Gab let out a hiss of disgust. "I wonder where its head is."

Something caught Gab's eye, and she leaned forward. At the corner of the jaw, just under some tubing, she could see what resembled a hinge. Reassured by the giant's lack of response to Berry's tug, Gab reached out, tapping it with her knuckles. The material felt fleshy, but underneath, it resonated like metal.

"They *built* this thing?"

"Looks like they hadn't gotten it completely right or were maybe doing some repairs, but I'd bet anything that it was modeled to look like our friend, Anubis." Berry had his fancy camera back up, and brilliant white flashes coated the giant in mini-novas.

"That's the stuff of nightmares right there." Renford joined them.

Gab glanced down the giant's massive flank and saw that Mendoza and Sloane were walking to the far end of the room. It made her nervous to see them so far from the group, though she didn't know why.

"Based on your theory, Berry, would you say that those weird animal-human hybrid gods made this thing?" Renford asked. "For what purpose?"

Gab pulled her Cognitool out and scanned the inside of the giant's maw.

The result that popped up on the small screen made Gab frown.

"This material was Earth-based," she said, offering the tool to Renford. "Circa 4,900 Pre-Calamity. Around the same time the pyramids were said to have been built."

Renford took the Cognitool and re-scanned it himself, standard procedure to check his commanding officer's initial read.

"I can't believe it, Gab! This is astounding—imagine what they'll say once we bring samples back to the station," he said.

Gab stared at the ceiling.

"Looks like the chamber took some damage. We should mention to the commander that an engineering team is needed down here to shore up the stability of the chamber," she said, pointing at a three-meter-long fissure in the thick stone ceiling.

Although she was physically still on Earth, her imagination pulled her up into the stars, into the space station. Her heart raced as she imagined all the accolades she might receive from the leadership council.

"Prof!"

Gab gazed down the giant's side where Sloane stood by its hip, her hand raised, finger pointing up.

"Do those look like impact marks to you, or is it just me?" Sloane asked.

Gab's eyes followed the woman's finger. The ceiling above the giant's knees were pockmarked deeply. The damage implied a struggle. A giant-sized struggle . . . perhaps out of rage, fear, a desire to escape? She looked further along and found great gouges raked into the stone above the giant's chest. Gab jogged down along the side of the giant's jaw, its shoulder, down its right arm, and to its right hand. A chill settled over her body. Its nails were torn, its fingertips raw-looking.

"Gab, I am going to start taking samples," Renford exclaimed. "We should collect as much as we can, and a secondary crew can come back for the rest. This is great though—between this and the advanced tech in the outer control room—we could really start to expand our research, maybe even our technology!"

"There's a room back here," Mendoza called.

"Let the next crew worry about that. We're going to grab some samples and get out of here." Gab was as surprised as the others to hear her voice crack.

A strong, undeniable desire to flee, to escape, consumed her. It overpowered the fantasies of promotions, of money, of talks, and travel to other colonies for lectures. She became convinced that if she were to remove her mask, this whole chamber would reek of an animal's hot musk, the kind of animal that stalked its prey and played with it before going for the killing blow. Her suit beeped, warning her of an accelerated breathing, reminding her to conserve her clean air.

"Get ready to go in fifteen," she barked at Sloane and Mendoza, who were still at the far side of the room, at the feet of the dead giant.

She returned to the head of the creature where Berry and Renford waited.

"This construction, it's—" Berry started.

"We are out of here in fifteen. That's an order."

The two men stared at her.

"We still have six hours left until we're expected back, Gab," Renford said.

Gab's initial desire was to tell them the truth, that she was frightened, and she felt like there was something very, very wrong in this room, but her training took over, first and foremost, so she hid her fear.

"It would be better if we came back with some engineers and biologists with tactical skill sets. Let's clean up and clear out."

Renford, ever loyal, nodded. He plucked out samples of synthetic hair, scraped miniscule segments of false flesh and muscle, sealing them into baggies. Berry, on the other hand, frowned.

"This is an important discovery," he said.

"It's waited for a few kiloyears, it can wait a couple days more," she snapped.

The student turned and gazed up at the gaping throat of the artificial giant.

"A tremor could bring this whole place down on it. We could lose everything."

"A tremor could bring this whole place down on *us*. With or without you, we are leaving."

Berry fixed her with a pure, unadulterated look of loathing.

"Of course, ma'am. I'll wrap up my specimen collection," he said.

The next moment was one she never forgot.

Berry, a look of utter disdain and frustration on his face, took his knife from his belt. He reached out and grabbed one of the tubes projecting from the giant's gullet. Gab realized, a second too late, what the student intended to do. The blade came down, a brilliant arc in the artificial alien light. It sliced through the strange tubing like it was nothing. Then he was holding just a section of it in his left hand, looking down at it with a reverence that bordered on mania.

Reality paused, sucked in, and held its breath. Gab's eyes grew so wide that they ached.

Then it all came crashing down.

The giant lurched, its chest rising, back arched, the lines of its great body contorted in the very image of agony. From the other side of the room, Sloane and Mendoza cried out.

"Run!" she screamed, to them, to everyone, to herself.

Her brain whirled with disbelief and terror. She lunged forward, grabbing Renford by his collar, and yanked.

The behemoth thrashed back and forth, and the whole chamber shuddered with its rage. Its great hands rose and dug into the ceiling, dragging ragged nails across the stone.

Gab looked across the room where Sloane and Mendoza were running for the door.

The monster rammed its knees into the ceiling, like living pistons, causing the whole chamber to shudder, stealing the floor from under Gab's feet with the shockwave. Her mind fizzed out in panic, then she landed on top of Renford.

Screaming.

She didn't know if it was her own or someone else's. Gab looked up. The giant jerked its jaw to the side. If it had had eyes, it would have been looking at her. A massive hand descended. Gab tried to call out to warn the others. Her eyes met Sloane's. The hand slammed down and Sloane was gone. The force of the impact painted the nearest wall in hues of crimson and burgundy. Chunks of bruised purple, shattered bone, and pinkish globs.

Mendoza, the faster runner, was only clipped. He flew forward and slammed into the top of the exit, his body folding around the frame. Gab heard the snap from across the room. Falling to the floor, he screamed in pain, in terror.

"Professor Richmond! We have to go, get up! Get your fat ass up!"

Even just the sound of his reedy voice was enough to snap her back to herself. Berry was yanking at her arm, pulling her off Renford, and then he jerked her assistant to his feet as well. Gab saw the construct's throat working, and the mess of tubing writhed against the floor, making a sickening pitter-patter. The monster rolled to one side, facing them.

A pause.

A moment of absolute certainty of death.

Then the giant braced a hand on the ceiling and one on the floor. Its tubing acted intelligently, like living things, reaching out with a probing hunger as it bent its knees and lunged off the wall.

Gab hadn't even realized she was running until she tripped over Mendoza at the base of the massive door. Renford was already stumbling through the control room to the opposite door that led to the narrow catwalk. Mendoza gripped her leg.

"Please," he said, blood painting his lips red.

Behind her rose a wet, hungry gurgle. Berry slammed into her, shoving her away from her student. She reached out for Mendoza, nonetheless.

"Leave him. He's dead weight now," hissed the student in her ear, and she hated him and was thankful to him that he had made this decision for her.

They raced through the control room to the other side, and Gab could see the catwalk. It was now lit by an ethereal violet light cast upon it by the gaping eyes of the many Anubis heads. She looked back as the giant picked up Mendoza. Her student stared at her, too weak to fight this final horror. Lacking an upper jaw to aid in chewing, the giant pressed Mendoza's back against its single row of teeth under a massive palm and proceeded to grind him back and forth.

The fangs sliced through Mendoza's skin, cut through his spine, tore him to dripping ribbons of flesh, bone, and organ. The blood poured down, and Gab looked away at the first soul-rending howl. She kept her eyes on Berry's back after that.

The remaining three ran as fast as was safe across the catwalk, between the glowing gazes of basalt heads. A meter from the end of the catwalk, the ground shuddered. Gab's right foot landed just on the edge of the catwalk, the boot failing to catch, slipping and plunging downward. She felt her body tilting, vertigo spinning, as gravity took control. Then she managed to fall to her left knee, saving herself, while her right leg dangled in the abyss.

She glanced over her shoulder. The goliath was trying to force itself through the doorway. It managed to jam its jaw through the opening but was stuck at the shoulders. Its fangs glistened with Mendoza's blood. A rope of intestines hung from them like a garland.

Renford knelt in front of her, pulling her up.

"It can't catch us," she said. "We're safe, it's too big!"

"I wouldn't bet on that." Berry was on the other side, his face obscured by his beloved camera as he documented the giant's struggle in the doorway.

Gab stood and ran with Renford to join the student. Behind them came a soft, wet sound.

She didn't want to look, but she did.

The beast was stretching, its body lengthening, slimming, sinuous and sinister as the tubes from its throat suctioned onto the surface of the catwalk and pulled. Its shoulders wrenched back, flattening, and its chest seemed boneless. In this state, it convulsed across the narrow bridge, slowly, but steadily. Like a snake.

"As I thought. Its body isn't made up of a conventional skeleton. I think those tubes can harden and soften at will," Berry said, his voice hushed with awe.

"Fuck this," Gab grabbed both men and jerked them away from the catwalk, into the tunnel.

"We're dead!" Renford cried out.

Gab ignored him, keeping a tight grip on his wrist. The tunnel was endless. Another crash sent chunks of limestone tumbling down. She glanced over her shoulder again.

The long, savage jaw was forcing its way in, moving faster now as if remembering all it was capable of. Several wriggling appendages launched from its throat, whipping toward them with terrifying speed. Gab threw herself on top of Renford, hurling them both to the ground, and the tubes swiped the air above them. She rolled onto her back and pulled her laser cutter from her belt, turning it to its highest setting.

A prayer on her lips, she flung it, and the brilliant blue blade struck true, burning its way into the very tip of the giant's jaw.

The giant reared back, smashing against the ceiling. Gab immediately regretted her decision to attack as dozens of fissures appeared in the stone above her and sand began to rain down.

Berry was already fleeing. Gab pulled herself up to follow with Renford on her heels.

The monstrous abomination thrashed behind her. A tremendous lurch shook the ground. Gab looked back to see that the brute had managed to punch through the wall, the ceiling crumbling from the assault.

The three were back in the large hieroglyphics chamber where giant orb lights mounted along the tops of the columns now shone brightly. With the room lit up entirely, it revealed a secret.

Sprinting to the staircase at the other side of the room, Gab happened to look up and see the rest of the monster's head suspended above her by fine golden chains. It was, indeed, the exact replica of the head of the Anubis figure depicted on the walls: dark, cruel, and intelligent. Its tall, pointed ears brushed against the top of the vaulted ceiling, its open eyes glinted like amber in the dim light that reached its height, and the upper row of teeth were savage porcelain stalactites hanging like guillotines as the head swung in its chains. The head was adorned with a crimson crown that framed its savage countenance. As she stared in awe and horror, its left golden eye flicked down and met her eyes—she could swear that its upper lip lifted in a half sneer.

Berry ascended the shaking stairs, but he stopped to pull out his camera and snap a few pictures of the head. Gab clung to the wall, feet spread for support as she tried not to be thrown from the stairs, screaming at Berry to keep moving.

A billow of dust exploded outwards as the giant's body burst into the room, a tsunami of malevolent flesh.

All the while its hanging head continued to watch the three humans struggling on the steps. Gab shoved at Berry, forcing him up step by step.

Finally, Gab scrambled off the exposed landing into the tight spiral stairs that led to the upper rooms. But any hope Gab had that the claustrophobic space would prevent the monster from following was soon dispelled as, with a horrible grinding noise, a completed snout soon appeared close behind them. The thing had found its head.

The three tumbled over each other out of the stairs into the small antechamber, to the next room, and finally into the lasered tunnel. Gab could see light at the very end of the passage, but it seemed long—too long.

A great howl, a blast of fetid breath with a storm's strength beat at their backs, actually helped them run faster, as the giant called out for blood. Gab's whole body thrummed in terror, convinced she would feel a great hand catch at her and pull her back into the darkness.

She ran, feet pounding on the rippled, faceted glass, while behind her came the whisper of flesh against stone as the monster gave chase. Any moment now.

Any moment it would catch her, catch them. It would grind her across teeth taller than herself, blood pouring down in a crimson waterfall.

Any moment—

—then they were out.

"To the ship! The ship!" Gab screamed.

Behind them, the whole ground humped upward, exploding into the sky as it birthed the subterranean leviathan. The manufactured god darkened the dim, ashen sky. Gab was frozen in a crouch as boulders fell all around her and she watched the beast reform itself from a twisted snake back into a muscular humanoid. Its black nostrils flared, its head lowered, turned, and she met its golden gaze again.

Next to her stood Berry. He stood without fear, camera gripped tight, snapping photos. The giant's jaws opened, and its writhing nest of tubing shot out. Gab grabbed the student's wrist and ran, but they wouldn't be fast enough, they couldn't escape. Boots pounding over rubble, she burst through a cloud of dust, and there was Renford, standing with legs spread wide and his little stun pistol in hand—its charge wasn't strong, meant more for deterring than killing.

"Renford! Run!" she commanded.

For once in their long careers together, in their lives together, Renford disobeyed. He opened fire, and bright red flashes of light glittered the air. She heard the impacts behind her as they struck the tubes.

"Get to the ship and launch!" Renford shouted as she passed him.

She tried to stop, to beg him to come with them, but now it was Berry pulling her forward, and he was stronger than her—or maybe she was too scared to resist. She looked over her shoulder.

The giant stood above Renford, murderous hands reaching, and he had time to make one more shot.

Gab was proud to see that he made it count as the small electrical shot pierced the horror's left eye, exploding it in a splatter of ichor. Then Renford was gone, crushed in an unfeeling, inhuman hand, without even a whimper to mark his passing.

Gab turned away, closed her eyes against the tears, and ran. She and Berry made it to their ship. The monster, perhaps hesitant after suffering such an attack, had not pursued them. It stood, towering over the bedrock crags and ruined buildings, watching them with its remaining eye. Its tubes slithered back up its body, tucking away once more, but its jaw worked as it chewed on its meal. Gab collapsed just inside the small ship, staring back, and as the bay door closed, she could have sworn she'd seen it smirk.

P.L. MCMILLAN is a Canadian expat living in the States after having taught English for three years in Asia. She is a victim of a deep infatuation with the works of H.P. Lovecraft, Shirley Jackson, and Algernon Blackwood. To her, every shadow is an entryway to a deeper look into the black heart of the world, and every night she rides with the mocking and friendly ghouls on the night-wind, bringing back dark stories to share with those brave enough to read them. Her stories have been published in various anthologies, such as *Terror at 5280'*, *Strange Lands Short Stories*, and Hinnom Magazine. Her fiction has also been adapted into audio episodes for Nocturnal Transmissions podcast and NoSleep Podcast. You can find her at her website: plmcmillan.com, on Twitter @AuthorPLM, or on Facebook.

Illustration by Joe Radkins

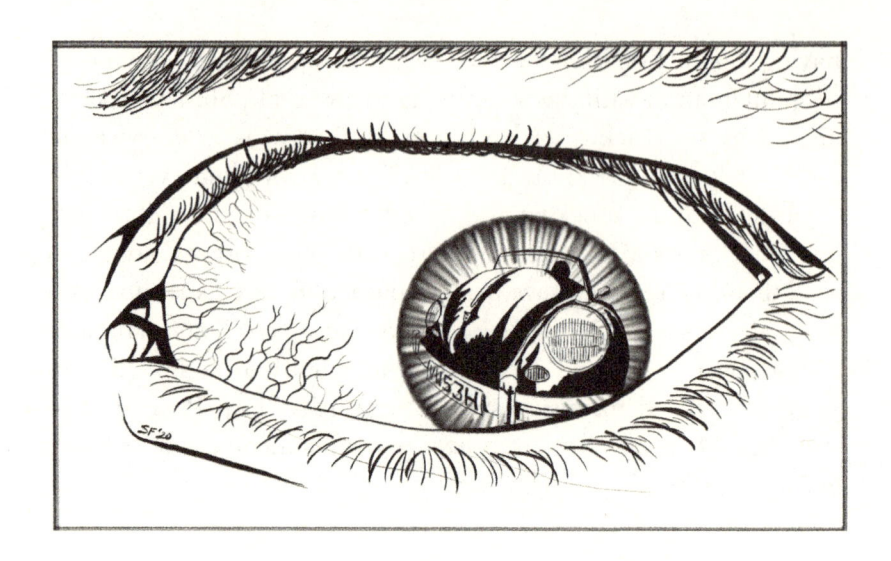

RED PUNCH BUGGY

B.O.B. JENKIN

Glass crunches beneath my flip-flops as I lurch across the steaming pavement. Already shouting, asking if he's okay before I reach the red door. Sun's never been more in my eyes as I fumble for the punch buggy's handle, missing twice before finally curling fingers around metal and throwing it open.

"And what do you think you're doing?" the man snarls.

I stop, stare. He stares back through a film of blood, sporting an oozing gash on his forehead where it bounced against the steering wheel.

"Geez, mister," I say. "I'll call 9-1-1."

"Excuse me?" he snaps. "First you break into my car, then you threaten to call the cops? What kind of holdup is this?"

"I think you're confused. I'm not a mugger—I'm the guy who hit you!"

"You hit me?" He feels his face, smears a red handprint around his wound. "Nobody's ever punched me before. What's your problem?"

"I didn't punch you, I rear-ended your car. You need an ambulance, dude. I think you're suffering brain damage."

Vehicles swerve around us, eager to make the green light regardless of the drama playing out along the side strip. A kid stares, their face pressed flat against the glass to render their gender undefinable, giant teeth squeegeeing the divider. Then they're gone, whisked along and into the never-ending roar of traffic.

"My brain has never been better," the balding man spits. "I don't know why you're bothering me, but the light has turned green and I refuse to engage in shenanigans any longer." With that he speeds off, tires squealing, front door still hanging wide.

"Wait," I cry. "We didn't even exchange insurance!"

Does he flip me off in reply, or is he only trying to close his door? Either way, it slams shut and his ride vanishes into the angry blur of rushing metal known as morning traffic. Leaving me alone, the sole dumbass on the side of a busy street.

I glare at my busted headlight as I stomp back to my crappy-as-crap Toyota. Yeah, the accident was my fault, but I still wanted to swap information. Dude's head was already swelling up around the impact point. If something bad happens, I should be held responsible, or at least made to pay for his paint job—I dinged utter hell into his bumper.

I slump into the driver's seat to shake with anxiety. My very first car accident, and what a weird one. Feels like I'm doing something wrong. Probably supposed to call the police, report the accident, tell them a man with a potential brain injury is out there operating heavy machinery. Then I catch a glimpse of the clock and realize how late I am. Shit!

Twist of key, roar of engine, stomp of gas. *Vroom vroom*, baby! Peel out like a banana and blare pop music from a singer who does the splits. At least, I assume that's how his voice goes so high.

I run into one glaring red light after another. Pass a donut shop whose drive-thru line is backed into the street. Pull over so a procession of wailing ambulances can pass, a too-scarlet fire truck in the rear. Drive, stop; drive again, stop again. A motorcycle passes me in flagrant disregard for the rules of the road. I know bumper stickers say MOTORCYCLES ARE EVERYWHERE but, rather than engendering sympathy, it makes them sound like cockroaches, an infestation in dire need of a pesticide holocaust.

Then, as I pass what's normally a vacant lot, I see it. The red punch buggy, gleaming in the sun like fresh-erupted magma, a flame from the pits of Hell bursting through the ground to say hello to its future denizens. Can't see the driver through the gleam of the windshield but I can feel his stare punching right through to me. I imagine his forehead still steaming blood, pouring waterfalls of crimson down his glowering face.

I almost pull over to see if he's okay, but the guy behind me is tailgating to the point I'm afraid to slow down. Don't want to get rear-ended. But when I peek at my side-mirror, do I see the red bug skittering out of the lot, falling into line in the traffic behind me? Hard to say.

"You better watch out." Not sure why the radio is playing Christmas music in July, but I'm too shaky to fiddle with the dial. "You better not cry." Santa is still *ho-ho-hoing* as I park at my work, his jingle bells chiming louder than ever. Or maybe that's a rattle in my engine. I'll take my car to the shop this weekend, see if I knocked some important internal mechanism out of place.

I get out only to be hammered by the sun. Need A/C! Flee to the shade of the building, gasping a sigh of relief to be bathed in shadow. Traffic roars around me, cars honking messages in Morse code while I wait for the world to stop spinning. When I finally make it through the front door, I've lost half my water weight in sweat.

"Look what the cat dragged in," says Jane, the worst secretary in the history of secretaries. Blabbing as she runs a gigantic file across her sharp pink claws, "Does someone need a shoulder rub?"

I've given up on reminding her I'm gay. If she wants to flirt with a human brick wall, she can knock herself out. "Need coffee." Eyes playing *Where's Waldo?* across the office. "Where's the pot?"

"Broken." She yawns. "Should've hit Dunks."

Except I was too busy hitting a red punch buggy. One I almost swear flashes past outside the window to the parking lot. I rush to the glass, whip the blinds aside. Is that a flash of red to the right? Something edging out of my line of sight, tucking itself away into the parking nook by the dumpster? Can't crane my neck far enough to tell. Should I go outside and check?

"Spaz much?" asks Jane as she stomps a spider once, twice, thrice. "Quit bird-watching and get to work."

"You aren't my boss," I grumble as I follow her orders anyway.

Speaking of bosses: enter Mr. Morris. Red tie dripping down his front like a bloodstain from a slashed throat. Charcoal suit that seems to sink into oblivion, a black hole in my vision. An odd duck, but he pays great. Dude hired me without an interview; apparently, he knew my grandfather through some sort of social club. "Top of the morning," he booms, never a fan of indoor voices.

"Ditto," I say, pretending I'm too engrossed with work to offer more.

Entering interrogation mode. "How are those spreadsheets looking?"

"They're well-spread. And they're definitely sheets."

"Mmm-hmm." He nods like a bobblehead. "And how about the numbers from Tokyo?"

"Hard to say. I'm bad with yen."

"Understandable. Keep up the good work, kid."

Pen scribbling manic spirals. "I'm not a kid."

"You only graduated high school a month ago!"

And college can't come soon enough—assuming I save enough money to afford tuition.

The morning dance plows onward. Papers fly, computers bleep, and eraser crumbs get stuck in the webbing between my fingers. When Jane screams that she saw a hand pressed against the window, Mr. Morris and I yell that it was only a tree branch. She starts crying, so the boss turns up the radio. Nothing like moldy oldies at max blast to make the day drag. I pop in headphones, drowning out Elvis with a hip-hop jam that urges bitches to move, get out of the way. The song features a guest verse from a rapper who did jail time for sexual battery.

"Russia just emailed," says Jane through sniffles. "They want to know how many crates we're sending."

"So tell them," Mr. Morris snaps.

"But I don't know the answer!" This kicks off a minor apocalypse. Luckily, like most movie apocalypses, we save the world at the last minute when a presumed-lost file turns up under the mini fridge. We wipe sweat from brows, pat one another on the back for keeping the machine called a company from imploding.

That's when the power goes out.

"Dammit, Jane," says Mr. Morris. "How did you forget to pay the electric bill?"

"I didn't! I set up automatic payments after the last time."

Outside, the sun is brighter than ever, filtering into the office in giant rectangles of light. Wonder if this means I'll get to go home early. I could use a nap. Or a hundred. Who am I kidding? I'll be playing video games until midnight like usual.

"Too bad about the power," I say, trying not to smile too blatantly. "I'll come back tomorrow when it's all squared away."

"Not so fast," Mr. Morris roars at his normal speaking level. "I'm going next door to see if they have electricity. We need to know if this is a town-wide blackout or if it's only happening to us."

It's only happening to us. Jane and I learn this when Mr. Morris crosses the room, rips the front door wide in the middle of telling us how the show must go on, only for another man to walk through that open door and block our boss's path. A hulk of a man, his figure blotting out the sun that tries to squirm in around him. A man whose face has been painted red.

"Excuse me," says Mr. Morris, "but this is a private office, not a hospital. Please depart at once."

The man smiles. Flashes blood-gunked teeth. Raises an arm.

Bonk!

I don't realize the man is holding a tire iron until he's already demolished Mr. Morris's forehead with it. One blow is all it takes to take the fight out of a man who preaches daily the benefits of a go-getter attitude. Manager material, now barely managing to keep his brains from materializing on the floor as he shakes, twitches. Until he stops.

The intruder's smile is practically spilling off his face. He scans the room before locking eyes with me. Winks. Red crust flaking from his brow, he says, "Thank you."

Then Jane goes absolutely batty, and shit gets slightly nuts. She's screaming, the psycho is charging, and I'm wishing more than ever that I had some coffee in my system. I grab Jane, or Jane grabs me; either way, we're flying as one into the depths of the office building.

Shadows swallow us, one backroom emptying into the next. Bare shelves shake with laughter, but surely it's a trick of the light —or the lack thereof. All the while, pursued by a doglike panting, a voice calling, "Wait!" A bulky body slamming into every table, corner, and doorway in the dark. A demented holler: "I want to reward you for freeing me!"

When my flip-flops try to trip me up, I kick them off and proceed barefoot. As Jane drags me deeper into the intestine of the building, she hisses, "Is this guy an ex of yours?"

"No! I just rear-ended him."

"Yeah. Your ex."

"Rear-ended with my car!"

We pass one perfectly good hiding spot after another. Empty bathrooms and shadowy nooks under desks wave to catch my attention, whispering, "We'll conceal you." As much as I'd love to stop and cower for a while, Jane isn't letting up in her flight. She mutters that there's a rear exit, has to be, she knows she's seen it, dammit, if only Mr. Morris would tidy up once in a while. If memory serves, cleaning is her job, but now's not the time to broach that subject. Pretty sure she's not even talking to me but rather to some invisible third party.

"Fools!" comes a shout overloaded with a preacher's righteousness. "I only want to open you up." Even *he* must realize this sounds wrong because he adds, "To new ways of thinking."

Well, mission accomplished, because I'm thinking all sorts of new things today. Like, who was the first person to punch a buddy over a punch buggy? Did that mythical first blow set off a chain of events which directly led to my current plight?

Jane kicks a box from our path, sends pamphlets scattering. Titles range from DO YOU HAVE SPIES IN YOUR ATTIC? to GERMANY DESERVES A THIRD CHANCE. Wasn't I supposed to mail those out last week? Whoopsie-daisy. I bump my skull on a lamp, and while trying to course-correct, a cluster of pens almost strips me of my balance.

"Here." In the dark, Jane's hiss sounds like a cigarette being extinguished in a glass of water. "The exit is through this next room. Has to be."

Lo and behold, she's right. Broken clocks, twice a day, yada yada. The exit: our big, strapping savior in the wooden flesh. We fly towards it, shoving one another out of the way in attempts to be the first one through. Jane wins; I'm a video game lover, not a fighter. And yet.

"It won't open," she wails, shaking the knob, throwing her body against the barrier. "Why the fuck won't it open?"

"Because I don't want it to," the man answers—the man who is already in the room with us, so close that his spittle splashes my ear. Jane screams, and the surrounding dark rushes for her, shouldering me aside with the ease of a shark gliding between a swimmer's legs in the ocean.

Bonk!

Jane isn't screaming anymore. I don't need my sight to know she's become another crumpled ball on the floor. I clamp my hand over my mouth, hold my breath, convinced the man doesn't know I'm here and will ignore me now.

No such luck.

"Finally." The man yawns. "I thought I'd never get rid of those pests. Now it's just the two of us. How I like it."

The heat in the black room feels like being smothered beneath a thousand blankets. I want to run but can barely summon the strength to say, "I'm sorry I hit your car, but you didn't have to kill Jane."

"She'll live," he says with a sniff. "Or she won't. That's in the universe's hands. For, you see, the universe does have hands. And I have become one of its fingers."

Talk of "fingers" and "just the two of us" has my STRANGER DANGER alarm ringing at top volume. I miss the time when I only thought he wanted to murder me. A hand caresses my cheek and my fight-or-flight instinct hits absurd new heights. Flight wins, obviously.

"Stop!" His massive body fumbling in the hall behind me sounds like tentacles blindly groping for prey. "I thought you understood!" As I propel myself back towards the front of the office building: "You did it to me—I only want to return the favor!"

It's time to blow this clambake. I haven't even started college; I'm too young to die for my job. Now I know how Peter Rabbit felt with the demon-eyed Mr. McGregor hot on his heels. I'm gonna get chopped into stew and fed to this psycho's punch buggy! Papers rustle their agreement in the gloom.

When the hand lands atop my skull, I'm almost not surprised. Almost. "Let go of me, you fucking freak! I'll kill you! You're dead!"

"Dead?" he hisses, fingers tightening around locks of my hair, pulling me in for a lover's embrace. "Death is a myth. A lot of things are. And I never would have known if you hadn't opened me up to it. Loosened my mind. Helped me re-learn how to think and interpret my surroundings. There are so many lies we allow to become facts. Mind over matter is what matters. But words aren't enough to explain it." A rush of wind as he jerks in the dark. "I'll show you instead."

Bonk!

"We've got a live one here!"

Fingers squirm into my armpits, drag me across a hard floor. "No," I beg. "Not again."

"It's okay, kid," a voice insists as multiple hands hold my writhing appendages in place. "You're safe now. He's gone."

That's not what I'm scared of. I want to tell him this, but my head goes a bit funny, leaving the next few minutes blurrier than a piece of stereogram art. EMTs and police buzz about, uniforms rendering them red-and-blue husks. They check my pulse, probe the massive lump that used to be my forehead. Say I'm lucky to be alive, that Mr. Morris is dead. Sounds like Jane is in the same boat as myself, fluttering in and out of consciousness. I wonder if she saw what I saw.

"His name was Joseph Stone," a cop says. "By the time we arrived, the 7-Eleven cashier had him subdued. Not before he smashed eight customers' skulls, unfortunately. From there, we followed the trail of dead and unconscious victims back to your office. Do you know this man? Or why he targeted your place of employment to begin his rampage?"

I know, all right. Know too much. And I can explain it all to this cop if I so choose, but why bother? As the red punch buggy driver said, it's much easier to show than tell.

When I pick up the tire iron that my new friend left behind for me, my mind flashes back to the cascading oceans of white I witnessed while unconscious. Flesh tingles as I recall the sensation of unseen fingers probing through the milky gulfs, the tickling as my brain rewires itself beneath the weight of the knowledge they impart. And that voice! A siren's song that melted my eardrums like butter, dripping into my brain, splashing my synapses with the forgotten history of history, the truth behind the truths around which humanity has spent their entire history building vast mental walls. Mental walls that a manic punch buggy driver somehow toppled.

I smile, thinking of the man's other "victims." The survivors must be waking to the same feelings I'm now experiencing. As I bring the tire iron down to crunch against the back of the cop's skull, I'm hoping the others will feel equally passionate about spreading our new faith. After all, why should we be the only ones who get to bear witness to that glorious, never-ending light?

B.O.B. JENKIN was a best-selling author on his own Earth, but after the apocalypse, he was forced to relocate to this timeline. He is now in the process of trying to republish all the classics his old Earth knew and loved. At present, this anthology is his only publication.

Illustration by Solomon Forse

SHE'S TAKEN AWAY

SHANE HAWK

[File #351b]
[Property of Wichita Police Department]
--REPRINT--
[Date: October 10, 1941]
[Time: 14:15 - 14:24]
[Official Law Enforcement Transcription]
[Transcribed by: Howard L. Phillips]
[Session: 4]
[Doctor: Jay M. Landry, PsyD]
[Patient: Annie Ellis]

JML: It's okay, Annie. Breathe. Let's start over. Can you describe your feelings regarding your sister's situation?

AE: Um, well. I hate it. I hate when she's taken away. Barbara and Father console me by saying she will be back in no time, but she never comes back that fast. It's always a while.

JML: I noticed this toward the end of our last session. Is there a reason you call your mother by her first name? She is your birth mother, correct?

AE: Yes . . . no reason.

JML: All right then. (*Scribbles on notepad.*) And when your sister is gone for all that time, do you feel alone? What goes through your mind?

AE: Well, yes and no. I miss spending time with her and having someone to talk to outside of my circle of friends. But I also cherish my alone time. Doesn't everybody? But now, my skin crawls every time I have to stare at that empty chair at the dinner table.

JML: You and your parents still eat together at the dinner table? That's good. I know you miss her often, but it is good to keep routines. Broken routines could lead to other things breaking apart. We should avoid disunity . . . besides, more leftovers for you, right?

AE: (*Clears throat. Offers a forced chuckle.*)

JML: I apologize. That wasn't very professional of me. I know—

AE: No, no. It's fine. You're trying to lighten the mood. I get it. But no, Barbara rarely prepares dinner anymore. No sharp objects and all. Lately, we have eaten little. Father's wallet can only stretch so far. Barbara has been ordering dinner from White Castle on Friday nights. We've been cutting corners where we can. Thank heavens the country is starting to recover.

JML: Ah, yes. President Roosevelt is doing wonders for us. I'm still sorry. You were saying you cherish your alone time. How do you use your time? Why the word "cherish"?

AE: Oh, I don't know. I sing along to Crosby and Sinatra on the radio, draw in my notebook, or go on short walks. Pay no mind to that last part. My parents don't let me go out anymore.

JML: Because of your sister?

AE: Neighbors stare at our house all hours of the day because of her—well, you know. They want us to leave the neighborhood, but I don't think we can. My sister's medical bills and my therapy with you must run their pockets dry. I reckon it's all very expensive. I hate how they all stare.

JML: Right. Can we broach that subject today? The incidents, I mean. Do you need more time? I figure it's the fourth session, and we're already making so much progress. I understand if you're hesitant.

AE: (*Long pause.*) I guess it's okay now. I've been trying to avoid it, but maybe today is the day. Let's proceed, then. Actually, could you fetch me some water, doctor? I'm parched.

JML: Um, yeah, yeah. Allow me to get you a glass.

(*Dr. Landry exits the room. The door clicks shut.*)

(*Shuffling. A repeated smacking of skin followed by forceful breathing. Hurried and indecipherable speech. The utterances abruptly cease.*)

(*Door clicks open and shut. Dr. Landry's chair swivels and creaks.*)

JML: All right, here we are.

AE: (*Gulps water. Slides glass onto table.*) Thank you.

JML: Let's start from the top.

AE: (*Shallow sigh.*) I never thought my sister would be capable of such things. When we were little, she would always set the best example: good grades, impeccable manners, and she never lied. Somewhere in our early teenage years, we switched. I got on the beam while she received bad marks in school and became a bit of an active crop.

JML: "Active . . . crop?"

AE: You know. A girl who becomes a bit boy-crazy.

JML: Ah, I see. Sometimes the newfangled colloquialisms escape me. Please proceed.

AE: (*Giggles.*) So, yes. Just crazy about boys. Later, she dated a certain boy, a troublemaker. I became infatuated with him too, that amazing head of hair . . . oh well. (*Long sigh.*) My grades were improving, but it was mostly because I used crib notes.

JML: How did that make you feel? Did your status of being viewed as the "good" twin influence you in any way?

AE: I don't know. It's complicated. I'm not sure what I could have done differently. Could I have prevented it all from happening? I don't know. I just know for all my efforts I get bupkis. What's the point?

JML: She did some horrific things. The institution's nurses have said that the chemicals in her brain aren't functioning as they should. Synapses, hormones. She has no control over what she does, and neither do you. Don't blame yourself for any of her actions.

AE: Oh, I don't. I know—she did what she did. There were early warning signs, mind you.

JML: Like what?

AE: Well, she would pull these schoolyard tricks. You know, harmless pranks. Tying kids' shoes together, placing thumbtacks on the teacher's chair, putting itching powder down the pants of schoolmates, pushing—

JML: Down their pants? Goodness.

AE: Yeah, well, that's all innocent in comparison, don't you think?

JML: Well, but—

AE: Then she began stealing greenbacks out of Barbara's purse when she wasn't looking. Peanuts at first, but more money later on. Barbara would snap her cap and scold both of us, but I'd always point my finger at her. She always protested it. She was so over the top. It was almost laughable. Who knows where she spent the money. I saw nothing new in her bedroom or at school.

JML: Laughable? Interesting word choice, Annie. We must remember that your sister isn't well. Her brain doesn't work like ours. It's out of order. God has a plan for all, and we must trust that He knows what's best. Perhaps . . . otherworldly beings influenced your sister. Demons? What else could drive a young female to perform such unspeakable acts?

AE: (*Laughter.*) Demons? You think demons made her nail all the neighborhood cats to trees? You think a little red devil forced her to put rat poison in the milkman's delivery bottles? To spread blood and feces all over the gymnasium walls at school?

JML: Well, I . . . okay, you're right. I—

AE: Do you know the worst thing she did?

JML: I have a list of her incidents in this folder, but I haven't reviewed them all.

AE: She made her boyfriend go to sleep forever. Yeah, the troublemaker one. She said she force-fed him stolen barbiturates. Soon after, he started slurring his words and gasping for breath. Then the euphoria kicked in and he could no longer move. Apparently, his pretty little eyes were dancing against his will.

(*Dr. Landry's chair squeaks.*)

AE: After that, she separated each of his fingernails from their nail bed and superglued them all to his chest in the shape of an M. Then she shaved his head, stuffed the hair into his throat, and watched his body writhe as he choked for air. She then carved M's all over his lower torso with a utility knife. She left a kiss on his forehead with her favorite red lipstick.

JML: (*Loudly clears throat.*)

AE: That's not even the weirdest part. She encircled his body with thirteen kerosene-soaked pigeon heads and set them aflame. And placed a queen of hearts playing card below his groin. (*Long pause.*) I've had dreams—I mean nightmares—about that ever since she told me. Rumor had it he was necking with our school's head cheerleader, Mary Miller, out at Griffin Park. (*Loud scoff.*)

JML: Excuse me, I feel a bit ill . . . (*Slurps from coffee mug.*) That's a level of detail I wasn't expecting. I don't see that on this list. She killed him? (*Shuffling of notes.*) I . . . wasn't told she was the prime suspect for the case. I'm—I'm just a therapist and their communication leaves much to be desired. This is . . . (*Pen scribbling. Clears throat.*) I must, um, report this additional information, you understand? This is above my pay grade. (*Long sigh.*) If she's not proven to be insane, they may execute her for murder. Now, I assure you, she is receiving help from the state's best physicians. I hear they're using novel methods to cure whatever awful disease has plagued her, beguiled her to do these nasty, demonic things.

AE: Yes, she told me before she went away last. I don't have any evidence myself, but I suspect the police can match the lipstick to the one on her nightstand. Maybe it's not a dysfunctional brain.

Maybe she's finally revealed her true self. There could be a bunch of things she's done that we've yet to discover.

JML: Why are you smiling?

AE: I didn't mean to. I don't know. Smiling, I guess, to keep the tears away?

JML: Hmm, yes. Could be your defense mechanism. These mechanisms are things we do to cope with our negative feelings. They mask them. Perfectly normal. I've seen patients smirking when speaking of their children drowning. The human body is not equipped to deal with such horrors.

AE: Defense mechanisms, interesting. Yes, I guess that's why I smile here and there. You said my sister is receiving top medical treatment. What exactly are they doing to her? Last time she went away, they shot electricity into her head. Are they still doing that?

JML: Ah, yes. I see it here . . . her last treatment of electroshock therapy was in June. I don't see another instance of it. That's not to say they haven't done it recently and have yet to fill out the paperwork. Oh, good. They're administering Metrazol—today's first line in mental instability treatment. It's a medication used to induce seizures. They were trying to shake her disease out of her brain. To fix her. Seizures can help rid the body of many illnesses, including schizophrenia. You said your sister has acted like many people in the past?

AE: Yes, she has acted like different people, not herself. Sometimes she would take on an unfamiliar accent or hold wildly different opinions on things. It was strange. It was only me who saw it, though. Whenever we were at school or in front of our parents, she always acted normal. She only revealed that side of her to me. No one else.

JML: Are you all right? Your eye is twitching uncontrollably.

AE: Oh, yes. Quite all right. It has been on the fritz lately . . . unsure why.

JML: Hmm, very interesting. Oh, my. It says here that one of her Metrazol-induced seizures broke a few of her vertebrae.

AE: Doctor, are you allowed to share her sensitive information with me?

JML: Yes, the current law states medical information can be shared among family members, and seeing as your sister is currently incapacitated, I don't see her objecting to it. Do you wish for me to stop?

AE: No, no. It's quite all right. Please do share.

JML: So, yes, her seizures. A pity. And afterward, it appears she suffered from episodic amnesia. (*Inaudible muttering.*) Yes, it looks like they are closer to her cure. She has had no violent episodes or bouts of cursing or crying since her last treatment.

AE: So, she's okay? (*Long pause.*) Do you think I can ever get my sister back? Do you think she will return home?

JML: She's done terrible deeds, monstrous deeds—and if what you've told me is true, far worse deeds than we've realized—she's a diagnosed schizophrenic. I'm uncertain, but I believe she will spend her life in the ward. I'm also not sure about visitations. She's in solitary confinement and on suicide watch.

AE: Suicide watch?

JML: Yes. Nurses and guards take extra precautions regarding their every interaction with your sister. It's terrible and upsetting, and I'm sorry. There's not much we can do about it. She's committed heinous acts. She belongs there and you belong here. You're the good sister.

AE: (*Sobbing. Sniffling.*) Good sister . . .

JML: Oh, dear. Did I put my foot in my mouth again? I sincerely apologize. I have disposable handkerchiefs in one of these drawers. (*Rustling in desk drawer.*) Ah, here we are. (*Shallow sigh.*) In all my years, none of my patients have progressed this much—at least this quickly. You've displayed such moxie today.

AE: (*An increasingly measured voice.*) I hate when she's taken away. And now it sounds like she'll be away forever.

(*Chair legs skid against linoleum floor.*)

JML: Wait, what in—what in God's name are you doing?

(*Shuffling. Shattering glass.*)

JML: Put the glass down. Down this instant! Annie . . .

AE: I don't want to pretend anymore!

JML: Pretend—pretend what? Jesus, Mary, and Joseph . . .

AE: That I didn't do all those things. That I'm the good twin!
(Papers scatter. Dr. Landry's chair screeches and crashes.)
JML: *(Gurgling. Labored inhalations.)* No, no, no, no, no . . .
(Hammering. Door slamming. Scuffling of feet.)
(A drawn out shriek. Indecipherable speech in a guttural voice.)
(Microphone levels peak. More shattering glass. Filing cabinet crashes to floor.)

[End of wire recording]
[Note: Original recording missing three days after initial transcription.]
[File #351b]
[Property of Wichita Police Department]

Shane Hawk is an emerging indigenous dark fiction writer. Shane received a BA in history from California State University San Marcos, as well as a single-subject credential for both social science and English. When he's not working with students or writing fiction, he enjoys the outdoors, photography, and watching classic '80s movies—all with his fiancée, Victoria Fletcher. You can find Shane on Twitter at @shanehawkk or at his author website shanehawk.com.

Illustration by Joe Radkins

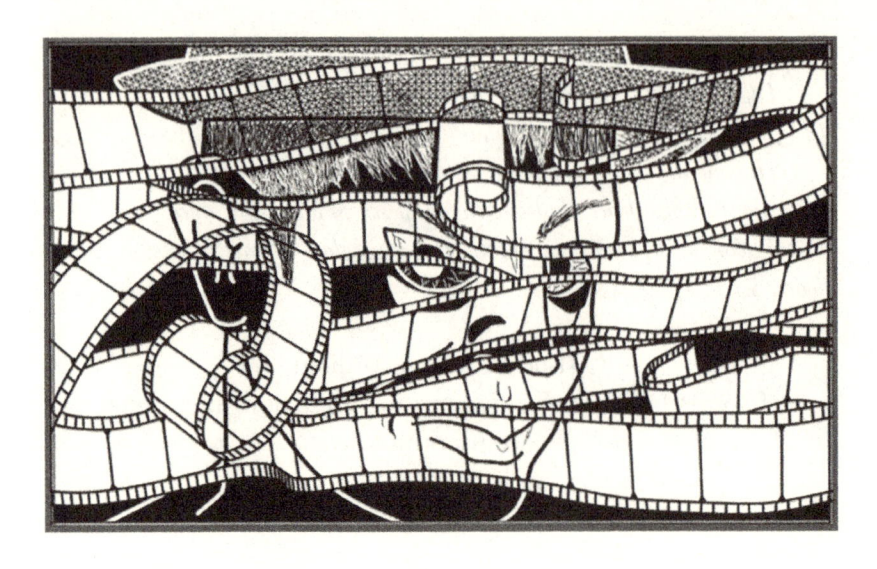

SUSPENDED IN LIGHT

ALEX WOLFGANG

JULIA'S NOSE stung with the vinegar scent of acetate, and she winced at its abrasive familiarity. Fumes wafted from the film while she searched the rusty canisters for clues, but neither titles, nor dates, nor anything else eased the task of identification. With nothing more to guide her, she began the careful process of threading the 16 mm reel into the projector.

Once the leader was secured around the take-up reel, she flipped on the machine and it whirred to life, the beam of light suspending particles in the air. For a moment she watched their lazy drift. She opened her notebook and leaned into her chair, relaxing as the hum of the projector filled the barren screening room. The stack of canisters, dust motes, and shadows would be her only Saturday companions.

The countdown flickered past, and the scene opened on a man sitting in a plain wooden chair who stared out of frame. An overcoat wrapped his lanky body, and a wide-brimmed hat concealed half his face in shadow. Idly, he stroked his mustache as if lost in thought. Behind his chair was a white backdrop, ruffled and parted like the closed curtain of a stage, and he did nothing but sit there for a full minute.

Feeling the weight of her eyelids, Julia gulped down coffee, chastising her formerly drunken self for accepting this job offer. She'd noticed her professor's email around eleven o'clock the night before. Twenty euros an hour to classify old, donated footage sounded like a dream when she was three Duvels deep at Cafe Thijssen, but it had since lost some appeal.

Dr. van der Meer's proposal of an impromptu—and illegal, if they were being honest—job opportunity was a surprise, especially on a weekend. But despite her discomfort, she was grateful for the chance to earn some cash. At the bar, while the two girls from her film program were in the restroom, she made the mistake of checking her bank account balance, and her beer lost its flavor. She could've turned down the invitation to go out, but she was too grateful they'd asked. Making film school friends had sounded so easy back home. God forbid she be forced to ask her parents for more help. Their generosity was the only reason she'd been able to leave Colorado at all, and that pool of guilt spilled across the Atlantic.

The man looked at the camera and jolted, the sudden movement jerky and exaggerated by the slow frame rate. Julia jumped too, her heart rate accelerating. The man leaned forward and peered at the camera. Surprise contorted into grim amusement. His nostrils flared with heavy, slow breaths.

His unfaltering stare was potent enough to instill the effects of observation. She squirmed in the hard seat—an awkward, unnatural struggle.

The man rose from his chair, not flinching when it silently toppled behind him. The hair on Julia's skin bristled—though she couldn't say exactly why—as he approached the camera, feet slow and deliberate as if stepping through molasses.

Unnerving as he was, Julia couldn't help noting the film was remarkably well-preserved: few cinch marks, no torn sprocket holes, beautiful contrast in the blacks and whites. The donor must have taken good care of it.

Closer and closer the man came, until his features were blurred patches of grey. The amorphous form of his mustache consumed the screen. Then he lowered his face and raised his hand to the lens, twisting it until he was in focus again. His gaze never left the camera, pupils dilating like he could see into the darkness and penetrate the inner workings of the machine.

He remained there another thirty seconds, eyes shifting as he examined the device's lens. As he did so, Julia imagined she could see through his pupils to his brain and examine the mechanisms of his biological camera, the curious mind that must have inspired such a creation.

Could this just be an experimental piece? An early counterpart to *cinéma vérité*? The reel wasn't dated, but her knowledge of film history placed it in the early 1920s. After four years at university and one in the graduate program, early filmmakers still fascinated her. Their creativity with the novel medium—from the fantastical works of Méliès to the slow cinema of whoever this guy was—always manifested in unexpected ways.

Despite his relative inactivity, she couldn't take her eyes off him.

He pulled back, grinning. He laughed hysterically. Was she witnessing the fruition of his life's work? The thought made her smile despite the situation, lessened the sting of being anywhere but home in bed.

He readjusted the lens and backed up to the center of the room beside the toppled-over chair, then held up a single finger as if to tell her "one moment" before walking offscreen.

Julia stared at the chair while nothing happened for over a minute. The waste of film was painful to witness. She bobbed her leg, bit down on her pen. Soon though, the man returned, lugging a piece of heavy equipment. The metal legs of a tripod gleamed as they reflected a light somewhere behind the camera. A dark box sat at the top, one taller than the man's head. A second camera.

She shivered beneath her sweater and folded her arms.

Occulted by the new camera, the man tinkered until, apparently satisfied, he stepped around it, grinning. He looked back and forth between the two machines and looked on proudly as they recorded each other for several minutes. Finally, he shut off the new camera, then came center-frame again. He stared at the first camera—at Julia—for a long time, arms folded in smug self-satisfaction, like he was the cleverest bastard in Europe. He disappeared off screen again, then returned with a projector.

"No fucking way," she said to the empty room, watching him transfer film from the camera to the projector. "There is no fucking way you're about to do this."

She laughed to herself, tried to brush off the creeping feeling. And yet, each movement on screen was stretched to infinity by the invisible tendrils sweeping across her skin.

He's just going to show the camera, she told herself. Anything else would be impossible.

He straightened the white curtain, then flipped on the projector to reveal footage of the camera—the one which recorded the images she now watched, a film within a film. But it zoomed in further and further, until the screening room was swallowed in darkness. Then, a point of light grew in the center of the screen, with a figure inside it.

She whimpered, the sound buried beneath the machine's din.

"Oh, shit."

Projected on the curtain was what she'd feared: a screening room with a lone occupant. A young American girl with thick-rimmed glasses, sitting alone beside a stack of reels, chewed-up pen and paper resting on her lap.

Her analytical mind attempted gymnastic feats. A film that filmed back? Briefly, she considered the possibility of a prank, but even that couldn't explain this. There was no machine, no technology, no possible way this could work. Nowhere in the annals of film history had someone created a device which could perform such a feat. Yet there she was, her own image displayed before her, on a film shot eighty years before her birth. She would have to examine it, frame by frame, under a microscope to see what was really there.

But first, a curiosity needed to be satisfied. What would come next? The projector spun on, and she made no move to stop it.

The camera zoomed out and the man peeked his head into the frame then grinned at her. He mouthed three words, and she read his lips clearly.

"You are mine."

He pointed to his chest as he said "mine."

She dropped the pen and paper. Sweat coated her palms.

The man held a handwritten sign to his chest—black, cursive ink on a white backdrop. On it was written: PLAY US FOREVER. He did not avert his gaze.

For a long moment, he held the sign there, willing her to read all three words again and again.

Her racing thoughts had no time to dissipate before her projector erupted into a spasm of crackling smoke and sizzling acetate. Julia cried out and lurched away. She jumped to stop the damage, but it was impossible. It wasn't just the section of film being projected that was destroyed; it was the entire reel. The only evidence of what had just transpired, proof of an impossibility.

Yet it didn't burn or melt, but dissolved into ash instead.

"No, no, fuck, no."

She tried to salvage some of the film, but it was no use. When she touched the greyish powder, it slipped through her fingers until there was nothing left.

🐾

FOR SEVERAL MINUTES, she sat in the dark room and tried to squeeze a rational explanation from her brain. She was dreaming. She was so tired that she'd fallen asleep in the chair and encountered a horrible nightmare, the unattended film burned at its conclusion. Yet a pinch to her skin did nothing. She was awake, sober, and alert—painfully so.

Play us forever.

The film was destroyed. How could she play it?

Then she remembered the other reels. They beckoned silently, as if they lived and breathed beside her.

Us.

With a shaking hand, she swiped the remaining powder from the projector.

A deep breath. A closing and opening of the eyes. She could figure this out. She just needed to stay calm.

She locked the next reel into place and guided its leader through the labyrinth of sprockets and gates. As it began to play, she clenched her teeth so tightly her head hurt.

Another lone person, this one a middle-aged woman. She stood before the same ruffled white backdrop. Clad in an elegant dress and labored curls, she shifted back and forth in discomfort. An arm reached into frame, beckoned her closer to the shot's center. She moved and stared into the camera. For several minutes, she only looked onward.

The woman turned to her side and stood still for another few minutes. Over and over, she raised her arms or changed her position slightly as if it was important that every inch of her body was recorded. Then she turned around, then again to the other side, then faced the camera once more.

The reel went blank before it reached its end.

Though less overtly disturbing, the reel formed a void in Julia's stomach, an anomalous sense of doom.

She put on the next reel. This one showed a young girl, perhaps six years old, also wearing a beautiful dress. Confused, she looked at someone off screen and nodded. For the next few minutes, she displayed every inch of herself, just as the woman had. Then it ended.

Every reel displayed more people doing the same. Other children. Elderly folks. All mildly confused, all instructed to turn and lift their arms and display themselves.

And that was it. Sixteen reels, one destroyed, the others all the same.

Play us forever.

She now understood who "us" was. If only she understood anything else.

🐾

EARLIER THAT MORNING, she'd wavered in the doorway of Dr. van der Meer's office.

"Where'd they come from?" she asked the old professor, clearing her throat.

Though he'd decked out his office at the University of Amsterdam in old movie posters and photos of his boat, this workspace at the film archive was empty beyond a desk, a chair, and a thin layer of dust.

"Anonymous donor," he said. "Are you okay?"

Julia's eyelids perked back up, but she didn't move from the doorway.

"Fine." She forced a smile. "Just a late night. I was going to sleep in, but this is honestly better. Thank you."

The old man shook his head, chuckling as he leaned back in his chair.

"Be careful," he said. "Americans—you don't know how to drink. They keep your beer away until you're twenty-one and then throw you out in the world and say, 'Drink up!' It's no wonder you keep vomiting in our canals."

"I'll aim my puke at a British stag party next time."

"Ah! That's how you'll gain your citizenship!" He both charmed and annoyed her. How could someone have so much energy this early on a Saturday?

"Not to question a good thing, but why me? Aren't there staff or interns who normally do stuff like this?"

"Well, to be honest, it isn't me or the university that's paying you," he said, leaning back into his chair. "The donor included a cash payment to have the films investigated on short notice. It must be done this weekend. Maybe they are hoping to uncover something special for the festival next weekend. *Ha!* Like they have room for last-minute programming . . . or maybe the donor has more money than patience. Either way, no one else was willing to work on a Saturday."

Julia laughed, feeling a jolt of caffeine finally enter her bloodstream. She sipped from the mug in her hand. "You took a bribe?"

Dr. van der Meer shrugged. "I prefer the term 'extra donation.' It seemed harmless enough. I assumed you could use the cash, too."

"No kidding. That woman at orientation underestimated how much I should've saved for Dutch socializing. Is there a screening room around here? I want to get started before this caffeine wears off."

"Just down the hall. There's a dolly for the canisters and a rolling projector in there as well," he said. "And take this."

He tossed her a bottle of water. She missed the catch, and her face went hot when she bent down to pick it up.

"Believe it or not," he said, "we drink water in Europe, too."

🐾

Now she stood outside Dr. van der Meer's door again, this time shaking and coated with sweat. He wasn't there. Not surprising considering it was late afternoon. A note on the door told her to leave the reels inside, so she pushed through and left them in a stack beside his desk.

He'd left his laptop open. Faint light from the screensaver beckoned her. Snooping felt wrong, but everything about this situation felt wrong.

I am fucking losing it.

This conclusion acted as permission. After what she'd seen, this seemed a minor—if not necessary—transgression.

She sat at the desk and tapped a key to bring the computer to life. It was unlocked. She scrolled through two pages of undeleted emails before the phrase *anoniem donatie* caught her eye. Anonymous donation. For a native English speaker, learning Dutch was all but pointless, but she'd learned to pick up on some patterns.

She copied the email and pasted it into an online translation program then interpreted the broken English.

A woman named "Emma Jansen" had asked a week prior when she could bring in the reels on behalf of a donor. Julia typed the woman's email address on her phone, then logged out.

As she left the building and strode through the cold streets of Amsterdam, the void in her gut spread throughout her body. Night had set in early. Wind gusts dug into her skin, tiny ice picks prying molecules from her body, one by one. She rode the ferry across the river, lamenting her decision to live on the darker side of Amsterdam. Two teenage boys spoke to her in Dutch, and when she responded with confusion, they laughed hysterically and spoke more. The words sounded like English that fell apart in her ears before they reached her brain.

She wanted to push them overboard.

The other side of the river was calm and quiet, the effect like a blanket of freshly fallen snow. The only visible occupant of her apartment complex was a man outside the entrance wearing a dark hoodie and smoking a joint, sending puffs billowing toward a flickering streetlight. He paid her no mind, but the scent of his smoke followed her into the elevator.

The plain white walls didn't usually bother her. She was only here a year, after all, and purchasing decor was impractical. Tonight she wished it felt less like a sanatorium. From her bed, she wrote an email:

DEAR EMMA JANSEN,

I'm the student assigned to the film donation you provided. This might sound strange, but I was wondering if you would be willing to tell me anything about the origins of the reels. I realize they were an anonymous donation, but I would very much like to discuss the contents with the donor. They would remain functionally anonymous, of course.

Sincerely,
Julia Williams

She stared at the blinking cursor for a moment before deciding to add: *Please, it is extremely important.*

Afterward, she took a shower hoping it could ease her anxiety. It was no use. No amount of soap could wash away what she'd seen. As the water ran down her skin, images flashed before her eyes—herself sitting in the screening room, watched by an impossible camera, the man's smile as he held his sign. She lathered the loofah and scrubbed herself thoroughly. When she was done, her skin was raw and pink, like she'd scraped roughly and removed too much skin. The stinging sensation followed her to bed. As she tried to drift off, the man's sign kept appearing in her mind.

PLAY US FOREVER.

She awoke to morning light streaming into her room and immediately checked her email. A new message.

Hello Julia,

I'm excited to hear there was something of interest on those films, but I'm afraid I cannot put you in contact with the donor. My grandmother was a bit of a hoarder who recently passed away, and I found them locked in a vault in her apartment. I thought maybe they would be worth something since they were so secured. Maybe I'm right? I hope so. If you are telling me that the films are important then I would be happy to help you however I can. Let me know if you want to chat more.

Sincerely,
Emma Jansen

Damn. Not what she was hoping for, but still a lead. Julia replied, asking if she could meet the woman at her grandmother's apartment sometime soon. Willing herself not to overthink the message, she quickly sent it.

Though she wasn't really hungry, Julia scrambled some eggs and made toast while she waited for a response. She needed something, anything to distract her. But soon her laptop dinged with a new email saying that, though it seemed a little strange, Emma would be cleaning up her grandmother's apartment all day and Julia was welcome to come by.

Once she copied the address into her phone, she left immediately.

The apartment was in Amstelveen, a suburb just south of Amsterdam. The bike ride took about an hour. Though it was warmer than the night before, bursts of wind still dug into her exposed flesh and stung her. Had she really scraped off so much skin in the shower? It didn't seem possible, but her mind had been in an awful place. Today, she felt more sane, like yesterday was a faraway dream that only needed interpretation.

She arrived at the address and stared up at the building. The bottom floor was an Indonesian restaurant called Toko Madjoe, where an old woman in a grey dress slowly swept dust across creaking floorboards. The upper floor's facade was a series of rotting green wood panels surrounding a boarded up window, where a hole was visible through the glass. She double checked the map on her phone. This was the place.

When she went upstairs and knocked on the door, a middle-aged woman in sweatpants and a t-shirt opened it. Her blonde hair was tied back into a ponytail.

"Julia? Come in."

The house was in a hell of a state. Emma hadn't exaggerated in calling her grandmother a hoarder. The rooms were so stuffed with objects that it was difficult to maneuver. Yet there was no stench of old food or animal droppings, no garbage at all. Instead, there were hundreds of books, small knick-knacks, photos, and other relics of a bygone era. Dust coated everything in sight, and beams of sunlight streamed in and illuminated airborne motes as they drifted. It was hard to believe anything had been removed at all, but Emma insisted she'd been working for more than a week already. The woman led her through the living room, carefully weaving through makeshift pathways between the stacks and into the kitchen.

"So what was on the reels?" Emma asked, sipping a Heineken she'd pulled from the fridge. She offered one to Julia, who briefly hesitated at the early hour, then accepted. "Grandma was kind enough to leave every object in existence behind except a working projector. She did leave a broken one, though."

Julia took a deep breath and a long pull from the beer bottle.

She hesitated but was surprised by how desperately she wanted to share the truth's burden. The story spilled out, from the impossible recording of herself and the cryptic message to its self-destruction and the contents of the other reels. Emma watched her, fascinated by the tale.

"Do you think I'm crazy?" Julia asked.

Emma sipped her beer and stared at Julia.

"So what, you think this very old, very dead person is going to make you . . . play a bunch of film reels?" Emma replied. "What's he going to do if you don't?"

"I don't know." Julia twisted her hair between her fingertips. The story sounded even less believable out loud. "Maybe nothing. But he *filmed me back*. I know it doesn't make any sense, but it's true."

"But that film he took of you is now mysteriously destroyed."

Neither woman spoke for a moment.

"You do think I'm crazy. Jesus, am I?"

Emma turned away and thumbed through a stack of books. "Hey, it's okay. My sister was crazy. She joined a cult in Cambodia three years ago. She either ascended to a higher dimension, or she's dead in a jungle somewhere."

Julia laughed and choked on her sip of beer. "Thanks, that's reassuring."

Emma shrugged. "Maybe I'm crazy too. To be honest, I was hoping those reels would be worth some money, like maybe that film festival would want to buy them. Wasting money in the hopes of making more, now that is its own kind of crazy."

Julia smiled. She liked Emma already, despite her misguided business venture. Did she not realize she *donated* the reels? Oh well, no need to mention it.

"But I don't understand," Emma said. "What made you want to come here?"

"I guess I just wanted to know if there were any clues. Assuming I'm not insane, I don't suppose you know why she had those reels?"

"I didn't really know her." Emma dug up a couple of chairs and offered one to Julia. They sat in a small clearing. "She lived here for like fifty years or something. Kind of a strange lady. Never tried to talk to me, even though I was her only relative and I lived in basically the same city. Then she insisted in her will that I be the one to handle her affairs. Not that there was anyone else to do it. Who knows, maybe I can turn this place around and sell it."

Julia scanned the room, noticing a pile of framed photos on a short table in the corner.

"Mind if I take a look at these?"

"I wouldn't mind if you took those, honestly. Take whatever you want."

Julia flipped through the pictures. Mostly scenes from around the city—canals, bridges, churches. Whoever took them clearly had an appreciation for Amsterdam, but none held any clues.

Emma resumed cleaning the kitchen, taking handfuls of dishes and stuffing them into sacks. For three hours, Julia looked through boxes. She found plenty of interesting photographs—more city scenes, portraits, still lifes, family gatherings—but nothing to help her understand what she'd seen. Her eyes became sore, and the constant clinking of dishes and plastic wore on her mind.

In one box, she found a stack of photos labeled *The Jansens*. One photo showed a young man and woman with their backs to the camera, looking out over a canal. A little girl stood between them, hands intertwined in theirs. On it, someone had written *Emma* and drawn a heart.

Julia entered the kitchen, where Emma had stopped cleaning to lean against a counter and scroll through her phone. "Thought you might want this."

Emma took the photo.

"Oh, shit." She almost dropped it, eyes lighting up. "I've never even seen this photo before."

"How long have they been gone?"

She placed the photo on the counter and stared at it.

"Twelve years. Car accident. My dad was drunk."

A brief silence.

"Well, maybe your grandmother did care about you," Julia said. "She kept that photo."

"Look around," Emma said, disgust seeping into her voice. "She kept everything. I doubt she even knew she had it. A word of advice, Julia. Don't have kids. All they do is inherit your baggage."

Emma pulled another beer from the fridge and sipped it. Her eyes explored the still-messy kitchen—plates and stacks of papers still covered the countertops so thoroughly the surface was barely visible—and sighed. She didn't meet Julia's gaze, instead stared at her shoes. Was she angry, or was it something else?

Unsure how to respond, Julia returned to her search in the living room. The clinking of dishes didn't resume.

🐾

AN HOUR LATER, Julia was on the verge of giving up when she spotted one last box with a photo sticking out of an edge. It was shoved into a corner of the bedroom, obscured by a vinyl raincoat. She flipped open the lid. More portraits. But her heart jumped when something caught her eye.

A familiar man with a familiar mustache. He stood beside a familiar projector, grinning proudly. She shuddered at the memory of him on screen. Though he held no sign now, his icy expression was just as piercing. She tried to call out, but choked on the words at first.

"This is him!" she managed to say. "The man from the reel!"

Emma sauntered into the room cautiously and looked at the photo.

"Huh," Emma said. "He does look a little familiar. So does his name. It's really faint though, maybe from when I was a kid."

A scribbled name and date on the back of the photo: *Hans Veldt, 1923.*

She kept looking through the box until she found more familiar faces. Fifteen of them. A stack of unframed photos wrapped in string. Each a simple portrait with a name and the year *1923* written on the back.

"Can I take these?" Julia asked.

"Like I said, take whatever you want."

"Still think I'm crazy?"

"Is this supposed to convince me otherwise?"

Julia shrugged and smiled. "No, I guess not."

Emma sighed. She flipped through the photos without expression. "What did he say again? 'You are mine'? 'Play us forever'?"

Julia nodded. Emma bit her lip.

"I don't know what's going on," she said. "But if I've done something . . . wrong, I'm sorry."

They were both silent a moment.

"What do you mean?" Julia asked. "How could you have done something wrong?"

Emma stared at the wall, struggled for words. "The projector here wasn't broken. I don't know why I lied. I broke it by accident because I had no idea what the fuck I was doing. I tried to fix it, but I only made it worse. So I just sent the reels to you all. I had too much else to do."

Another silence. Emma sipped a freshly opened beer. Once again, she wouldn't meet Julia's eyes.

"Oh, so *you* were going to watch them."

Emma cleared her throat, but didn't respond.

They exchanged phone numbers in case anything else came up.

※

For the next two days, Julia was swamped with schoolwork. Dr. van der Meer mentioned nothing about the reels, even after Julia emailed him to explain their contents. She'd left out the first one. If Emma thought she was crazy, she didn't want the man guiding her education to reach the same conclusion. At the end of each long day, she showered, and each time, the loofah and hot water abraded her skin. A new brand of lotion didn't help. When the red splotches lasted for hours afterward, she stopped using the loofah altogether.

Her brain shifted seemingly at random between lucid clarity and muddled confusion, like neurons were firing through a milky membrane. At times she caught herself staring at a textbook page for several minutes without comprehending a word.

Once, while studying at home, she realized she'd been staring at a patch of red on her paper for some unknown duration without noticing it was blood. She wiped her nose and examined the dark red streak across her hand, then rushed to the bathroom to clean it off.

That was strange; she never got nosebleeds.

※

"Have you heard of an early filmmaker named Hans Veldt?"

Dr. van der Meer looked up from his computer screen and peered at her while she leaned in the doorway. He looked much more natural when bookended by posters for Ciske de Rat and Soldaat van Oranje. In the fluorescent light of his office, she hoped the dark circles beneath her eyes weren't obvious. He hesitated at the sight of her, but when he gestured to the chair in front of his desk, she slunk into it.

"Veldt." He fiddled with a pen on his desk. "I'm not sure. I take it a web search wasn't helpful?"

"No." Two hours of scrolling through pages had turned up nothing but passing mentions from journal articles, and those were only references. Nothing concrete or helpful, but at least they confirmed he was real.

"I assume he's Dutch?"

She smiled. "With a name like Hans Veldt?"

"Ah, we weren't always so peaceful, you know." He leaned back. "We have a reputation of spreading to lands we weren't invited to."

"Fair, but those reels from the anonymous donor were his. I'm pretty sure he was Dutch."

As soon as the words left her lips, she wondered at their truth. *Play us forever* was written in English. For some reason she hadn't considered that earlier.

"Hmm." The old professor's eyes glazed as his mind wandered. "Well, there's no guarantee you'll find anything, but there is a section of the library with old, undigitized texts. I haven't looked through them myself, but I know it's almost all Dutch, and I seem to remember being told there were some historical film documents. You'll need an appointment, but I think I can probably get you one."

"Yes, yes please. That would be amazing."

"Why so interested? From what you told me, those reels sounded rather boring."

She squirmed in her seat, searching for a suitable answer.

"I get these weird obsessions sometimes. The more niche something is, the more desperate I am to follow the rabbit hole."

Dr. van der Meer laughed and slapped a hand against his desk.

"Ah, I know that feeling well! It is because of obsessions like this that we end up studying obscure fields like film preservation."

He scribbled out a note in Dutch and handed it to her.

"Give this to the librarian. She will help. Perhaps if you ask nicely, she'll even translate the results for you."

"All you have is a name?" The librarian raised an eyebrow beneath her blonde bangs. Her smooth skin and smirk made her look too young for the profession. "You might find this . . . challenging."

Julia nodded. The library room was smaller than her apartment, but the shelves lining every inch of wallspace were jam-packed with old tomes. Their entrance stirred up dust, and she sneezed into her hand. When she pulled her hand away, red painted her fingers, but she wiped them clean with a handkerchief from her jeans pocket before the librarian noticed. The warm liquid seeped through the fabric and clung to her skin.

"I have more patience than most," Julia said. "Just going to search through the indexes. If I find his name, will you help me read it?"

The woman raised her eyebrows in annoyance. "You can't read *any* Dutch? You didn't bring someone who could translate for you?"

Dutch brusqueness still caught her off guard sometimes.

"No, I didn't bring a translator, but considering I'm the only one here, it looks to me like you can spare a few minutes."

"Fine." The woman rolled her eyes. "You know where to find me."

Thankfully, most of the books had clear indexes, and when she passed through the V's and found nothing, they were easy enough to discard into an ever growing stack of rejects. She soon discovered they were loosely divided into similar lengths of shelves. Dutch history, governmental procedures, and art history all had their own subsection of the room.

She pulled out her phone to translate a few titular words from a book, but the screen wouldn't unlock. Two more times, her fingerprint failed. She resorted to typing her PIN. After she logged in, she examined her finger closely, wondering if it was still smudged with blood. She could make nothing out—no striations in the flesh, no looping patterns—just smooth skin. Even when she held her finger up to the fluorescent light, her print wasn't there. Other fingers showed the same absence.

"What the fuck is happening to me?" she breathed.

The room didn't respond, so she distracted herself by continuing the search.

Eventually she encountered a technical manual for early cameras, and her adrenaline surged. After digging through the stack for fifteen more minutes, she spotted the name "Veldt" in an index, and rushed to the librarian's desk.

"I guess he made documentaries," the librarian told her after reading through his article. "That's what this whole book is about. Let's see. His style was 'direct cinema,' minimal intervention. He wanted to film people and places as they were, to preserve them. Lots of shots of Dutch streets and stuff. Maybe he predicted the war. But since you couldn't find his stuff online, it wouldn't surprise me if all the films got destroyed anyway."

"Anything else?" Julia asked.

"Uh, looks like he had one popular film called *'The Balance of Decay.'* That's basically it though, it's a short article."

Julia shuddered. He was a preservationist like her. *The Balance of Decay.* Veldt's films must have been a counterbalance, tools to keep the past suspended in light on a movie screen.

Julia thanked the librarian and headed toward the large study room of the library. She needed to walk, to pace. In an area full of desks and chatting students, she went to a window between two bookcases then gazed through it. A rare sunny day in Amsterdam's October. Laughing students whizzed by on bicycles. A group of tourists—likely drunk or high already—giggled as they approached the entrance to the Torture Museum nearby.

A man in a gray overcoat and a wide-brimmed hat stood in the middle of a bike path, facing away from her as he looked out over the water.

Idiot, she thought, remembering the many times she'd lamented absent-minded tourists who walked through bike lanes.

One cyclist flew by the man, yet he didn't flinch. Didn't move a muscle until, slowly, he turned to face her. Julia could have sworn he was looking directly at her, but his face was obscured in shadow.

Three girls with bulging backpacks and determined expressions sped toward him, but they seemed not to notice. Julia waited for the inevitable collision, only a little guilty at the voyeuristic pleasure. It wasn't like she could stop them.

But they passed right through the man as if he wasn't there. She blinked and rubbed her eyes. He didn't move, just stood and faced her.

Her cheeks went hot. She gulped and forced herself to look away.

On Thursday, she hacked up blood. She leaned along the railing of a canal in the Jordaan—half-lit by the evening gloaming—when a bout of coughs turned violent. She spat what she assumed was phlegm into the canal, but it was tinged with a dark crimson that looked almost black in the wall's shadow. None of the other pedestrians noticed, so she carried on as if nothing was wrong and hurried home, wondering at what point she should see a doctor. If it would even help.

When she got there, she opened her laptop and put on an episode of *Star Trek*. A hot plate in the kitchen boiled water for spaghetti. The episode was one she'd seen before, but even so, her mind repeatedly wandered, and she couldn't keep track of the plot. Finally, she paused the show and let Hans Veldt's words fill her head: *Play us forever.*

Ignoring the impossibility of being recorded by the first reel, she couldn't even make sense of the situation on its own terms.

You are mine.

Was she meant to constantly play the reels? It didn't add up. If Hans truly wanted these films—these people—to be preserved, she should never play them. Each viewing degraded them slightly, brought them closer to their demise. Tucked away in a temperature and moisture-controlled environment, they could survive indefinitely.

But could that be called surviving?

Perhaps she could digitize the reels. Play them on a loop in some corner, forever ignored. Yet somehow, she knew that wouldn't work either. What's the purpose of a film nobody ever watches? What good is an unperceived life? Besides, something told her a reproduction wouldn't cut it. There was no true way to digitize film without losing something inherent from the original. Dr. Sanchez had taught her that in Intro to Film Theory, what felt like a million years ago.

She rested her forehead on her palm and closed her eyes, thoughts spinning so quickly she couldn't make them out for a moment. These bouts of fuzziness were becoming more frequent, often accompanied by more blood from her mouth and nose. She was degrading quickly, losing her essence like a photograph left out in the sun. Whatever Hans had done, it was working.

Forever.

What was forever, anyway? Julia was only human. Someday she would die. Even if Hans could force her to keep playing the reels until then, they'd still eventually be lost to the torrents of time. And the reel that had tethered her was gone, now scattered ashes spread throughout the screening room and a nearby garbage can. How could it hook someone else? Was Emma's grandmother tethered? If so, what happened to the reel that hooked her?

"Fuck. Fuck. Fuck." So many questions. So few answers. The most immediate: how the hell was she going to get those reels back? She'd already asked Dr. van der Meer for access again, but he told her they were stuck in the archive for another week.

She unpaused the episode and desperately tried to let it distract her. It didn't work.

When she finished preparing her meal and stuffed the first bite of spaghetti into her mouth, it was so tasteless she thought she'd forgotten the sauce. The sight of red smeared across the noodles nearly made her retch. But she hadn't hacked up more blood. It was tomato sauce; she just couldn't taste it. The two meatballs also proved flavorless.

She forced the bland dinner down anyway, then shut her laptop and cried. For almost half an hour, she let herself feel it, let the tears come.

"How is this happening?" The words, over and over, coaxed no answers.

In the bathroom mirror, she saw where the blood now came from. It streaked down her face from her lower eyelids to her chin, eyes sunken above the crimson cascade. Her skin was pale, almost grey.

Her phone buzzed in her pocket. She pulled it out and read a text through the faint pink veil across her eyes. A request from Leonie, one of a couple film school acquaintances straddling the cusp of friendship: *Niamh and I are going for espresso martinis tonight, care to join?*

She tossed the phone aside. Her guts twisted, desperate for the warmth of cocktails and companionship, but they couldn't see her like this. She hadn't even been able to confess the situation to her loved ones back home, whose correspondences were already suffering from distance and time-zone disparities.

When she left the bathroom, she approached her window without thinking. It made no difference if she saw him; she already knew he was there, waiting. Though she was four stories up, she could make out his silhouette standing across the street. Faint traces of a bushy mustache were visible under the golden glow of a streetlight.

She shut the curtains and tried to pretend he wasn't there, but his hidden gaze permeated the thin-walled apartment. She needed to leave anyway. There was only so long she could pretend she was okay, that she didn't desperately need a hospital.

🐾

ONCE AGAIN, alone. Her faded face looked back at her from the doctor's office mirror—a sunken, hollow expression. The ubiquitous glow of the fluorescent lights did little to soften the blow. Now she could only wait to see if modern medicine could deter her ailment—fat chance, but a chance all the same. She shivered in the cold, sterile examination room, where muffled beeps and voices permeated the walls and a sickly clean odor wafted in under the door.

The door swung open and a spectacled man entered the room, not looking up from his clipboard. "Julia Williams?"

"Yeah."

He paused for a long moment while he continued to look over her chart.

"What can you tell me about your symptoms?"

She told him about coughing and weeping blood, about her fingerprints and raw skin. The doctor said nothing, just examined her closely—first her throat, then her eyes, ears, skin, and fingertips.

"Hmm."

Anger welled. "Is that all you have to say?"

Immediately, she regretted the outburst, but the doctor didn't even look up.

"Julia, I'm going to write a recommendation for a psychiatric specialist," he said, jotting something down in Dutch.

"W-Why?"

He glanced up at her, then back to his clipboard.

"You said your fingerprints were fading. I brought an inkpad, would you like to test it?" He held it out, a moist, spongy blue rectangle. She dipped her left pointer finger and pressed it to a sheet of blank paper. When she lifted it, she gasped—the looped striations were all there.

"Like I said, Ms. Williams, I think it would be best if—"

A sizzle and crack. The lights flickered violently and Julia jolted. Artificial yellow transformed to the blood-red glow of a photographic darkroom, and the doctor's features receded into his silhouette. The red light strobed, and she stifled a scream as she scooted backward on the examination table. Closer and closer the silhouette came, until his tousle of hair spread into the wide brim of a hat. She couldn't see his face, but she didn't need to.

From some unseen source, an image projected onto the wall, where a human anatomy chart was smothered by a familiar scene: Julia in the screening room.

Her mouth went dry; she could not decide whether to look at Hans or her phantom image. The impossible camera zoomed in like a movie star's close-up. The youth and luster drained from her face. It shriveled and wrinkled like a timelapse of a rotting corpse. The version of Julia on screen did not notice, not when her hair fell to her shoulders and drifted to the floor, not when her eyeballs liquified and poured from their sockets, not when her skin dissolved like ash and her bone-white remains received air for the first time.

She couldn't stifle the scream—didn't even register it was happening. The whirring, absent projector and the flashing red lights swirled into a sensory maelstrom, and the vinegar smell of spectral acetate drowned out the hospital scent. Pressure built in her brain, threatened to explode. All the while, Hans stood still and silent because his punishment said it all.

She closed her eyes and willed herself to stop screaming, and when all went silent, she opened them.

The doctor was no longer stoic. His hands shook, eyes watered with fatherly concern.

"Julia, call this doctor as soon as possible and set up an appointment. Please."

"Yeah. Sure. Okay."

When she got home, there was still a little ink on her fingertip. She pressed it against a page in her notebook. Solid blue.

She cried reddened tears.

WHILE SHE WAITED for the ferry, Julia's phone buzzed in her pocket. Emma's number.

"Hey."

"Julia? How are you?"

I'm literally falling apart, she wanted to say.

"I'm okay. How are you?"

"Something else turned up today," Emma said. "I found another box with a picture of that man with a little girl. I can't say for sure, but she looks like my grandmother. I think she was his daughter."

"Holy shit," Julia said. "He cursed his own daughter?"

Silence on the line.

"'Cursed'? Wait, what? Julia, what's really going on?"

After a brief hesitation, Julia spilled her guts—blood, skin, fingerprints, tastebuds. Her belief that she must play the reels, now more urgent than before. She only left out her visions of Hans.

Silence again.

"What the fuck did I do to you?"

"It wasn't you, Emma."

"I still can't help but feel responsible. Is there something I can do?"

Julia hesitated. Though Emma had triggered this situation, she couldn't help but gravitate toward her anyway. The only person she could talk to. The ferry arrived and lowered its gate. Bikes, scooters, and pedestrians all moved in a huddled mass to board it.

"I don't suppose you know anything about breaking and entering."

Emma didn't respond for a few moments.

"Where are the reels?"

🐾

A STEADY MIST rained down on Julia as she walked through the city's dark industrial center, where grey buildings idled as they awaited working hours. Julia wanted to twirl her hair or bite her nails, anything to occupy her nervousness, but the strands were coming out in thick locks, and three of her fingernails had already detached. Instead, she repeatedly wiped water from her glasses, a useless task which only defined the amorphous shapes surrounding her for a few seconds before the lenses were saturated again. When she could identify nothing, every shape was Hans.

In her weakened state, the portable projector she carried was even more difficult to lug than usual, but she was degrading so quickly that she didn't know how long she could make it. A thin layer of vinyl protected it from the water. She hoped it was enough.

Finally, she saw Emma huddled under a streetlight, tiny droplets of rain visible in its yellow glow. If the older woman noticed her horrific state, she made no mention of it, and Julia could scarcely meet her eyes to search for truth.

She led Emma down the street until they reached the archive. The lobby glowed faintly, but the rest of the building was as cold and dead as the others surrounding it. The brutalist facade wasn't much to look at even in daylight. While the Eye Filmmuseum jutted up gloriously along the waterfront like a spaceship blasting off, this offshoot had no reason to appeal itself to tourists.

Inside stood the silhouette of a man in a hat, waiting between the two double doors. Though she couldn't make out his face, his eyes bored into her, looking through the tiny pieces of flesh he'd stripped away. He turned his head to her left, at Emma, then back to Julia.

"Can you see anybody inside?" Julia asked, testing her.

"Not yet. Do you?"

Silence resumed for a moment.

"No," she lied, not knowing why. A desire to tell the truth surged, but she caught it on the tip of her tongue and suppressed it. "Come on."

They reached the front door, and on an impulse, Julia opened it.

"Why is it unlocked?" Emma asked.

Julia ignored her and pushed forward through the door, toward Hans and his reels, but Emma hesitated, eyes watering in fear.

"I—you don't have to stay," Julia said. "You can go if you want . . ."

It would have been okay if Emma had turned away, relieving in some small way, but she didn't, and this comforted Julia to an extent she didn't understand. The woman followed through the doors and into the archive. Julia relished the warmth of her presence.

Nobody was there. Inexplicably, the security guard at the front desk was absent, and nothing was locked. Julia walked quietly through the building's empty hallways, Emma behind her, awaiting the moment when an alarm would go off or a rough voice would shout, "You there, stop!"

The doors to the archive hallways, the individual rooms, all unlocked. How had Hans done this? It was a silly question. How had he done any of it?

"Isn't this dangerous?" Emma asked. "Anybody could come in and steal these things. Aren't old reels worth a lot?"

"Some are." She started to explain further, but her thoughts dissolved to mush in her mind. She stopped, clutched her forehead, tried to think straight.

Hans peeked from distant hallway corners, ajar doorways, never getting close. She felt his eyes on her, sure any false move would further incur his wrath. It was hard not to look. Would it matter if Emma knew she could see him? Maybe not, but the desire to conceal her insanity beckoned. It made him feel less real.

When they reached the hallway that housed the archival rooms, she easily knew which one to enter. Hans stood, half in, half out of the doorway.

"In here," she told Emma.

Inside, Hans lurked beside her reels, arms folded. No longer obscuring his face, he watched them enter, his mouth a straight line. His eyes pierced Julia's mind, as if to say, *you'd better hurry.* There were hundreds of other reels in the room, but she paid them no mind. Nothing else was housed in the archive, no posters, windows, or seats. Just a plain, cool room to keep the reels safe.

"These are the—"

Julia cut off her words when she felt something hard and small come loose in her mouth.

A tooth. She spat it into her hand and stuck it in her pocket, turning away to keep Emma from noticing. A few steps toward the stack of reels made her go woozy again. Coppery blood dripped into her mouth from the tooth cavity, and for an instant, the entire room flashed red.

Her stomach lurched, but there was nothing to vomit. She hadn't eaten in two days.

"Julia?"

Julia turned to Emma, who stared at her in horror, as if now, under fluorescent lights, she had a full view of the person Julia had become. The person who was afraid to look at herself. Julia's eyes blinked in and out of focus.

"We have to play them."

"Now? Here?"

"I'm not gonna make it much longer."

"Yes, that's why you need to go to a hospital!"

Squatting on the floor to maintain her balance, Julia ignored her and unfolded the projector, then told Emma to bring her the first reel. Emma did as she was told, and Julia prepared it. Her hands were so clammy it nearly slipped through her fingers. At her instructions, Emma hit the lights, and Julia flipped the switch on the projector. It hummed to life.

The first woman. Hans's wife? Emma's great-grandmother?

The relief was immediate. Her nausea passed. Like an opiate entering her bloodstream, euphoria consumed the pain. She teared up, and when she wiped her eyes, the liquid was barely pink.

She started laughing. She must have looked insane, but that only made her laugh harder. Emma said nothing, and Julia didn't bother to look at her until the reel ended.

Emma's eyes were two full moons. She trembled.

"Another reel," Julia said, no longer caring how she was perceived.

"I don't—"

"Another reel."

Reluctantly, Emma handed one to her, and Julia played it. A child. More bliss. More laughter. More intoxicating relief.

"Next one."

"Julia, please."

"Give it to me!"

After three reels, Emma started crying.

Julia ignored her. She stood, walked to the light switch and turned it on. Then she looked at the fingers still without nails, felt the empty spot in her mouth where the tooth was before.

Nothing had gotten better.

When she turned back, Emma picked up a reel, held it like a venomous snake.

"I think we should destroy these."

At that, Hans whipped his head toward Emma.

"No," Julia said. "We can't! I can't."

"These are . . . fucked up! I don't think you see what they're doing to you. We have to destr—"

"*Don't!*"

Emma lurched forward and grabbed several more reels, but Julia was too invigorated to let her get away. She tackled Emma in the doorway, sending the reels flying into the hall. They smacked against the walls and linoleum floor. Emma fell too, but Julia paid her no mind, instead dropping to her knees and gathering the dented canisters. Hans watched her, and she no longer hid her gaze. She turned, stared into his grey eyes, and felt the bridge of time warp between them. He smiled with teeth like television static.

"Please, fix me!" she said. "I'm playing them, I'm playing them!"

Emma moved aside as Julia reentered the room and faced the projector toward a blank wall again. She flipped it on. One of the children appeared and spun around and around and around.

"Julia," said Emma gently, "Stop. Don't let this haunt you forever."

"Let it?" Julia asked, crying again. "Like I have a choice?"

"Destroy them," she said. "I think . . . I think if the reels are all gone, maybe you'll be okay."

"Maybe? And what if it kills me? You don't know a goddamn thing! It should have been *you!*" She jutted a finger at Emma.

"Julia, I'm sorry." The older woman stepped back.

Julia put a hand to her heart and felt her pulse slow as the film's effects took a deeper hold.

"I'm . . . sorry too. Please, please just sit and watch with me. I don't want to be alone."

Emma sat on the floor next to her, placed a hand on Julia's shoulder. For the next several hours, the two watched reel after reel. Men, women, and children who should have disappeared into the annals of history. Julia tried not to notice that her body still wasn't changing back to normal, that Hans kept watching behind them. Time stretched to agonizing lengths, but even when Emma shifted in discomfort, looked on the verge of speaking, she said nothing and waited patiently for the end.

When the last reel approached its conclusion, Julia looked at her hands. They were the same, just as bad as before. Fingernails were still missing. Her tooth hadn't regrown. She ran her finger across her phone scanner to no avail.

"What are you doing?" Emma asked.

"It didn't work. I can't undo it."

Hans walked behind Emma, looked to make sure Julia was watching. He raised a hand above the older woman's head and held it there for a moment. Julia stared up at him.

"What are you looking at?" Emma asked.

"I . . . you . . ."

Emma suddenly made a strange choking sound. Eyes bulged. Her lips opened and closed like a fish pulled from water. Beside her, the reel ended and the projector spat out plain white light. Emma's face went pale, her eyes grey. She tried to speak, but her teeth dissolved into bone dust. It spilled from her mouth to the floor while Julia watched in bewilderment.

The woman's skin sunk inward as if all the moisture was sucked from it, like Julia's face in the hospital reel: pulled until every patch was concave, until flesh became ash. Locks of blonde hair fell to the floor.

Above Emma, Hans still held out his hand. Now, Julia could see his face more clearly, the details in his eyes and mustache and pores. He looked at her with more intensity than ever before, a gaze so potent it pierced her from the distant past. A look that said, *you could have avoided this. I suggest you don't let it happen again.*

Soon Emma was nothing but a skeleton beneath a pile of clothing. Then the bones disintegrated into more dust. Julia buried her head in her hands to gather herself.

"Why? She didn't do anything!"

Hans stepped closer. When she looked up, his eyes widened into perfect circles of strobing blacks and whites. She couldn't turn away. In them she saw an infinite plane of time; chronology jumbled until linearity became meaningless. But somewhere in the swirling clouds of static was a circular motion, a cyclical ratio indicating order.

His eyes brightened until they were so blinding she had to turn away. When she finally looked again, beams of light projected from his sockets onto the wall behind her. He hummed like a machine, the sound spilling from his fully agape mouth.

The image of her face covered the wall, her features contorted into agonized horror. The peaks and valleys in her expression were lined with textures only time would bring.

The camera panned across a living room, turned to a young woman seated before a screen. Beside her, a projector cast an image she'd seen before—Hans and his sign: PLAY US FOREVER. The film disintegrated as it spun on beside the girl, who turned wide-eyed to Julia, stammering inaudible excuses, face pained by guilt.

That face—so familiar yet so distant. A face half her own that would not exist for years, one she hadn't been sure ever *would* exist. A girl she didn't yet know but already adored. The images disappeared, and his eyes went dark. She buried her face in her hands.

"Why?" She wanted to scream the word, but she barely

muttered it.

The name of his film entered her mind: *The Balance of Decay*. The loop of punishing time spinning eternally, degrading what remained of her until there was nothing left. The weight of infinity pressed down on her—the past, present, and future pulling in all directions at once. In an entropic universe, there is no restoration without destruction, no give without take.

When she finally looked up, Hans was gone. She shook her head involuntarily, again and again. As she packed up the projector, then gathered the reels, she muttered the same phrase.

"Never again, never again, never again, please, Hans, I won't let it happen again."

She scooped Emma's ashes into the woman's clothing and left to toss the bundle into the chilly waters of a canal.

"I'm so sorry . . ."

It wasn't until she stashed the projector and all the reels away in her apartment that she finally looked in the mirror. Staring back was the self she knew, the one from a week ago. But in her eyes she saw the slow decay of her body, the rate at which nature would unravel her into bone and stardust and then come for who was next. Until then, she would see a scar that would never heal, that would reopen again and again and again as she played those reels until forever's end finally came.

ALEX WOLFGANG is a horror author from Oklahoma City. When not reading and writing horror, you'll find him camping, playing the drums, watching movies with his wife, and backpacking around the world. His debut collection *Splinter and Other Stories* is available now. He's been a member of HOWL Society since May 2020 and is proud to call it his horror home. Follow him on Amazon and Twitter.

Illustration by P.L. McMillan

GOOSEBERRY BRAMBLE

SOLOMON FORSE

WELL, Yer Honor, I s'pose that was when it all began—with that warnin my grandmammy gave me some sixty years ago. She looked me right in the eye, wavin that switch in her hand, sayin, "Boy, ya stay away from Gooseberry Bramble, ya hear?"

She said them words near a hunnerd times that summer, back when I stayed at her ol lean-to out in the Black Cobb backwoods while my pappy, come to find out, went philanderin.

But, Yer Honor, if I may address these folks before us today—

Y'all folks know, like any youngin with a noggin full a dreams an desire, that warnin from my grandmammy only tickled my curiosities—built em up like a heck lotta scratchin grows a skeeter bite.

An if y'all ever had somebody put the fear a God in y'all durin yer childhood, no matter if it was with a switch, belt, or open hand, then y'all know what I mean when I say it wun't even til the sixth or seventh time my grandmammy fell asleep in her rockin chair on the porch that I finally screwed up the courage to sneak off to Gooseberry Bramble.

I member that afferrnoon like it was yesterday, tip-toein an squeakin down them crooked porch steps ev'ry time my grandmammy took a gulp a air, snorin ev'ry sev'ral seconds or so. But when I finally got to the foot a them steps, feelin them pine needles crunchin unner my shoes, I reckoned I was scot-free. Had the same crooked grin I got now, too, cept back then I wun't much more than two beanpole legs with a wild bunch a blond hair. But I figure all y'all men out there member bein boys, so y'all know that feelin I had—headin out fer an adventure, even if it meant riskin a whuppin.

Now, I reckon y'all think the last thing this murder trial needs is some ramblin ol geezer yarnin bout his boyhood, drawin out the proceedins. Seems like no matter what I say, y'all got yer sights set on Mr. Ramblewood over there fer the deaths a them dozen children. But I might just change yer minds, so listen close. When I swore on that Bible just now, I swore to tell y'all the truth—an that's what I'm fixin to do, so help me God.

Anyhow, back to that summer afternoon. So some half hour later, affer I got down them steps an done a whole lotta runnin an hurryin—mosely cause I didn't know when my grandmammy'd startle awake an come a-hollerin—I made it to the river.

I member standin there on the shoreline next to that ol fishin boat tied up to a tree. Never did find out who owned it. But there I was, dog-tired an covered in scrapes an scratches from my neck down to my ankles cause I ran through all them nettle patches an oak scrub. Made it to that shoreline in record time, though, an I member standin there, seein them pine trees wavin in the wind above a patch a gooseberry bushes right out cross the water.

Now, all y'all know that sensation ya git when yer somewhere ya don't belong. Specially as a child. An maybe it was a chill risin up off the water, or some kinda breeze, but as I looked out at that thicket cross the river, a shiverin somethin awful ran up my back —like a stranger done snapped off an icicle an slid it up my spine, all terrible an slow. Affer that I reckoned goin in them bushes wun't a good idea. There was somethin over there I wun't s'posed to see.

But how come my grandmammy got to know bout it an not me? I wun't a baby no more. Considerin all the chores I was doin round the lean-to—choppin wood, fixin fence, haulin scrap—I was halfway to manhood.

An heck, by the time I got through all that scrub, my tummy was a rumblin anyhow. Them berries were gonna hit the spot, no matter what was over there.

So I unhitched that ol boat an went cross that river.

Folks, I'll tell ya even today I don't blame my grandmammy none fer fallin asleep when she shoulda been watchin me. She done her best to warn me bout that place in ev'ry damn way she known. Now some a y'all sittin out there might reckon me a simple man—or a simple boy at that time—specially fer not listenin to my grandmammy, or fer not learnin nothin from a whuppin neither, but I was sharp as a tack—an I still am to this day. Y'all can see I ain't got no hair an I ain't got many teeth neither—hell, my eyesight is just bout near gone, too—but I know fer damn certain I got my mind. That ain't gone just yet.

Since alotta y'all folks got faces like fresh pails a mornin milk, I can't reckon ya knew my grandmammy. But if y'all was acquainted, then ya'll woulda known she'd drum up any ol story to keep a youngin like me outta trouble. Such as tellin me if I stuck my hand in her pickle jar one too many times then my whole arm'd turn green. But I was as slick a boy there ever was, an I learned right quick her warnins were just some made-up hogwash, specially given all them pickles I done snuck outta the cellar that summer. No green arm to show fer it neither.

So when my grandmammy told me bout all them children gone missin afer playin round them gooseberries, names like "Caleb" an "Mea" an boys an girls I ain't never heard of, I didn't take no stock in it. Pickles or gooseberries, truths or tall tales, ain't nothin was gonna git between a boy an his inclinations. I was like a huntin dog hot on a coon trail.

So I got in that boat, an I paddled right on over to Gooseberry Bramble.

Affer shiftin the oar from side to side fer a while, drippin water on my knees ev'ry time I switched, I was bout halfway cross that water. I member stoppin fer a minute, eyein a fat ol carp swimmin right beside the boat—sun reflectin off all them yeller scales. I member wishin I had my pole, cause I'd reckoned if I brought that sucker back to the lean-to, my grandmammy wouldn't a got me with no switch. She'd a fried up that sonuva gun an fergot all bout me sneakin off. But I ain't had nothin but that pocket knife that my pappy gave me, an that wun't gonna catch me no fish. I s'pose that was the last thing I member thinkin bout just when I noticed somethin queer.

Well, not noticed, but *heard*. Comin from them gooseberry bushes on the shore ahead. I fixed my ears on that sound an done fergot all bout that carp.

Now I reckon mose y'all sittin out there is churchfolk, so y'all can magine what it was I heard. If y'all ever been outside the church doors durin mass—maybe cause y'all were runnin late on Sunday mornin, or maybe cause y'all had to step out fer one reason or another—then y'all can magine it.

First off, listenin to folks singin the Word a God is somethin beautiful when yer standin there inside the church, surrounded by all them angelic voices a yer schoolmates an neighbors an such. I won't deny that—specially affer me swearin on this here Bible. But when yer *outside* the church, it sounds somethin unnatural. The way them harmonizin voices bleed through them walls an leak out them windows an unner the door—it's right devilish. Maybe stretchin the notes or changin the pitch—I don't rightly know—but what I *do* reckon fer certain is that's just the funny sound I heard. Comin straight from that clump a gooseberries. Cept the only difference was, least from what I member, it wun't all men an women singin. It was just the women, all high-pitched an waverin.

An there ain't never was no church out there by the river. An ain't no women neither.

Y'all folks prolly reckon that right then I shoulda turned that boat round an hurried on back to my grandmammy's lean-to. But like I done already said, I was a youngin, an my curiosities got the best a me. An besides, I was practically touchin the other side. Might as well a finished what I set out to do.

So I kept paddlin.

When I got to the shore, just before my boat pushed up on the mud, I felt that chill again—but this time it wun't just a moment, an it wun't just up an down my spine. It draped round me an sunk into my bones, like I just done gone in that walk-in freezer at the five an dime. Like summer had jumped right over autumn an landed smack dab in the middle a winter. I ain't never took a coat with me out in the woods durin July, an I reckon none a y'all'd do the same, but right then I was wishin I had anythin to wrap round my shoulders—heck, even that ratty ol quilt in the lean-to if I coulda got it.

I climbed on over the bow, rubbin my arms up an down, teeth a chatterin an mud a suckin at my shoes, an the singin got louder. Like they's just on the other side a the bramble. But I wun't plannin on stickin my neck in there to find out—I was just hungry. An I thought maybe I'd just mosey on up the bank an snatch me a few a them berries right quick, stash em in my shirt all folded up like a make-do bucket. Then I'd eat em on the boat while I went back cross the river an got warmed up in the sun.

Affer I scrambled up to the top a the bank, I realized the singin wun't women—it was children. An it wun't like the voices—wun't like they's comin from *behind* the bushes, but instead directly out of em. Like children stooped down in that scrub all hummin some ugly lullaby.

An just as I thought bout divin right back in that boat, the bramble went all quiet. It was like when ya hear some crickets chirpin in the grass, an soon as ya set foot near em, they all go silent, like they's never there. Them voices stopped just like that, an all I heard was the soft splishin an splashin a the river behind me. I started thinkin maybe it was just a figment a my magination affer all. But one thing was fer sure—I was cold. An I was hungry, too. So right then, them gooseberries were lookin round an ripe, ready to pop in my mouth an slide on down my gullet.

So I done picked one at first, a fat ol berry, plump an purple, turnin it over in my hand. But then I seen them funny ridges on the skin. There was somethin familiar bout em. I coulda sworn they's arranged just like a—well, like a lil face or somethin. Now, maybe my mind was playin tricks on me, but that wun't the only thing, cause the berry felt warm against my fingers, too. I just told myself I was seein things, an maybe the sun had caught them berries just right, at least before that chill swept over.

As I brought that berry up to my nose, I can't say I fancied the smell neither—magined it'd be somethin like a grape, but it was more like a peppery kinda apple.

Feelin my tummy rumblin an grouchin, I said heck with it an flung it in my mouth.

But when I squoze it between my teeth, I heard a lil peep—somethin like a mouse caught in a trap. Then it popped an the warm juice ran over my tongue—not thin an runny—more like thick an soupy, but tastin all silvery an metallic, like them ol spoons my grandmammy served with a bowl a grits. When I spat out that berry, I seen the juice that dripped down my shirt an speckled the ground, dottin all the leaves an grass. Reminded me of a time I shot an ol squirrel outta some tree an it bled all over the damn place.

As I stood there lookin at all that juice I done spat out, some rotten odor started burnin my nostrils, stinkin to high heaven. It wun't that gooseberry neither—it stunk like a dirty ol dog an a rotten can a worms. I ain't never fergot that smell.

But right then, somethin wicked reached out from that thicket an grabbed hold a my ankle.

I yelped an tried to make a dash fer the boat, but whatever it was had me gripped, squeezin so hard it damn near tore my foot off. I couldn't do much but grit my teeth an try an kick the damn thing. But then it swiped my leg out from unner me, an I slammed flat on my face. My nose crunched against the ground, tears stingin my eyes as I gasped fer air. Before I could even git a breath, it started tuggin me in the bushes, an all I could do was claw at the ground, my fingernails jarrin loose as they scraped cross the dirt.

When I looked behind me, even though I was squintin through my tears, I seen somethin worse than my magination coulda ever dreamed up—vines an roots an leaves all twisted up like wiry muscles in some diabolical shape, one a them stringy arms wrapped clean round my leg an squeezin ten times harder than my pappy ever could.

An it was my pappy that saved me, cause he was the one who gave me that ol pocket knife.

Just before that wretched arm yanked me full into the bramble where I'd a been trapped in a tangle a brushwood, I dug a free hand down in my pocket an fetched that knife. As the creature hauled me cross the ground, my body draggin through the dirt, I had that blade out with a flick a my thumb. Reachin down, I slashed that knife straight away into them vines wrapped round my ankle. I done sliced my foot a handful a times, sawin back an forth with a mad fury—hell, I still got the scars to show fer it. But I knew I cut myself free when a nasty spurt a black goo run over my hand, the vines uncoilin fer a second.

When I scrambled to my feet, that demon lashed out with more tendrils, clutchin em all over my body like the legs a some big ol spider. But this time I was ready. Heart poundin against my chest, blood roarin in my ears, I squirmed through the vines an hustled down the bank, divin into that boat like someone shot me out a cannon. I slammed into the bottom so hard it pushed me right off the shore.

As I swiped the paddle from unner the bench, I seen how them root-fingers had followed me, grippin at the sides a the boat, curlin up round the edges, tryin to pull me back to the shore. Couldn't find my knife, but I swatted at em with the paddle like I seen my grandmammy clobberin at possums with her porch broom. I screamed at ev'ry last one of em, somethin primal boilin up inside a me. An affer I slapped the last a them stringy arms away, them tendrils went suckin themselves back over the water an up the shore into the bramble, like a burrow-spider crawlin backward down a hole.

I turned back to the opposite shore an never looked back. I paddled an paddled til my arms burned an til I couldn't feel my fingers round the shaft no more. I member crawlin outta the boat an collapsin on the shore, huggin at the ground an warmin up in the sun as my breath came in gulps.

Any y'all can magine what happened when I got back to my grandmammy's. What happened when she seen my shoes all mucked a muddy-brown an my shirt all stained a purple-red, specially figurin the way she waved that switch at me before.

I was due fer a whuppin.

But if y'all think she scolded me or spanked my bottom somethin raw, then yer wrong.

My grandmammy wrapped her slender arms round me an squeezed me tight—like if she let me go I might melt away. I member her warm tears drippin down her cheeks an into my hair. I didn't say a word. It mighta been a half hour. I just let her hold me like that til she was done.

Fer the rest a that summer my grandmammy treated me polite as pie. Gave me all the pickles I wanted. She knew I wun't ever gonna go back round that river.

Now y'all wanna pile up all this—whaddaya call it—"circumstantial evidence," an prosecute Mr. Ramblewood over there fer the murders a all them children. Well, I ain't no attorney, but I tell ya that ain't somethin y'all can do. Cause them children ain't dead. They're alive as much as y'all an me. But stead a sittin here inhabitin human bodies like we all is, them children is livin in them gooseberries—trapped by that *thing*. Trapped fer all eternity like a livin Hell.

I see some a y'all smilin, thinkin I ain't got all my facts straight affer so many years. But I ain't told y'all bout what I seen just a few years back—right affer my pappy passed. It was a hot summer day when I buried 'im right next to my grandmammy's headstone—out there in the field a black-eyed susans next to the ol lean-to that ain't nothin but a pile a sticks these days. An course I wun't a boy no more, but my curiosities still got the best a me, cause I headed on out there again. To Gooseberry Bramble. But I didn't go cross the river—I at least knew better'n that—I just strained my ears, listenin real hard fer an hour or so. An at some point, when the wind blew just right, driftin over the water from the other side, I could make out the singin, soundin just the same as it did in my boyhood, like a choir a women—cept this time I knew it was children. Missin children.

Yer Honor, I do unnerstan we're in the middle a this here trial. An I unnerstan I ain't nothin but a witness, but let's just say we took one a them recesses, I think ya call it, an ya done took yerself on a field trip a sorts, drivin on up to Black Cobb. If ya parked off the side a the county highway an walked out into them backwoods past the ruins a that lean-to, an if ya tramped west through them fields an then ducked through that grove a all them pines an oaks —a course mindin the scrub—an made yer way down to the shoreline a that river, ya'd hear all them children a cryin like they been doin fer the last sixty-odd years.

An if ya got in that ol boat—assumin it's still there an as sturdy as I member—an paddled cross that water, an if ya wun't scared a that devil-thing, ya might crouch down an set yer eyes real close, just like I did when I was a youngin. If ya did that, I betcha'd see them same tiny faces danglin from the clusters, one a them Caleb Campbell, one a them Mea Jayson—the faces a all the other children ya have up there on that list.

There's one face ya won't see, though, an that's the poor child I popped between my teeth all them years ago. But I'd rather see it like I put em outta their misery.

So I reckon if anyone's a murderer in this here courtroom, well then, I guess it's me.

SOLOMON FORSE is the founder of HOWL Society. After serving in Alaska with the US Army and completing a deployment to Iraq, Solomon moved back to his home state of Colorado to attain a master's degree in education. He now lives among the lakes and forests of the Rocky Mountains where he teaches literature and writes fiction. If Solomon isn't reading, watching, or writing horror, you'll find him role-playing horror with tabletop RPGs like Call of Cthulhu—or shredding horror on the guitar in his Lovecraftian metal band Crafteon. Follow him on Twitter @SolomonForse.

Illustration by P.L. McMillan

CLEMENT & SONS

JOE RADKINS

For years, families had moved in and out of the ancient home so much so that the neighbors were as accustomed to seeing U-Hauls as they were the weekly mail truck. The community welcome wagon had long grown tired of introducing themselves to each new inhabitant, and after a while, they simply ignored the new faces coming and going. While the house wasn't necessarily a place parents would tell their children to stay away from, it didn't matter because the neighborhood kids avoided it anyway.

The unique eighteenth-century building sat on the corner of Walnut and Third behind a row of disordered shrubs. Cracked shutters clattered against the stone walls, hanging from rusted hinges. The foundation sagged into the mud beneath the unkempt lawn. Vines clung to the veranda like a kraken engulfing a ship, and the small front yard was filled with knee-high clumps of grass. Every type of weed under the sun inhabited the overgrown chaos, which provided the perfect home for crawling ticks, slithering snakes, and swarming cicadas.

Surrounding the front of the property, a faded wooden fence leaned forward, backward, and forward again because of the rolling cement of the sidewalk.

Lydia Carrigan couldn't have found a better fixer-upper.

And for once, she needed to feel in control.

No one took notice when the middle-aged woman with brittle, dark-brown hair pulled up in her station wagon. The behemoth of a car lurched to a standstill in front of the dilapidated house. Had anyone noticed, they might have mistaken the woman for an English teacher, at least if they saw the dozen-or-so boxes labeled BOOKS piled in the back of her car.

Taking a minute with both hands on the steering wheel, rays of morning sunlight cascading across her knuckles, Lydia glanced at her reflection in the rearview mirror. Tired eyes reflected back at her, hiding behind dark circles and her massive, clear-framed glasses. She remembered the day she bought them—dragging Michael along to her appointment because the high school had suspended him. The secretary ogled her son's bloodied and battered knuckles. Lydia had never expected Michael to grieve for his father that way.

The growl of a truck zooming past the car ripped her from the memory.

After climbing out of the station wagon, Lydia walked around to the passenger side, pulled out a brown box full of hardbacks, and turned to gaze up at her new home. She wanted to savor the start of this new chapter in her life.

As she sauntered across the uneven walkway, the blades of grass from the neglected lawn tickled the sides of her legs. The wind blew Lydia's linen skirt around her knees, emphasizing her petite frame. When she reached the end of the walkway, she found the porch steps surprisingly silent. Under a corner of the faded welcome mat, Lydia uncovered an envelope with her name scribbled in blue ink. Before she could bend down to grab it, her ears caught a muffled ticking sound coming from the other side of the door. *Had someone left a clock behind?*

Shifting her balance, she placed the box on the porch and picked up the envelope. Excitedly tearing it apart, she discovered the deed and three keys, which she slid out into her cupped palm. As the first key landed in her hand, the taste of metal swarmed about in her mouth, dancing to the tip of her tongue and sliding against the back of her teeth. She shrugged away the curious feeling and inserted a key into the brass lock.

Lydia pushed the massive oak door open with ease and stepped through the threshold, greeted with the smell of something sweet in the air. A light, crisp aroma filled her nose, reminding her of the homemade butter rolls that David used to beg for—she couldn't remember the last time she'd made them.

She took in her new home.

Well, it looks just like the pictures.

Last month, Lydia had worried about not being able to tour the house, but now that she saw it with her own eyes, she knew her intuition had been right.

A spacious, open kitchen with an island occupying the center stretched out before her, and to the left there was a dining room lined with faded yellow wallpaper. Around the corner to her right was a gorgeous living room with windows big enough to let the sun paint the floors and furniture. The rays of light swam with motes of dust.

I could put a couch there, a couple of shelves over here for my books.

On the far wall stood a brick fireplace stretching to the ceiling. And to its left, a staircase with a meticulously carved banister led to the second floor.

Besides a couple of scratches and the need for a fresh coat of paint, Lydia thought the place wasn't too bad.

She softly stepped through the open living room adorned with windows that seemed to sprout from the baseboards and reach to the ceiling. She found herself at the base of the stairs.

Again, the bizarre ticking—seemingly coming from above—interrupted her thoughts.

As Lydia looked to the staircase, she marked how it showed its years through many scuffs and dents. Curiously, when she moved to investigate the second floor, she found the steps didn't make a sound. As Lydia climbed them, she used the railing to keep her balance.

A ringing came alive that made Lydia jump and bring her slender hands to her chest.

Was there a phone here? Was it left behind? It couldn't still be in service.

A second round of ringing blared from the first floor. With it carried the dreadful memory of the worst day of her life.

Lydia had just walked through the door of her previous home after a late night at the office when the phone rang.

"Yes, may I speak to Lydia Carrigan?" the gravelly voice on the other end had asked as she cradled the kitchen landline phone to her ear. It must have been the abrupt sternness in this man's voice, but Lydia never forgot the lump in her throat and the chill down her spine at that question.

". . . Speaking."

"Ma'am, my name is Officer Belardo. Is your husband a 'David Carrigan'?"

She remembered dropping the knife on the cutting board, sliced carrots spilling onto the tile floor.

"Yes."

"And does he drive a silver Toyota Tacoma?" Her heart froze as cold as the chicken she had just pulled out of the freezer.

"Yes, that's him," she said, nearly choking on her words.

"There's been an accident. We are going to need you to come down to the hospital."

"My god, what happened? Is he okay?" she asked, sobbing into the phone.

"Ma'am, we are going to need you to come down here," he said, and then in a softer tone, "I suggest you clear the rest of your day."

The last thing she remembered was standing there in the morgue, her husband lying across a metal table, a gloved hand peeling back the blanket that had covered his pale, bruised body.

As the ringing came to a halt, Lydia was out of breath.

How long did it take me to get up the stairs?

Lydia took a moment at the top of the staircase to steady herself and look down to the first floor. If she wasn't mistaken, the surrounding windows seemed darker now, as if dusk had already fallen.

That's when the ticking grabbed her attention yet again.

At the end of the hallway sat a massive grandfather clock crafted from beautiful dark walnut. A miniature roof crested the top of the clock with faux shingles burned into the wood, crisscrossed by what looked like vines. The face of the clock was the size of a dinner plate, with long, slender Roman numerals lining its perimeter—a regal gold trim boasting a sheen that reflected light like that of a lighthouse guiding ships. As Lydia walked toward the captivating clock, she discovered her footsteps falling in perfect sync with the pendulum's swing.

Perched on four legs that resembled the paws of a mighty lion, the body of the clock was hollowed out to display the reflective pendulum. Kneeling and looking up into the space, Lydia observed a hanging brass rod as thick as her forearm swaying from left to right. It reminded her of peering into her own open mouth in the mirror, the dangling rod like a giant uvula. Attached at the end of the swinging rod was a weight made of the same brass composite, and as Lydia followed it with her eyes, she discerned a peculiarly carved pattern—the head of a rose. In complete transfixion, Lydia's eyes imitated the swing of the pendulum, following its movements from side to side. She admired the color, the finish, the carvings, and especially the brass rose.

As she marveled at the clock, the loud ticking bore its way into her skull, and an image of David blipped across her mind, maybe from one of their first dates—a memory of him walking toward her with a single rose that bobbed in his hands with every step.

Step.

Step.

Step.

As Lydia stood, her reflection distorted and bowed across the curved glass that housed the face of the clock. Her button nose now elongated to that of a witch, her almond eyes rounding out to the sides of her head. She chuckled to herself and gently placed a hand on the side of the clock, the clicking of the pendulum pulsating against her palm like a heartbeat.

LATER THAT NIGHT, after dragging in the mattress from her station wagon, she finally set her last box on the aging laminate kitchen counter. Hands on her hips, Lydia looked around the place and smiled.

If only younger me could be here to see it.

She'd finally got her blank slate.

Lydia then lay in the cool darkness of her new bedroom, grateful for her new life. A light warmth filled her body, the ticking down the hall transfixing her, ushering her into a gentle reverie.

Drifting off to the clicking, Lydia dreamed of the day she met David.

AT HER FRESHMAN orientation she had noticed a man wearing a green-and-black checkered flannel, sleeves rolled up, and holes worn through the knees of his pants. She wanted to scoff, but then he turned and smiled at her. She couldn't ignore his piercing eyes. And that was all it took.

He leaned over and said something to his group of friends before standing and crossing the crowded room to greet Lydia himself.

"Hey, I'm David," he said, the words seeming to float from his mouth, fluttering toward her ears. His eyes dropped to a textbook she was holding to her chest. The edge of the book peeked out from underneath her arm.

"I have First-Year Seminar too," said David, lowering his gaze, likely to admire the rest of her.

"Would you want to get some coffee? On me?" he asked.

Five minutes later, they found themselves on the busy sidewalk leading to Addams Hall, paper cups in hand. Lydia had ordered her usual latte with milk and sweetener but was surprised to find that David wasn't a fan of coffee—he had ordered a hot tea with honey and vanilla instead. As they walked side by side down the footpath, their steps fell together in unison.

Left.

Right.

Left.

Right.

After pointing out a woman and her golden retriever on the path before them, David told Lydia about his ailing dog he had put down only a few weeks prior. Lydia sympathized, but fought the urge to console him. Her thought was interrupted when she marked the faces of the people surrounding her—their contorted expressions painted with shock and disgust.

As if a dam had burst, a flood of people rushed toward her, knocking into her without concern. Lydia stumbled and tripped over her own feet. Inundated with a wave of panic, Lydia looked over to see David reaching out to her. Suddenly, strange hands grabbed and grasped all over her body, one after another. Each grip stronger than the last, the hands pulled at her hair; Lydia's scalp nearly tore away from her skull before her vision faded to black.

She couldn't see, she couldn't move, she couldn't even scream —but she could still hear.

All she could do was listen.

A chorus of a hundred feet surrounded her and stamped the sidewalk in reverberating lockstep.

Knock.

Knock.

Knock.

LYDIA'S EYES JOLTED OPEN, sweat beading on her forehead. Three heavy knocks on the front door broke the morning silence. Another round of hammering pulled Lydia from her daze, and she forced herself to rise and answer the door. As she walked down the hall to the stairs, the ticking reverberated inside her skull. Her body pulsated with every click. Head throbbing, eyes squinting, teeth clenching, she shuffled down the steps.

Lydia opened it to find a stocky man in a crimson shirt standing on the veranda.

"Mrs. Carrigan?" asked the man.

"Yes. Hi, I'm so sorry for the wait." She peered at the moving truck parked in the street beside her station wagon. "Should I move my car?"

"No need, we'll bring everything in." He glanced back to the truck for a moment, revealing a tattoo of a rose on the side of his neck. She could see the petals quivering with each tick of the clock that echoed behind her.

"Just as soon as you let us know what goes where."

Lydia could see two other men dressed in the same crimson uniform waiting by the moving truck. The bold black letters that clung to its side read CLEMENT & SONS.

"Of course. Thank you," she replied with unease.

A couple hours and a few signatures later, the house was looking more like a home. Organizing bookshelves always brought her joy—she gazed at them and smiled, admiring the numerous rows of hardback novels organized into genres. Beyond the books, the knick-knacks were all sorted, her clothes folded and put away. Framed photos of David and the boys dressed up the home as a finishing touch.

As night crept in, she went from room to room turning on lamps; the light revealed more and more of her hard work. Weary from the unpacking, Lydia eventually moved to her favorite couch that had been pushed against the living room wall. As she lay down and leaned her head against the cushion, the weight of her eyelids transported her to a much-needed sleep.

🐾

THE ECHO of the swinging pendulum upstairs hurled itself down the hall, bouncing down the steps and rippling through the living room. Lydia jerked awake, gasping for breath, her hands reaching down to the couch to center herself. Her eyes immediately darted to the stairs.

The hair on the back of her neck prickled as she listened to the clicking from the floor above. Lydia pushed herself off the couch and paused after a couple of shaky steps. Crowning the top of the steps on unsteady legs, she stared down the hall, unable to help herself from gawking at the clock's beauty—the carvings, the color, the lustrous wood finish. But what mesmerized her most was the rose at the end of the pendulum. Clicking from side to side, it almost beckoned her. Her feet shuffled toward the clock against her will, her eyes following the pendulum's swing. The closer she got, the faster her heart pounded against her chest.

🐾

LYDIA SQUEEZED the last globule of her travel-size shampoo bottle into her palm. The hum of the mower outside the bathroom window blended with the steady torrent of the showerhead to create a soothing effect. She felt dazed, almost like she had fallen into a stupor. As Lydia drifted into a trance, she bore deep into her memories.

She recalled sitting at the end of a dock, David at her side. The Minnesota lake house stood behind them while they both gazed out toward the sun as it dipped over the lake. Lydia remembered it vividly, resting her head on David's shoulder as her legs hung over the edge, swinging back and forth above the dark green water. The smell of David's cologne filled her nostrils. He reached behind his back for a moment, then his hand reappeared, a single rose rippling in the wind from the lake. Lydia plucked it from his gentle grasp. Roses were her favorite so she kissed him.

Lydia looked down at the water, and the image of her swinging legs in the lake's reflection burned into her mind.

Back and forth.
Back and forth.
Back and forth.

The sudden sting from hot to ice-cold water shocked Lydia back to the present. She slammed the stainless steel knob sideways, and the full force of the blast immediately quieted. She no longer heard the mower. The drops from the showerhead beat against the bottom of the tub, echoing in a synchronized pattern. She wrung the excess water from her hair while her eyes followed each free-falling drop to the drain below.

From down the hall, the sound of the pendulum joined with the droplets, keeping time.

After the water stopped dripping, Lydia eventually stepped out of the tub and got dressed. When she later passed through the hallway, hair still wrapped in a towel, she examined the clock in the morning's gentle glow. The ticking greeted her.

With dreamy eyes, she whispered, "Morning, my love."

Once again she caressed the side of the grandfather clock. A strange set of grooves tickled her fingertips, so she removed her hand and leaned closer. Engraved into the paneling were the words CLEMENT & SONS.

A shiver rippled across her skin.

LATER THAT NIGHT, part of the golden moon peeked through the trees in Lydia's front yard. As she came down the stairs, a familiar scent wafted through the air. She tried to place the aroma, her brow furrowing as remnants of nostalgia flickered through her mind.

Vanilla. And . . . honey.

Almost too dark to see anything, she gingerly entered the

kitchen. Between the stainless steel sink and the still-hot coil of the stove top was her favorite mug filled almost to the top with milky water. A swirl of vapor rose from the cup.

That can't be possible.

Lydia's heart rate quickened as a brick formed in her chest. Finding herself holding her breath, she forced herself to relax then reached out for the handle.

Lydia turned off the stove with a shaky hand and dumped the tea down the drain. During the process, she smacked the bottom of the mug against the kitchen sink. The sound sang through the house. Lydia flinched from the noise then placed the mug in the dishwasher, effectively erasing the evidence of what she was already telling herself was a hallucination.

Tick.

Tick.

Tick.

She thought how odd it was that only at certain moments she could consciously hear the clock or how it crept into her ears out of nowhere when she was busying herself with everyday chores. It felt like a deceiving hug from a parent, reassuring her but at the same time squeezing her tighter and tighter with each breath.

Lost in thought, she wandered into the living room. The plush threads of the thick area rug tickled her bare feet, pulling her from her trance and pushing her into the present. Out of her peripheral vision, Lydia detected something through the banister rails at the top of the stairs—a pair of black leather shoes topped with navy work pants.

"Hello?" she croaked.

The stranger didn't answer, only stood there without moving. Lydia waited in the stillness. Her throat was dry. Blood pumped harder through her ears. Every muscle in her body tightened.

"I'm going to call the police," she announced to the stranger.

The ticking grew louder, and she felt compelled to see who the mysterious individual was. But something inside her already knew the answer. She took a deep breath to gather what courage she had and trudged up the staircase as if wading through a swamp.

An urge to investigate swelled in her chest and consumed her against her better judgement.

Lydia reached the first step, looked up, and discovered the stranger was now facing away from her. She could hear the intruder, who she took to be a man, tapping his hand on the banister with a distinct clicking sound—as if he was wearing a ring.

Tap.

Tap.

Tap.

With the same beat as the man's hand, the same rhythm as the clock, Lydia unconsciously swayed her head from side to side and took the steps one at a time. The man on the stairs suddenly raised his foot, turned, and meandered down the hall. His footsteps, her swaying head, the pulsing in her ears—all were synchronous.

Lydia reached the second floor and followed the man's direction. Down the hall, the stranger's body was staggering back and forth between the walls in concert with the clicking pendulum.

The intruder was now at the end of the corridor, standing toe to toe with the clock. He turned around and faced Lydia before delivering a massive grin, the rest of his face painted black from the shadows.

Her stomach dropped with recognition as her heart swelled, and all the stress that balled up in her chest melted away.

There he stood, not looking any older than their wedding day. She couldn't mistake him for anyone else: the dark hair, the small dimple when he smiled. She moved toward him with a soft shuffling, and as she got closer, the unmistakable scent of his cologne enveloped her. It was her David.

"Hi, sweetheart. You're right on time," he whispered in the soft tone that crawled out from the past and into her heart.

Their eyes locked. The closer Lydia floated toward him, the wider his smile grew—stretching to almost unnatural proportions. The hallway seemed to be three times longer than usual. Lydia extended her hand, and David reciprocated with his own—now a sculpted rose at the end of a long, brass arm.

Dread smothered the hope and longing within her heart. She would not lose the love of her life again.

She moved to within a couple feet of her husband. David was now the size of the face of the clock, and he beckoned her from the other side of the glass. His smile and the sway of his head stirred the deep longing she held within her heart since his departure from this world. But here he was—he had come back for her. Lydia's hands gripped either side of the clock, knuckles white, standing inches from its glass face. Her head rocked along with David and the rose of the pendulum.

With a smile on her face, she exhaled with a breathy voice, "My love."

THE COMMUNITY WELCOME WAGON—WHO had long since abandoned paying attention to the house and its occupants—neither noticed the abating cicadas nor the new abundance of ticks and snakes in their own yards. It wasn't until neighbors became curious about the rusty station wagon with expired plates that sat outside the home that anyone heard the rhythmic, muffled ticking. The sound leaked through the broken windows shattered by neighborhood kids who had hurled rocks from across the street. If only they had the courage to enter, they may have found their way upstairs, followed the noise down the hall, and discovered the most gorgeous of grandfather clocks. Below its face, they wouldn't have seen a swinging pendulum, but the severed leg of a woman who gave everything for her past—swaying back and forth, blood dripping to the dark puddle below.

Drip.
Drip.
Drip.

JOE RADKINS IS AN ILLUSTRATOR, horror writer, and a cheesecake connoisseur. Born and raised in Florida, he now resides in Pennsylvania with his wife and son. At a young age he discovered his love for film, stories, and art, leading him to attend Columbia College Chicago to study cinematography. He spends his days training his Padawan, writing, and fulfilling art commissions. You can find his work on Instagram @thecinemaddiction or contact him at radkinsjoseph@gmail.com.

Illustration by Drew Nault

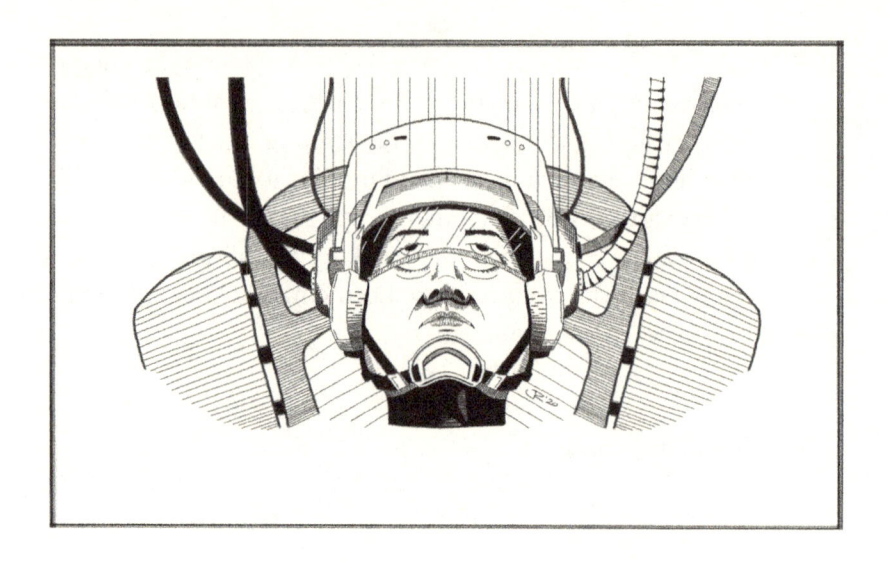

POSSESS AND SERVE

CHRISTOPHER O'HALLORAN

1

Sarah opened her eyes behind the counter of a convenience store, the dirty barrel of a .38 Special inches from her face. The snub-nose peeked above a skeletal fist. It was close enough to smell—rusty, like ore pulled straight from the earth, dirty and raw. A scrap of faded brown fabric clung to the front sight where it had ripped when the homeless man tore the gun from his pocket.

Outside, traffic zipped by. People tried not to stop on East Hastings; it wasn't one of Vancouver's nicer streets.

The Summoner was taped under the counter to the left of the register. Her finger released the button.

She was fucked.

It was her duty to de-escalate situations to which she had been summoned. The man whose body she inhabited could have a family. People who might rely on him. People who could suffer if he took a bullet to the head.

The robber's snarl fell away, his mouth dropping open.

The man she possessed had brown skin. That likely meant brown eyes. The rings around the pupils that indicated possession by an officer of the Assumed Control Unit were light-blue.

They would be as glaring as white paint on a chalkboard.

Sweat coated her face. She didn't dare wipe it away. It collected in her goatee.

She couldn't disarm the robber. Couldn't move out of the way or duck behind the counter before he had time to pull the trigger.

The clerk should have handed over the money.

The robber closed his mouth and tightened his jaw.

"Let's take a moment—"

The robber's finger flexed. A flash of light swelled from the end of his barrel and whited out her world. Lead punched through her forehead, igniting a blaze that was thankfully brief.

🐾

SARAH AWOKE IN HER RIG, sweat sticking her shirt to the hollow of her back. Her helmet was a vice. She yanked it off, neglecting to loosen the knob on the rear strap so that it pulled strands of hair from her scalp.

"Fuck," she said. "Fuck!"

She slammed a hand into the soft plastic cushion on which she lay.

It wasn't the first time she had failed in a moment of Assumed Control, but it never got easier. The situation had been hopeless. She hadn't stood a chance.

That didn't make it easy.

She checked her watch. Almost quitting time. Throwing in the towel would be acceptable, but it would ruin her day. Better to cleanse her palate with another summoning.

Sarah needed a win.

She slipped her helmet back on and accepted the next call.

White light washed over her vision. Three long seconds passed as her consciousness flowed from her body into that of a fit young man.

He was the type of guy who could take control of a situation. Body like a firefighter. Strong forearms, large biceps. A chest that could jump on command.

Why did he summon her?

"You are such a fucking loser! Am I not enough for you? People you've never met are more important than your *fiancée?*"

Sarah turned around. A woman stood before her, beautiful and furious. A PlayStation controller was in her hand, lifted as if to bludgeon.

Sarah was there to de-escalate. If nothing else, she could serve as a witness in the unlikely event he filed charges.

The woman looked to the Summoner in Sarah's hand. Looked into her eyes. Recognized the blue rings.

"Ma'am," Sarah began, "I am an officer of the Assumed Control Unit. Can we speak about—"

His fiancée shrieked in frustration. She hurled the controller into the stone mantle of their fireplace and stormed out of the apartment. Problem solved, at least until she returned.

How many times would an ACU officer be called to this apartment throughout their hopefully brief marriage? It didn't matter; the man paid for their service, so they were obligated to provide assistance.

Sarah was about to relinquish control when she caught her own eye in the mirror hung over the mantle. The reflection revealed a handsome face with a sharp chin and eyes only a shade darker than the blue rings around the pupils—*his* pupils. Sarah rubbed her hands over the stubble of his cheeks, flexing his biceps, and running fingers over his abs.

She walked through his apartment, now running her hands over his things. The stone mantle, its rough edges like little teeth against her palm. The sharp corners of ornately framed photos depicting their doomed relationship.

What would it be like living this man's life?

In his kitchen, Sarah opened up the double doors of their giant fridge. There was a shelf dedicated to kombucha and other health drinks—all organic, of course. This beautiful couple didn't put anything toxic in their body. Something else must have poisoned their relationship.

On the top shelf sat the unhealthiest thing in the kitchen: a plate of tiramisu, thickly layered with cream and soft cookie. She took it out and sat it on the counter.

One of the benefits to possessing another person was that you tasted anything you put in your mouth while the body left behind dealt with the calories. It wasn't professional, but it was harmless compared to the guys in the unit who she'd overheard bragging about the "racks" they'd felt up when assuming control.

The perks of the job were few. This man could handle a couple extra calories.

2

"You think Anderson knows his fly is undone?"

Sarah had been listening raptly when Otto pointed out the fashion faux pas. Anderson was large and commanding behind the podium. There was a sheet of printed notes on the clear surface, but not once did he consult them while introducing training courses in Krav Maga and Improvised Weaponry. The open fly undermined his competency and professionalism.

He gave the weekly briefing in the same, immaculate boardroom he always used. The constant lemony scent of Pledge hung in the air.

Sarah's eyes flicked from his face to his pants.

"Ah, look at that." White cloth with a red pattern showed between open zipper teeth in Anderson's crisply pressed pants. "Maple leaves or hearts?"

Otto leaned forward, putting his newly Lasiked eyes to the test.

"My guess is maple leaves. I wouldn't peg Anderson as a romantic."

"Very patriotic." She looked up. Anderson caught her eye. He smiled at her.

She smiled back and looked away, her face growing hot.

Among the Assumed Control Unit's fifty officers, Sarah was one of only five women. Instead of banding together, they all sat at separate tables in the packed boardroom to distance themselves from one another.

They wore baggy clothes to straighten curves. Hoodies and sweats. The unofficial uniform of the ACU. The other four women cut their hair short in conservative hairstyles, but Sarah wasn't prepared to go that far. She had been growing her hair out since high school.

Her dark locks were one of her best features, and she hadn't given up on love quite yet.

However, none of that mattered in the ACU; when you possessed someone else, you wore the body of whoever summoned you like a well-tailored suit.

It didn't matter what you looked like, what clothes you wore, your gender or race. How strong you were. When you were called, all externals were stripped away and left in your rig. What remained was your mind. Your training. Discipline. That was all that was needed, all an officer brought with them.

Sarah brought her knowledge of boxing, jiu-jitsu, and conflict resolution into each encounter. Most people who purchased and utilized a Summoner were timid and weak. If Sarah couldn't talk her way out of a dangerous situation alone, she was prepared to use their body to fight.

They feared injury. They feared death.

When she possessed these people, Sarah did not inherit that fear.

"In the few years the ACU has been established," Captain Anderson said, "we have been able to take pride in the honour of our officers. Your record-keeping has been astounding, and we appreciate that. Performance in the field has been exemplary; most Assumed-Control situations are resolved in a professional manner with minimal casualties." For the first time during his presentation, Anderson looked at the podium. "But recently we have been receiving some complaints."

Sarah stiffened at Captain Anderson's words, ice forming from the base of her skull to her tailbone.

They caught me.

Sarah dropped the pen she had been taking notes with. Her last call. The tiramisu. What if it was the fiancée's? What if she'd come home looking forward to her one indulgence, and the empty plate in the sink pushed her over the edge? She was violent enough to have her outburst in front of Sarah. What was she like without outside intervention?

I'm fired.

She shook off the paranoid thoughts. Surely most officers did the same. It was a snack; it wasn't like she cleared out the pantry.

"A local woman claims her jewelry was missing when she came to after a B&E," Captain Anderson continued, his voice low. "She searched her house after the encounter and found them outside her first-floor bathroom. They were under a bush, presumably in a place where the offending officer could come back and retrieve them in his—or her—own body. I do not need to explain to you why actions like these reflect terribly on the department."

His face grew severe. "Officers acting in a way not befitting of the badge will be summarily terminated and prosecuted to the full extent of the law. A great deal of trust is placed in your hands every time a victim presses that button. They relinquish consciousness with the hope *you* perform better in *their* body. The amount of trepidation they must overcome before activating their Summoner is something we can only guess at, and it is up to us to resolve the situation as effectively and professionally as possible. You do not have to deal with the ramifications of your actions after the situation. They do. There are ways to audit your calls, so let's not go down that path.

"Remember your oath. Do not give my superiors reason to dismantle the program. You all know how valuable it is."

Indeed, they did. How many times had Sarah and Otto shown up late to a call while working for the city police? Their cruiser reached too many situations where minutes had been the difference between life and death—minutes they lost in traffic, moments of mental agony sitting in a roaring car while they could only guess at the horrors occurring in the time between call and arrival. She and Otto jumped at the opportunity to join the new unit. It was a chance to make a difference. To save lives in seconds.

———

THE OFFICERS FILED out of the conference room after the speech, each one taking time to shake the captain's hand as they left.

"Should I tell him about his fly?" Otto asked quietly.

"*No*," Sarah hissed back, closing her binder and tucking it under her arm. "Let him be embarrassed in private. Have some decency."

Otto rolled his eyes. "Okay, okay. Meet you in the ring, padawan. Got your gear?"

"Mhm. It's gotta be a quick session though. I have a date tonight, and my *Hot-Girl* disguise takes time putting on."

Otto chuckled and walked towards the door. He shook hands with the captain and said a few words before heading off to the men's locker room.

"Forrester!"

She glanced over her shoulder.

Mark Taylor. He strutted towards her, shaker cup in hand and head held high as if the act of sitting through a meeting made him noble. Tall and well-built, another recruit from the police force. Guys like him had a hero complex. They thought they were God's gift to mankind, like Superman sent to protect the city. He had a trendy blond haircut, long on the top, short on the sides.

I hope he goes bald. Sarah turned and began to walk off. He caught up easily.

"Why are you ignoring me?" His coy look of manufactured confusion seemed to ask, *What reason could anyone have not to talk to little ol' me?*

"I'm not," Sarah replied. "Guess I didn't hear you."

"Sure. What are you doing tonight?"

"I'm busy." They reached the captain. Mark stepped ahead, transferred his shaker cup to his left hand, and enthusiastically shook hands with his superior.

"Taylor," Anderson said, "They told me about that three-man mugging you neutralized yesterday. Great work, son. That's the kind of story fit for the newsletter. A couple more of those and our funding should double, if not triple."

Mark beamed. Those pearly whites shone like polished plastic.

"Thank you, sir. It was a little touch-and-go for a bit there. The woman who summoned me was on the older side. A bit stiff."

"You'd never let a little thing like old age hold you back," said Anderson.

They laughed. Mark stepped through the door. Just a couple guys, shooting the shit.

Sarah stepped to the captain, feeling like a dwarf before the tall man. He grasped her hand delicately, his large palm swallowing hers.

"Forrester. You're off now, correct? I hope you've had a productive day."

"Yes, sir. A teenager got into a fender bender but didn't know how to trade insurance information." She could've told him about the gas station robbery, but didn't want to highlight her failure. "Those possessions always feel like a waste."

She had taken over the scrawny boy while a short, fat woman was in the middle of reaming him out. When the woman saw the blue rings appear in his eyes, her agitation disappeared, leaving behind only heaps of respect for the officer inside the boy's body.

"Yes," said Anderson, "but we are here to assist in all situations, life-threatening or trivial."

Trivial was becoming the norm.

Sarah thanked the captain and walked toward the women's modest locker room. As she approached the door, she felt a tap on the shoulder. Sarah turned in the direction of the tap but saw nobody. Rolling her eyes, she turned in the other direction to find Mark leaning against the wall beside the men's locker room.

"Blow it off," he said.

"Excuse me?"

"Whatever you're doing tonight, blow it off. What can be so important on a Wednesday night that you can't go out to dinner with me?"

"I have a date."

"When?"

"Dinner time."

He looked at his watch. "Come out with me now. I'll buy you a smorgasbord so when you go out with the next schmuck you can act all ladylike and order a watercress salad or something."

"You should talk to Anderson about these strategies you come up with. Maybe he can put you in charge of an all-female strike team. You certainly know how to talk to them."

He smiled with the corner of his mouth. "I can't talk to those bulldogs. They scare me."

"Maybe I'll blow off the seven o'clock schmuck after all and schedule an appointment with a barber. Would you still annoy the shit out of me if I had a buzz cut?"

"You'd have to put on about thirty pounds to get rid of me."

"I'll make sure to order the entire menu tonight then."

"Save the schmuck that bill. Come out. If we leave now, we can still make happy hour."

"She can't," said Otto. The door to the men's locker room swung shut, air whooshing out of the room in a defeated sigh. He stood outside it, cinching tight the rope on his sweats. "We've got a date in the gym."

Mark looked at Otto, then looked back at Sarah, raising his eyebrows.

"If you leave now, you can still make happy hour, Taylor." She disappeared inside her own empty locker room.

3

Sarah panted as her blows landed like butterfly kisses upon the training pads Otto held.

"Who do you think the thief is?" she asked.

"Could be anyone."

"If I got my hands on that asshole—"

Sarah swung extra hard. The pad moved an inch and a half. Otto smiled.

"Seriously," Sarah said, bouncing on the balls of her feet. "Who do you think it is? Think it could be—"

"You always want to talk about work."

Otto swung his left pad at her head. Sarah ducked. His right followed, and she leaned back out of his reach.

The air smelled of fresh rubber. The gym had brand new punching bags, speed bags, weightlifting equipment, and state-of-the-art cardio machines. They had it all to themselves, but Sarah was so focused that she wouldn't have noticed a full marching band performing around the ring in which they sparred.

Otto's arms barely moved as she sent jab after jab. Left, left, right, then a hook. A lock of hair came loose and fell in front of her eyes, but she ignored it, sending one inconsequential punch after another, never quite hitting as hard as she hoped. She longed for control over someone strong. To spar inside a body built for fighting would be heaven.

But Sarah trained for technique, not to build muscle. If she could be faster, if her reflexes could be better, maybe looking down the dark barrel of a gun wouldn't mean defeat. Maybe she would have a chance.

She pushed harder. For the job. For herself.

Otto swung the pads at her head, one after the other. Sarah

evaded, bending at the waist. When she popped back up, she led with an uppercut.

It connected with the pad, rotating Otto's arm like a speeding windmill. Sarah gawked at it.

It finally moved!

The other pad was still in motion, however. It smacked her on the side of the head, sending her sprawling onto her knees.

"Oh my god," Otto exclaimed, ripping the pads off and rushing to her aid. "I'm so, so sorry."

"It's fine," Sarah replied, waving away his attempts to help. "My fault. I lost focus." She stood blinking back tears. "You really got a swing on you, Otto."

He blushed, looking at his palms. "I guess all the training is starting to pay off." He laughed. "Where was all this a year ago?"

Sarah didn't know what to say. Otto had been chunky as long as she knew him. His discipline had been scant. When they served on the police force, she frequently cleaned out junk-food wrappers from their cruiser at the end of their shift.

Ironically, it was only when his personal health stopped mattering as much that he started to improve his lifestyle. A month after joining the Assumed Control Unit, Sarah started seeing him in the gym. At first, he walked the treadmill, binge-watching *Game of Thrones* when people were around, and anime when they weren't. Eventually, he started jogging, then mixing in dumbbell curls and bodyweight exercises. He ditched the specs and paid a doctor to zap his eyes to perfection. Before long, the pounds started to shed, leaving behind thick muscle and a happier man.

"I'm really proud of you, Otto. We all are."

He blushed even harder, rubbing at the back of his neck. "At least I don't grunt getting in and out of my rig anymore."

Sarah chuckled, removing her headgear and pulling her ponytail tight. "I've noticed some of the girls sneaking glances at you from time to time. You should talk to one of them. I'm sure once you get past those haircuts, they're lovely people."

Otto held the middle rope of the sparring ring and Sarah stepped underneath, dropping to the ground.

"You women are awful to each other," he said through a wide smile, following her out. "You would think you'd look out for each other with how much testosterone flows around here."

"You'd be wrong." She tossed her gear into her duffel then rummaged through it and brought out a water bottle. She sat on a bench against the wall and drank deeply.

"Who's the guy?"

Sarah wiped at her mouth. "The guy?"

"Your date tonight." Otto plopped next to her.

"Some guy my sister thinks I'll get along with. I can't remember his name, but he's a supervisor at some data-entry firm."

"Ah, upper management. I didn't think people like that *had* lives outside of work." He stood, stretching his arms wide. His shirt lifted an inch, and Sarah's eyes were drawn to the suggestion of a six-pack there.

Looks like the days of Slim Jims and potato chips are long gone.

"I was thinking," Otto asked, stretching his neck, "maybe if things don't go well tonight, you and I could grab dinner tomorrow. Think of it as a palate cleanser."

"Otto, my man, you're starting to sound like Mark—so forward."

"Mark? Oh no, you got me all wrong." He nearly dropped his bag. "I just wouldn't want you to think all men are as dull as this 'Melvin in Accounting' or whatever. It would just be two friends, enjoying each other's company."

Sarah's face grew hot. She didn't mean to insult him. It was self-defence. Keeping a friend at arm's length so as not to ruin the relationship.

"I'm sorry, Otto. Dinner sounds nice. They say you should do it every night."

He stumbled, and for a second Sarah thought he might stop right in his steps.

"Really?"

"Sure," she said. "I mean, that's assuming I don't fall in love with Melvin and elope with him this very night. I'll send you a wedding invitation if we do."

He laughed, catching up to her. "I'll have to mail my present to you at a later date. I picked up a second shift tonight."

"You work too hard."

Otto opened the door with his back and held it as she passed through.

"When you love what you do, Sarah, you don't work a day in your life."

4

"Not the dreamboat you hoped for?"

Otto offered Sarah the bag of chips that came with his meal. The large cafeteria was almost empty apart from a few officers who sat alone with their simple meals—bland-looking beef, neon heaps of corn, and pale mashed potatoes. All funding went toward the high-tech possession rigs, leaving the food service to suffer.

"I feel bad for him, you know?" She pulled open the bag. "How does someone like that find love?"

"He's probably a really interesting guy once you get to know him."

"That's the thing," she replied, mouth full of chips. "Most everyone is, but what if that awkward stage lingers past the first date? What if he's a stammering mess at your wedding, stepping all over your feet on the first dance? Then you guys have kids, and they're all awkward and boring, little clones of him."

"I guess that's the chance you take in the dating world."

"I guess." She shook crumbs from the bottom of the bag into her mouth. "I bet you got up to no good last night. Save any damsels in distress? Stop any affronts to our civilized society?"

"A few," he replied, leaning back. He laced his fingers together behind his head. The motion put his chest on display. Where fat used to hang, fleshy and weak, there was now hard muscle, built by strict discipline in both the gym and the kitchen. Why was she only noticing this now?

"The only damsel I'm looking to save tonight is you. Save you from a boring night."

Sarah rolled her eyes and flicked a kernel of corn at him. He dodged. It sailed over his shoulder and hit Mark on the thigh a couple feet behind him.

Oh God, Sarah thought, *here we go.*

"Boys and girls," he said. He sat on the fixed chair next to Otto and placed his bottle full of some sort of protein shake on the table.

"Oh, hi, Mark," Otto replied.

"What do you want?" Sarah crossed her arms.

Mark raised his hands, palms out. "What the hell? What's with the hostility?"

She leaned forward, raising the pitch of her voice as if talking to a child. "I'm so sorry, Marky, what can I do for you? Do you need Mommy to open the lid on your juice?" She leaned forward and popped the top open on his protein shake. "There you go. Drink it up, it'll make you big and strong." Otto laughed behind a muffling hand.

Mark wasn't bothered. He smiled at Sarah.

"Careful with that mommy-talk. I don't need a sexual awakening this late in the game." He grabbed the protein shake and raised it to his lips, his Adam's apple bobbing as he downed half the drink. When he finished, he wiped his lips. "I know you want to roll your eyes at me. Don't hold back to spare my feelings."

Sarah complied.

"You do that so often, I'm surprised they don't get stuck back there," Mark said. "How'd your date go?"

"Otto and I were talking about how much of a pompous cock you were—"

Otto's eyebrows shot up. "I wasn't!"

"—but here you go, proving me wrong. You *do* care. You *do* listen. Someday you'll make some little sorority girl the happiest wifey ever."

"I'm over my college-girl phase, Forrester. I'm into women now." He dropped a wink at her, and she felt like simultaneously laughing and puking.

"Well, I'm into real men who don't get their eyebrows threaded." She lifted a fist to Otto, who reluctantly bumped knuckles.

A fresh-faced officer with close-cropped hair approached Mark from behind.

"Marcus Taylor? The captain would like to speak with you."

Mark's mouth turned downwards in a comical frown.

"Uh oh," he whispered to Sarah and Otto. "As if the mommy-talk wasn't worrying enough, it looks like I'm in for a spanking. What are the odds of me coming out of this day with a weird, diaper-wearing, baby-talking fetish?"

Sarah burst out laughing. It just slipped out. She didn't want to give Mark the satisfaction, but it was too late.

Mark stood, smiling.

"Do good out there, boys and girls," he said and walked off.

"See ya, Mark," Otto said, and Mark lifted a hand over his shoulder in a lazy farewell. "Guy's a bit of a prick, huh?"

Sarah wiped a tear from her eye. "Uh-huh. He's relentless."

"Gotta admire that." He looked uncomfortable. She should've tried harder not to laugh at Mark's joke. "I figured you and I could check out this new restaurant a couple blocks from my place. It's supposed to be pretty good, all organic and stuff."

"That sounds nice."

Otto smiled at her then looked at the table. Mark's shaker cup remained there, forgotten. "Guess the baby forgot his bottle. I'll bring it to him."

Sarah chuckled. "I'll see you tonight, Otto."

He lifted his hand over his shoulder as he walked away. The gesture lacked something present in Mark's wave, a certain confidence that didn't have to be forced or displayed for the benefit of others.

Sarah blushed. *Don't you dare compare them.* Otto was a nice guy. He didn't deserve that.

The joke wasn't even that funny. But later, when she thought of it, she couldn't help but chuckle.

5

"We were hoping to get someone who knew how to fix computers."

Sarah had been called into the body of a boy who was deep within the clutches of puberty. The computer monitor before her was filled edge to edge with pop-ups advertising erotic video games, easy hookups in *your* town, and pills to increase your dick size by one to three inches. The faux-leather chair beneath her was uncomfortably warm.

"What the hell were you kids doing on this thing?" Her pubescent voice cracked.

"Nothing! We were, um, just on YouTube, watching videos."

Sure, thought Sarah, *and those crusty socks your mom finds under your bed are that way because your sweat is 50% corn starch.*

"Please, you have to help. This is my dad's computer. It was all *your* idea anyway. I mean, Josh's idea, sir."

"The Summoner is for emergencies only."

"This is an emergency!"

Sarah smacked her forehead with a sweaty hand. Not her hand, not her forehead.

The customer was always right. Summoners weren't cheap. If this kid's dad was willing to shell out the money, it was her responsibility to provide assistance.

Sarah located the offending program, shut it down, found the file location, and uninstalled it. All that was left was to close the pop-ups and install a parental lock. When she did, the boy's disappointment paid better than any money his dad could provide.

"You spend too much time looking at that stuff, you're going to be bored when you finally get to touch a real woman."

She basked in the embarrassment that washed over the young boy as he turned a bright shade of red. His glasses had fallen halfway down his nose, and Sarah noticed the cluster of pimples forming between his eyebrows. High school would be tough for him.

"Maybe you guys should find different hobbies," she said. "Watching porn with your buddy is a little fucked up."

Before the boy could stutter his response to her, Sarah relinquished control. She opened the visor on the control helmet and let her eyes adjust to the lighting in her area. The clock next to her rig reassured her that her shift was half an hour from being over. *Thank God,* she thought. Her stomach rumbled in agreement.

A light on her HUD notified her of a call. *One more.* She lifted her fingers to the helmet, secured it, and assumed control.

There was a flash of white. It faded, revealing a modern kitchen equipped with stainless steel appliances, granite countertops, and a row of sharpened knives hanging by a magnetic strip. She scanned the room for signs of distress but found nothing.

Not nothing. Smoke. The smell hung in the air like a cloud. On top of the stove lay the charred corpse of either a large chicken or a small turkey. Other than the bird, she was completely alone. In the body of a fifteen-year-old boy.

"What—"

A dry erase board hung on the fridge, an uncapped marker hanging from a string. THAT'S NOT MY DAD was scrawled in clumsy capital letters. An arrow beneath pointed down a short hall that ended in a closed door.

What did it mean? Was it for her?

She walked towards the door and tried the knob. Locked. She put her ear against the cold wood.

A woman's muffled pleas came from the other side.

Sarah backed up a step, lifted a thin leg, and drove her heel into the door beneath the knob.

It swung open, revealing the naked backside of an overweight man. His pants were around his ankles. He leaned over a woman lying on her back at the edge of a king-sized bed. His large, hairy hand covered her mouth. The woman's crying eyes met Sarah's.

Sarah didn't think. She rushed forward and grabbed the man by his thick work shirt. He was heavy but unbalanced as he struggled to get his pants back on. She rolled him over her back onto the ground and dropped a knee on his neck. The rolls of fat surrounding it softened the blow, however. The man got to his feet, raging and shaking her off.

Blue rings glowed around his pupils.

She stopped, stunned. He wasn't in control of his own body.

This man had summoned an ACU officer, most likely to put out the fire in the oven, and whoever answered the call took advantage of the situation. Was this the same officer who stole from those he—or she—swore to help?

They'll relinquish control now, Sarah thought with clenched fists as she prepared to give this body back to the teenaged boy who owned it. She would catch this monster on the other side and punish them. *It's over. They're caught.*

The rings remained, glowing fiercely like a cold, blue fire. The man hiked up his pants, covering the fading erection. He balled his fists and charged.

Sarah braced herself. The officer would be trained. She could only hope they were less diligent with their practice than herself.

He grabbed her by the arm, shoving her into the kitchen.

Sarah dropped beneath his legs. She used her entire body weight to flip him, and he flew onto the counter, knocking pans and knives from where they hung. Metal and cast iron crashed around him, the sound of a destroyed wind chime.

Sarah knelt, catching her breath.

The man slipped off the counter and grabbed a non-stick frying pan. He swung it sideways at her head.

Sarah ducked underneath, feeling the whoosh of air as the pan nearly caught the back of her skull.

Her hand fell on the handle of a knife. Scrambling to her feet, she wielded it before her to find the blade only a couple of inches long.

A chef's selection and you grab a paring knife. She flipped it so it stuck out the bottom of her fist.

"Relinquish control," she ordered at the man, but he advanced in a blind rage. The officer controlling his body was someone used to getting their way.

She slashed out, but he deflected the blow with the pan. He swung it back and hit her on the shoulder, sending pain shooting outward in a fractured spiderweb of agony. It would be someone else's problem when she relinquished control.

He swung high, and she ducked. When she came back up, she swiped at the inside of the man's bicep, the thin blade cutting through fabric, skin, fat, and—her target—his brachial artery.

BLOOD POURED OUT IMMEDIATELY, spreading dark rouge along the thick shirt and spilling out onto the kitchen's white tiles. The man slipped and fell onto his back, sending the pan flying. He grimaced but didn't rise.

Sarah investigated his face. Gone were the blue rings around the man's pupils, replaced by dark brown and confusion.

Sobbing came from the doorway to the bedroom. The woman stood holding the broken strap of a tank top to her shoulder.

"Call 9-1-1," Sarah instructed, reaching into the man's arm to pinch the artery shut. "Police and ambulance."

"Archie?" The woman seemed to be in a trance. "What—"

"Now!"

She rocked backwards as if slapped, then raced toward a side table in the bedroom. Sarah turned her attention back to the man.

"The fire," he blubbered. "Did I . . . did he get it? Why am I bleeding?"

"Listen closely. You need to tell your son something when he comes back."

"Archie? Where did you come from?" His eyelids were closing, but Sarah slapped him back to attention.

"The police are on their way. Tell Archie to keep his fingers pinched the way they are right now. If he lets go, you will die in less than a minute." She held the slick artery tight, watching the confusion on the man's face as tears began to slip from the corners of his eyes.

"Why can't you—"

"I'm so sorry."

She relinquished control.

BACK IN HER OWN BODY, Sarah pulled the control helmet off and jumped out of her rig. She stumbled out of her office, blinking rapidly at the bright, fluorescent light.

"Otto," she called, stepping into her partner's room.

He lay in his rig, helmet on.

It didn't matter. She could handle it herself.

Sarah rushed down the hall with open offices on either side. In every room, an officer sat in a padded rig, eyes closed, becoming the hero in someone else's conflict. She peeked into each room, one after the other. There were no empty rigs until she got to the second last office on the right. Next to the empty rig on the ground was a shaker cup with the last half inch of protein shake sitting at the bottom.

"Mark . . ."

"Yeah." To her left, the door to the men's washroom swung shut. Mark stood in front of it looking sweaty and uncomfortable. His eyes remained fixed on the floor.

"What were you doing?"

"Do I really need to explain what goes on in men's bathrooms? Picture the women's, just with more urinals and fewer tampon dispensers."

"What was your last call?" She stepped to him, and he took a step back.

"Fuck, I don't know. I'd humour you, Forrester, but my guts are practically running down my leg. Can we discuss this another time?" He walked away.

She followed.

"Wait," Sarah said, but he kept walking. "Your shift isn't over."

"I'm taking a sick day."

She wanted to stop him, but to fight in your own body meant to suffer the consequences. There was no walking away from yourself.

How dangerous would he become if confronted? He was so much bigger. So much stronger. The preoccupied officers wouldn't hear her cries for help if he attacked. They would remain engrossed in whatever situation demanded their attention.

Otto wouldn't hear her.

The fire alarm would boot them all from their rigs, but that meant admitting she couldn't handle the situation.

Mark reached the stairs at the end of the hall and ran down them, feet falling in rapid descent. She hurried after him.

At the bottom, she watched Mark disappear out the glass doors and jog to his car.

She walked to the full-length windowpane facing the parking lot.

Mark slid into his old, restored Mustang, which was parked close enough for Sarah to see the multiple donut-shaped air fresheners dangling from the rear-view mirror.

For months, he had tried to convince Sarah to go for a ride in it, bragging about the power of the engine. How it made the car *vibrate*.

He sped off. The muffler rattled and roared, the sound rumbling through the glass.

"Still on for dinner?" Otto said, coming down the stairs.

Sarah lifted the back of her hand to her forehead. All colour drained from the world. Her knees threatened to buckle and send her crashing to the floor. Instead, she found a hard wooden bench and dropped. Her teeth clicked painfully.

"He did it. He fucking did it."

"Did what?" Otto sat beside her and placed a hand on her shoulder. He squeezed gently. She closed her eyes. The gesture helped center her, bringing her back into the realm of consciousness.

Sarah told him everything.

She opened her eyes, tears spilling out, and she hated herself for them.

"He was . . ." Sarah's breath caught in her chest. She pushed it out in a racking sob. She couldn't say the word. "The kid's mom, Otto!"

She collapsed. Otto held her.

6

Captain Anderson slid a box of tissues across the desk, but Sarah slid them right back.

"I don't want any fucking Kleenex, sir, I want an APB put out on him." The air conditioning hummed in the large office. Anderson sat across from Sarah, the considerable man nervously tenting his fingers and tapping them against each other.

"We have officers keeping an eye out. This is a very serious allegation you're leveling against Officer Taylor, however, so we need to do our due diligence by not assuming his guilt before he gets the chance to defend himself."

"He wouldn't have run if he was innocent."

"Forrester, you know that kind of evidence wouldn't hold up in any court. All we can do is go to him and ask him some questions."

"Do you have any officers stationed at his home?"

The captain shifted in his chair. "I'll send someone to check in on him as soon as we're done here."

Sarah sat bolt upright. "Send them now."

"Forrester, let me remind you I am your superior officer—"

"He's probably packing a bag and heading south as we speak!"

"—and I will not take orders from someone so emotional that they can't—"

"*Emotional?*" She glared at him, finally understanding. "Because I'm not a man, you don't have to take me seriously." More tears threatened to seep out, and she hated them, hated the fact she couldn't show rage for rage, that when she found conflict those tears wanted to dance on her face, undermining her.

"How dare you." Anderson returned her gaze, jaw clenched. "I spearheaded the ACU initiative to level the playing field. This program gives everyone the chance to make a difference, the chance to help—even if you're not as strong as your colleagues— so for you to insinuate that I am treating your accusation any different than I would a man's makes me sick to my stomach."

He slammed a clenched fist on the desk. "I personally went through the file of every officer who applied for a position with the ACU, spent *my* own time evaluating and interviewing every single one of my officers, so this isn't personal for just *you*, Sarah." His hands rested on the table, still clenched into fists that blanched his knuckles.

Anderson sighed and relaxed them so they laid flat.

"You said there were ways to audit the calls," Sarah said.

"The neural connection is strong, but only peer-to-peer. What information is saved after the call is . . . spotty."

"Spotty?"

"We can get visuals, though nothing in HD. We can get metadata—"

"Then you can see who the possessing officer was."

Anderson's gaze faltered. He tapped his fingers on the desk.

"Scrambled."

"What?" Sarah leaned forward. Suddenly, Anderson's commanding voice was hard to hear.

"The information is scrambled. Metadata, visual feed, everything. It might be some sort of encryption, but tech hasn't been able to decode it." He sighed. "They're saying it's all corrupted."

"So," said Sarah, head swimming, "there's no way to catch him?"

"It'll be hard. The only evidence a rape kit will reveal is that a husband had intercourse with his wife, and we can't exactly charge *him* for what one of our officers did in his body. There will be no DNA from the actual perpetrator, and the higher we go with this incident, the worse our division looks. It was like pulling teeth getting approval for the ACU, so my superiors are always looking for a reason to shut it down."

He lifted a hand and rubbed it over his shaven head, small hairs rasping against his touch.

"The victim, Mrs. Vance," he continued, "is recovering with the support of her family. I could never understand how she feels, but it seems less severe than your traditional case, I assume, because she knew and loved the man our officer controlled."

"You think it's any different because he's her husband? Captain, you don't get what something like that does to—"

"No, I don't. You'll have to forgive my ignorance. It's not okay because they're married, and that's not what I'm saying. I'm saying our trained counselors are working with Mrs. Vance. The situation is complicated, but it's between her, her family, and the support they choose to receive." He got to his feet and stretched his back.

Sarah stood, her legs numb. Her entire body was numb, like she was summoned herself, but controlling it from above like a puppeteer.

Mark would get away with it.

"Thank God Mr. Vance survived. Your emergency treatment saved his life, Sarah. You should be proud of that."

Sarah felt no pride when she left his office. Instead, she was filled with disgust—disgust for Mark, an officer bringing to this new force the corruption she had naively hoped would remain in conventional law enforcement. Disgust for her superior, willing to turn a blind eye and reinforce the code of silence that protected vile men only in the job for the power trip. Disgust for the bureaucracy that allowed injustice to reign over reason. That allowed rape to slip through the cracks. Injustice that finally dried her tears, but left her fiery as a bull, poked and prodded beyond its breaking point.

🐾

"He can't get away with it," Sarah told Otto from his passenger seat. He had offered to drive her home after finding her sitting mute behind her steering wheel.

"He won't. If he comes back, they'll figure out what he did and make him pay. If he doesn't come back, then he's already paid with his job and the life he's built here. He'd be a fugitive forever."

"That's not enough, Otto." He didn't get it, didn't see the look in the man's eyes when she caught him. "He didn't relinquish control. He was outraged that I had the nerve to interrupt him. He thought he deserved it." She looked at Otto, but he focused on the traffic, clearly uncomfortable at the topic. "You don't get it."

"I'm sorry," he replied as they came to a red light.

"No, I'm sorry. It's not *your* fault." She closed her eyes and leaned back against her headrest.

"Not to be insensitive, but I guess we'll need a rain check for tonight?"

Oh shit, I forgot all about our plans. Sarah turned her head to look at her friend. His slim face was focused on driving, but she could feel his attention on her. "I'm sorry, I'm just not feeling up to eating in some pretentious restaurant that avoids gluten like it's rat poison." Eating was the furthest thing from her mind, though it had been hours since lunch.

Otto's face drooped, then lifted, the gleam of an idea in his eye. In his crooked smile.

"A home-cooked meal, then. Where we can just relax." He turned his face to her.

She could stay mad, but what was the point? It all amounted to wasted energy, and at that moment she was out of energy to waste.

Otto was helping. He was a good man. Without his glasses,

without the baby fat, he was something else, too. The heart of her old friend, in a body that was taken care of. Sarah didn't want to be thinking about him like that. Didn't want to be thinking of *anyone* like that, not after what she saw Mark do, but Otto was her friend. She didn't want to be alone.

"You cook?" she asked.

"You'll see." His smile grew wider.

The light ahead turned green while Otto was busy looking at her, and a lifted Ford F-250 behind him blared its horn. Otto raised his fist at the truck, middle finger sticking straight as he leaned out his window and screamed, "Go fuck yourself, baby-dick! You're not impressing anyone with that truck!"

He sped away before Sarah could hear baby-dick's reply.

I guess nice guys aren't immune to road rage. She hid her smile so as not to offend Otto.

7

THE SMELL of artificial cotton sprayed out of an automated air freshener. Otto led her from the noisy, dim hallway into his apartment. After they were through the door, he closed it, slid a chain lock home, locked two separate deadbolts, and used his foot to lower a metal bar into the flooring.

"Tough neighbourhood?" she asked.

"Somebody thought so." Instead of tossing his keys on the table next to the door, Otto dropped them into his pocket. "Guy that sold me this place had it all installed. Bit of a . . . you know . . ." He twirled a finger around an ear and whistled.

Despite the closed door, Sarah could still hear the music coming from a party down the hall. The warble of a police siren rose and fell on the street outside.

"Very nice." Sarah hung her coat on the hook next to the door and gestured at the floor lock. "I thought they only had those in cafes."

"Crazy people can be resourceful," Otto replied. "Ever had turkey burgers?" He strode down a hallway flanked by nerdy knick-knacks perched on simple shelving and through an archway on the right into the kitchen.

"Probably," she replied, following.

Here was a Mario figurine next to a collection of *Game of Thrones* Pop! figures. There was a nativity scene set up with various Star Wars action figures. Yoda was in Baby Jesus' bassinet. Princess Leia played the role of Virgin Mary.

"Well, you haven't had mine." Otto removed some ground turkey from the fridge and threw it into a bowl. He reached into a cupboard, grabbing three spice jars with one hand before taking an egg from the fridge.

Where was Mark now? What was *he* eating?

"They'll catch him," Otto said, as if reading her mind. "Sooner or later, scumbags like that always get caught. The surveillance state we live in, I'm sure he's been seen on like a dozen CCTVs."

"I know, I know."

Otto ground the ingredients in the bowl, the smell of raw meat mingling with the spices.

"Let me tell you though, if that prick decides to show his face at the station, I'll make sure he feels the weight of his actions." Otto flexed his hands into fists, raising them. Egg white dripped from his pinky.

Sarah laughed, brushing her hair behind her ear. His hands still looked small despite the muscle he put on.

"Do your neighbors have kitchens this nice?" There was a gas stove, a huge, double-doored fridge, a deep freezer that could hold an entire cow, cupboards with frosted glass, and an island in the center. Sarah placed her purse on the quartz countertop that crowned the island.

"My neighbours look like the kind of people whose cooking skills top out with Kraft Dinner." Laughter came from the outside hallway, followed by the sound of running footsteps. "I'm surrounded by assholes."

He opened a cupboard and brought out a head of garlic.

"Can you grab a red onion from the pantry?" he asked, pulling off one clove after another before putting away the diminished head. There were two doors in the direction Otto indicated. Sarah opened one. The wrong one. Coats hung before her, shoes on the ground. Tucked away to the side of the closet was a life-sized Stormtrooper costume.

Sarah smiled. She closed the door on the Star Wars cosplay and turned around to grab an onion from the pantry opposite the closet.

"Why don't you sell this place?" Sarah said, coming around the corner. He could afford better than this. They had both received a considerable pay raise after accepting the transfer to the new unit.

"And commute like everyone else?" he asked, smiling as he crushed the garlic with the blade of a chef's knife. "I'm used to it. It's home." He chopped the garlic and dropped it into the bowl.

"Why did you start hiding the things you like?" Sarah asked. She knew he was a nerd, but the only evidence now was here in his apartment.

"I changed," he said, peeling the skin from the onion. "I bettered myself."

"Nerds can have muscles. You don't have to completely reinvent yourself to change."

"It wouldn't have been that easy. I needed something dramatic. A new identity."

"I'm just saying you don't need to be ashamed of any of these things. If anybody judges you for it, it's because they themselves are afraid of getting shit on." She put her hand on his arm. "You deserve to treat yourself. You're doing so well."

He pulled away, grabbing the knife and dicing the onion.

"Sarah, I *used* to treat myself. I treated myself every day, from middle school till the day I joined the ACU. Every value meal I crammed into my gob was a treat that made me fatter, lazier, and more disgusting." He tossed the knife in the sink with a clatter. "Do you know how it felt, assuming control of someone thinner than you? Someone who could run, jump, climb stairs without losing their breath and getting stitches in both sides?" He lifted the chopping board and dumped the diced onion into the bowl of meat. None spilled. "You either break the mold, or the mold breaks you. I treat myself by taking care of myself. If that means laying off the fried foods and sweet drinks, so be it. If it means keeping the things I like private, then oh well."

"That sounds lonely."

Otto smiled. He shrugged. His hands sunk into the meat with a squish. The smells of garlic and onion filled the air, mingling with the air freshener to form a sickly potpourri that made Sarah queasy.

"Where's the bathroom?" she asked.

"Through the living room, down the hall, and on your left."

Sarah crossed through a room obviously furnished by a bachelor. Mounted on the wall was a sixty-inch, curved TV facing a large sectional with cup holders set in the armrests. Beneath the TV were all sorts of toys: an Xbox, PlayStation, a charging iPad, and an HDMI cable that led to a large desktop PC humming away beneath a modest desk.

Why did she nag him? Just because he didn't show off his passions anymore didn't mean he abandoned them.

"I hope you like red wine," Otto called. "I've got a bottle of cabernet from the Napa Valley with our name on it."

Red wine gave Sarah headaches. Otto didn't know that.

What a hypocrite. Sarah chastised him for not sharing, but how much of *herself* did she really put out there?

Red wine. Sharing red wine was something you did on a date, not something you did to comfort a friend after they experienced a trauma.

Trauma craved the hard stuff in the cupboard above her sink.

Sarah would stay for an hour or so, then get a rideshare home. She didn't want Otto thinking this was a date.

She stepped into the bathroom and closed the door behind her. The room was large, a bathtub/shower combo against the far wall with the sink to her left. A bar of soap sat in a stone dish stained white from its residue. It wasn't lavender, vanilla, or any sort of flower. It just smelled like *clean*.

She washed her hands and examined her face in the mirror. Pinching her cheeks, she wondered if she might benefit from a regimen like Otto's. Though she trained often, she wasn't as strict with her diet as when she first joined the ACU. It wasn't necessary since her body played no part in the calls.

A smudge in the corner of the mirror distracted her from the thought, a mark left behind by a greasy finger.

The old, messy Otto isn't completely dead, she thought, grabbing the hand towel from the rack. Sarah pushed the cloth against the mirror to wipe away the mark, but in doing so, pressed the opening mechanism for the medicine cabinet behind it.

The mirror pressed inward, activated with a click, and sprung open a crack, revealing a hint of the contents within. Through the opening, she saw pill bottles, lotions, creams, and a curious stack of objects that looked like folded leather.

Don't snoop, Sarah. The man deserves his privacy.

She wouldn't judge him for anything. Like the well-muscled man she saved from the domestic dispute. Looking was as harmless as tiramisu.

Sarah opened the cabinet fully and revealed a stack of wallets of various lengths and colours. Men's styles, women's styles, cloth wallets and leather wallets. There was even a wallet made from duct-tape, a novelty item only a teenager would be interested in. Her sensibilities told her she already went too far, already pried into his personal belongings more than a friend had any right to, but her curiosity got the better of her. She took a wallet from the top of the pile, opening it to read the name on the cards within.

Verne Sommerville was the name on the Visa within the first wallet. The driver's license showed a balding man with thin lips.

The second wallet belonged to *Fiona Walters*, an overweight woman with red cheeks and hair to match.

The third wallet belonged to *Jack Washington*, a black man dressed in a sharp vest.

Why do you have these, Otto?

She opened them all, dropping them into the sink as she examined the insides. No wallet held cash—only credit cards, driver's licenses, forklift certifications, loyalty cards to sandwich shops. At the bottom of the pile was a small wooden box. When she opened it, Sarah was momentarily dazzled by the light reflecting off the gold and gems within. Wedding rings, earrings, necklaces, and bracelets. She dropped the box onto the pile of wallets and stood before the filled sink as the obvious conclusion stared Sarah in the face like a dog caught rooting through the garbage.

"It was you." Her mouth went dry. The room seemed to grow small.

Otto is the thief Captain Anderson told us about, she reasoned, *but that doesn't make him the officer who possessed that woman's husband.* That was *Mark*. She caught *Mark* outside of his rig, guilty of something. Sweaty and nervous, running like a man with something to hide.

Otto had been on a call in that moment.

She had rushed into his room for help to find him busy in his rig.

But it would have been easy for him to abandon the man she fought, then jump right into a new call. Or to access the system through his helmet and encrypt the metadata, like Anderson said.

Sarah hadn't suspected him for a moment. How could a mild-mannered, nice guy like Otto do something like *that*?

Only that wasn't him anymore. That old Otto had fallen away like a molted shell as the new, evolved Otto broke through with the help of a bench press and a few bottles of cologne.

Sarah grabbed a handful of wallets and jewelry from the sink and stormed out. Something in her head told her to document the evidence and call in for backup, but for once she wanted to resolve something on her own. If she couldn't protect people herself, if she couldn't even get a date without the help of her sister, then at least she could confront someone she once considered a friend.

She retraced her steps to the kitchen but stopped short when she saw him.

"Sarah." Otto faced her, his back against the food he had been preparing, arms held stiffly out to his side, and his knees locked straight. Vegetable oil sizzled in a skillet to his side.

Sarah dropped the wallets. They fell to the floor with a collective *fwap*.

"Otto?"

Light-blue rings shone out of the sunken pits that were Otto's eyes.

"No. It's Mark."

"Mark? What are you doing?" How was he possessing him? Did Otto even own a Summoner?

"You won't want to hear this. Otto's the one who's been taking advantage of his position. He's been hiding valuables during assignments, putting them in places where he can find them after his shift."

"How are you controlling him?"

"I'm using his rig. They're synced to us, and I always had my suspicions they could be used in different ways, but Sarah, I managed to get the visual logs from his last call."

"Anderson said they couldn't do that, the connection was—"

"Since when did those in charge have a better understanding of the machines used by those who actually operate them? The data from that call was scrambled, but not erased. Unless you knew how to operate the rig, how to *really* operate it, you couldn't access it." Otto's fingers twitched, curling briefly into a fist before straightening out again. "Sarah, he's dangerous. This woman, after he put out a fire, he—"

"I know." Tears welled up at the corners of her eyes. She wanted to wipe them away, to blink them into nonexistence, but she held back, and they spilled over, cutting hot tracks down her cheeks. "I saw him."

"Their son?"

She squeezed her eyes shut, nodding.

"Sarah . . . I'm so sorry . . . you need to restrain him. *Now.*"

Her eyes shot open, and she stared at the man before her. Otto was big, much bigger than her. Soft, flabby flesh had been replaced by hard muscle, capable of strength she often witnessed in their training sessions. The adrenaline of her discovery had blinded her to the danger, but now—

"I—Why can't you do it yourself?"

"He's fighting me." Otto's body trembled all over, micro-movements rippling through his muscles. The rings in his eyes flickered like a loose light bulb. "I only have limited control. He knows the system."

"Okay . . ." Sarah rushed to the cupboards, flung them open and started pulling out cans of vegetables, boxes of pasta, and protein powders before finding a roll of butcher's twine. She turned back to him, twine in hand, but stopped.

Otto's hands were moving, raising slowly, shaking as if they weighed an incredible amount.

"Mark?"

His hands cupped his ears. His mouth pulled downward into a painful grimace, and his eyes squeezed shut as his own tears began to flow.

"Run," Mark grunted through Otto's gritted teeth.

Sarah stumbled backwards, dropping the twine.

"*Run!*" he screamed. Somehow, the two men's voices came from one throat, erupting through one set of vocal cords.

She spun on her heels and darted out of the kitchen, her foot catching the edge of the wall, sending her stumbling. The sounds of a struggle—animal snarls, a scrape as the hot pan was shoved off the stove—came from behind, but Sarah was running down the narrow hall where the nerdy army of figurines loomed over her, shrinking the already claustrophobic area until she felt like she was breathing thick liquid.

When she reached the door, she began throwing open the locks. The chain lock slid out of its track.

A fist slammed against a wall.

She turned the deadlocks, retracting bolts with solid, metal thuds.

Footfalls pounded along the hardwood towards her.

Sarah turned the knob and pulled, but nothing happened. The door shuddered in its frame but remained closed.

Her head jerked back. Electricity shot along her scalp as she was pulled off her feet by her hair. It became fire, burning up every thought but one:

The other women in the unit were right to cut their hair.

She screamed, kicking wildly, but the sound only lasted a moment. Otto's hand, diminutive but strong, clapped over her mouth as he dragged her back into the apartment. The door shrank smaller and smaller as she was pulled away.

There was her mistake: the bar slid into the floor at the base of the door—the lock usually found in cafes. One of her kicks had knocked it open. The door was unlocked but too late.

Otto was big. Much bigger than her.

8

He hurled her through the bathroom door.

Sarah flew past the sink and into the bathtub, tearing down the shower curtain as she toppled over the ceramic edge. She fell forward, slamming her forehead on the tile wall and landing in a crumpled heap with her legs sticking out of the tub at an awkward angle. A door slammed.

Sarah lost her bearings. On weak legs, she stood, but the curtain tangled around her. She unravelled herself so she wouldn't trip over the cheap plastic. Finally freed, head clearer, she ran to the door with no plan of what she would do when she got it open. It didn't budge.

"You piece of shit!"

She slammed her weight against the door. The impact shook blood from her forehead into her eye, and Sarah squinted hard against the sting. She lifted a palm to the cut and winced. There was a crack in the tile where her forehead smashed the wall. *Good,* she thought, *at least he won't get his damage deposit back.*

She quickly examined her cut in the mirror. Shallow, but the forehead always bled more than it needed to. Sarah dabbed at it with a hand towel that needed washing. Red blossoms bloomed on the white fabric.

Good, Sarah thought, *I'll stain everything you have. I'll leave enough evidence here for any jury to put you away.* When the bleeding slowed, she threw the towel into the sink where it covered the heap of wallets like a sheet over a mass grave. Blood still welled up on her forehead, but she couldn't stand the smell of mildew in the towel any longer.

"Sarah, you need to calm down," Otto shouted through the door.

"Fuck you," she muttered under her breath, looking for a way to escape. There were no windows, nothing she could use to bust through the door, but she remembered the noise that had bled through from the hallway into Otto's apartment.

Sarah stepped over the shower curtain, over the lip of the tub, and put her ear against the tile wall. Loud music played on the other side. Her mouth almost tasting-distance from the wall, she yelled.

"Help!" she screamed, "I'm being attacked! *Help!*"

The music blared on, in fact, even seemed to grow louder. "Help," she continued, but the sound washed away in the heavy bass.

"Sarah." His voice came through the door clear as a bell. "I didn't want it to happen like this." The bass in his voice reached her as easily as if he were at her side.

He wanted her to catch him. Why else put all the evidence where a visitor could easily find it?

Then again, Otto didn't have many visitors. Otto didn't have many friends. Only Sarah.

"You're a monster." She slid down the wall, ending up perched on the edge of the tub, shoulders hunched. "We trusted you. We served with you."

"Oh please, don't give me any of that shit. Nobody in the ACU serves together. When you're out there, it's every man for himself. I don't get any backup in the field. Any failure is mine. Any success is mine."

"Your crimes are yours, too."

"Do you know how many lives I save, Sarah? I'm out there every goddamn day, most nights, putting in the work. Do you think I don't suffer? I feel the pain those people feel, I feel it for them. I feel the fear in a hold-up, though I know I won't die. I feel the heat in a blaze, though I know it won't be my burnt body they find. I feel the—"

"The lust when you save a family from a scorched kitchen? You get so worked up in the moment, you have to fuck the woman standing next to you. What, did she hug you? Give you a little kiss on the cheek? I bet she deserved it, didn't she? She *wanted* it. Wanted the stranger possessing her husband's body to take her into the next room and give it to her the way only an officer could. Never mind her son in the next fucking room." Sarah stood now, had stalked up to the door in her rage, not even remembering doing it.

When Otto spoke, it was further from the door. "It wasn't like that," he said, his voice small.

"What was it like?"

"She . . . she did want it. She went to the room. The kid wasn't even there. She did want it at first."

"Wanted it so bad she cried?"

"Stop. It wasn't like that. I was her husband. I was her—"

"You weren't, Otto. You were not. Don't pull that shit with me. Don't try to justify it. I know you. You were *weak*. You felt like a hero. You felt powerful, and that's not something you're used to, is it?"

He sniffled on the other side of the door. He had moved closer while she was talking.

"I did, Sarah. I was weak. I've been weak. You know how it feels, don't you? You're what, five-three, five-four, a hundred and twenty pounds? I've seen you in a crisis, face to face with a jumped-up tweaker. I've seen the fear in your eyes before you joined the ACU. You try to hide it—we all do—but the eyes give it away if you know what to look for." He breathed heavy. His hands rasped against the door. "You know how it feels to be weak."

He was right in a way. Hadn't she joined so she could shed the small body that held her back? Emotions always welled up when faced with confrontation. No matter how strong she tried to be, there were always tears dancing behind shaky eyelids. Sarah's weakness compelled her to join the Assumed Control Unit, but her reasons had to be more altruistic than Otto's. She wanted the strength so she could make a difference, not lord her power over others smaller than herself.

"You're a coward." She slammed a fist against the door. "Let me out of here. Let's see how strong you really are." If she could just get him to open the door, she could slip past and get out of there.

"I don't want to hurt you, Sarah. I'll figure out what to do with you. Just let me think."

"How does it feel to have power over someone in your very own body? I bet it's a lot better. Knowing it was *your* muscles that grabbed me, *your* strength that carried me here. I bet you feel *real* powerful."

"Just let me think."

Outside, someone's souped-up car pulled into the parking lot, the muffler announcing the driver's arrival.

Of course. That cut through the noise. The partygoers probably had no trouble hearing that.

"You did it, Otto. You got yourself a woman. All you had to do was lock her in your fucking bathroom. Bravo, my friend, this success is yours, revel in it you—"

A door banged open, deeper inside the condo.

She put her ear to the door. There was a struggle, grunts from Otto and another man. The crunching of a fist driven into someone's nose, shattering bone. Soft body shots and accompanying grunts. Furniture scraping the ground, overturning with a clatter. Another cracking sound, much louder than the nose, followed by a yell.

Heavy EDM seeped through the shared wall in the shower like soft background noise with a low beat. The music became the only sound in the room. *The only sound in the apartment.*

No.

Here was heavy breathing. Footsteps, coming closer and closer. Sarah backed away from the door, lifting her hands to defend herself. The doorknob jiggled, and something wooden, a chair maybe, slid along the ground. Then the door opened.

🐾

MARK TAYLOR STOOD on the other side. A thin trickle of blood ran out of the corner of his mouth, but other than that he looked unscathed. *Unscathed, but pale.*

"Otto?"

Mark shook his head. "Down and out."

Sarah breathed heavily for a moment before dropping her guard.

"You're going to get a fat lip, pretty boy."

"It won't look as bad as that goose egg growing on your forehead, Forrester."

She lifted a hand to her cut and probed the swollen lump. "Fuck," she swore. "No more dates for a while."

"But they've been going *so* well."

She brushed past him. "Come on, Taylor. Let's get out of here." They walked through the living room. Otto was there, unconscious on his stomach. "What do we do with him?"

"The cops are on the way. I'll watch him until then." He was walking Sarah to the door. "You go down to the car. I'll stay here."

"No, Mark, come on. You don't look so good."

"I'm fine, just a little nauseous. I think your friend over there put some eye drops in my protein shake when he gave it back to me. Must've been jealous of our tremendous rapport."

"You all right?"

"I might shit my pants again, but that would work in my favour. Nobody wants to tussle with a man in soiled drawers."

"That's attractive."

"I'm still attractive with a clothespin over your nose." He smiled a bloody smile.

Behind him, a drawer scraped open. His smile faded.

Before Mark could turn around, three gunshots exploded from the living room, shoving his body towards Sarah. He fell into her, grunting. Three red spots grew on his shirt, inches above his pelvis. She held him for a moment but couldn't carry his weight.

"No no no," she begged, lowering him to the ground.

Mark fell the last six inches, landing face down. A puddle of blood expanded around him, running over Sarah's hands and soaking her sleeves. "No," she whimpered as she began to turn him over.

"Don't," warned the cold voice in the living room.

Sarah raised her head.

Otto was on one knee in a shooter's stance, the drawer to his side table open beside him. In his small hands was a Glock 19, little more than a shadow. An aberration in Sarah's vision.

"Don't move," Otto said, getting to his feet. His leg buckled beneath him, and he shifted his weight onto the other. "Don't. Move."

She got to her feet.

"What did I say?" he asked, raising the gun so that he was aiming at her head.

She lifted her fists. There was nothing else to be done.

"Come on, Otto. One last sparring session between friends. What do you say?"

"I'm not stupid, Sarah."

"No, stupidity was never your flaw. You're a coward. Always have been." She needed to make him mad. Needed to throw him off his game. "You're a self-entitled little shit who will always be a pockmarked, greasy-haired, fat boy no matter how many weights you lift. No matter how many times you get that unibrow waxed, no matter how much you change. There's no amount of showering that can wash the stink off you, Otto."

"Shut up."

"I can smell you now."

"I don't want to hurt you."

"Smells like weakness. Smells like shit."

Otto ran at her in an injured loping gait, gun dropped. Forgotten.

Anger wasn't expressed with bullets. Bullets flew on fear. Anger ripped and tore and strangled. Anger had claws.

Sarah ducked under Otto's outstretched arms, kicking at the leg he favoured.

With a roar, Otto stumbled, dropped.

The momentum of Sarah's kick brought her down as well. Scrambling away, she reached for the gun, but he jumped over her and smacked it clumsily into the bathroom.

Sarah rose to run after it, but Otto grabbed her by the shirt and fell onto his back, throwing her clear over himself. She soared through the air and into the kitchen, landing and sliding along the linoleum until the fridge stopped her. *The gun,* she thought, *he's closer to it now.*

But Otto didn't go after the gun. He stumbled toward her, his face a mask of hatred. Though he didn't share any features with the man he had possessed, the look was the same. The fury controlled him, the self-entitlement, the rage at events not unfolding as planned.

When he approached, Sarah tried to kick out at his leg again, but he expected that.

He fell on her knee with all his weight. Bone shattered, knives exploding into Sarah's flesh like contained shrapnel. She let loose a piercing scream as the pain shot up her thigh and through her body. The knee was fire, but Otto wasn't going to let her focus on it.

"I didn't want to hurt you," he said, and drove his fist into her face. Sarah's lips smashed against her teeth.

She tried to lift her hands in defence, but the fire in her knee was burning the colour out of her vision.

"I love you," he said, punching her square in the nose. It broke, another source of heat. She tasted blood.

"I love you, Sarah," he said, crying. He drove his fist down once more, landing it squarely on Sarah's chin. Her jaw clicked. She saw stars.

"Stop . . ." she stammered, lips already swelling. His weight pinned her down, grinding the bone fragments in her knee against flesh and tendons.

Otto rolled off.

Sarah began to crawl. She moved forward, inching away from her old friend, but couldn't resist looking back.

Tears flowed freely down his face. He pawed at his eyes with small hands, looking like a giant kid, unaware of the destruction he was capable of. It was as if *he* was a victim in all this. She turned her attention forward, continuing her crawl.

"Sarah, no," Otto said, regaining control. "Come back, baby." He was sniffling behind her, getting to his feet.

Just a little farther, she thought, pulling herself along with her arms and the one good leg remaining. Her face rubbed against the kitchen tile. There was something beneath it, coarse and fibrous— the butcher's twine she was going to use to restrain Otto.

"Let's go to bed. Come on." There was a limping shuffle behind her. She reached out with her right hand, grabbing blindly just as Otto clutched her by her left.

Sarah grabbed Otto's narrow wrist and torqued her body. He was propelled over her, pushed along by Sarah's good leg.

Otto landed on his back, air rushing out of his lungs. He rolled over, but Sarah leapt onto his back before he could get up.

She unraveled the butcher's twine and looped it around his neck, but his fingers slid between it and his throat.

Sarah pulled back with all her weight, but it wasn't enough. He was pulling the twine away. He was stronger.

If only I was in the body of someone else.

He pulled more and more, the twine coming away from his neck. It slipped a little through her fingers—she gripped it desperately.

Otto would get out of her hold and finish what he started.

Her leg ached. Couldn't she give up? She could sit back, say she tried her best and let Otto do whatever he wanted. After all, wouldn't she wake up in her rig? Wouldn't she open her eyes, blink at the bright lights a bit, and then go on with her day?

Her vision was cloudy. The cut on her head was dripping again. Her ears rung like the high-pitched alarm of a faulty smoke detector.

No, this was the real world. Nobody to deal with the consequences but her. The fallout was coming, and it didn't look good.

Her grip was slipping.

I'm sorry, Mark. I'm sorry you got dragged into this.

Sarah looked over at him expecting to see his limp body, but he was *moving*.

He reached towards the door. It was a feeble gesture, but he was trying. He had reason to give up, three oozing ones in his gut, three valid excuses to call it a night, but he was still trying.

You either break the mold, or the mold breaks you.

Sarah redoubled her grip, giving the twine a turn with each hand. It tightened, pressing Otto's fingers against his own neck. She pulled hard, bending his back with all her strength as the fingers near the side of his neck turned first crimson, then a dull, dark violet.

He groped at her with his free hand, but Sarah used her good leg to kick him in his swollen knee. Otto shrieked in pain and, with a great effort, slid his hand out from under the twine.

Sarah looped the twine around another turn, crossed her hands behind his neck, and pulled even harder as he used both hands to get to his feet. She held on as he stumbled through the living room, smashing her into the TV mounted on the wall. She held on as he fell forward, crashing through his coffee table, sending coasters flying across the hardwood.

He shifted his body and began to crawl towards the bathroom, towards the gun that had come to rest in the piled-up shower curtain, yet still, Sarah held on.

He collapsed a foot away from the firearm, yet still, Sarah held on.

She held on through the music coming from next door.

She held on while sirens wailed outside. While heavy boots fell outside the apartment, while the music shut off, and while the door swung open, she held on.

It was only when Captain Anderson himself kneeled next to her that she let go. His large, soft hands pulled her fingers open.

"You're okay, Forrester. You did it." Anderson unwrapped the twine from her bleeding fingers. It bit into her skin the same way it had bitten into Otto's. Paramedics lifted Sarah onto a stretcher. Another tended to Mark, pressing gauze against his wounds and calling for help.

"Otto," she stammered, colour fading from the world as she looked at Anderson from half-closed eyes. "It was Otto."

"We know. Mark called us on his way here." He placed his hand over hers. "Everything is going to be okay. You can rest now."

She rested.

9

Sarah used her crutches to hobble down the hall and visit Mark. He watched a *M*A*S*H* rerun on a small, wall-mounted TV.

"Knock-knock," she said, awkwardly pushing her way through the door to his room.

"Hey, Forrester. You look like shit." He was lying in bed, shirtless, his stomach wrapped in bandages. Colourless hospital food sat before him untouched on a plastic tray: a loosely wrapped sandwich loaded with mayo, a carton of milk, some cereal, and a pudding cup.

"You *smell* like shit," she shot back, lowering herself into the chair at his bedside.

"Do I?" he said, frantically pushing the blue hospital blanket to his waist and checking the ostomy bag on his stomach.

Sarah laughed. "No, I'm just teasing."

"You may look worse than me, but my gut's going to pay the price for our little date for years to come."

She *did* look worse than him. Her lips were swollen large, like two fat earthworms dried out and cracked by the sun. The break in her nose had been reset, bandaged with a metal splint running along the bridge. She had two black eyes, bruised cheeks, and a leg wrapped in a heavy cast.

But she was alive. She needed to breathe through her mouth, but at least she still breathed.

"If that's what you consider a date," she said, "I'm not surprised you're still single."

"Maybe I've just been waiting for the right one to come along." He held a plastic container out to her. "Pudding cup?"

She took it. "Look at that," she said, peeling off the top, "you finally got to buy me dinner. Does that make this date number two?"

"Sure," Mark said, "Maybe for our third we can get our hands on some wheelchairs and wreak havoc on these hard-ass nurses."

"You sure know how to treat a girl," Sarah said, licking the top of the lid. "Any news?"

"Nothing from Anderson himself, but Janine said they're keeping things hush-hush. They don't want news of Otto getting out of hand. Nothing about his actions while on duty."

"No complaints from the woman he assaulted? Her family?"

"None. The man he possessed is going to make a full recovery and won't have to work for a *very* long time. From what I hear, the ACU has some deep pockets. Funded by some big-name donors. They're trying to open units all over the country, possibly international. Get ready for the threat of outsourcing a major police force."

"What are they saying about Otto?" Sarah asked.

Mark rubbed a hand along his jaw, feeling the stubble there. "From what I hear, they're going to call it an isolated incident. A domestic argument that got out of control. I'm sure they'll be talking to you soon so you can get your story straight."

"And the wallets? The jewelry?"

"I don't know. Mailed back to their owners? A cynical person would assume they would just drop them in the trash and forget about it."

"I still can't believe—"

"Hey," he said, interrupting her. "There's no way you could've known, so don't go kicking your own ass about it. You're a fucking hero, Forrester. Don't try to convince yourself otherwise. If you weren't such a badass, I wouldn't be here right now. Janine says the officers are going to be throwing you one hell of a party when you're back in fighting shape."

Sarah's smirk stung her busted lips. "I thought you said you couldn't talk to those bulldogs. Said they emasculate you."

Mark smiled at her. "I guess my ego isn't as big as people assume."

"Nobody wants to hear about your 'ego,' Taylor. Your euphemisms are as disgusting as your shit bag."

That set him off. He laughed until he was holding his stomach and crying through his chuckles. Smiling, Sarah turned up the TV to drown him out, but an older nurse walking by heard his uproarious laughter and walked in, frowning.

"Excuse me, miss, you need to leave. Mr. Taylor needs rest so his stomach can heal." The nurse tended to Mark, whose laughter died off when the matronly woman walked in. She reached into a cupboard and pulled out what looked like a deflated, beige whoopie cushion. "We're going to change your ostomy bag, Mr. Taylor."

It was a procedure Sarah had very little interest in watching.

"Sorry! Mark, I'll come back when you're feeling a little bit better."

"Thank you, Mommy," he replied in a baby voice. Sarah rolled her eyes as she began to hobble out. "There it is. The patented Forrester eye-roll. She reads her own mind as if reading the paper."

At the door, Sarah turned around to flip him the bird. A glint in the nurse's eye stopped her.

Blue rings around the older woman's pupils shone accusingly as she swapped out the bags.

"This TV is way too loud," the nurse muttered, turning around to press a button on the side of the flatscreen. When she turned back, the blue rings were gone. "I'm going to wipe you down now, sweetie."

"I could get used to this," Mark replied, rolling onto his side. "Some dignity, please?" he said, looking innocently at Sarah.

She shook her head.

"Right, sorry. See you later."

The blue rings were never there. They couldn't be. She hobbled away, certain of it, but felt cold eyes on her as she moved down the hallway to her own room all the same.

CHRISTOPHER O'HALLORAN—HWA and HOWLS member—is a Canadian actor-turned-author who has been published by Hellbound Books, Tales to Terrify Podcast, The Dread Machine, and others. Despite making the transition to writing, Chris still puts his acting diploma to use; he acts like a fool for chuckles from his wife and son at home in British Columbia. His work can be read at COauthor.ca where fans can find updates on his upcoming novel, *Pushing Daisy*. Follow him on Twitter @BurgleInfernal.

Illustration by Joe Radkins

DUPLICITOUS WINGS

AMANDA NEVADA DEMEL

AFTER THREE MONTHS, Lisa was still stewing in rage. She knew there must be something she could do about the atrocious injustice. If her relatives wouldn't help her, and if her lawyers couldn't revert the will to its original state, then she would have to take matters into her own hands.

A brilliant idea occurred to her one night as she was watching a reality television show. The brash nature of the women onscreen spurred Lisa's fantasies. Consuming mindless entertainment had become part of her nightly routine, but she was more than willing to interrupt the monotony to fulfill her idea.

She poured herself a third shot of whiskey and swallowed it in one gulp. Springing from the couch, she swept everything off the coffee table and dashed into the tiny bedroom of her wretched, temporary apartment. She regarded her surroundings with disgust as usual. The state of the whole building was disgraceful. The apartment was small and prone to pests. Every nook and cranny hosted swarms of cockroaches, always fleeing down the drain before Lisa could get a chance to crush even one of them. The hovel was also devoid of décor. Boxes still lined the walls from her move-in day. She simply didn't have the energy to go through everything or the will to put it all away. It was all such a drastic change from her previous home, which her brother Marcus had usurped.

As she settled her hand on the closet doorknob, rustling sounded from behind the door. A shudder came over her body. She was tempted to lock the creature inside, but she needed to retrieve her hidden materials. She took a deep breath and turned the doorknob. The bitter smell of rat feces wafted out from the closet. A large, dark shape scurried into the corner, followed by several smaller shapes. She normally would have set more traps, but she didn't have patience tonight. She was on a mission, and she would not tolerate distractions.

Her cloak hung in the corner of the closet, hidden behind her work suits. After quickly dressing in the proper attire, Lisa checked the mirror. She hardly recognized herself. A smile, though small, lit up her face. Lisa hadn't seen herself smile since before her father died. It encouraged her. If she was able to smile and feel excitement again, what could stop her from reclaiming her rightful haunt?

She stooped to get the shoebox from the ground, brushing away some pellets of feces and holding back a gag. A corner of the box had been nibbled away by the family of rats, no doubt. She opened the box to find an old, untitled book. The faded cover of the tome was some sort of leather, obviously cut by an amateur. The material did not fit the dimensions of the book well; the corners puckered with flaps of extra leather, and even the flatter areas had ample room to sag and shift. Lisa stroked the soft cover, her heart pounding through her fingertips, and took the book into the living room.

She had marked the page more than two months ago, when the lawyers read her father's will to her and Marcus. She hadn't planned on reading the passages the day she tagged them, but she acknowledged the possibility of needing to act. Her brother, meanwhile, accepted the terms of the will without argument. He had sat in the lawyer's office, arms folded, and grinned.

Why should he have complained? He got the house, despite knowing nothing of its potential. To him, it was simply a large, fully furnished home for his wife and kids. To Lisa, however, the house offered a far more important opportunity. It lay in the center of a huge plot of land surrounded by strong, thick trees. She wouldn't have to worry about nosy neighbors there, and she would have access to all her mother's relics. Marcus believed they were collectibles, but Lisa knew better. She was well acquainted with their power, and she even knew how to wield some of it.

Lisa had tried to change the will with minor incantations, but they were not strong enough. Each time an attempt failed, she would down a few drinks of whatever half-empty liquor bottles she could find in her apartment, swearing to never open the book again. Even so, she kept it in the closet with her cloak, unwilling to throw away that bit of her heritage. Her mother must have taught her dark alchemy for this very reason: to provide for herself. She always said that to live was to look out for oneself, never for another. "You must protect yourself," her mother told her, "no matter the cost."

The events of tonight, fueled by alcohol, ambition, and ire, would right the wrongs of the past. She would have to use major spells, forceful spells, far beyond anything she had previously practiced. Marcus and his wife Gabriella would become aware of their crimes. They would receive retribution. However, she was determined not to wreak any undue havoc tonight. She only needed to punish the parents.

Their children were innocent, especially little Will. Just four months ago, Lisa had vowed never to be the cause of his tears. She had made her gentle promise on Thanksgiving, when Marcus lost his temper because Will spilled gravy on his new shirt. Marcus was incensed, already under the stress of hosting the festive meal. Will ran outside to cry on the porch while his parents cleaned up the mess. Lisa followed him and eventually soothed his tears. She could still hear her brother's loud frustrations from outside, all his cursing and insults. Not even the elderly patriarch of the family could get Marcus to calm down. Although Lisa had never felt much of a connection to her niece, Amelia, something about Will pulled at her heart. Maybe it was because he resembled his grandmother.

Lisa now had to make Will's grandmother proud. Kneeling next to the coffee table, she opened the book to the passage marked with a red ribbon. The yellowed pages were thin, the outer margins nearly transparent from decades of oily fingers riffling through them. Although the text was not in the Latin alphabet, or any language that still had fluent speakers, the symbols made sense to Lisa.

Accompanying the alternately jagged and swirling characters were countless illustrations, each drawn with excruciating detail and rich color. Some images seemed to depict plants, though they didn't resemble any known flora or fauna. Others were intricate, abstract designs, often weaving through the lines of script. Still more pictures showed humanoid figures with exaggeratedly long limbs, extra facial features, or extremities that connected to larger plant-like effigies. The drawings had always mesmerized Lisa, as she knew they held ancient, mystic power.

Grotesque visages and unnatural limbs occupied the upper half of the page that Lisa needed. The lower portion featured a tower of red and blue rings. Flanking either side of the pillar were three strings of tiny symbols.

Lisa read the six lines in her head. A few words were unfamiliar to her, so she tried to sound them out. There was no way to confirm her pronunciation. Her mother had advised her time and time again about the gravity of articulating the incantations with accuracy. The unearthly, conniving beings that fulfilled spells always took advantage of ignorance. The High Court could sort out some mishaps, but much like the mortal courts, one couldn't rely on them for justice. But Lisa had confidence in her abilities on this night. She closed her eyes and chanted the words aloud. With each repetition her speech strengthened, starting as a murmur and growing into a boisterous, passionate song.

A hot wind blew through the room. Lisa's skin buzzed. She smelled an unfamiliar burning, bitter odor. She opened her eyes and jerked backward.

Standing on top of the coffee table was a gorgeous woman, though she was not quite human. She had two arms, two legs, and such, but there were also large wings sprouting from her back. There were four wide wings, almost like a dragonfly's. Instead of being filmy and thin, these appendages were solid and sturdy. Even so, they were strangely translucent. Looking through them was akin to looking through a glass block window. Thick veins traced across each wing, forming a network of pumping blood. As they twitched, candlelight glinted off the ridges. Examining this woman, Lisa saw two other inhuman traits: a pair of fiery orange eyes and a set of long, sharp fingernails, almost like talons. The conjurer gazed up in awe, taken aback by the power of her spell. *She* was the one who called the creature into being. This fact bolstered her confidence even more.

"Anza, you are now at my command," Lisa said, shoulders rolled back and chin turned upward. "I have a task for you."

The winged woman looked down, away from the window. Her eyes brimmed with fury and her lips pressed into a tight line.

"Why have you summoned me?"

"My brother has betrayed my honor, stolen what is rightfully mine," she explained in a steady voice that grew with vigor as she continued. "You will retrieve it. Go to him while he sleeps and show him the consequences of his actions. Do whatever you see fit to make him leave. Frighten him and punish him. He must flee the house and never return. I only ask that he be left alive."

"Yes, Master," the winged woman said. She stared past Lisa for a moment, and her lips perked up a trifle. "What of his wife and children?"

"Leave the children," Lisa said, emphasizing each word. "As for the wife, you will discipline her as well. She has allowed her husband to dominate and control all he desires. Let the bystander suffer. Use whatever measures you must to make them leave. Just spare the children."

"Yes, Master."

"Now, find Marcus and Gabriella Carrey. Go!"

The flames of the candles suddenly rose like pyrotechnics. The hot gust of wind made Lisa screw her eyes shut. When she opened them again, only a pile of ash remained where Anza had stood. The candles had extinguished, leaving her in darkness, save for the artificial light bleeding into the apartment from the streetlamps.

She rushed to the window. The winds picked up outside, sending the trees into a frenzy. Their branches flailed and their leaves shuddered. Up in the light-polluted sky, clouds covered the emerging stars. How Lisa missed the vivid colors of an untainted sky! Soon enough, she reasoned, she would once again revel in the pure night, far away from the contaminations of the city.

Turning on a lamp and returning to the book on the table, she flipped the page. This passage had far more words than the previous one. The illustrations on the bottom half of the page showed two large circles atop thick stalks that crossed over one another. One winding strand sprouted from the top of each circle, and a woman was cradled by each of them. The woman being held on the left side of the page peered into the end of the vine as if it were a telescope. On the right side, the tail of the strand seemed to envelop the back of the woman's head, leaving only the profile of her face exposed.

She recited the spell more quickly this time, excitement and confidence growing. As she spoke, her surroundings faded away and her vision filled with another familiar background. The conjurer and the conjured began to share a line of sight. Anza soon descended on the secluded house. Lisa's heart rate increased as the winged woman headed toward the open window of the master bedroom. Little did Marcus know that his paltry life would soon change irrevocably, and it would all start with that small aperture where Anza entered.

Standing at the foot of the grand bed, they saw Marcus and Gabriella sleeping soundly. Anza blew out a long, freezing breath, causing the husband to shiver and grimace in discomfort. When the gust didn't let up after a few seconds, he opened his eyes and got up to close the window. He scanned the moonlit room and almost overlooked the interloper. Lisa delighted in his small jerk of fear.

"Who are you?" he whispered, careful not to alarm Gabriella. "How did you get here?"

Anza remained silent. Marcus scrutinized her face, but quickly looked away from her luminescent orange eyes.

"*What* are you? Answer me!" he hissed, still averting his eyes.

Lisa chuckled at his belief that he could handle the situation. It would only make his downfall more amusing.

The winged woman took a single step. Marcus walked backward until he bumped against the windowsill. He bit his lips into a thin, worried line, and it was obvious that it took a great deal of effort to stand still. His jaw shivered and his brows knit together over bulging eyes as he took in Anza's form. Lisa grinned at his foolishness, his helplessness. Anza advanced silently, stopping but a foot away from him. Perspiration clung to his skin and glistened in the moonlight. He drew his hands into fists, but before he could strike, the winged woman lifted a hand to his throat. She didn't apply pressure. Lisa knew that the important part was the threat. Anza straightened her index finger, moving it back and forth on his jaw. Marcus shuddered but kept his shoulders squared and his fists tight.

"I was sent to reclaim what you have stolen. You must leave this place," Anza said.

"Now? In the middle of the night?" Marcus asked incredulously. He continued before he could get a response. Barreling onward had always been his fighting tactic. "You have no right to come in here and evict us!"

Anza released Marcus and glided to the shadowed part of the room. She leaned over Gabriella, sending images of her fitful rest to Lisa. Without permission, the winged woman grabbed Gabriella's arm and hoisted her to a standing position. Gabriella yelped, suddenly wide awake, and looked up to see the assailant. Her eyes opened wide and darted to her husband. He was frozen to the spot.

"Good thinking," Lisa said. "Get them together. I want to see them cower before us."

Anza hauled Gabriella to the window with little difficulty. The couple looked at each other with frantic eyes and fumbled around to find each other's hands. Gabriella quietly wept.

"What does she want?" she asked.

"You will address *me*," Anza responded. "Do you understand?"

"Yes, yes. Please, just tell us what you want," Gabriella begged. "Is it money? I'll write a check, I'll give you our credit cards, you can take all our cash. Please! Let us go."

Of course she thinks it's about money, Lisa thought.

"Leave this place. You do not belong here."

"Honey, you can't help here," Marcus said, pushing her to stand behind him. "Just stay quiet. I'll handle this."

"You will address *me*," the winged woman repeated. "Will you all leave peacefully, or do I need to convince you? You do have children . . ."

Lisa gasped. "Wait! I said to leave the children alone. Don't you dare touch them."

Anza bared her teeth in a twisted grin. Lisa could not see the smile, but she deduced from the couple's reaction that Anza had shown them something terrifying. She knew Anza had set a new plan in motion. Gabriella now openly and loudly sobbed. Marcus stepped back and put his arm around her, keeping silent. His eyes bounced around the room, seemingly in search of a flashlight, a baseball bat, anything he could use as a weapon. When he reached out to grab the lamp on the bedside table, Anza swiped at his arm. Gabriella screamed, and he reeled back, staring at the burning, bloody gashes from the creature's talons.

Anza turned around, then said, "Stand in front of me. Summon your children."

"You leave them out of this," Marcus said. Lisa knew he would have been ashamed of the tremor in his voice if he could hear it, though the thought brought her no joy.

"Stand in front of me and summon your children," Anza commanded, "unless you would like me to get them myself."

"What if she hurts them?" Gabriella whispered. "We have to do what she wants."

Nodding, Marcus led her by the hand to stand before the winged woman. As they walked, Lisa saw his tears shining in the glow of evening, his chin wrinkling from the stress. She shook her head, trying to clear the image of imminent disaster, but the sight endured.

Anza stared into the dark hallway, waiting for the children to appear. A moment passed. No one spoke. Then she lifted a talon to the back of Gabriella's neck, whispering, "Summon them, or I will do it for you."

"Amelia!" Gabriella shouted, the name involuntarily bursting from her lips. Her husband attempted to argue, his mouth opening and closing and quivering, but no words could escape his throat. "Will!"

"Stop!" Lisa cried. "I order you to stop! Listen to your master."

Lisa could not see her living room. The disconnect between feeling and seeing was jarring. Desperation creeped in. She felt for the table, found the book, and slammed it shut. Still, only the dark corridor of her childhood home, blocked by two huddling figures, lay in front of her.

Now both parents were calling for their kids. Sobs broke Gabriella's high-pitched shrieks. Marcus's usually deep voice cracked and wavered, making him sound like an adolescent boy. Even Lisa shouted, though her words were not names. She recited every spell she could remember, but nothing changed.

Amelia emerged from her room in a panic. She turned on the hall light and began to ask what was wrong but quickly silenced herself when she saw the large, winged creature behind her parents. The blood drained from her face. She backtracked a step, swaying on her feet.

"Go get your brother, Amelia," Marcus said, choking on his words. "It'll be okay."

Their daughter nodded at the same rate as her chest rose and fell. She burst into her brother's room and dragged him out. Both children were silent, and little Will was crying. The sight of the young boy's red, puffy face made Lisa's chest constrict.

"Stop this!" she bawled, still trying to exert control over Anza.

The family huddled together on their knees before the mighty woman. Amelia was now crying, shaking, trying to hold herself together. Gabriella held Will, rocking him side to side, both of them wailing. Marcus made an effort to look angry, but he only looked pathetic.

"Let us go," Gabriella pleaded. "Take whatever you want, just let us go!"

"Yes, let them go," Lisa directed. She needed to regain some authority. All she could do was give orders that would not be followed, but she would not relinquish her last sliver of hope. "Get them out of the house and *leave them alone.*"

Anza grabbed Gabriella's arm and lifted her again. Gabriella looked at her children and assured them she would be fine. Her manic promises fell flat.

With an abrupt movement, Anza seized the mother's throat. Clenching her fist, her sharp talons pierced skin, and blood trickled onto Gabriella's shoulders. It stained the collar of her pale night shirt, starting with a small seed and blossoming into a dark flower. The children screamed. The pounding of Lisa's heart was the only thing that grounded her. She knew her control of the situation and of herself was rapidly evaporating.

Finally, Gabriella fainted, going limp in Anza's grasp. Anza threw the body against the wall without bothering to look where she fell. Lisa only heard the thud.

"Mommy!" Will shouted. He wriggled out of his father's grasp and ran to the body. "Wake up, Mommy! Wake up, wake up, wake up."

"Rise," Anza said, ignoring the incessant torrent of Lisa's commands.

The family stood on wobbling legs, leaning on one another for support.

"You," she said, pointing at Marcus. "You refused to leave. Your children may thank you for their future."

"We'll leave," Marcus said. "We'll leave right now. Come on, let's go."

He walked over to Will, grabbed his hand, and pulled him away from his mother.

"What about Mommy?"

"We'll come back for her," Marcus promised.

"Run," the winged woman ordered.

Marcus hauled his son onto his shoulder and yelled at Amelia to run to the car. The woman calmly followed them to the top of the staircase where she watched them stumble downward. After a minute, she heard the car engine start and the wheels kick up the rocks of the driveway as it raced off the property.

"Is that enough?" Lisa asked. "Have you done enough damage? All I wanted was my home. I didn't want anyone hurt or . . . or fucking traumatized! I told you to leave them alive. You disobeyed me. The High Court will find out, and you'll be damned. Just you wait."

"There is no evidence. We shall see justice." She barked a laugh.

"There is plenty of evidence against you! *I* am evidence of your perfidy, of your recklessness, of your crimes. Those poor children are evidence too. You'll never see this world again."

"You are mistaken," Anza said. "Your drunken, stuttering recitation of my conjuring spell has given us free rein of this realm. You spoke without grace. Your gibbering blunder will be your demise. You convinced yourself that you were so skilled and so powerful, but you are no one's true master."

Lisa's eyes widened. She had been warned about the sanctity of the spells, and she now realized the consequences. Anza escaped through the window. She flew up to the top of the trees and followed the only road leading away from the house. It didn't take long to find the new Mercedes-Benz weaving across the median.

"No," Lisa whispered.

The winged woman dived like a hunting kingfisher. She righted her position before reaching the tarmac and landed on her feet in the middle of the narrow road. The Mercedes-Benz barreled forward.

"Dad, watch out!" Amelia's shout could be heard from Anza's distance.

Marcus cut the wheel to the left. The few seconds he had were not enough to register the figure as Anza. Lisa squeezed her eyes shut, but she knew her vision could never separate from the winged woman. They both watched the car charge through the trees lining the road. They watched the car slam into the wide trunk of an oak. They watched the car disappear in billows of smoke.

The winged woman remained in the middle of the road, waiting for the smoke to clear. Lisa cried and screamed, begged and pleaded for Anza to leave the scene. The sight of the burning car on its side made her chest tighten, her throat constrict. Through the thinning smoke, she spied a tiny, limp arm hanging out of a shattered window. Her throat suddenly opened. A wail, louder than what she thought her body could produce, erupted. The force was strong enough that she tasted blood in her mouth. Anza's eyes lingered on the crash for another minute, basking in the glory of her work. Then she took flight.

"Why?" Lisa asked. "Why would you do this?"

The landscape changed from forest to suburbia to the buildings of the city as the woman glided to her next destination. Lisa felt like her heart caved in. Anza entered the apartment through the open window, not bothering to show even a modicum of respect with a formal reentrance. It was bizarre for Lisa to see herself through another's eyes. Her face was red and splotchy, her hair a greasy mess. She looked so small. The only orderly part of her appearance was the velvet cloak she wore.

"Well?" Lisa croaked. "Have you destroyed enough?"

The winged woman strode up to her conjurer. In one swift movement, she brought her talons up and dug them into the soft flesh under Lisa's chin. The piercing pain made her body go rigid, made her head feel light and heavy at the same time. She tried to breathe through the blood flowing out of her mouth to no avail. She only produced a gurgling sound. The weightless feeling behind her eyes spread and overtook the sensation of gravity pulling her body down. The last image to register in her mind was of her broken, limp body sagging from Anza's hand.

AMANDA NEVADA DEMEL is a born-and-raised New Yorker, though she currently lives in New Jersey. Aside from being a lifelong reader and visual artist, she has been relentlessly writing since she was thirteen years old. Her favorite genre is horror, thanks to her father and much to the confusion of her mother. She especially appreciates media that can simultaneously scare her and make her cry. Amanda also loves reptiles, musicals, and breakfast foods. You can find her on Instagram @amanda.nevada.demel and on Twitter @AmandaDemel.

Illustration by Joe Radkins

IT GETS IN YOUR EYES

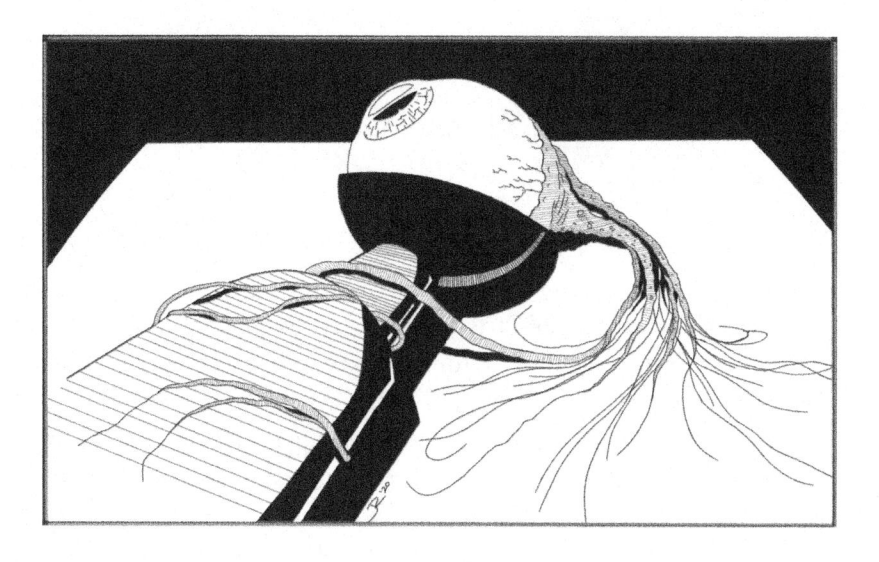

JOSEPH ANDRE THOMAS

I HEARD Marnie before I saw her, her boots clomping down the building hallway. Immediately upon entering our apartment, she slammed her two big travel bags against the wall.

"Hey lady, how was your vaca—"

I managed only a couple of garbled half-sentences before we made it to the bed. She'd just been on an Alaskan cruise with her family and was ready to "fucking explode," she said. I didn't last very long. Marnie did most of the work.

When we were finished, she threw on a big t-shirt and rolled over, examining herself in her makeup mirror.

"I think," she said, "that there's something in my eye."

I leaned over her shoulder to see the reflection. Her left eye twitched slightly. The veins were bright red and thin, like stress cracks on a window.

"It's been bugging me the last couple of days. There's *definitely* something in there," she said. In the freaky, enlarged reflection, her tear ducts looked like something out of one of those nasty surgery videos they used to make us watch back in AP Bio. "Dirt, maybe, or . . . ?"

"Stop touching it," I told her. "You're only going to make it worse."

"Fuck you."

"Maybe dust?" I suggested. "Have you tried flushing it out with water?"

"No, dude, I haven't tried flushing it out with water," she responded dryly. She ran a finger around her eye, pulling her eyelid down to reveal the wet, fleshy redness beneath.

After a bit, we rolled out of bed. I whipped up a taco salad for dinner while Marnie took a shower. When she sat down at the dinner table, the skin around her eye was puffy and pink.

"So," I said, staring at my bottle of homemade chili-lime dressing, "how was the trip? Anything exciting to report?"

"We had to social distance the entire time, so I had no one to speak to but my cousins for three weeks. We also had to share bunk beds. There isn't an open bar in the world worth that torture. Not sure I would've wanted to talk to anyone else on that cruise, though. I've never seen so many pear-shaped people in one place."

"Nice of your family to pay for a vacation, though."

"True, I drank my bodyweight in free Bud Light. I'm not complain—" her hand wavered awkwardly, nearly stabbing herself in the cheek with a forkful of salad, as if her brain and eyes had miscommunicated "—not complaining about that."

"Well." I gave her a smile. "I'm happy to have you home."

"Happy to be home," she said. "And the fucking *employees*. I thought cruise workers would be fun." As she spoke, she started rubbing her eye. "They were so . . . vacant, robotic, like members of some pelagic cult."

"I really don't think it's a good idea to keep touching it."

"Yeah? I think it's a good idea to keep it to yourself," she snapped, fixing that eye on me like a laser.

"I'm sorry," I said, surprised at her ferocity. "I'm just worried that it'll—"

"I'm fine, sorry," she said. "I didn't mean to yell. I'm just uncomfortable. It *itches*."

She fully mashed her palm into her eye.

I nodded and forced a smile. We finished the rest of our dinner in silence.

I GOT up early the next day to cook Marnie a welcome-home brunch. To make up for last night's tiff, I whipped her up her favorite—eggs Benedict.

As I stood there cracking eggs, all I could think was how much they resembled eyeballs. I passed yolks and whites between half-shells in a borderline trance . . . big yellow pupils slowly separating from globs of white sclera.

Marnie shambled into the kitchen just as I was whisking an unethical amount of butter into the hollandaise. She moved with the gait of the undead, as if brutally hungover. When she looked at me, my stomach lurched. Her eye looked like it should be floating above a tower in Mordor.

She barely ate anything, just half a poached egg, then pushed the rest around the plate like it was prison food. We'd been together for five years, Marnie and I, and I had still yet to give her a present that made her happier than my homemade eggs Benedict. Evidently not this morning.

"What's that?" she said, indicating a gift basket sitting on the living room table.

"Oh, that. Housewarming present from my mom," I said. "I've been waiting for you to open it up."

"All right," she said, worriedly lifting it up and unraveling the wrapping. "Let's get weird."

My mother had a penchant for giving her loved ones uncomfortably personal, high-concept gifts. A couple Christmases ago, to the horror of the entire family, she stuffed Marnie's and my stockings with various flavored contraceptives —condoms, dental dams, etc. Whether this was a ghastly attempt at a joke or a jab at our childlessness, Marnie never got over it.

This gift basket was at least less disturbing—a basket of kitchen supplies we'd have—per her handwritten note—"never thought to get" for ourselves: a melon baller, an egg timer, avocado savers, a sponge holder, and a bunch of other stuff I'd give good odds on being lost in the back of the utensil drawer within a year.

"Oh wow," said Marnie, bouncing an elaborate apple corer in her hands. "Is all this stuff so that I can have really nice dinners waiting for you when you come home from work?"

"If you want to?"

She gave me a look that said: *You're an idiot.* I scratched my neck. Sometimes Marnie said things that went over my head.

I got dressed for work, opening a pack of masks and tossing my freshly-washed Steak Frites apron into my knife bag, while Marnie lay on the bed looking at her laptop.

"Need anything on my way home?" I asked.

"Yeah, could you toss a Molotov cocktail into The Cheesecake Factory's front window?"

"Uhh . . . ?"

"I'm kidding," she huffed, closing her laptop, "but those fuckers *still* haven't officially laid me off."

"Fuckers," I echoed. "No unemployment check, then?"

She shook her head. She'd been a server at The Cheesecake Factory until a couple weeks before her vacation and was hoping to get her job back when things settled down. "I'll call them later."

"Hey, at least you don't have to go to work," I said, examining the glinting silver blade of my beautiful *Grand Maître* knife. "Some of us still have to!"

"Yeah, you'd rather be jobless, worried about where your money's going to come from, while the entire ugly, awful, apocalyptic world burns to a crispy turd around you?"

I blinked at her. "It'd be nice to have some time off?"

I CAME home that evening with a cornucopia from the pharmacy: all the eye drops, allergy pills, and skin ointments I could fit on our credit card.

"Thanks," she said, applying some stinky oregano oil around her eye, "but I think I need something stronger. Something's really wrong. I'm going to go see my doctor tomorrow."

I was going to ask how she was so sure it was that serious, then noticed her laptop open on the couch.

"Have you been diagnosing yourself on Google? I'm not sure that's a great idea . . ."

"Look, look, look," she said, grabbing her computer and clicking through about forty open tabs. She landed on an enlarged photo of an insect: a creepy, red-and-orange monstrosity. It looked as though several other insects had come together to form an insect-Megazord. "This is *malleus e oculum*, a gnat native to the Amazon. It gets in your eyes and feeds on the white eye jelly—the *vitreous humor*."

"Jesus Christ," I said. "But you didn't go to the Amazon."

She shrugged. "So? There are something like seven thousand billion undiscovered insect species. What if there are other genuses of this motherfucker in other parts of the world?"

"I think you might be making your anxiety worse by looking at this."

"My anxiety . . . ?" she asked with a sidelong glance.

Her eye had turned the color of red wine dregs. I choked back a gag and gave her an apologetic smile.

🐾

"*HORSESHIT*," Marnie said, bursting through the door.

I startled, fumbling the book I'd been reading—*Jamie's Comfort Food!*—like a bad wide receiver. "Hi, um, how'd it go?"

"It went," she said, whipping her purse into the couch, "like horseshit." After a thirty-second exam, she explained, her family doctor had concluded it was a simple infection. Minor periorbital puffiness—nothing too bad. An infection of the sclera or of the macula, possibly, had spread into the vitreous humor, thereby making it difficult to treat with over-the-counter medications. She gritted her teeth. "He didn't take me seriously at all."

"Sorry, lady."

"At least he prescribed these," she said, revealing a big white pill bottle. "Sweet, sweet, prescription drugs."

THREE DAYS LATER, she asked me to examine her eye again in the mirror.

"Looks a little better, right?" she said. She'd been taking the pills and applying ointments and cream pretty much hourly.

I leaned in close and inspected her eye. It did *not* look better. If anything, it was more inflamed. The blood vessels were such a bright red I worried she was going to weep blood.

I coughed, hiding my grimace, and said, "Yup, definite improvement."

WHEN THE WEEKEND came and the problem still hadn't gone away, Marnie called the cruise line to see if anyone else had reported any medical issues. She left the call on speaker.

"No," the man said. "No recent vacationers have reported any medical issues." He sounded thoroughly disinterested in the conversation.

Marnie asked if she could possibly be put in touch with other people on the cruise to confirm that fact, to which the man chuckled.

"No. Guest confidentiality is the company's top priority," he said.

"Higher priority than a guest's health?" she asked.

"Guest health is our absolute, top, *highest* priority," he said. "However, given that the cruise you took was at one-third capacity, and that family units were required to social distance—outside of regularly scheduled Luaus and Limbo Competitions, of course—it is highly unlikely that infections were passed between guests. Perhaps you have a preexisting condition?"

"A preexisting fucking thing in my eye?"

"I don't know. I'm not a doctor," he said, then explained that she could be in touch with the cruise line's legal department if she felt the need. Though he added, with a smirk you could actually hear, that the waivers she had signed divesting the company of medical responsibility were "remarkably ironclad."

I never realized how many tiny parts were inside a cell phone until I watched Marnie pitch hers against the wall.

※

"Well, there are no infections, and nothing is lodged in there," Dr. Fulci concluded flatly. "I see that the periorbital skin has become raw, though I do not see a clear cause. Perhaps the abrupt change in climate after returning from the cruise?"

Dr. Fulci, a well-reviewed optometrist Marnie had found online, was kind but slightly terrifying. Her voice was an octave too high, her posture sharp and stiff from years of sitting behind a desk. She brought to mind a hungry eagle.

As the doctor spoke, Marnie sat twisting up various medical pamphlets while muttering beneath her mask. I'd driven Marnie to the appointment, as she could barely see out of her left eye.

Dr. Fulci's office was crammed with a wide array of optometric machinery (nearly all of which Marnie would have her head stuck in by the end of the visit) and graphic medical posters. On her desk sat a sliced-up eyeball preserved in plastic casing. A light smell of vinegar hung in the stuffy office air. I tried not to think about it possibly emanating from the eyeball slivers.

Though Marnie didn't say much—mostly just muttered incoherently to herself—I could tell she was frustrated by Dr. Fulci's vague conclusions. After the appointment, we walked across the street to a pharmacy and picked up a number of different medications and eyewashes, as well as a pair of thick, tinted goggles that made Marnie look like she should be driving an airship in some strange steampunk fantasy world.

None of it helped.

🐾

"It's shaking," she said a few days later, yanking the skin around her eye in front of the mirror. "I feel it *shaking*."

By that point, she spent most of her days sitting in the dark living room watching television with the sound off. She flipped channels constantly, obviously unable to concentrate on anything for long. The discomfort sapped both her attention span and her stamina. Sometimes I caught her crying, but whenever I asked about it, she said it was nothing.

When The Cheesecake Factory announced they were reopening, they offered Marnie shifts, but she turned them down. She did not think she would be able to effectively do her job like this, she said. Probably no one would want to be served by that globulous red eye anyway, I thought (but kept to myself).

I wanted to help but couldn't think how. This person simply was not her. Marnie did *not* pass up work. I had seen her, after drunkenly pitching herself down a two-story flight of stairs, wake up for a 7:00 a.m. brunch shift. When a coworker quit abruptly, Marnie had picked up three double-shifts during her midterm week. Seeing her so lethargic unsettled me.

And the problems were not confined to her waking hours. Usually a solid eight-to-nine-hour sleeper, she became impossible to lie next to at night. She twisted up the sheets in distress, and when she did fall asleep, even in dreams, she'd worry at her eye with her palm. She had to start wearing the goggles in bed. Our sex life—previously healthy, although short-lived at times—became non-existent. I examined her eye so uncomfortably closely, for so long, and so often, that we achieved a level of intimacy that sex could only dream of, though intimacy of a far less pleasant kind.

THE DOCTORS at the hospital lay Marnie on a stretcher and strapped a thick leather band across her forehead. Then she was thrust, like some huge, oblong phallus, into various pieces of whirring machinery. I watched it all from behind a viewing pane. The first few doctor's visits had already drained our out-of-pocket expenses. Thank God for my Steak Frites medical coverage.

Dr. Fulci had ordered a full electrodiagnostic examination of her eye after Marnie wouldn't stop calling her office. Once Marnie had gone through a few exams, the optometrist put a gloved hand on my shoulder and asked, conspiratorially, if we could speak in the hallway.

"I'd like you to know that these tests we're running on her are unnecessary," she said in that slightly too-high voice.

"Oh." I awkwardly adjusted the straps of my mask.

"I have all the equipment in my office necessary to find anything that might be wrong with her eye, as would any of my optometric colleagues. These machines might be more powerful, but I'm confident they won't tell us anything new." She leaned against the wall, fidgeting like a pack-a-day smoker gone cold turkey. "There is nothing wrong with her eye. Nothing that I can find."

"Why did you bring her to the hospital then?"

Dr. Fulci took a step towards me. She spoke low, voice muffled by her mask. "I had to do something else to back up my prognosis. No matter what I've explained to her or showed her, Marnie has remained insistent that something is wrong. At first, of course, I believed her. But I've run every conceivable test I can imagine. I told her that, but she won't listen."

"Oh. Wow. Okay," I said. "You said 'believed,' as in, like, past tense . . . ?"

"You have to understand that I'm technically breaking doctor-patient confidentiality right now. I'm also making medical recommendations outside my area of expertise. But I think it's possible that the problem is psychosomatic—a psychological issue."

"The thing in her eye is . . . in her head?"

"Possibly."

"You're saying she's nuts?" I asked.

"No," she said firmly.

Dr. Fulci sat me down on a nearby bench. "It is not uncommon for psychological issues to manifest themselves physically, even if the person in question has no underlying or undiagnosed mental illness," she said, sternly patting my gloved hand with hers like I was a misbehaving child. "It can be actively harmful to think of such people as being 'crazy.' The relationship between mental and physical health is a complex beast, one that modern science has barely even come close to truly understanding. It's a relationship of such extreme complexity that most of our current treatments will probably be viewed by future generations the way we would look at, say, treating tuberculosis with leeches."

I could tell Dr. Fulci had more to say, but a crackling intercom announcement informed us that Marnie's exam was finished. In retrospect, I wished I had picked a better word than "nuts."

WE WERE in the living room watching some interchangeable Netflix show when I was finally able to bring up the whole "psychosomatic" thing and show Marnie the literature Dr. Fulci had emailed me.

"Oh. You think I'm crazy?" she said, not looking up from her laptop.

"No—God, no," I said, turning my attention from the movie to her. "The relationship between mind and body is, like, a way-misunderstood beast? That modern medicine is still only beginning to wrap around—uh—wrap its head around?"

"What the fuck are you talking about?"

My eyes darted around the room stupidly, looking at anything but her furiously red left eye. "I'm just saying that there are other things that maybe—?"

"There is something," said Marnie, pointing at her face, "*in my fucking eye.*"

"Because you won't leave it alone!" My forehead glowed and voice rose, unbidden. "You keep rubbing it and touching it and staring at it—every day. Even with the glasses. *Of course* it's going to look bad! You need to leave it alone."

She didn't seem shocked that I'd yelled, just kept a hard face, staying silent and staring at me with that Mars-esque eyeball. After a few seconds, she said, "You know why no one ever believes the girl in horror movies?"

"What? No?"

"Because it's true to life. I'm Virginia Madsen in fucking *Candyman*."

"What do you mean?" I was so confused. I'd never seen *Candyman*.

But she didn't answer. She got off the couch, saying something about buying yellow wallpaper for the bedroom.

AFTER A COUPLE more weeks of useless eyewashes, antibiotics, and steampunk eyewear, Marnie started to deteriorate. She did nothing but crawl from the bed to the couch, leaving all the lights off in the apartment. She was so inanimate, lying there with those enormous black goggles on, that I sometimes worried she was dead, except I'd often see her kicking the couch armrest, an involuntary tick.

Her communication with me wilted to monosyllables. The few things she did say made no sense at all. I'd overhear her muttering stuff about "literal hellscapes" and "divine punishment." Unable to touch her eyes with the goggles on, she'd often dig her nails so deeply into her palms that it would draw stigmatic blood.

I started bumming smokes off the dishies at work and letting the line guys go home early while I stayed late into the evening. Somehow endless piles of uncut beef carcasses seemed preferable to facing the problems at home.

Then one evening, Marnie came to me in tears.

"M-maybe Dr. Fulci was right," she said. "Maybe this is all in my head. I can't do this anymore. I *can't*. I'll try anything."

I blinked at her, surprised. It was the most she'd spoken in weeks.

"I can't do it," she said, barely audible. "Will you help me?"

"Yes—yeah, of course. I'll do whatever I can."

I embraced her and told her we'd get through this together. I felt her tears seeping into my shirt but was afraid to look at the stain.

🐾

"Hey, come here!" Marnie called from the bedroom. "I want to show you something."

When I entered, she was sitting on the bed with her laptop, practically bouncing with excitement. She spun the computer to me.

"Dr. Hardy," she said. "He's this big-shot psychologist working in the city who specializes in 'psycho-oculus' studies: the relationship between the brain and the eyes."

I sneered. "That seems a bit pseudo-scientific. Are you going to Google again . . . ?"

"Just shut the fuck up and listen," she said, sounding more like the girl I fell in love with than she had in ages. "'The connection between the mind and the eye is one of the most poorly understood areas of physiology—and one of the most fascinating,'" she read off Dr. Hardy's website. "'Hallucinations, blurring, selective memory, spots—all of these can occur without any obvious physical trauma, yet they are undeniably physical symptoms. It is our practice's goal to help patients improve through better understanding of the psycho-oculus, or mind-eye, connection.'"

When she looked up from the screen, smiling, her optimism was only somewhat diminished by the blazing meteor that was her left eye.

"Oh yes, I see," said Dr. Hardy, looking at Marnie's eye through a device that looked like a tiny version of the Hubble Telescope. His minimalistic, white, open-concept office projected quite a bit more professionalism than Dr. Fulci's Frankensteinian laboratory, though I was beginning to wonder why this profession seemed to require such a wide array of weird, scary machinery.

"Inflammation. Redness," the doctor continued. "Is it sore?"

"Yes," she said, neck cranked back, shoulders at a geometrically bizarre angle, her eye being widened by a claw-like apparatus. I watched this all furtively from a chair up against the wall of his office.

"Is it tender?"

"Yes."

"And you say you've tried calodrexidyn, polyspelimen, and topical adreno-ocolus lubricant?"

"Yes, yes, and yes," she repeated.

I was unsure of why he was asking these questions because, so far as I could tell, we'd included all of that information on the intake forms. Though his bedside manner was an improvement on Dr. Fulci's, just being around him distressed me. He gesticulated inhumanly, like a giant praying mantis in human skin. He spoke pedantically, as if we were children who would be impressed by any little scientific fact. Like did you know that if you add vinegar to baking soda it makes a pretty great volcano?

After a while, he freed Marnie from the strange device and bid us both sit across from him at his desk.

"You made the right decision coming to see me," Dr. Hardy said, his arms flailing like he was trying to get attention outside a used car lot. "Based on what you've told me, the problem could very well be psychological. I'm going to recommend a treatment plan that balances physical and mental therapy. Around here, we like to say that the *mentis oculi*—the mind's eye—is your body's sixth vital organ." He smiled coyly and tapped his temple. "After all, what could be more vital than this bad-boy?"

Then he deposited a box of eye-care supplies into Marnie's arms, including a plastic medicinal pad that would lock around her head for fourteen hours a day.

"I know you don't *mean* to scratch," he said, arms akimbo, "but sometimes our hands have a mind of their own!"

🐾

IN ADDITION to a wide array of prescription medication, Dr. Hardy scheduled weekly meetings and meditation sessions, aided by various "calming" mantras. He prescribed phone calls with his assistants. ("I call them my 'clear-eyed' gurus!") He advised daily engagement with the *Tao Te Ching*.

And he got all the same results.

Marnie never touched the pad or missed a meeting. Every day, she was a "leaf floating on a river parted by a stone" or a "serpent not yet a snake." Dr. Hardy's gurus instructed her to draw her feelings via art therapy. Her drawings were inchoate, colorless, vaguely infernal. They looked to me like smears of charcoal pencil on parchment.

Her eye did, however, begin to improve. The swelling and redness reduced. The skin around it softened. The blood vessels attenuated. After a while, it looked almost back to normal.

Each day, I could tell that Marnie put serious effort into seeming fine. She turned the lights back on in the living room, the sound on the television. She didn't cry anymore, at least that I could see. She never grimaced, but also never smiled. She told The Cheesecake Factory she might be able to pick up a few hosting shifts soon.

Little by little, her face became a mask of alrightness, until she almost seemed back to her old self.

Almost.

🐾

ONE EVENING, after she'd laughed a couple of times over dinner, after a few glasses of pinot grigio, after I'd just—*just*—allowed myself to believe we might be getting back to normal, I asked how she was feeling.

She replied, smiling, "There are circles of hell more comfortable than this."

         🐾

I CAME home from work a couple of days later, exhausted.

"Hey babe," I called out. It'd been a long shift, but I had two tables send back compliments, so despite my fatigue, I was in a good mood. "I'm starving. Want to go to The Rathskellar for dinner? Wing night! My treat."

No response.

"Marnie?" I said, letting my bag slump awkwardly to the hallway floor.

Which was when I saw the blood.

It was all over the kitchen floor, trailing from the sink to the bathroom and into the living room. So much of it, as if mortally wounded soldiers had been dragged through the apartment.

"Marnie!" I called again.

Laughter erupted from the living room.

My sweaty hand slipped off the doorknob. Ants scurried down my spine. An iron, sour stink wafted through the apartment—the pungent odor I'd imagine in a nail-polish factory.

Several of my steak knives of varying sizes lay in the kitchen sink, all bloody. The melon baller, from my mom's gift basket, sat amongst the knives, covered in beet-colored viscera.

I called out to Marnie again, but her laughter continued from the other room.

Blood smeared the bathroom sink and mirror. All of this seemed unreal, like I was watching it on video, my head just a swivel for a movie camera.

I stepped into the living room.

Marnie leaned over the coffee table, hair covering her face. She tittered to herself—high-pitched, almost drunken laughter.

Red soaked everything: her hair and forearms, the coffee table and the carpet.

"Marnie . . . ?" I croaked, stomach corkscrewing.

She stopped laughing, as if just realizing I was there. She slowly turned her head towards me and brushed the hair out of her face.

I puked all over the floor.

Her left eye was gone, a black-and-bloody hole where it should have been. The surgery had been imprecise. Slits and gashes decorated her brow and nose and cheeks. Fresh blood striated her chin and neck.

And on her lips, the widest smile I'd ever seen—an expression of absolute joy. Blood had drained into her mouth, between her teeth and gums. She didn't seem to mind.

In her left hand was an apple corer. On the table in front of her was what had once been an eyeball, completely hollowed out and mangled.

"M—Marnie? Wha—?" My voice echoed from miles away.

She had her right hand shut tight. Dropping the corer with a gory clatter, she cradled her wrist as though the hand might pop off and run away. She stood and held her hand out to me, giggling.

"I knew it . . . I knew it . . ." she said.

She opened her hand.

In her palm lay a translucent glob of . . . something. Something about the size of a dime. She held it up to my face, and I could see that the "something" was actually a small, spider-like creature. It had too many legs to be a spider, though—fifteen or twenty. The appendages wriggled as if the creature were drowning in the open air. Its flesh was completely clear, like gelatin or silicone, and its head looked a bit like that of a tiny, elongated turtle.

The thing craned its neck into the air, making a wet and sickening *hsssssssssssss*.

"I knew it!"

Then Marnie screamed—a shrieking, pealing laughter of unbridled relief.

The last thing I registered before the world went black was the sheer, unadulterated ecstasy in her remaining eye.

JOSEPH ANDRE THOMAS is a writer and literature teacher living in Vancouver, British Columbia. He is a graduate of the University of Toronto's MA in Creative Writing program. A recipient of the Avie Bennett Emerging Writer scholarship and the Canada Master's scholarship, Joseph's writing has appeared in *The Puritan's Town Crier* and *Untethered* magazine.

Illustration by Joe Radkins

RED AND THE BEAST

THEA MAEVE

Once upon a time, a girl threw a knife and impaled a rabbit through its eye. Pinned to the ground, the small beast made no movement or sound; it merely ceased to live. Red skipped to her latest kill, crunching the dried leaves beneath her boots. The blade slid out of the rabbit's head with a wet scraping of bone against metal. Before sheathing the knife, she wiped it clean against her cloak, the blood camouflaging into the red fabric. Then she slung the corpse into a leather bag. Grandma would be happy with her haul that day: three rabbits, a pigeon, and a bunch of blackberries.

Red walked on the path through the tall oak trees until a small clearing gave way to a cottage. A cobblestone path led through a vegetable garden planted by her grandma with plenty of carrots, cabbage, cauliflower, and herbs. Her grandpa had built the house of light-gray stones from the river, with two front-facing windows split in the middle by an oaken door. Bundles of straw dangled from the roof, and a long chimney rose on the right, which fumed woodsmoke into the sky as Red approached.

When she neared the door, a faint slurping noise came from inside the cottage. Was Grandma eating leftover stew? She pushed the door open further and froze. Before her was an animal—or so she thought at first. Long tusks jutted out from the head of a boar covered in ragged brown fur drooping atop thick, human legs. In its enormous claws was her grandma's body, soaked in blood. Her head hung low from her neck, her eyes locked in a vacant stare. The monster pulled its giant fangs from her chest. Flesh dangled from its teeth as it glared at Red. With a booming roar, the creature spewed the foul stench of blood and carnage throughout the room.

Red responded with her own roar, smaller but just as primal. She pulled her throwing knife from its sheath and in one swift motion threw it at the creature. The blade plunged into the fleshy snout between its long tusks. Rearing back its head, the creature dropped her grandma to the floor, blood spurting from her mouth. Red ran at the monster with another dagger already unsheathed. The grisly animal staggered backwards, pawing at the handle sticking from its face.

"You little shit!" the creature spat in a low guttural voice.

Before Red could attack, it turned and burst through the wall, the stones collapsing beneath its weight. As the creature fled into the forest, the chimney tilted into the new gap in the wall, pulling half of the cottage with it.

Red scrambled to her grandma's side, but a falling stone crushed the old woman's skull like a melon. Guts and brains splattered across the floor. Red choked on her breath and fell to her knees.

She stared in disbelief at her grandma's headless, crimson-stained corpse. It took a few seconds for the stones and straw to settle into ruins, but to Red, it was an eternity. She touched her grandma's dress and tugged at the fabric, hoping somehow the action would bring her only remaining relative back to life. When the body stayed motionless, she bent forward and cried until her tear ducts ran dry.

When the sun dipped behind the trees, casting a shadow over the remains of the cottage, Red decided there was no better resting place for her grandma than the home where they'd both spent their lives together. Red first gathered the fallen straw from the roof and laid it on her body. Then one by one laid the stones on top.

As Red worked, deep in her gut emerged a bitter aching that, with the laying of each stone, grew into a great anger. *Kill the beast.*

When she finished, she opened her weapons chest, which was battered from the rubble but still intact. The lid groaned as she opened it. Red equipped herself with a shoulder strap of throwing knives, a belt with two short blades in scabbards on either side, and wrist armor with sheathed daggers.

Before donning the armor and weapons, Red ran her fingers over the handiwork, recalling the hours her grandma had poured into making them. She remembered listening to the stitching of leather as she sipped hot soup by the fire on cold, wintry nights.

Red covered the weaponry with her cloak. Then she put on her rucksack with her travel gear: canteen, cook set, and a bedroll.

As Red entered the forest, she looked back one last time at the ruined cottage—once her home, now forever a tomb.

"I love you, Grandma," Red said.

She needed to follow the monster before its trail went cold. Hoping to make up ground, she sprinted through the woods with leaves and sticks lashing her legs. At first, Red needed only to follow the blood-splattered blades of grass. However, the sky soon grew dark as rain clouds shrouded the moonlight, making tracking impossible in the low visibility.

Even though adrenaline and anger still coursed through her veins, she needed to stop for the moment and take shelter. Red found an overgrown bush and propped it up with sticks until she had a suitable shelter. Inside, she slid under her blanket with her hands on her daggers. Smelling the soft rainfall and listening to fairies dance upon their mushrooms, Red breathed deeply until finally settling into sleep.

🐾

RED WAS ALREADY AWAKE when the morning sun filtered through the trees. She hastened after the creature's trail, inspecting branches and leaves for signs of disturbance.

It was the early afternoon when Red tracked the trail to a tiny village. A narrow road sliced through dilapidated cottages lining both sides, leading to a tall steeple. The entire town reeked of the aged urine, excrement, and food waste filling the street gutters.

Red walked down the main road, hoping to find someone she could ask about a bloodthirsty monster. She stepped over a man who snored near an empty cup in the street. Red had no idea how anybody could live in these conditions. She clenched her nose and followed the steeple to the town's center.

When she stood beneath the church, she found a small plaza full of villagers. Red climbed the church steps to get a better view. In the center of the crowd, a beautiful woman stood with long red hair cascading halfway down her blue peasant's dress. She stood by a stone well in the middle of the plaza as she pleaded with the other townsfolk.

"We have to save him," the woman said.

"He's a crazy old man," said a burly man with a booming voice. "Better him than us."

"The Beast probably took him for a slave," said another.

"For his bedroom," a fat man croaked.

The crowd laughed.

"Even the Beast has higher standards."

"Please. Please, I need my father. He's everything to me." She fell to her knees and cried into her hands.

"You can come home with me," said the burly man. He wore a fur jacket with a wolf's head hanging from the back. "I'll protect you from the Beast."

"I need my father back."

"Oh, come on, Beauty," an elder woman said. "Just look at him! A strong man. Your father isn't coming back. You'll need some protection."

"Forget it! You're all useless!" Beauty, or so Red thought was her name, stormed off to the east of the church, rounding a small graveyard.

"Look at her go," said a man in the crowd.

"You don't have to tell me twice." Another voice, accompanied by laughter.

"I'd love to bend her over."

"Think she could handle us all at once?"

"And the next village over, too."

"And the Beast."

Disgusted, Red left the crowd to follow Beauty around the graveyard. She saw the blue dress turn on a side street, and as Red followed, she found her collapsed on the porch of a quaint home. Irises, lilies, and poppies decorated the front garden, and ivy crawled up the walls. The woman lay on the front step, sobbing into her palms.

"I saw what happened back there," Red said, unsure of how else to approach her.

"Yes. They were awful. They would never have said those things if my father was here." The woman rubbed her eyes and turned to Red. "Do you know him?"

"I . . ." As she looked up at Red, her scarlet hair brushed away from her face, revealing deep hazel eyes that shone in the sunlight. Red's body tensed as tingles ran up her arms. Never had she beheld such a beautiful woman. "I don't know your father. My name is Red. I live . . . well, *lived* in a cottage south of here."

"Oh. Well, my father is a great man," she paused. "I don't want to lose him."

"I understand," Red said.

A moment of silence passed between the two of them.

"Is your name Beauty? I think they called you that back there."

"Yes. That's my name."

"Okay, Beauty, I think I can help," Red said. "I am going to kill the Beast you spoke about earlier. Maybe I can save your father."

"You?" Her eyes analyzed Red head to toe. "Aren't you a bit small?"

"I see it as an advantage."

"Hilarious. Did Hunter put you up to this?"

"I don't know who Hunter is. All I know is that thing killed my grandma, and I won't stop until it's dead."

"Oh," Beauty said. "I'm sorry. I didn't mean to be disrespectful. I just . . ." She broke down in tears.

Red reached out, but after thinking twice, pulled her hand back and rubbed her forehead.

"You've had a run-in with the Beast yourself," Red said.

"Yes, he took my father. I don't know if he's alive or dead or what. I just want to get him back." Beauty sniffled and wiped her eyes with her blue dress.

"Do you know where the Beast is?" Red asked.

Beauty nodded.

"His castle."

"Castle?"

"He's the Prince. He's ruled over us for as long as I can remember. Just takes a sacrifice now and then instead of taxes." Beauty sighed with an exasperated smile.

"Well, can you tell me how to get there?"

"If you promise to save my father." Beauty stood up.

"If he's alive, we'll save him," Red said.

"We?" Beauty asked.

Rather than answering her question, Red only told Beauty to bring a bowl to prepare for their journey. Beauty didn't have a canteen or any other supplies, so they decided they would share Red's.

Beauty ran inside her house. Red stood awkwardly, looking around. She noticed some movement behind the houses and realized it was one of those men stalking Beauty. Red tucked a hand into her cloak and rested it on a throwing knife.

"Will these work?" Beauty stood in the front door, holding a small bowl and utensils.

"Yes. Definitely." Red took off her rucksack and stashed Beauty's belongings before slinging it back onto her shoulder. "Are you ready to go?"

"Yes," Beauty said. "The castle is to the east."

Together, they walked out of the village. Red didn't notice any suspicious movements and figured the men had let them be.

RED AND BEAUTY moved along a narrow path enclosed by thick walls of oak, pine, and beech trees. The midday sun filtered through the branches upon juniper, heath, and lavender where the beetles and spiders lived. The brush rustled as squirrels gathered nuts and birds hopped between branches. And Red much preferred the bright fragrances of poppies and tree sap over the waste in the dreadful town.

"I'm getting hungry," Red said after hours of walking.

"Me too. What do we have to eat?"

"Rabbit." Red tilted her head toward a rabbit that grazed on the ryegrass only a dozen paces away. She held her arm out and stopped Beauty from moving.

"Oh," Beauty said.

"Shh," Red hissed, her eyes locked on the small critter.

In one quick motion, Red withdrew a knife, flicked her wrist, and sent the blade flying at the creature. Beauty's jaw dropped. As Red went to collect her kill, Beauty stayed motionless until Red was back by her side.

"How did you do that?" Beauty asked.

"Lots and lots of practice," Red said.

They settled for dinner in a small grassy clearing with a rock jutting out of the middle. Red took off her rucksack and gathered sticks, dried leaves, and small twigs from the forest floor.

"I've read so many stories about women like you. I never dreamt I'd actually meet one of them," Beauty said as she unpacked the pot and bowls.

"What do you mean?" Red piled the materials together. "Can you pass me the flint?"

"You're a warrior." Beauty pulled out the flint and handed it to Red.

"I don't really know. I just always wanted to be a hunter." Red started striking at the flint with a rock, watching the sparks fly onto the bundle of tinder, kindling, and sticks.

"Well, I've never seen somebody so skilled with knives. You killed a rabbit from twenty feet away!" Beauty said. She leaned forward, elbows on her knees, chin in her palms.

"Ever since I was a kid, I've always practiced. It's instinct for me now."

"Oh, I hope they write songs about you. People love a fighting woman."

"Not in my experience," Red said as the kindling crackled and popped, tendrils of smoke curling into the air.

"What do you mean?"

"Everywhere I go, men have to show me they are tougher." The wood caught fire. "I don't go to towns much anymore, was never one for hunting guilds. I just keep to myself because men are always wretches with me around."

"Well, I love it," Beauty said. "Maybe I'll write your song."

"You'd write about me?" Red leaned back, surprised. She never felt her life was special enough to be accounted for. Would she even want the attention garnered by such a thing?

"Absolutely. A female warrior who slays the Beast and rescues a young woman's captive father! That's a story worth telling, don't you think?" Beauty poured water into the pot and set it over the fire to boil.

"I suppose. I just want to avenge my grandma." Red stared down at the ground again. An image of the Beast towering over her grandma flashed through her mind.

"Maybe I can write about you, and you can teach me some things."

"Teach you? About what?" Red decapitated and skinned the rabbit. Then she sliced it into short strips of meat and plopped it into the pot for cooking.

"You can teach me how to fight." Beauty walked over to Red. "I don't know if I'd be any good at it, but I've always been a quick learner. Had to learn to sew all by myself since my father isn't any good at those sorts of things."

She grasped Red's empty hand and pointed to the small sheath strapped to Red's wrist.

"Can you show me how to use one of those?"

Red's heart thundered in her chest. She pulled out a dagger and turned the handle to Beauty, who gripped it tight as Red let her take its full weight.

"You want to loosen your grip a bit. And adjust your thumb. Here." Red helped Beauty position her hand correctly, touching her smooth skin. "Does that feel more comfortable?"

"A little." Beauty breathed a sigh of relief. "Okay, you can take it back before I accidentally stab one of us." Her arm was shaking.

"Good idea," Red said, nervous herself. She took the dagger from Beauty and slipped it into its sheath. "That was step one. You'll get better in no time."

"Thanks, that was terrifying." Beauty laughed and hugged Red. Not knowing what to do with her arms, Red let them hang by her sides, blushing as Beauty squeezed tightly.

"Maybe tonight I'll show you how to thrust. That's step two."

"I'd like that." Beauty released Red and clasped her hands into her lap.

Once the rabbit was finished cooking, they ate in silence, listening to crickets chirping in the distance, broken by the occasional croak of a frog.

"I think we should rest here for the night," Red said.

"Okay," Beauty said. "We should get to the castle late tomorrow."

"You can use the pillow and blanket. I don't really need them." Red handed them to Beauty.

"Nonsense. I think they're big enough to share."

"You're right." Red swallowed her spit. "They're probably big enough."

Beauty laid the pillow at the foot of the rock and rested her head on the downy cushion. She held the blanket up so Red could slide under, and Red did so. They lay with their backs to each other and fell asleep.

Through the night, fairies danced on their bodies, and by the morning, their arms were wrapped around each other as they slept face to face.

RED LEFT the campfire to hunt for breakfast while Beauty collected berries. She kept thinking about how she awoke in the tender embrace of Beauty's body, staring into her peaceful face, admiring Beauty's glowing skin and luscious eyelashes. She wondered if Beauty had the same images running through her mind—if Beauty also looked at Red and admired her body, her face, her personality. Was that even possible with a girl like Red?

Then, drowning her thoughts, came the drumbeat of horse hooves.

Red ran back to the campfire, but Beauty was still gone. The hooves were beating closer, so Red bolted across the clearing into the woods. She hid behind a bush and watched.

Three horses galloped into the clearing. The first man she recognized from the town. He still wore his wolf-skin jacket. With him were two shorter men, one skinny, one fat, both faces she'd seen in the crowd.

"All right. I think we found her," said the man with the wolf jacket. He leapt off his horse and walked up to the campfire.

"What if she already left?" the fat man said.

"Their stuff is still here," the wolf man said as he inspected the area.

The other two men dismounted. The skinnier one peered into the trees, his gaze nearing Red, then glossing over her and continuing along.

A tree branch snapped on the other side of the clearing.

Each man's head turned in unison. A moment of silence followed, Red's own heartbeat the only sound she could hear.

"Let's get her." The wolf man ran into the trees, with his two companions trailing behind.

Red bolted after them. She scanned the ground as she ran, plotting her footsteps to avoid leaves and sticks, but she couldn't keep up. The men were much quicker as they crashed through the trees.

"Hello, Beauty," the wolf man said.

"Hunter?" Beauty said. They were a short distance ahead of Red. "What are you doing here?"

Red followed the voices until she neared, then slowed down to avoid detection as she listened to the unfolding situation. Hunter stood in front of Beauty, his hands on his hips, grin stretched wide. His two friends flanked Beauty on either side.

"I just came to check up on you. Where's your friend?"

"What friend?" Beauty asked.

"We saw you leave town with a little girl in a red hood." Hunter looked around the trees, but Red ducked behind a juniper bush before he could spot her.

"Oh, her? I was just showing her the game trails my father had shown me before. She's long gone now."

"The game trails? So you know you're close to viper territory here. Correct?"

"Of course, I know."

Hunter scoffed.

"Gonna get yourself bit. Shouldn't be out here all by yourself." His eyes looked her up and down.

"As you can see, I'm just fine. You can leave now."

Hunter laughed.

"Oh, you are not," he said. "If I was a bear, or . . . the Beast, you would be dead already."

"That's right," the fat man said. "I've seen it happen to George. Remember him? Got mauled by the Beast."

"I remember that. Torn to shreds," the skinny man said.

"Stop it, you two." Hunter glared at each of them before stepping forward. "Of course, that won't happen to Beauty. I apologize if they're scaring you. Let's get you back to town."

"No. I'm fine, Hunter. Really." Beauty stepped back but bumped into the fat man.

All along, Red had been moving closer, now within ten feet. Her fingers were on her daggers, ready to pull them and charge.

"I would feel better knowing you weren't out here all alone. As they say, 'the woods ain't a good place for a pretty gal.'" Hunter squeezed Beauty's shoulders and leaned his face close to hers. "I'll protect you, love."

"Get off of me!" Beauty pushed at Hunter's chest with no effect.

"You shouldn't refuse help like that," the fat man said.

"No. She shouldn't," Hunter said, his hands now wrapping behind Beauty's back.

"You disgust me," Beauty said, and she spat in Hunter's face.

Hunter released her and stood back, mouth agape. He wiped the spit with the sleeve of his wolf-skin jacket and flung it to the ground. As he did so, Beauty turned to run, but the other men grabbed her. Red balanced on the balls of her feet and unsheathed her daggers.

"Now, now. Bad manners, Beauty. I thought you were a lady, not an animal."

"Help!" Beauty screamed.

Hunter grabbed Beauty by the neck and pulled her to his body.

Red lunged out of the woods and, sliding between the two accomplices, flashed her knives to each side with arms outstretched. Using her forward momentum, she sliced both men through their guts. The fat man's intestines spooled into the dirt. As the skinny man wrapped his arms around his gaping wound, blood oozed between them and dripped to the ground. Both men looked at each other, their eyes glazed in wonderment and shock. They collapsed.

"Red!" Beauty screamed.

Hunter's eyes jumped wildly from the bodies to Red to Beauty to the trees.

"Let her go," Red said. She pointed a dagger at Hunter's face.

Hunter pushed Beauty forward, her body slamming against Red's. They both fell between the two dead men. As Red got up, Hunter was running back through the trees to the campfire and his horse. Red held her hand out to Beauty, who took it and rose to her feet.

"Are you okay?" Red asked.

"I—Yes. I'm so thankful you came." Tears welled up in her eyes.

Red hugged her, letting Beauty's tears run through her hair.

"I think it's time to teach you how to use a dagger," Red said.

"Yes." Beauty chuckled through her tears. "Probably, it's time."

"You're okay," Red said.

"Thank you." Beauty kissed Red on the forehead. Red blushed.

"Let's head back," Red said.

As they walked, Red unstrapped her wrist armor and handed it to Beauty.

"You strap it on like this, and you can cover it with your dress sleeves so nobody even notices it's there." Red strapped the armor onto Beauty's wrist, buckled it in, and pulled Beauty's sleeve down to show her how it was done.

"Okay, now this is how you pull the dagger from the sheath with the same hand. It's a bit tricky on these, but if you get the hang of it, you can draw it out quickly without notice." Red demonstrated by reaching for the handle with her middle finger and drawing it out until she could grip it with her thumb. Then she reached with her fingers to the end of the handle and slid it further.

"This is the part where you need to be careful or you'll cut yourself." Pinching her thumb and middle finger around the base of the handle, she flicked her wrist backward and the entire dagger glided out from the sheath. Then she pushed down with her thumb, and the dagger rotated around her fingers, the handle falling into her palm.

"That looks incredibly difficult," Beauty said, her eyes staring blankly at Red's hand.

"You've just got to practice. It's easy once you get the hang of it. Now you try."

Beauty attempted to mimic the motion, but when she needed to flick the knife handle into her palm, she only dropped it.

"Close," Red said. "Just keep practicing and you'll get it."

As they walked to their campsite, Beauty practiced unsheathing her wrist dagger over and over. To Red's surprise, she never cut herself, although she never completed it successfully. When they reached the clearing, the two dead men's horses remained, and Hunter was nowhere to be found. The fat man's horse still had plenty of bread and berries among its effects. Red and Beauty sat and ate their breakfast in silence.

"Do you know how to ride?" Beauty asked.

"No," Red said. "I've never been around horses."

"Do you think I could teach you someday, like you taught me to use the dagger? We might need a little more time though." Beauty ran her hand up and down the brown nose of one of the horses. It whinnied beneath her touch. "For now, you can just hop on with me."

"Hop on with you?" Red didn't know two people could ride the same horse.

"Of course, just get behind and wrap your arms around me. We can both fit on this saddle." Beauty walked around and pulled herself up on the horse. She smiled down at Red.

"Trust me," Beauty said.

"Okay," Red said. "But first . . ."

Red took the water and put out the campfire, then collected her gear. She triple-checked all her weapons, feeling a bit naked without one of her wrist daggers. At some point, she realized she was delaying the inevitable. She wasn't sure if she was more scared of the horse or of being so close to Beauty, arms wrapped tightly around her waist. Red took a drink from the canteen and let the water flow down her throat.

"Ready?" Beauty asked.

"Yes. I'm ready." Red approached Beauty, who held out her hand again. Red grabbed on and took care to slip her foot into the stirrup. She hopped and lifted her leg over the horse, her cape swirling in a circle. She nearly launched herself too far, grabbing Beauty to stop herself from falling over the other side.

Beauty laughed, which calmed Red's nerves. Red righted herself and found her arms already wrapped around Beauty's waist.

"You all right back there?" Beauty asked.

"Yes. Fine," Red said.

Beauty shouted, "Yah!" and dug in her heels. The horse kicked forward, and Red squeezed tighter, pressing her head into Beauty's back.

THE FOREST OPENED into a wide plain with a dark looming castle scratching the sky with haphazard spires. It seemed as if it was designed to intimidate all those who beheld it. At every corner, its architecture featured sharp spikes that could impale anyone who displeased its occupants. It was built of dark stone and black iron, nearly impenetrable to the eye.

As they galloped toward the castle, an overgrown garden of red and white roses split by a winding path replaced the ryegrass. Red found the cloying scent overbearing as they passed through the countless blossoms. She was lost in their beauty until they stopped at the gates. All the windows were pitch black, neither torches nor candles seeming to blaze inside, as if the castle had been long abandoned. They both dismounted the horse.

"Here goes nothing," Beauty said.

Black iron ribbons stretched across the dark wooden doors.

Red tried to push them open, but they didn't budge. Muffled voices muttered from the other side of the doors. Red reached into her cloak pocket, ready to draw her throwing knives. Then the doors swung open.

"Welcome! Welcome!"

Red stared into the dark castle, and in the middle of the entryway stood an antique vanity painted white with a red rose pattern decorating the sides of an oval mirror.

"Hi there!" the voice said. The mirror, which reflected Red and Beauty's faces, made their mouths appear to speak, as if they were the ones greeting themselves, although the voice that came out was unquestionably masculine. "I presume you two are here to court the Prince?"

"Uh . . ." Red looked at Beauty, surprised at her unfazed expression.

"Yes, yes. I am here to court the Prince," Beauty said.

"Very well then," the mirror said. "Please come in. We haven't had visitors in a long time. I presume this is your servant."

"She's my friend," Beauty said. "Her name is Red."

"Red, how lovely to make your acquaintances. We are already preparing you some fine dining." The vanity shifted its weight from side to side. Each step took a full second, signified by the rattling of jewelry sliding in its drawers. It turned away from them and shuffled slowly through the hall. Red and Beauty looked at each other in disbelief. Then Beauty took Red's hand, and together they followed the vanity.

Even though the house appeared abandoned, inside there was no sense of musk or dusty air. In fact, the entire place smelled like it was freshly cleaned. From within resounded a clamor, and when they turned the corner to find the main dining hall, they saw why.

Everything was in motion. Plates, chairs, silverware, cups, cookware, and brooms all moved around fervently preparing the table with a grand banquet. Red touched the daggers inside her cloak.

"Come sit, you two," the vanity said.

"Hello, mademoiselle," said a passing plate to Beauty.

Two chairs slid beneath the legs of Beauty and Red, buckling their knees so they fell back into the seats. The furniture carried them to their respective places at the table. Beauty sat at the head, with Red on her right-hand side. Within seconds, all the furniture ceased, as if it had never moved to begin with.

The vanity announced the foods presented on the table. "We have Nicoise salad, mushroom bisque, tourin, bottles of both muscadet and pinot noir, and of course our delicious meats for you to enjoy." As the vanity spoke, the platters and bowls tossed some of their food onto two plates, which then slid in front of Red and Beauty. All the foods looked magnificent, especially the mouth-watering cuts of meat.

"Bon appétit. The Prince will be down in a few minutes. Sorry to keep you waiting," the vanity said, its mirror showing them eating the food. Then it waddled up the stairs. Each step still took exactly one second, even though Red was certain it would fall backwards into ruin, but it trudged up the steps without fault.

Red and Beauty grabbed the utensils and were astonished at how easily they could pick up their food. They started with the salad and soup, drank some wine, and then finally cut pieces of the meat to chew on. It was juicy, tender, and tasted a little sweet.

Satisfied, Red left her seat to walk around the room.

"What are you doing?" Beauty asked.

"Just checking out the castle," Red said. "What did you mean when you said you're courting the Prince?"

"That's the tale," Beauty whispered. "The Beast is the son of a forgotten king who was cursed to live this way until he finds true love and breaks the spell."

"Sounds awful."

Red ambled around the room, surveying her surroundings. The architecture of the castle was disorienting, as if the floors were slanted and the walls leaned inward. The longer she stared at the ceiling, the more it seemed to bow at the center. Did any inanimate objects exist within the castle at all, or could the curtains, the rugs, or even the walls move as well?

One side of the room featured windows overlooking a courtyard. Opposite the windows was a grand marble staircase with a descending purple carpet. It split at the top into each wing of the castle; the hallways faded into darkness as if they never ended at all.

If Beauty's father was truly concealed in the castle, Red wondered if they would ever find him in the labyrinth of rooms. Red made her way back to the table, sat down, and put her hand on Beauty's.

Above them, a door slammed violently, and footsteps rumbled behind the castle walls. Red tucked her hand into her cloak, and none other than the Beast himself rounded the top of the steps. She seethed with hatred at the sight of him, recalling how he roared in her grandma's cottage. The light shone off his tusks, a bright white haze hovering in front of a husky silhouette. As the rest of his body stepped into the illumination, he flaunted a long purple robe with gold accents, although his bulging feet were bare.

Red wanted nothing more than to carve the Beast into a thousand pieces. To pry the horns out of his head and stick them into his heart.

"What are you doing here?" the Beast's voice echoed. He was larger than Red remembered—built like a bull and tall as a tree.

"To switch places with my father," Beauty said.

"Your father?"

"Yes. The man you abducted from my village."

The Beast scratched the scab on his snout from where Red's knife had stabbed him days earlier. Then he burst into laughter, the furniture following suit.

"What's so funny?" Beauty asked.

"Well, you'll have to crawl onto that serving platter to replace him." The Beast's cackles grew so loud the floor shook like the castle was rocking on its foundation.

Beauty stared at the slab of meat, her eyes growing wide in horror. Red heaved forward and spewed bile onto the rug. Broken from her trance, Beauty joined Red by coating the table, her food, and her father's flesh with vomit and gobbets of half-digested food. Both their stomachs churned as if to devour themselves until pain cramped down deep inside. Red glanced at Beauty, who bawled, spilling tears into the remains of her father, her mouth muttering a tragic, inaudible eulogy.

Red pushed herself up from the chair, her face flushed with fury. The Beast was now at the bottom of the stairs, still cackling hysterically. Red grabbed her knives and jumped onto the table, spilling the pinot noir. With one swift motion, she threw both the knives. The Beast dodged one of them, but the second stuck into his right shoulder.

A booming roar ceased the laughter, the furniture falling dead silent. Red was already retrieving another knife when the Beast charged her. She tossed the knife and heard it thump into the Beast's hide before he rammed into her. As the table snapped under the Beast's weight, Red skittered across the room until she slammed into a wall. Beauty's chair veered back from the table, but she remained seated, her face glazed over and wet with tears.

The Beast roared again, then turned to Beauty. Red stood from her position, drawing another throwing knife, but when she looked back, Beast was holding Beauty between the both of them, his claws nearly puncturing Beauty's neck.

"I will kill her," the Beast said.

"Please, don't. I'll love you. I'll break the curse," Beauty said.

"Fuck the curse," the Beast said. "I have everything I need now."

Red held a throwing knife in each hand as she stepped closer. Blood poured from the crimson-stained knife that jutted out from the Beast's left arm, coating his fur and dripping to the granite floor. Her other knife handle stood like a short black horn on top of his head. He seemed not to mind their presence in his body, or was too distracted to do anything about them.

"You stop right there, you little shit," the Beast said.

Red complied.

Out of the corner of her eye, Red saw Beauty's wrist flick quickly, and a glint of metal flashed beneath her sleeve. Beauty stabbed wildly while reaching behind her, jutting the blade into the Beast's leg over and over.

The Beast yelped as he dropped her, and she collapsed to the floor. He groaned as he crouched down to grip his wound. Red rushed forward, but the Beast moved quickly. He swiped at Beauty with his claws and tore into her shoulder. Beauty screeched in pain. Red slid across the floor as the Beast opened his mouth to bite Beauty. His yellow fangs loomed large from his mouth. Saliva dripped from them, landing on Beauty's dress.

Red envisioned her grandma hanging limp in the Beast's claws. Except it wasn't her grandma this time. It was Beauty, with her red hair falling to the floor and her hazel eyes locked in a death stare with Red. Crimson liquid drained from her neck and chest. Red erased the vision from her mind and focused on the Beast's open mouth.

She threw the knives in a swift motion, and they missed, only slicing his right cheek before skidding across the floor. The Beast stumbled backwards, groaning, the skin on his right cheek now flapping below his jaw. Red gripped her last two throwing knives and hopped over Beauty. The Beast pounced. Red leapt upward and planted her feet upon the Beast's arms before jumping and flipping over his head. As her cloak arched over him with a swirl of red, she pegged her knives downward.

The throwing knives split the air before impaling the Beast through both his eyes with one resounding *schlunk*. The Beast's head snapped backward, his feet launching out from beneath him. With a loud thud, his body walloped on the granite. Red landed graciously on the balls of her feet.

Wasting no time, Red pulled the long dagger from her belt, jumped onto the Beast, and burrowed it between his tusks. The skull cracked beneath her blade, and she leaned down, listening to the sticky movement of the metal sinking deep into his brain.

After several violent shudders, the Beast lay motionless on the stone floor. For a moment, the entire room was silent. Then, in a raucous clatter, all the furniture howled in mourning. They clattered in their places, making the entire castle tremble with their grief. Sensing hostility, Red quickly bounced to her feet.

"Come on."

Red grabbed Beauty, and together they ran out of the dining hall. After a moment, the furniture piled behind them, filling the halls with blustering noise. It was deafening. Red feared the walls themselves were caving in. A flash of pain seared her calf as something sharp slashed at her skin. She stumbled, pushing Beauty forward, close to the door. Red glanced behind her. There, a tidal wave of ceramic, wood, metal, and glass rushed towards her. Red sprang forward, doing her best to ignore the throbbing in her leg. A knife slashed past her ear, missing and lodging itself into one of the doors.

Beauty heaved the same door open slightly as plates shattered around them. She reached out to Red, but Red tackled her, and they tumbled through the door into the rose garden. The furniture scratched at the doors behind them, unwilling, or unable, to leave.

"You have brought torment upon us all!" The vanity berated them. Then it slammed the door shut. Wails of anguish bellowed from inside the castle walls.

Red and Beauty gazed at the doors in disbelief, then simultaneously lay back in the grass.

"I'm sorry," Red said, "about what happened in there to your . . . your . . ."

"I know," Beauty said shortly. She breathed deeply. Her skin, Red noticed, which previously shone, was now drained of all color. Beauty closed her eyes, and in that moment, she appeared dead. The only sound in the air was the furniture scratching, snapping, and shattering ruthlessly behind the door. Then Beauty rolled over and looked back at Red. She attempted a smile, but it was weak.

"Let me see your wound," Beauty said.

Red rolled to her side so Beauty could examine the back of her leg. Beauty bent down to look closely. Her fingers pressed into Red's skin on both sides of the wound, causing Red to wince.

"It isn't too deep. You'll be fine."

"What about yours?" Red asked.

"Tell me how bad it is."

Red sat up and examined Beauty. She pulled the fabric over

Beauty's shoulder and saw three gashes across the skin, but the blood had stopped leaking from the lacerations. Subconsciously guiding her hand down Beauty's back, she looked up and saw Beauty, head turned, staring into her eyes. Red inhaled, suddenly aware of her hand and how close they were to one another.

"It looks fine. It's stopped bleeding," Red said, taking her hand off Beauty's back and shifting her gaze to the castle.

Beauty slid over and hugged her. They held each other tightly, both possessing immense grief, both too shocked to cry, both accepting the only comfort available in the aftermath of such chaos.

After a long time there in the dirt, Beauty rose to her feet. She held her hand out to Red, who winced as she stood, her leg still in pain. Beauty supported Red with an arm around her side, and they limped down the pathway to their horse.

"Can you stand?" Beauty asked.

"I think I can. It just hurts." Red pressed her hand into the horse's side, and Beauty let her go. She tested her weight on her injured leg, and while it still hurt, she could stand.

Beauty plucked a rose from the garden, her fingertip pricking on a thorn. A droplet of blood trickled down her palm as she raised the rose to her nose and took in its scent. Her face melted with pleasure, and her cheeks filled again with life. She walked back to Red, clutching it between her thumb and forefinger.

Beauty extended the rose to Red.

Red blushed. She grew lightheaded, no longer sensing the pain in her leg. No longer sensing her legs at all. She leaned into the horse to keep her balance. Beauty giggled.

Red took the rose, pulling it close.

Beauty kissed Red. Euphoria washed over them. The world, for a moment, drifted away. Their grief, anger, exhaustion—all phased out—replaced with joy, love . . . and lust. They wished the kiss would never end. If they could have frozen there as statues, beholden only to the erosion of time, they would have been happy.

Alas, the world and all its responsibilities came back into existence as they released their embrace. They climbed onto the horse. This time, Red struggled to get over, and Beauty pulled her up.

They galloped out of the garden and into the woods where they would build themselves a cottage and live together, with their traumas and their love, surrounded by wild beasts and fairies, until death do them part.

THEA MAEVE (SHE/THEY) is a transgender woman currently living in Phoenix, Arizona. She occasionally posts poetry on her Instagram and Twitter under the username @TheaMaeveTV. But mostly she can be found day-dreaming about the upcoming queer communist revolution or cuddling with her dog, Fred.

Illustration by P.L. McMillan

THE INTRUDER

JUSTIN FAULL

I smile into the yellow, orange, and red. Sometimes a simple squinting of the eyes can transform the ugliest aspects of life, fusing them into a thing of beauty. My eyes half-closed, I take my mind half-elsewhere. Cars, trucks, motorbikes, and streetlights consolidate into a galactic communal mechanism of glowing rush-hour traffic. But once I focus upon the finer details, it all becomes so much more sinister. Cogs lost in the machine—or some other cliché shit like that.

I open my eyes. The motorway's cold and calculated shape overwhelms my vision once again, its intricate parts now in full view. A black four-wheel drive is to the left of me; a stressed mother wearing an overtly formal blazer intermittently looks over her shoulder to yell at her squealing children in the back. Should've thought about these things before having kids, sweetie. Up ahead, horns blare at a tradie in a run-down ute as he swerves across four lanes to get ahead of the traffic. Does he think he's better than everyone else?

My train of thought derails as I realise that the idiot in front of me is doing a hundred instead of a hundred and ten. Fucking moron, acting as if everyone has all day to get home. I slam my palm on the horn until they look in their rearview mirror. I shift my left hand to the bottom of the steering wheel, exerting the least energy possible, and grab a spliff I made earlier for this very moment. Hammering on the horn some more, I can see it's a young kid, probably just off his P-plates. He swerves into the left lane and gives me a dirty look as I pass him. I give him the finger.

The traffic ahead then slows to a crawl, and I hit the brakes nearly too late, inches away from a blue hatchback. The deafening roar of a motorbike just behind me, I look into the rearview mirror and see a broad-chested twentysomething slink between the lanes, quickly approaching on my right, veering on the edge of the emergency stopping lane. My hand makes its way to the car door with a mind of its own. Pulling on the handle, I imagine him colliding with the car door, his cocky smile wiped away as the glass strips the skin from his face. I push the door a fraction too slowly as he zooms past without a clue how close he was to death. I shake my head violently—what the fuck am I doing?

The traffic moves again, and I crank the radio till the music dissolves my wandering thoughts, shifting my focus back towards the road. Rock music plays—what sounds like a Nine Inch Nails song. Besides the spliff hanging between my fingers, music is the only other medication for my dangerous tendencies. Sometimes I get so lost in the music that I arrive at my destination, an hour having passed, with no recollection of actually driving. But this song does none of that, and it muffles and distorts, the vocals becoming unintelligible. Shitty radio antenna—I need to get that fixed. I change the station, but the song remains the same. The vocals deepen and slur as if some demonic force consumes the band, and the melody twists itself into a sort of blaring emergency alarm. This is too fucking weird. There must be some interference or something. I shut the radio off.

My headlights flash over a passing exit sign; I'm stuck in Ipswich for at least another half an hour till I get home. Not sure how long I've been daydreaming—haven't crashed the car yet, so it can't have been too long. The glare of the setting sun stings my eyes, so I pull down the sun visor. I look back over at the kid from earlier who is now behind me. I wonder what it would sound like if I were to suddenly swerve in front of him and brake, the squeal of screeching tires and the thunder of twisting metal. He looks a bit like Terrance from that shitty pizza place all those years ago, always giving me and the guys shit for every little thing so he could suck up to the owner.

I see my sign up ahead and veer into the exit lane, not bothering to indicate. Had I always been like this? If I'd changed, then I'd never noticed it—changes in a person are barely noticeable because they always occur simultaneously, constantly reacting to the present and intertwining with the past. Does everyone feel this way? Perhaps some are just better at stuffing it inside. I leave the exit ramp.

My car twists and turns around the dimly lit streets. I occasionally glance at those making the treacherous walk home, darkness lapping at their feet like a rising tide. I pass a house that has been for sale for months. Someone has graffitied the word SCUM over the face of the real estate agent.

A stop sign ahead, I briefly slow down, and my headlights illuminate a dead bird lying in the middle of the street. It appears to be someone's pet cockatoo, its white feathers now maroon from the blood and dirt. As I accelerate, I see its beak widen and eyes glisten. I speed closer, seeing tiny, grey, wriggling maggots erupting from its mouth like liquified television static spilling out of a screen. A bloody screech pierces my ears as the tires flatten its feathery corpse. The music plays again—the radio has turned itself back on at full volume. I turn it off with a trembling hand. Surely it was just a glitch of the stereo. Guess I need to get that fixed too.

I park my car in a cramped spot on the street, squeezing it between a decrepit Holden Commodore and a weathered Mitsubishi Magna. One of the Magna's windows is missing, a duct-taped garbage bag peeling from the corner, flapping in the wind like a trashy flag for the neighbourhood. Opposite from it is a playground with a broken swing set, the seat missing, its loose chains flailing and clinking.

I live in a large apartment complex, sandwiched somewhere on the third floor between a multitude of identical rooms. When it was being built, someone fucked up and failed to account for the number of rooms when paving the car park—so it's first come, first serve. And once again, I'm late getting home, so all the parks are probably taken. I switch off the ignition, and the streetlight flickers, blinding camera flashes pulsating through the car window.

As I slam my car door, the sound breaks the eerie silence like a stone thrown in a placid lake. Crooked trees reach out onto the sidewalk, roots bursting decaying pavement. No moon glows in the black sky. No stars pierce the clouds. The silence is so palpable that I am conscious of each step I make, heavy thumps on the sidewalk.

As I look up at the towering apartment building, dark windows stare back at me, no light behind the glass. My hands slick with sweat, I imagine the building empty and echoing, everyone having agreed to leave, together and all at once. Was there a bomb threat? A fire? I take a quick peek into the car park. From where I can see, it's full, the cars crammed together like chickens in a coop. Where the fuck is everyone? Was there some stupid party I wasn't invited to? Doesn't matter, I don't need them. Perhaps my loneliness is manifesting paranoia.

I make my way into the apartment stairway. Each footstep reverberates off the stairs as I ascend, and the bright, clinical lights of the stairway waver rhythmically as if spirits are following me. I wipe a bead of sweat off my brow. My body is reacting without my permission. There is nothing wrong. It's all in my head. And then I see my apartment door. A cold wave washes over me. I freeze. My arm hair prickles as my mouth goes dry.

The door is wide open; the intruder—if my suspicions are correct—made no attempt at concealing the break-in. The yellow glow of my living room lamp spills out into the hallway. I creep towards the door, ready for anything. I have no instinct to retreat. This is my home. The police would roll their eyes at me; another drunk povo shitting where they eat. This dilapidated apartment is all I have.

I slip my car keys between my fingers like claws, the cold metal digging into my skin as I form a tight fist. I'm eager for a physical encounter; it's been too long since I've truly felt alive. Someone I can finally lay into, a vessel for all the shitty bosses and gossiping colleagues. Lost in thought, I step into the kitchen, barely aware of the open drawers, scattered cutlery, broken glasses, dirty dishes, and half-drunk beer bottles. I'll punch the greasy robber in his neck, slam him to the floor, and jam my keys into the whites of his eyes until I feel the blood and jelly splatter on my fingers—I will be the final image burnt into his brain. "Self-defence," I can say. These thoughts leave my mind as I enter the living room, dissipating the moment I see the intruder.

Heart in my throat, time stops for a split second. Sitting on the couch is a thing not of this world.

It appears to be in the shape of a human, except for the absence of any perceivable matter—as if some deity has sculpted a fourth-dimensional hole in the image of a man. What fills the space between is a moving, living static—all gradients of grey dancing and seething, like, I realise in terror, the bird in the street. There is no sound between us but the whirring spin of the ceiling fan.

My exhilaration spills out in an audible gasp. The intruder turns its head—looks directly at me with eyes it does not have, yet I know it stares into my soul. Any idea of escape enters my head a moment too late. The door to my apartment slams shut. I scramble towards it, grappling at the knob as if I were dangling from a cliff. Clammy hands slipping, I steal a look back at the intruder. It sits still. Unmoving. Its absent stare unrelenting. To the left is the living room window—my last resort. I imagine the glass breaking and my bones shattering. Or my brains spilling over the concrete, a neighbour awaking to a nasty surprise. Either seems infinitely better than staying here with the intruder. As I consider the window, my stomach suddenly churns, and I fall to my knees, my throat constricting as the air turns toxic, an evil energy threatening to suffocate me.

I push myself up with all the power I can muster and attempt a sprint towards the window. I am so close now. My hand inches from the latch, a crack resonates through the air like a whip. The intruder appears before me, and I fall into its emptiness like a neck through a noose.

I free-fall through the blinding depths of an infinite dark. Thousands of otherworldly worms wriggle over me, digging tiny, corrupted needles into my skin. I try to cry out, some kind of pathetic whimper, but the worms seize the opportunity for entry. The pain passes beyond the physical, a war on my being, digging into the synapses. I want to cry, but the intruder will not even allow me these simple comforts. Instead, I see the image of my body breaking down from afar—convulsing, then spasming and dribbling like a dying child.

My body slams into the ground. My vision returns, but it's blurred, filtered through something charcoal-like, like a black rubbish bag. The fleshy darkness compresses rapidly until it clings to me like a second skin, paralysing me. And then it breaks through my skin. My consciousness refuses to leave despite an overwhelming desire. My organs collapse, bones break, and blood dries. I am but a tiny glimmer within myself. I hear myself laughing, and I feel my body move under its control as it lies on the floor of my apartment, drinking wine with my throat, laughing with my mouth.

I WAKE UP. I get out of bed. I have a shower. I put the kettle on for coffee. Last night's horrific ordeal now feels like a distant dream. Perhaps it was. I pour the kettle.

Later, when I arrive at work, a co-worker makes a risqué joke at the water cooler. I laugh. I don't know if it is funny. I can't quite tell what my laugh is. I finish work.

This goes on. Things happen to me, but I don't understand my reactions. The intruder sits within me now. Most days it remains subdued, but every day it influences me. Days pass more rapidly now. The longer I live with it, the more familiar it becomes. I now wear expressions like fresh coats of paint on a dilapidated house. I don't know what lays inside me, but I'm not sure that it matters anymore. I remember something from the dream now.

I must have left the door open.

JUSTIN FAULL IS an emerging writer from Gold Coast, Australia. Having recently graduated with a dual degree in Law and Arts, majoring in Literary Studies and Journalism, he now finds himself drawn to dark fiction. You can find him on Twitter @JustinFaull.

AN EARLIER VERSION of this story was originally published in Issue Five of *3 Moon Magazine*.

Illustration by Joe Radkins

SPROUT

M. DAVID CLARKSON

When my right testicle popped, I think that's when I realized how serious the situation was. That I wasn't getting out of this alive. That I was going to die here. Maybe *popped* isn't the right word. Burst. Exploded. You know how you can roll up a ketchup packet tighter and tighter, building pressure at the seams? Then one small weakness gives way to a sudden spray of red.

I couldn't move my head to see the gore that painted my inner thigh. That was probably for the best.

See, I'd always had a thing for hippie girls. Maybe I was too young the first time I watched *Dazed and Confused*. Too impressionable when I saw that documentary about Woodstock. Whatever it was, whatever switch got flipped, it worked for me. Give me hairy armpits and flowing skirts, chunky hair and the scent of patchouli. Gets me going every time. Everybody's got a thing, I guess.

The first time I saw Lilian, I was at a friend's birthday party. Well, I knew someone who knew someone, and somehow I ended up standing around a bonfire in a dried-up cornfield surrounded by strangers in the middle of October. The beer was free, and there were enough joints being passed around that for once I didn't feel like leaving as soon as we got there.

Someone had strung together a series of extension cords from the nearby farmhouse to power a makeshift stage, and it was far enough outside of town to avoid any noise complaints. The music sounded like a mix between surf rock and doom metal, but if you didn't listen closely, it wasn't too bad. The microphone had cut out soon after the band took the stage, so the singer wandered off into the crowd with a tambourine while the other members kept playing.

"I really should've worn a jacket." Troy rubbed his bare arms, then stuffed his hands back in his pockets. He had texted me for over an hour to convince me to come out that night, but couldn't be bothered to check the weather. "Why aren't any of these chicks dancing?"

"I've seen three people trip just trying to walk out here," I said, kicking at a rut left in the ground by the harvester. The soil was already hardening as temperatures cooled. "I don't think anyone wants to break their ankle dancing." I took a sip of beer and used my free hand to make sure my stocking cap was covering my ears, watching my breath float away from me in the frigid air. Even though the bonfire was raging, I couldn't feel the heat from where I stood. "You ready to go yet? We've been here for hours, and I want to get at least a *little* sleep—I'm picking up an overtime shift at the mill tomorrow."

Troy hopped back and forth a bit, trying to warm up. "Yeah, I gotta go piss first. And see if I can find Doug to tell him happy birthday." He turned to walk away, then stopped. "Wanna come talk to him?"

I shook my head and stood watching the fire. Doug had always been more Troy's friend than mine. He shrugged and walked off. I finished my beer and absently toyed with the knife in my coat pocket. A nervous habit, but other than a couple of scars, it was the only thing my old man gave me before he bailed.

A sudden chill shuddered up my spine, as though a vibration had crawled from the fertile earth to burrow into my body. Despite the cold, I started sweating. Dread overcame me—the "I'm going to be in so much trouble when Mom gets home" terror that I hadn't felt since I was a kid. That icy, heavy stone that lodges in your stomach when you realize that both fight and flight have left you defenseless.

Standing there, slightly buzzed, a little high, and wishing desperately to be somewhere else, the feeling passed.

I dropped my empty beer cup on the ground and stared into the flickering fire. My eyes followed embers floating into the night until I noticed a strange movement.

A slender, feminine shadow spun in front of the fire. Twirling, twisting like a leaf on the wind. Dancing. She moved as if her life depended on it. As if her body were designed only to dance. She weaved through the crowd unnoticed, her movements graceful and violent in equal measure, her bare feet kicking up dirt with every step as she circled the fire.

I was transfixed. Hypnotized. She was the feather from *Forrest Gump*. The plastic bag from *American Beauty*. My eyes watered. I hadn't blinked. I didn't want to. She spun around to the opposite side of the fire again, and our eyes met briefly. Flowers graced her hair. Tears rimmed her eyes.

"Ready?" Troy smacked me on the shoulder.

I looked from the fire to him. From him back to the fire. I rubbed my eyes, but she was gone.

🐾

My body convulsed against the bed of moss and soft earth beneath me. I felt the skin on my arms splitting, muscles flexed to the point of tearing, bones dislocating. The webbing between my fingers ripped as my hands clenched and spread repeatedly. My fingers bent backwards and dug into the warm soil, taking root like tendrils searching for water.

I tried to scream. Tried to draw in oxygen with lungs that no longer functioned.

🐾

I scoured my friends' social media accounts, looking for anyone that knew her. Adding friends of friends, looking for even a single tagged photo or comment. Searching desperately for her name, or a place to find her. She was a ghost. An illusion, floating away from me like snowy ashes in the night sky. Dandelion seeds in a summer wind.

I barely worked the next week. The few shifts I showed up for, my boss sent me home early. Something about "distraction causes workplace accidents" and how I needed to "focus on my future in the industry." For all I cared, the paper mill could die right alongside printed media. I stopped calling in.

I didn't speak to my friends. I drove around town in a daze, not knowing where I was going, not caring where I ended up. I hardly ate. Food bored me. The memory of her sustained me. Her silhouette against the bonfire planted a seed in my mind. Her eyes and tears, the sun and rain. Giving life. The days passed. The seed split. Grew. Became a sprout of obsession.

One particular day, I found myself on the eastern edge of town, passing by the rundown strip mall there. The long, low brick building sat mostly vacant, and the few stores that remained held no interest for me. I tossed my cigarette out the window and pulled into the parking lot next to the empty husk of a video store. I put the truck in park and rolled my window the rest of the way down, enjoying the cool air in my lungs.

I think it was the smell that hit me first: lavender. Vegetables and flowers. A perfume of nature. Every scent seeking dominance, but weaving with every other into a tapestry of life. Growth. A wave of smell, ebbing and flowing, so full and calming that I could almost see it. A mist surrounding me and pulling me out of the pickup and into its depths.

It was a nursery. A greenhouse. An oasis of life among the orange, red, and brown leaves that littered the parking lot where I stood. A breath of life across the street from a world that was slowly dying around me. Numbly, I stumbled forward, crossing the threshold into the lush garden.

I walked along rows and rows of flowers, vines, and vegetation. Out-of-season blooms and exotic fruits. My skin prickled, and I shivered, despite the humidity in the building. I felt unwelcome, but unable to leave. The greenhouse was silent, a miniature jungle whose inhabitants sensed an approaching predator. The only sound, the sleeves of my hoodie brushing against branches that seemed to reach out to grasp me.

"Hi."

Her voice rustled like leaves, spinning in a circle, caught by an errant gust of wind. Part whisper, part sigh. Suddenly lightheaded, I reached to steady myself with a nearby shelf as the blood left my extremities to pool in my loins. I knew it was her before I even turned around.

"Umm." *Real smooth, asshole.*

She turned a corner beside two flowers I couldn't name. That could not exist in any sane world. As she passed between them, long magenta petals parted and spread to reveal waving cone-shaped leaves. I could have sworn they weren't there when I had passed that way a few seconds ago. As if satisfied with what I'd seen, the petals lowered back down. She smiled.

"I'm Lilian."

She walked to me, her long skirt wafting above her bare feet, as though caught in a breeze that flowed only around her. She was at home, in her element. She reached out, brushing the leaves and thorns around us.

"Hello," I said, my voice cracking into a pubescent squeak on the second syllable. Some of my blood found its way to my face, and my cheeks flushed.

She moved past me, indifferent to my embarrassment. She

smelled like peat moss, like the bottom layer of leaves on a forest floor. Wet and musty and already composting. She smelled of the earth. Of growth, ripeness, fertility. Of life and death, rebirth and decay. I leaned in closer to pull more of her scent into my lungs, not caring how blatant the gesture looked, and unable to stop myself. The flower in her hair seemed to angle toward me as she turned, a cobra bobbing its head hypnotically. The dark red petals seemed to spiral around a thick green stalk. It smelled sweet, with a hint of something darker. Heavier. The sweetness caught in my throat, holding on. Scratching. Squeezing.

She was everything I had ever wanted, but yet the only things I'd ever truly feared. The first hint of sunlight after a rainstorm, yet the creeping shadows behind trees at night.

"What are you looking for?" When her green eyes locked with mine, I realized I was holding my breath.

"Flowers? A bouquet?" I didn't know what to say. "How long have you been here? I don't think I've ever seen this place before."

"I don't sell bouquets," she sighed. "Only living plants." She pulled a small bottle from a shelf and began spraying a fine mist on a few nearby leaves. "If you want a bouquet, you'll need to go somewhere else."

"I'm sorry, I didn't mean—"

"And I've always been here. Maybe you didn't need anything before now." She turned her back on me, walking away, picking leaves and petals to spray, seemingly at random. "So what do you need?"

"I need you." The words just came out. I smacked a hand over my mouth to keep any more from escaping.

"I'm sorry?" She stopped, looking over her shoulder at me.

I stuttered. I mumbled. Eventually, "I mean, I need your help. I want houseplants. Greenery. For my house. Like, plants." *You're doing great, buddy.*

She walked me through the rows, explaining the best way to care for this ficus, or the optimal sunlight exposure for that succulent. She explained the perfect temperature variation for a prehistoric-looking fern, and I joked I would be better off getting some plants made from plastic or fabric.

She didn't laugh.

When she led me to the cash register, my arms were full. Bags of soil and fertilizer, a tray of weeds she claimed would turn into something beautiful. A few strands of lemongrass, an odd mixture of jade and ivy, a small jalapeño plant. She walked ahead of me, an empty hanging planter slung over each shoulder, bouncing off of her hips rhythmically as she walked. Swayed. Glided.

She only accepted cash and gave no change. "Exact payment only," she said. "We will use anything left over for expansion or donation. Spread life and beauty."

I paid nearly double what I owed and started carrying the items to the bed of my truck. I felt a slight panic. A hitch in my breath and a sudden tightness in my chest. Fully awake, but feeling like I just sat up in bed, startled by a dream of falling.

Foreign thoughts pushed into my mind. I needed more time with her. I hadn't left, but I missed her already. I had to see her again. Know her. Have her. Possess her. I shook my head to clear the fog that had collected there. To rid my thoughts of this influence.

I walked back inside. "Do you have pumpkins?"

"Pumpkins?" She held the last of my purchases out to me— the hanging pots, wrapped delicately in yellowed newspaper and brown string.

"Pumpkins," I nodded. "You know, for jack-o'-lanterns? My girlfriend wants to carve—" *Shit.* "Shit. I mean—"

"Girlfriend?" She raised an eyebrow. Not upset. Not caring. Aloof. Curious.

"Ex-girlfriend. She wants to carve pumpkins. For the baby. Baby girl. Daughter." *Oh my god, stop talking.*

She smiled slightly at that. Relieved, maybe? I could not read her expression at all.

"Giving life is a beautiful thing." Her smile fell. Leaving her face as quickly as it came, as if it were an intruder. A party guest that realized it wasn't welcome. That it never belonged there. "I don't have pumpkins. Not for carving." She held the planters out to me again as punctuation. Full stop. This conversation is over.

"I didn't mean to . . ." I trailed off, taking the wrapped package from her, and turning away to leave. A fresh wave of longing spilled over me, and I turned back to her. "Can I call you? Can I see you again?"

She started walking back to the rows of plants, the spray bottle already in her hand. "I don't have a phone," she said, not turning to face me, and my heart nearly cracked. She glanced over her shoulder. "But you'll see me again."

With those words, she walked away, turning a corner and disappearing from my view.

I set the last of the supplies in the back of the truck and sat inside, an idea forming in my mind. A plan taking root. I lit a cigarette and slammed on the accelerator, taking a corner too quickly and hearing the terracotta pottery breaking as it rolled and shattered against the tailgate behind me.

THE THING most people don't mention when they describe spinal injuries is the sudden sense of loss. The feeling that, between one moment and the next, some part of you has vanished. Disappeared. There is pain. There is fire. Then there is nothing at all. Just an echo, reflecting your shouts back at you from the distant canyon wall at the other side of your mind. Silence.

When the twisting, tightening grip in the small of my back finally severed my spinal cord, I sighed. When all the pain below my belly button became a memory. When the agony of my ravaged lower half disappeared.

I was relieved.

And then every nerve ending in my upper body and torso screamed as the pain I *could* feel intensified tenfold.

PEOPLE REALLY DON'T PAY enough attention to their surroundings. Even in a small midwestern town like Hawthorn, where some old folks still don't lock their doors. As I was drawn, night after night, to Lilian's greenhouse, I assumed she never saw me. Never knew I was there. Every day, I tried to stay away. Tried to resist the pull. Every night, I stood in the darkness, a mock fairy ring of my discarded cigarette butts around me. I was her thrall. As the power she held over me strengthened, I could no longer watch her from afar. She was drawing me closer.

Most nights, after closing the greenhouse doors, Lilian would walk a meandering route through the outskirts of town. I was forced to follow her as she walked across lawns and smelled the rose bushes at a few of the wealthier homes. Her path took her from the eastern edge of town, where the air was heavy with the stench of the paper mill, to the western side, undeveloped and clean.

The mill was five miles from town, and on a humid day, there was no escaping the smell. A cross between dried manure and wet cardboard. The ammonia stench of cat piss mixed with rotting cabbage. The smell of loss. That box of keepsakes you left in the basement a little too long that was destroyed when an old pipe burst and flooded everything. Your grandmother's photo album, falling apart. Your dad's old army uniform, a patchwork of holes and mold. I hadn't been to work there in so long, I'd probably been fired by now. They stopped calling me days ago. The ties that connected me to the rest of the world were falling away as the one Lilian placed around me grew stronger. Pulled tighter. There wouldn't be anyone left to miss me.

I always lost her trail after she entered a small copse of trees just outside of town. A few nights, I tried circling around to catch her on the other side but never did. It always took me longer than I expected. The grip she had on me wasn't strong enough to drag me into those depths, yet every night it tightened more and more.

The woods were a dark hole, like the bottom of a drain, my life spiraling inexorably downward into the void.

After a week, it seemed Lilian was no longer content letting me see her from a distance. She needed me close. Intimate. She turned and smiled at me, beautiful and terrible, before disappearing into the trees.

I followed her into the woods.

I LOST MY WAY IMMEDIATELY. I'd never had a great sense of direction, but something about moving among the trees triggered a dislocation. There was a *wrongness* to my surroundings. The trees were taller. More densely packed. And covering much more land than the small grove where I'd followed Lilian. My initial attempts at stealth were abandoned, and I quickened my pace.

There were no sounds coming from the trees. No birds. No insects. There were no dried leaves or fallen branches littering the ground to amplify my pounding footfalls, which seemed muffled in the still air. I held one hand in front of my face as I stumbled forward while the other nervously pulled my father's knife from my pocket. I was a frightened child again, running up the basement steps, convinced there was a monster chasing me. I felt hot, hungry breath on my neck. Branches seemed to reach for me, slapping at my face. Thorns threatened to hold me back like cruel, sharp fingers pulling at my clothes.

I tripped over an exposed root and nearly fell into a large clearing, grunting and cursing under my breath. I nearly dropped the knife as I caught myself. The glade sloped into a small moss-covered mound where, in a circle of bright moonlight, Lilian stood. Still as a statue. The soft ground seemed to pulse and vibrate beneath me as I stood to face her, pressing the blade flat against my inner arm as I hid my hands in my pockets.

"I knew you would see me again."

I took a few steps closer and stopped. "I had to," I said. "You forced me."

She spun in circles, her long dress fanning out, exposing more of her legs and casting an eclipse onto the forest floor. "Then come closer," she said. "And see me." Waves of her dark hair fell over her face as she stopped spinning, and her green eyes were sparkling emeralds behind them. Her dress stilled, the hem now even with the ground. She seemed to be a part of the clearing, a single entity growing to a focal point of intoxicating beauty. Reaching out with one slender arm, she waved me closer.

My body obeyed her as my mind resisted. It screamed in rapture and absolute terror. Some type of fight-or-flight reaction threatened to overwhelm me, but something much larger dragged it down and swallowed it whole. Lust. *There's always a bigger fish.*

"Come," she repeated. Steadily, confidently, I walked to her. I moved with more certainty of purpose than I ever had with anything in my life. My eyes filled with tears, and my groin ached with longing. Grabbing her shoulder, I pulled her close to me, surprised by the odd chill of her skin. I held her there in the clearing of that impossibly large grove of trees. Her breath on my neck. Her arms wrapped around me.

In a sudden burst of resistance, I thrust my right hand forward, burying the knife blade into her side. As soon as the warm fluid covered my hand, her power over me waned. Her grip loosened, and my willpower returned.

Lilian let go of me slowly and stepped back. Her green eyes widened, but her expression remained indecipherable.

"You shouldn't have done that," her soft voice turning into a growl as she pressed her hands to her side, covering the wound. I could see a spreading shadow on the pale green fabric of her gown as blood flowed from beneath her clutching fingers. Dark and wet in the moonlight.

"I had to!" I brandished the knife and began backing away.

"No." She stopped me with a word, the mental grip tightening again as her anger flared. Her voice grew hoarser. "You are a destroyer. A defiler." She paced around me, and I pivoted to watch her. "You do not respect life," she whispered. "You only take."

I reached for her, and she looked pointedly at my hand. At the knife that had pierced her skin, opened her side. Penetrated her flesh. That was covered in her blood.

"I—" the words stopped in my throat as I looked down. Turned into a questioning grunt when the gore I expected to see was not there. An opalescent syrup ran down the blade and dripped from my fingertips. A golden and milky fluid that tingled on my skin as it reflected in the bright night.

"Taste me," she said, her voice easing into a sensual purr. She took a step closer. Her breathing was heavy, and her cheeks were flushed. "Taste me. Now." There was a pang of longing in her voice. Pleading. Seductive.

"Lilian, I—"

She sprang forward, wrenching the knife from my hand and thrusting it into my open mouth, the very tip of the blade nicking my tongue and clicking between my teeth. The fluid tasted of honey, milk, and rotting fruit. I struggled against my gag reflex as the blood from my tongue curdled everything together. Yet I needed more.

I licked my fingers desperately, trying to taste as much of her as possible. I was vaguely aware of Lilian smiling and stepping back to watch as I consumed her cursed blood. Tears ran from my eyes, blinding me as my fingernails scratched the back of my throat. I rubbed the flat of the blade against my tongue, gorging myself on her. My knees buckled as I ejaculated violently, and I collapsed, panting before her.

"There," she said with a quiet laugh, brushing my hair back from my forehead. "There, there." Her laugh echoed from the surrounding trees. A chuckle from behind me, a series of giggles from the canopies. I hadn't seen her disrobe, but the moonlight now swam along her dark, nude skin, casting subtle shadows along her curves and muscles. No blemishes marred her flawless flesh. There was no wound in her side.

"How did you—" I couldn't seem to catch my breath. I was shaking. Sweating. *When had it gotten so warm?*

I craned my neck around to follow her as she walked a slow circle around me. She spiraled outward until she nearly reached the trees. "You shouldn't have followed me here." More laughter reverberated from the forest. "But you really couldn't help yourself, could you? And now you have taken from us. Eaten from us." She smiled. "And now you cannot leave."

Us? I tried to stand, and got one foot planted as shadows crept into my peripheral, lithe forms that seemed to slink from the treeline.

"Come, sisters," Lilian spread her arms wide. "See the offering I have provided. The seed I have given us. The servant we will prepare for Mother."

The shadowy forms around us took shape as the women walked into the clearing. Leapt down from branches. They were beautiful, every one of them. Their skin was the color of marble, quartz, slate. Granite, obsidian, and every shade between. Hair like golden wheat, freshly tilled soil, and falling cherry blossoms. The colors of tree bark and sunsets and sandy river beds surrounded me.

I struggled to my feet, and Lilian was upon me in an instant, her lips pressed against mine. Kissing me. Tasting me. Her sharp tongue forced my lips apart, and I felt her breathing into me. "Shh," she whispered, pulling back. I could see her breath as a small cloud of dust escaped our parting lips. *Not dust. Pollen. Spores* —the words rose fully formed in my mind as her breath filled me. Spread into me. Infected me. She held me as my strength left, lowering me to the ground and straddling me as my lungs hardened in my chest.

"Lilian," I wheezed, "please don't kill me."

She smiled at me. Warmly. With hatred and pride in her eyes. "Never." I felt hands pulling off my clothes. So many hands. "This won't kill you." I felt her skin against mine as she slid her body down my own. "But this is really, *really*," she let out a long sigh as she slowly filled herself with me, "going to hurt."

I couldn't tell you how long it lasted, Lilian and her sisters clawing and thrashing against my broken flesh in the moonlight. My body was slick with the pungent scent of their assault and the coppery stench of my blood. My mind struggled vainly to distance itself from their attack. Receding into unconsciousness only to be thrust painfully back into wakefulness as the sisters grew more ferocious. Each moment my mind threatened to break, and each moment their terrible hunger stole away the relief of oblivion. Every inch of exposed flesh was a source of wretched pleasure to them and incredible pain to me.

They fought over me. Bit me. Broke me. As every spasming, thrashing orgasm sent a sister into quivering ecstasy, a sharp dagger of pain drove through my body. The anguish dulled as each of them rolled away, only to be doubled as another took their place. After what seemed like hours, all that existed was the static of pins and needles. And still that stabbing pain everywhere at once. Torment pierced my body. A stigmata of my soul. A life sentence of dull pain punctuated by a jagged spike of agony.

As the warm sun rose to fill the clearing, our fluids dried up. Some evaporated. Others hardened into a flaky crust, a blackening scab.

Lilian and I were alone again. Her head was on my chest, no longer rising and falling with breath. She cuddled close to me and whispered, "I'll come back to see you."

Then she was gone, and I was alone.

And then the real pain started.

I WAS WRONG. I would not die here. No matter how often I wished I would.

It started with a twitch. That weak little head bob from a member that was used too strenuously the night before. Flaccid, but with just enough strength left over to roll onto my thigh. I stared as the skin of my penis started distending. Stretching. Tearing. Unable to look away as the first stalk of green slithered out of my urethra, rolling back the fleshy tip as it reached for sunlight. The limb thickened. The first branch sprouted just beneath the head.

As it grew, the hardening bark smeared red. Bits of pink flesh clinging at irregular intervals. Small, black, curly hairs waved in the breeze.

Little by little, my body changed. What began quickly that night in the clearing slowed to an excruciating crawl. Over the days, months, and years, the form that I had for most of my life withered, twisted, and decayed, becoming food for my new self. Every moment was torture. Every moment was a lifetime.

I was an outside observer to my transformation, my vestigial consciousness still connected to my new form. Obsolete, but watching as, over the course of a decade, my ribcage burst open and the main trunk grew forth. The spores in my lungs spread and formed around the decayed muscle that had once been my heart. As it grew, that blackened knot was embedded in the bark.

My brain and eyes slowly liquified, giving life to a third limb, growing out of my mouth. The first gift Lilian had given me. The first curse, the night of the fire. As the seed of obsession grew larger, it slowly pushed away the brittle remnants of my jaw and stretched outward to the sky.

THE SUN and rain give me life. The soil, sustenance. The pain of my leftover body slowly fades away as I grow, while the pain of my current form remains constant. Every new limb is another excruciating appendage. Every ring in my trunk is another circle of hell.

Lilian still visits me. Sometimes she whispers into my trunk, her delicate lips brushing against me. She tells me about Mother's plans.

Sometimes Lilian climbs. Higher and higher into the canopy every time. Mother's children grow from my branches. Lilian picks the fruit. Nurses them. Teaches them.

Lilian is ancient, born when this world was young. She tells me that Mother is unknowable. Mother is infinite.

And Mother is furious.

Every year there are more sprouts in the clearing.

M. DAVID CLARKSON lives in the Midwest, where he pretends to be grown-up about things. He collects toys and comics and obsesses over horror movies, and works in a trailer factory. Despite all of that, someone actually married him. He has been making up stories all his life, and can be found lurking HOWL Society or Twitter @vagrant6942.

Illustration by Joe Radkins

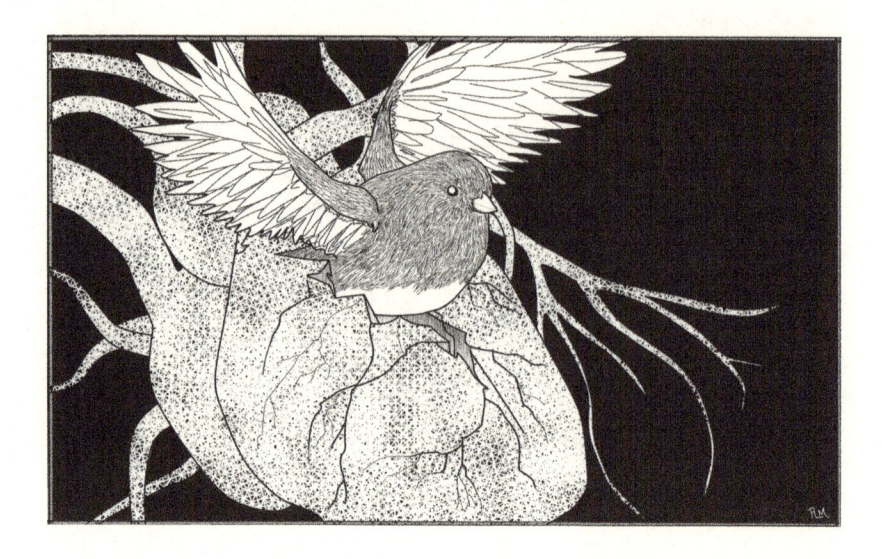

JUNCO CREEK

S.E. DENTON

MILES OF UGLINESS smeared past the car windows. Dusty lands full of oil wells and arid citrus groves. Rickety towns compiled of worn churches, gas stations, fast food restaurants, and ratty dogs. Leigh glanced at her son Ben, who studied the blurring desolation.

"How's Boy Scouts?" Leigh asked.

Ben shifted in the passenger seat, continuing to stare out the window.

"It's fine."

"Are you going on any backpacking trips this summer?"

"Yeah."

"When is that?"

"August. Before school starts."

"With your troop?"

"Yeah."

As sparse as his communication was, it was the most he'd said to her in months.

It was no one's fault. Things simply fell apart. Or rather, things *changed*.

Leigh was in the thick of becoming her "true self," as her therapist put it. However, Leigh had become a stranger on the inside. A new person she had to get to know from the start. Signs were there all along, of course: the way Leigh felt light and floaty back in seventh grade whenever Melissa Foster talked to her during science class; her borderline-weird fascination with her female basketball coach in college; the way her coworker, Mona, made her face and neck grow hot and her palms sweat whenever they talked. These clues were easy to make excuses for or flat out ignore for decades.

However, the affair with Theresa, whom she met in her Thursday-night painting class—well, that made things crystal clear.

"And where is your troop going?"

"Joshua Tree."

"In *August*?"

"Yeah."

"Isn't that . . . sort of *extreme*?" Leigh asked. "Backpacking in a desert during summer?"

"That's the point. It's about survival."

For the past three months, she'd been trying to survive herself —temporarily moved into her older sister's guest house to give Russ and Ben space. But no contact proved impossible. She called. She texted. Neither of them responded. The rejection was excruciating. But she had plenty of processing to do, and she did so alone.

First there was a period of overwhelming self-loathing. Layers of shame to peel off like sunburned skin. Then there were weeks where she desperately tried to cling onto who she was *before* the realization, tried to cram herself back into that persona again, but she no longer fit. Finally, she reached a state of numb acceptance. As of the past two weeks, that had shifted into an anxious willingness to let herself become whoever it was she'd been suppressing all along.

The boy was going through changes himself. He seemed as uncomfortable in his own skin as Leigh. His forehead was broken out and oily. He smelled different, like decaying childhood.

But these transformations only made Leigh love him more.

The getaway was a chance for them to reconnect.

Would it be all right if I took Ben on a trip? Just the two of us? Leigh had texted Russ.

Russ finally replied and said he would ask Ben.

Days later, she received a text from her son: *Okay, I'll go.*

It would be enough, Leigh decided.

GRADUALLY, the landscape outside the car changed, shifting from hulking oil wells to monstrous ponderosa pines as they drove up a winding, mountainous road. The higher they ascended into the Sierra Nevada range, the more Leigh's ears popped. She eventually turned onto a dirt road that serpentined towards the cabin, supposedly perched near Junco Creek, which the schlocky property rental website described as a "woodsey owaysis."

She'd decided on the cabin because of Ben's zeal for the outdoors, which had manifested when he joined Cub Scouts in the third grade.

They drove past a few other cabins tucked back into the pines. Eventually the dirt road ended near their rental, as the caretaker's directions stated in the email.

When Leigh pulled up to the cabin, Ben's eyes lit up.

"Do you like it?" Leigh asked.

"It's cool," Ben told her.

The cabin sat at the top of a shady slope overlooking Junco Creek, which flowed beneath a thick canopy of pines and river birches. The single-story cabin was made of wood shingles with a covered front porch. Aged, rustic, and remote. Clearly built by hand from the foundation up to the last stone placed atop the chimney.

As she exited her car, the fragrance of the Sierra Nevada pines soothed her, as did the faint chatter of the creek.

Ben walked down to the water while Leigh carried a few bags from the car.

She dug out the key hidden beneath a carved wooden owl statue that sat near the door. The statue looked as if it had been there as long as the cabin, the wood dry and aged. As she opened the front door, the cabin exhaled a musty breath. It was ugly inside—knotty pine in every direction, tattered rugs and shabby furniture—but at least there was a bathroom, running water, and a kitchen. It didn't feel homey, but it was perfect for a teenage boy, which was all that mattered to Leigh. If anything, she admired the massive stone fireplace. Despite the summer temperatures, it demanded to be used.

There were two bedrooms on either side of the short hallway. Plenty of windows in both, although the pines and the tattered red curtains filtered most of the sunlight. On each mattress were folded stacks of linens and blankets, which Leigh had forgotten to pack. When she returned to the kitchen, she saw a jar of honey sitting on the counter with a note: "Welcome to Junco Creek!" signed by Douglas Sable, that same name from the email exchanges.

Ben entered the cabin. Looked everything up and down while Leigh explored the kitchen.

"How was the creek?" Leigh asked.

"It's nice," he said, his voice tepid. "I saw an owl in one of the trees by the water."

"Are they usually out in the daytime?"

"This one was."

Ben disappeared down the short hallway to check out the bedrooms and the bathroom.

"Hungry?" Leigh asked when he returned.

"Sure."

"I can make you a peanut butter and honey sandwich," Leigh said, holding up the jar. "Your favorite."

"That's not my favorite anymore," Ben told her. "But I'll eat it."

"What's your favorite now?"

"Melted ham and swiss," Ben said. "The way Dad makes it."

He intended the comment to nick her. And it did. She expected there would be plenty more thorny remarks during the trip, but she hoped they could talk. If he could hear her side of the story, then maybe he could come to some sort of understanding that she wasn't doing this to hurt him, that it wasn't a choice. Surely Russ had explained that to him, but Ben needed to hear it from her.

But now wasn't the time for that conversation. Instead, she busied herself making him lunch. She made a sandwich for herself as well, even though she wasn't hungry.

They ate in silence on the front porch.

The porch swing creaked beneath Leigh. Ben leaned against the railing, his back toward the creek. Despite being thirteen, he still smeared peanut butter on his cheek and dribbled honey down his shirt.

"Tomorrow it might be nice to—" Leigh began, but a snapping branch interrupted her.

Ben turned and looked down toward the woods.

"There's a man walking up here," he whispered.

Leigh stood and saw a large man ascending the slope to the cabin. Shaggy, silver hair snaked out from beneath a dark cowboy hat. He wore faded black jeans and black boots splotched with fresh mud. The sleeves of his black button-up shirt were rolled up to the elbows, revealing tattooed forearms.

"Hello," Leigh called down to him from the edge of the porch, still holding her sandwich.

"Hello," the man echoed.

"Are you . . ."

"Douglas Sable," the man said, cresting the slope and approaching the porch steps.

He took off his hat and placed it against his chest. Up close, his brown skin looked eroded. His smile, however, was oddly white, glowing against his leathered complexion. His eyes were amber, the same color as the dead pine needles crunching beneath his boots. She glanced at his faded tattoos: a snake coiled around a rose on his right forearm and a long bird feather on his left.

"I hope the cabin is to your liking," he said.

A smile sprawled across his face, unnaturally still. He winked at Ben.

Ben only stared back at Douglas Sable, still unaware of the peanut butter on his face.

Leigh's tongue felt suddenly dry. The lingering residue of peanut butter and honey in her mouth made the act of speaking sticky and strained.

"Thank you for the honey," she told him.

"Of course," he said. "I keep bees. A little hobby of mine."

His smile remained intact. Carved into his skin.

"Do you live around here?" Leigh asked.

"About a quarter mile down the creek."

"And you own all the property? The other cabins?"

"That's right," Douglas Sable told her. "My family has owned this property for generations. Just me now, though. And the occasional visitors, like yourselves."

Cicadas chirped, the only dominant sound. Beneath it, the muttering of the creek below. Leigh was suddenly aware of their isolation in an entirely new form. Whereas before it was a welcomed environment for Ben to open up to her, now the unpopulated space made her feel vulnerable. They were the only ones around for miles.

Leigh stopped herself. There was no direct threat. Douglas Sable appeared to be in his sixties and was likely checking in and making sure they were comfortable. Hospitable, no doubt. Lonely perhaps. Still, Leigh didn't like the idea of him lingering around, monitoring their visit. His eyes. His *smile*.

"It's a good place for a boy to run around," Douglas Sable said. "Plenty of woods. No end to them, really. And the creek is always full of fish. There's fishing gear in the shed over there. Do you like fishing?"

"Sure," Ben said, his tone stiff.

"Well, just be careful when you're in the woods. Lots of critters. Plenty of snakes. More importantly, mountain lions. They'll rip you apart if you aren't ready for them."

Before Leigh could admonish the man for speaking that way to her son, Ben replied with enthusiasm. "What about bears?"

"Oh yes," Douglas Sable said. "I've seen one of those, too."

He winked at Ben. Leigh felt a chill needle the back of her neck.

"Thank you, Mr. Sable," Leigh said. "We'll be careful."

Still smiling, the man placed his black hat onto his silvery head.

"Nice meeting you folks," he said, and turned towards the creek.

Leigh and Ben watched his imposing figure move back down the slope in lean strides.

🐾

BEN RAIDED THE SHED, and after finding a fishing pole and tackle box, he spent the afternoon alone by the creek. Leigh busied herself with cleaning the inside of the cabin—removing cobwebs, dusting the furniture, disinfecting the bathroom. Beyond leaving honey, fresh linens, and toilet paper, Douglas Sable had not made the cabin very hospitable. But Leigh didn't care. Cleaning kept her mind off things.

Sweeping dust bunnies from beneath the bed in the bedroom, Leigh found a woman's thin gold wedding band. Crouched on the faded southwestern patterned rug, she held up the ring, wondering about the woman who had lost it. It wasn't much different from the one Russ gave her fifteen years before. They were babies then. Right out of college. Now her ring was in a small wooden box at home.

She doubted there would ever be another ring on her finger, but it was too soon to know that. Eventually she would stop living within the void.

She placed the ring on the nightstand and continued battling the dust.

🐾

As TWILIGHT SET IN, Leigh walked down to the creek and followed the narrow trail along the bank, looking for Ben. She found him leaning against a birch near the creek which ran slow and deep. He heard her approach and turned to look at her but didn't give Leigh any acknowledgement beyond a fleeting cool glance.

"Have you caught anything?" she asked.

"A few."

"Are you ready for dinner?"

"No. This is the best time to fish. I don't want to go."

"It's getting dark," she told him.

"Mom, come on. A few more minutes."

"Fine," she said, but she didn't leave.

Instead, she found a log near the bank and sat quietly watching her son reel in the lure and then cast it delicately back into the creek. The mosquitos were thick. Next to the tackle box was a bottle of bug spray. Leigh doused herself, and once the mosquitos left her alone, she was able to relax.

The twilight teemed with melodies: the shrill stridulation of crickets, the soft babbling of the creek, the buzzing whine of mosquitos, the rustle of wind in the trees. Leigh closed her eyes and listened intently. All the disparate melodies were woven so intricately together—even the sound of Ben's intermittent sniffs, evidence of allergies he insisted did not exist. Everything elegantly harmonized.

And then the hoot of an owl pierced the polyphony, disrupting the balance.

Leigh opened her eyes and looked upward.

Perched on one of the birch branches jutting over Junco Creek sat an owl, staring down at them with its amber eyes.

"Is that the owl you saw earlier?" Leigh asked.

"Same one," Ben told her, reeling in his line. "It's been watching me all day."

The owl hooted again; the sound filled Leigh with a cold, hollowing sensation.

Ben didn't cast. Instead, he stood gazing up at the owl.

"Maybe we should go back," he told Leigh. "It *is* getting pretty dark."

She helped gather the fishing supplies and together they walked the meandering trail along the creek bank toward the cabin.

Although she didn't look back, Leigh sensed the owl following.

"I wonder why it's called 'Junco Creek.'" Leigh said, settling in front of the fireplace. "Maybe Junco was someone's last name?"

"It's a bird," Ben told her. "Although, I didn't see any juncos today. Or any other birds, really. Maybe the owl scared them off."

Leigh didn't want to think or talk about the owl, so she said nothing.

To put the fireplace to use, Leigh suggested they make s'mores. Leigh had converted some wire hangers in one of the bedroom closets into roasting sticks.

She watched Ben's face closely as he tore open the thin plastic bag and jabbed two marshmallows on the tip of the straightened coat hanger. Ben sat on the hearth and eased the marshmallows into the flames. Leigh continued to study Ben's face in silence. In the flickering firelight, she saw ripples of her soon-to-be-ex-husband's face, ripples of her own. And hints of someone else. Perhaps hints of the man Ben was becoming, developing quietly beneath the boy's changing skin.

Ben did not look at her. He fixated on the distending white puffs charring in the flames.

"Ben," Leigh said.

"What?"

"I want you to know that the last thing I ever want to do is hurt you."

His jaw tightened.

"I know."

"It's just . . . I mean, it's who I am, you know? I realize now that I spent my whole life fighting to not be who I am."

Although she had rehearsed the lines in her head innumerable times, they still came out awkwardly and like bad dialogue from a *Lifetime* movie.

"I understand it, Mom," Ben said, but not warmly. "You don't have to explain it."

"But I'm still your mother. I'm still here for you."

"You're not really," he said. "Not how I need you to be."

"How do you need me to be?"

"Like you were."

He was trying hard to keep his face hardened, as if this alone would protect the softness inside him. Like the time last year when she'd walked to the end of the driveway to get the mail and witnessed Ben fall off his bike while performing a stunt for his friends.

He'd calmly stood after the crash and inspected his bleeding hands. His face was hard as granite at that moment. He walked toward the house, calling over his shoulder to his friends, telling them he was going to wash the blood off and would return in a minute. She followed him inside after witnessing everything. She barely had time to set the mail on the table before he fell apart in her arms. When he was done crying, she helped him wash and bandage the scrapes on his hands, and then his face hardened up again just before he ran back outside to face the other boys.

"But, Ben, I'm still the same person."

He looked her squarely in the eye. "No, you're not. You've changed."

"How have I changed?" Leigh asked, a strange fear creeping into her chest.

"You're just . . . different," he said.

"How?"

Ben sighed and set the clothes hanger down on the hearth, the marshmallows immersed in the flames. He stood and left the living room, his form dissipating into the darkness of the hallway. A second later, she heard one of the bedroom doors close.

While her heart tolled painfully in her chest for the first few seconds of being left alone, the pain shifted into something cold and frightening.

What exactly had *changed* about her? What was it that Ben saw?

Whatever it was had caused him to retreat and close the door.

She searched desperately inside herself, doing a quick scan of any abnormalities that maybe she hadn't picked up on. Other than anxiety and heartache, which were so prevalent in her life over the past few months that both felt normal, she *felt* something deep inside her. Lurking beneath the agitated surface. There was no label to attach to it. She could not identify the emotion. The inability to do so rendered it a threat. A heavy, cold lump. A burgeoning mutation.

Leigh noticed Ben's abandoned marshmallows, discarded in the fire. She picked up the clothes hanger and withdrew it. The marshmallows were shriveled, ashy black, still toasting within a fidgeting flame. She watched the blackening metamorphosis for several seconds, sad and entranced, then mustered a breath and extinguished the tiny flame.

AFTER BREAKFAST, they decided on a hike.

Fresh air seemed to be the answer for the unresolved tension between them. And she liked being outdoors with Ben. He knew so much about nature—the plants, animals, mushrooms, bugs, rocks. There would be plenty to talk about in the woods.

Pines and alders and the occasional sycamore kept the shadows plentiful on the ground. Above, sunlight speckled the foliage. Everything smelled fresh. Earthy. Their feet crunched on dried pine needles. Either side of the trail was thick with overgrowth. Birds fluttered in the branches, filled the air with a mix of songs. For the first time since the trip began, or maybe in weeks, Leigh felt peace.

"If you see a junco, will you tell me?" Leigh asked. "I don't think I've ever seen one."

"Sure," Ben said.

"It would be a shame to be at Junco Creek and not see a single junco."

"If you're meant to see one, it'll happen."

"What do you mean?"

"Scoutmaster Mike had this guy come talk to the troop, a Native American named . . ." Ben stopped. "Well, I forgot his name. But he talked about how animals appear to you when you need to learn a lesson. Spirit animals."

"How do you know if an animal you see is a spirit animal and not just an animal?"

"You just know," Ben said, and stopped walking. "Hey, look at this."

He left the trail, veered around some plants, and bent over a small decomposing animal, covering his lower face with the collar of his t-shirt. Leigh walked toward Ben, holding her nose. The dead animal's eyes were gone. Thousands of maggots writhed in the remaining fur, working on the dead tissue. The sight made her stomach clench, but it was too engrossing to look away.

What remained looked like a beaver or some sort of gigantic chipmunk.

"What is it?" Leigh asked. "Or what was it?"

"I mean . . . for where we are, I'm going to guess that it's maybe a marmot . . ."

"What's a marmot?"

"It's like a fat gopher-type animal . . . or kind of like a beaver, without the big tail."

Ben leaned closer, as if it was the first time he was seeing active decay up close and every detail was being scrutinized and memorized. Leigh left him to it, unable to stomach the sight of the maggots any longer.

Ben joined her a minute later, back on the trail.

"That was absolutely disgusting," he told her.

"It's disturbing to see anything in that state," Leigh said.

"You mean death?"

"Yes."

Ben shrugged.

"It's all a cycle," he said. "That kind of death, anyway. More like a change."

"What? Marmots don't have an afterlife?"

Ben barely smiled at her attempt at a joke.

"Circle of life or whatever. Dead marmots feed the maggots and then the soil. Become plants. And feed more things. The marmot changes into something else."

"I like that," Leigh said. "Constant change."

After she said it, she immediately vetoed the statement in her mind. She didn't like change at all. It caused Ben to pull away from her.

You've changed.

Leigh heard cracking branches to her left. Heavy breathing. She stopped cold.

Ben stopped as well, squinting through the clusters of shrubs.

"It's a black bear," he told Leigh.

Leigh's stomach twisted. "A bear?"

"Yes, but don't worry. They rarely attack people."

The comment did not reassure Leigh. Maybe it was the bear's unexpected presence, but the surroundings, which had seemed so tranquil only minutes before, were suddenly bereft of bird song and sparkles of sunlight. The hair on the back of Leigh's neck bristled.

The bear came into view, maneuvering around trees. It headed straight for them.

Ben stood tall, facing the bear, and waved his arms in the air.

"Hey, Bear! Go on! Piss off!" Ben yelled.

The bear did not stop.

"Ben," Leigh said.

"Stay calm and don't run," Ben told her. "Stand tall. It's just testing us."

Leigh stretched herself out, tried to make herself tall, but she felt smaller than ever. Like her spine was made of dough.

The bear took a few steps back and gnashed its teeth. Stood on its back legs.

Ben yelled again, waving his arms. "Get out of here!"

Suddenly, the bear returned his weight on all fours and charged, heading straight for Ben.

Stunned, Ben jumped out of the way and rolled. The bear didn't stop. Instead, its gaze homed in on Leigh, barreling toward her.

She backed up. Straight into a tree. Instinctively, Leigh covered her face with her arms and closed her eyes, not moving.

The stench of the bear struck her first. Beastly. Foul.

A blur of hot, fiery pain slashed through her above her right breast.

Leigh screamed and fell to the ground, curling into a ball. She braced for another strike, for a chunk of flesh to be ripped from her body.

Instead, the bear let out a pain-infused roar. She heard it stagger backward.

When she turned to look, she saw Ben holding a bloody hunting knife above his head.

The bear snarled again, lunging at him, and Ben brought the knife down once more, this time stabbing the bear in its right shoulder. The animal let out another painful roar and then turned away, barreling back through the woods.

Ben hurried over to Leigh, still clutching his knife.

"How bad did it get you?" Ben asked, examining the bloody tear in Leigh's shirt.

Leigh peeked down at the wound. It was too bloody to determine the actual damage.

"I don't know," Leigh said.

Ben grabbed her hand and pulled her up off the ground.

"Let's get out of here in case it comes back."

Although bloody, the claw marks weren't deep. She'd had worse encounters with kitchen cutlery. She cleaned out each gash, added some disinfectant, and taped a thick layer of gauze over the mess.

It wasn't until she was putting away the first-aid kit that it sank in how close she'd come to being ripped apart by a bear. The whole thing seemed surreal.

She thought of Ben holding the bloody knife above his head.

Like some primeval force had overtaken him.

Thank god it had.

When she exited the bathroom and walked back into the living room, she found him sitting on the couch, staring up blankly at the knotty pine wall.

"Are you okay?" he asked. "Do you need to go to the hospital?"

"Actually, it's not that bad," she told him. "There was just a lot of bleeding."

She sat on the couch and sighed, feeling abruptly exhausted now that the adrenaline was waning.

"It's so strange that a black bear attacked you," Ben said. "Black bears never do that unless their cubs are threatened."

"Maybe there were cubs."

"No," Ben said. "There weren't. It was a male."

"Maybe it was just me it didn't like," Leigh said.

Without warning, like the bear, Ben lunged, wrapping his arms tightly around her. He squeezed her, burying his face into her neck.

Leigh hugged him back tightly.

"I'm okay, Ben," she told him again. "Really. Thanks to you."

"I think we should leave," Ben said, finally loosening his grip. "Even if you're not that hurt, you should see a doctor."

"Let's get packed up then," she told him.

Ben stood up and hurried down the hallway, leaving Leigh alone to process. Their time may have been cut in half, but at least the attack had brought them together in a way that the cabin and roasting marshmallows could not.

Maybe this would help mend things between them.

Beneath Leigh's bandage, her skin began to crawl.

She rubbed her hand over the spot until the sensation went away.

It was midafternoon when Leigh locked the front door and placed the key next to the old wooden owl statue on the porch instead of beneath it. She couldn't bring herself to touch the owl.

"I think it's going to rain," Ben said, looking up through the pines.

Leigh descended the porch steps and looked upward. Gray clouds congealed, blotting out the pale blue sky.

"Hopefully, we'll beat the rain," she said.

Together, they walked towards the car.

"Hey, there's one," Ben said, pointing to a small bird with a black head and brown body. It perched on a spindly sapling branch only a few feet from them.

The bird was unimpressive compared to a blue jay or a cardinal, but there was something honest about its presence.

"That's a junco?" Leigh asked.

"Yep," Ben told her. "I guess you got to see one after all."

Leigh watched the bird quietly. Its dark eyes stared back at her. Pure.

"Leaving?" a gravelly voice blurted out of nowhere.

Leigh and Ben jumped and looked over to see Douglas Sable standing a few feet away. Leigh had not heard or seen him approach. He wore a charcoal gray t-shirt. The same grungy, black jeans and boots. Dark colors. Perhaps he'd blended into the shade.

"Yes . . ." she said.

"The lease is for the week," Sable said.

"A bear attacked me this morning," Leigh said. "On a hike."

She pulled down the collar of her shirt to reveal part of the bandaging.

"We have to go to the hospital," Ben added.

"Of course," Douglas Sable said. "There's an urgent care center in the next town over."

Although the information was helpful, his voice was void of concern.

Leigh wanted to mention a refund, but the domineering gleam in Sable's amber eyes made the hairs on the back of her neck stand up. She was filled with the overwhelming urge to flee.

She nudged Ben toward the car.

"Bye," Leigh said. "Thank you."

Douglas Sable muttered something, although she couldn't make out the words beneath the rustling of the wind in the pines. A storm was definitely blowing in. They might not even make it to town before the first drops fell.

They climbed into the car, and Leigh automatically locked the doors.

"That guy gives me the creeps," she said.

She jabbed the key into the ignition and turned. The car wouldn't start.

"Seriously?" Ben said from the passenger's seat.

Leigh tried several times. Nothing.

"Shit."

She popped the lever for the hood and climbed back out of the car. Ben followed.

"Car trouble?" Douglas Sable asked.

"Yes."

She propped open the hood and studied the car's innards. Ben stood by her side.

"Battery?" Sable asked.

"The battery isn't old," Leigh told him.

"Did you leave a light on in the car?"

"No," she said. "I don't think so."

"Let me have a look," Sable said, walking to the front of the car.

Leigh stepped aside. Ben backed away, wiping grease onto his shorts. They exchanged a quick, uncomfortable glance with one another.

Douglas Sable stooped beneath the hood and prodded. The faded tattoos on his forearms—the snake coiled around a rose on one and the feather on the other—writhed as he tinkered with Leigh's car.

"I see what it is," he said, seconds later.

"What?" Leigh asked.

"You got some wires that've been chewed through."

"By what?"

"Marmots most likely," he told them. "They like to climb up into the engine block. They're addicted to the taste of antifreeze."

"But that's poisonous," Leigh said.

"That don't stop 'em. Fat little bastards can't get enough of the stuff," Douglas Sable told them. "You'll have to get a tow truck up here."

"Our phones don't have service."

"I know." His amberish eyes glinted despite the stifled sunlight. "No one has service up here. I've got a landline."

Leigh took in a deep breath, completely vexed by the situation. She in no way wanted to walk with Douglas Sable to his home to use his phone. His presence made something recoil inside of her. His smell alone was unpleasant. A mix of sweat and earth and something animalistic. The way a large dog smells in the summer when it's long overdue for a bath. The stench was bold and familiar and made her pulse quicken.

"I can drive you to urgent care," Douglas Sable continued.

He removed the rod propping open the hood and let it slam shut. His hand glided up and massaged his own shoulder, as if soothing a pained muscle.

Despite her silent aversion, Leigh heard herself say, "I guess we—"

"It's all right," Ben said. "We don't need a ride."

Ben's face remained wan and glistened with sweat. He did not take his eyes off Douglas Sable.

"My dad will be here soon," he said. "He can help us."

"Oh," Sable said, giving Leigh's ring finger a hard glance. "I didn't realize you were married."

"Separated," Leigh said, but she followed Ben's cue. "But Ben's right. Russ is meeting us here today. In a few hours. He can help us fix the car situation and drive me to a doctor."

Douglas Sable stopped rubbing his shoulder. He brushed a strand of bristly gray-and-white hair from his forehead and stepped away from the car.

"All right then." He took a few slow steps backwards. "If you need anything, my house is right down the way."

"Thank you," Leigh said.

She didn't take her eyes off him as he walked back down the road in the shadows of the tall trees. Leigh was once again unsettled by how large and muscular he was for a man his age. He seemed younger than he had been only days before. Maybe he wasn't as old as she originally thought. Maybe it was only his silvery hair and dark, sun-scorched face that made him seem older.

After a dozen feet, Douglas Sable looked back over his shoulder, directly at Ben.

He winked.

When she glanced at Ben, the boy had lost all color in his face.

🐾

"Goddamn marmots," Leigh said, once they were back inside the cabin.

"It wasn't a marmot that messed up the car," Ben said.

"What do you mean? You think *he* cut the wires?"

"I know he did."

"How do you know?"

"Did you notice how he was rubbing his shoulder?" Ben asked.

"What about it?"

"Do you remember where I stabbed the bear yesterday?"

An image of Ben flashed through her mind, the knife going into the bear's shoulder. She remembered the animal's pained roar. And then the animal's smell.

It was Douglas Sable's smell.

"That's—" She stopped herself from using the word *crazy*. "That's not possible, Ben. People can't turn into animals. That's folklore. Myth."

But even as she said it, she believed Ben. She knew it deep down.

A burning itch blazed beneath her bandage. Perhaps agitated by her sweat.

"Regardless, we need to get out of here," she said. "I don't feel safe with him around."

"It's miles and miles back to the base of the mountain, Mom," Ben said. "It will take us a day to walk back to town. Especially if it storms."

"There were other cabins, right? Maybe there are people nearby."

"The other rental cabins were empty," Ben told her. "And there weren't any other houses. Only Douglas Sable's house."

Leigh suddenly realized how intentional it all was. Luring tourists way up a mountain surrounded by acre after acre of nature. Renting only one cabin at a time and leaving the others empty. Junco Creek was a place where people could easily vanish without a trace.

Douglas Sable was toying with them—prolonging the death of his prey for fun.

Even if they ventured out during the storm to make a run for it, they'd never make it back to civilization before dark, and she did not want to be anywhere out here in the night. Not with him prowling the woods. At least the cabin provided some sort of protection. Walls. A locking door. Sable would have a key, of course, but a shelter was better than being hunted in the night by an animal.

"We'll wait until the morning," Leigh told Ben. "At dawn, we'll leave."

※

THE STORM ROLLED in an hour later and continued into the evening. Thunder rattled the cabin. Rain and the occasional pine cone pounded against the old, shingled roof.

Ben had thought to haul several pieces of firewood from the woodpile to the front porch so they could keep a fire going through the storm. It was the only thing that kept them calm—watching the flames, tending to the fire—even if it made the cabin entirely too warm.

By the time the weather tapered to a steady rain after nightfall, Leigh felt dizzy. Her body temperature had steadily climbed over the past few hours, and sweat oozed from every pore. Infection. Her body crawled with it. It ate her up from the inside.

To fill the silence, Leigh tried to tell Ben about a movie she saw recently, but she was having a hard time describing it, and he only looked at her as if she was speaking gibberish.

"You aren't making any sense," Ben finally told her and placed the back of his hand on her forehead. It felt like a cold stone against her skin. "Mom, you're burning up."

She was sitting too close to the fire, wrapped in a blanket. One minute she was insufferably hot, baking in front of the flames, the next she was so cold she wanted to crawl inside the fireplace.

"Maybe your wound got infected or something. What's it look like?"

Leigh hadn't checked on it since that morning. She was afraid to inspect it. The four claw marks felt like living organisms, eating away at the flesh beneath the gauze.

"Maybe I should look at it," Ben said.

"No."

"Well, take some Tylenol and drink a lot of fluids. Keep your fever down."

Ben vanished and then reappeared with a bottle of water and pills.

Leigh could barely keep her eyes open long enough to place the pills in her mouth and swallow them with a few sips from the water bottle.

"You need to lie down," Ben said. "You need to sleep."

He helped Leigh to her feet, pulled her left arm over his shoulder and wrapped his right arm around her waist. They ambled together down the hallway, back to the bedroom she'd been staying in. Leigh fell onto the bed, still wrapped in the blanket. She suddenly needed to be free of its suffocating grip. She kicked and thrashed, but it was tangled all around her. Ben pulled it off and laid it beside her.

"Go to sleep, Mom. I'll wake you up if anything happens."

Leigh's head found the pillow.

Slowly, her mind melted into a feverish slumber.

"Mom," Ben said. "Wake up."

He shook her. The whole world seemed to move beneath her.

Leigh opened her eyes, but all she saw was darkness.

"Mom?"

"What?"

Her tongue was completely dry. A crusty lump in her mouth.

Ben stopped shaking her.

"There's somebody under the cabin."

She had no idea what he was talking about. There were colors in the darkness, swirling all around her, or inside her. She couldn't discern what was inside her mind from what was outside. She wanted to blend in with the colors, melt into them.

There was a massive thud, coming from somewhere below.

"Did you hear that?" Ben whispered.

"It's the bear," Leigh said, and drifted back into the swirling colors.

"It's *him*, Mom."

She felt herself pulled back into the mess of swirling blues and pinks and oranges. Swimming through them, diving deep down into a gyre of churning hues.

"Mom!"

Leigh's arms thrashed out in front of her, reaching for Ben.

He wasn't there.

"He's coming through the front door!" Ben screamed.

His voice was somewhere in the dark, far away.

Her boiling brain struggled to put something sensible together. The stench of her own sickness and sweat hit her nose. She moved her legs, rolled onto her side, and pushed herself upward into a sitting position.

Ben screamed.

The sound brought Leigh to her feet, sending her stumbling toward the bedroom doorway. There was light coming from the living room, and she moved down the hallway, bracing herself against the wall, toward the pale luminescence, the swirling colors dissipating as the darkness receded.

Something crashed. Shattered.

Reality was soft, like a wet oil painting. Surreal. Disordered.

In the firelight, she saw Ben, holding up what appeared to be a piece of firewood, fending off a beast near the small dining area. Leigh strained to see, to understand what was happening. The beast was Douglas Sable, naked, with his silver hair reflecting the flickering firelight. The next second, he was an animal unlike anything Leigh had ever seen, covered with thick, bristling fur, its growls filling the room.

"Ben!"

Ben saw Leigh and made a run for her. Leigh watched in slow motion as Ben tripped on the shabby rug on the living room floor. He seemed to swim through the air. He floated downward, his forehead crashing into the long edge of the stone fireplace before his body finally thudded on the floor. In the light, she saw blood stream from Ben's head, filling her with an electric sensation.

She started toward him, only to see the Douglas Sable-creature lunge toward her, its claws poised to slash. A nerve-splitting roar, like a mountain lion on fire, filled the living room, sent Leigh stumbling backwards. She fell onto the hearth, nearly toppling into the fire.

Beneath her fingers, Leigh felt something sharp and metallic. In the maelstrom of her fever, she remembered the marshmallows from the night before, watching them distend and blacken with flames. Time drifted around her, illusory and viscous.

The monstrosity came at her again on two legs, its fur scintillating in the firelight, its presence a confusing blur of teeth and fur and growls.

She grabbed the straightened wire hanger and brought it around in front of her just as the gnashing face descended.

Leigh felt the pressure in the hanger give as it pierced the animal's left eye.

The shrill, fiery shriek filled the cabin once again, more ferocious than before.

She thrust the hanger as far as it would go, shoving it deeper into the creature's brain. The monster let out another scream, this one more human than animal. It stumbled backward and crashed onto the coffee table. The floorboards vibrated beneath her feet as the table fell apart beneath the beast's weight and sent the monster crashing to the ground.

Leigh closed her eyes, feeling as if she might faint.

The crackling fire was the only sound in the room other than her own panicked breathing.

The colors were still there, swirling, but she didn't let herself melt into them.

When she reopened her eyes, Douglas Sable was on the floor, completely naked. The hanger jutted out of his eye, pointing straight toward the beamed ceiling. The sight of it did not belong in reality. She was unsure if any of it was actually happening, or if she was still swimming deep down inside a dream.

Leigh fell to her knees next to Ben. She shook him. Wiped blood from his forehead.

Ben's eyes stayed closed, but she could feel his chest moving. He was breathing.

She stood upright, but she could not feel her legs. She could not feel much of anything, except for a horrible slithering sensation inside her. It scurried through her veins like a million fire ants, urging her to vacate her body entirely. Tear off her own flesh to the bone.

Some sort of change was happening inside of her. Unstoppable. She moved away from the fire, toward the front door. And then she was out in the night, everything still wet with rain. There was no moon. The trees made dripping sounds in the darkness. The blaze inside her skull burned hotter, and the colors were more vivid. Blues, violets, greens smearing around her. Directly above her heart, her wound throbbed, forcing more of its poison through her blood. The change was happening.

THE NEXT MORNING Ben found Leigh lying along the bank of Junco Creek.

She'd ripped off her shirt and bandage during the night, and her exposed, festering gashes attracted flies. Ben brushed them away, covered Leigh up with her shirt, and shook her awake.

Leigh stared up at him. There was a bloody lump on Ben's forehead. She didn't understand why it was there. Beyond him, sunlight was streaming through birch leaves, glistening in his hair. It was the most beautiful thing she'd ever seen. The sound of the creek chattered directly next to her head in urgent, fluid sentences.

"What am I doing here?" she asked.

"You had a fever."

"What happened to your head?"

"I think I fell."

She sat up, clutching her shirt to her body, hiding her wound. Ben turned around, and she put her shirt on, not noticing it was backwards.

"I'm going to take you back to the cabin," Ben said. "Do you think you can walk?"

Leigh took a deep breath and stood.

Her feet were leaden. Her head was both light and pulsing.

They walked in silence, out of the trees, slowly up the muddy slope back to the cabin.

He helped ease her down onto the porch swing and went inside. He returned moments later with a bottle of water and a wet rag to clean her wounds.

"I'm going to walk to his house," Ben told her. "To call the police and an ambulance."

"Okay."

"Don't go inside. Just stay here."

"Okay."

Ben kissed Leigh on the forehead and left her. She heard his footsteps smacking on the wet dirt road behind her as he ran toward Douglas Sable's house, somewhere down the way.

Leigh closed her eyes and leaned back into the old porch swing. The chains holding it up let out a rusty melody. She vaguely remembered the events of the night before. An animal attack. Douglas Sable. She remembered the wire hanger sticking out from his eye, but none of it seemed real. Part of her wanted to go back into the cabin and see for herself, but mostly it felt like a dream that would dissipate as more minutes ticked by.

Instead, she remained on the porch swing, swaying with her eyes closed.

There was a loud fluttering sensation nearby.

Leigh opened her eyes, startled, and saw a bird flutter through her periphery and land on the porch railing, only an arm's length away. It was brown and black with dark eyes. A junco.

It studied her, and she stared back, consumed by its presence.

In those brief seconds, amid her sickness and confusion, Leigh felt a blooming convalescence deep in her heart, beneath her wound.

In the blink of an eye, the junco flapped its wings and flew away.

S.E. DENTON BEGAN STASHING Stephen King and R.L. Stine books under her mattress in middle school and grew into a lifelong horror junkie. Recently, Sarah transitioned into a career in product design. She writes fiction on the side and lives in Los Angeles with her two cats and some plants. You can find her on Twitter @InfiniteDent.

Illustration by P.L. McMillan

A Fistful of Murder

Lindsey Ragsdale

KILL.

It was written in the middle of the bill with a thick, red marker. I only saw it for a moment as the cashier counted out a stack of tens for my change. She said nothing; if she saw it, she was extremely good at pretending she hadn't. The red letters disappeared into the middle of the pile as she tapped the small bundle on the counter and handed it to me.

"Sixty dollars, in tens, cash back. Do you want a bag?"

I only stared at her. "What?"

"Do you want a plastic bag for your purchase?" She tore the receipt from the machine before folding it into thirds and holding it out to me along with the bills. I didn't move. My eyes were still fixed on the cash in her hand. She paused and set the receipt and money on the glossy countertop. Then she glanced up at me, eyebrows raised, and her smile began to dim.

"No, that's okay, thanks," I mumbled.

She turned away a second time.

I contemplated shuffling through the bills to verify if I had actually seen what I'd only glimpsed before. I didn't know what I would've done, however, if I'd fully inspected the bill. Even the one small peek at the red letters had caused the hair to raise all along my spine and my pulse to throb in my throat. It was unnerving because I didn't know where this burst of feeling could've possibly come from. I prided myself on being a fairly level-headed, unflappable human being. Always had. I decided to fold the bills and slip them into my jeans pocket.

The cashier was saying something, and I managed to catch the end of her sentence. "Did you want me to put some extra oxygen in here for your little guy? We don't recommend waiting longer than an hour before you put him in your aquarium tank."

"It's fine," I replied, holding up the plastic bag and gazing at my new angelfish. She was drifting in the water-filled, tubular plastic bag, flitting to each corner and exploring her temporary prison. Her silver and black scales rippled as I carefully supported the bulging bag with my left hand. "I'm going straight home after this."

"Well, thanks for stopping by, and we'll see you next time." The transaction completed, my cashier left her post and disappeared into the almost-empty PetSmart aisles.

I eyed her register warily. Did I really see that red word scrawled on a simple bill? Where had it come from? Or perhaps I was imagining things.

I was probably fretting over nothing. The uneasy feeling passed, each tense muscle in my body relaxing more with every step that carried me through the doors and out into the sunshine.

THE INCIDENT HAD FADED from my memory by the time I stopped for a quick bite on my way home twenty minutes later. The first Saturday of the month was my official errand day. After loading the car with groceries, buying craft supplies for my wife, and picking up the newest resident of my freshwater aquarium, I decided to treat myself. My indulgence, when I was alone, was greasy, comforting fast food. There was a spectacular hot dog place several miles away from the PetSmart, and after two circuits of the parking lot, I finally spotted a car backing out. What luck!

I turned off the engine and patted my pockets. Everything seemed to be in place. I glanced over at my angelfish, bobbing about in her bag in the passenger seat, which I'd placed inside a shallow box for support. She seemed a bit listless, and I reminded myself to be quick. The sooner I got her home and into her new aquarium, the better.

As I got out of the car, stuffing my keys in my back pocket, my mind was filled with thoughts of the menu. A familiar internal dialogue began. *Should I get the Cleveland Dog again? I got that last week. Maybe a classic Chicago dog, hold the neon-green relish? Hell, maybe I'll get two. Why not? My reward for a busy day.*

I stepped up to the ordering window. Fatso's was a small hotdog stand with window service and outdoor seating. Though paint peeled off the bricks and weeds sprouted freely from cracks in the asphalt, the place was famous for its delicious hot dogs, and rarely did one wait in line for less than five minutes. Families and friends enjoying the late summer day sweltered at tables in the sun, mouths full of fries, meat, and soda.

The man in front of me got his order and stepped to the side. I nodded to the familiar face in the window. "Hey, Marty," I said, greeting the skinny teenage boy standing behind the register. I was a regular and knew all the cashiers by name.

"Hey, Dave," the kid replied. "How's it going?"

"Can't complain, now that I'm here. You guys seem busy, huh?"

Marty shrugged. "I think people weren't expecting such a nice day, but when the sun came out, they decided to do the same."

I smiled. "Guess so. Hey, I'm getting two Chicago dogs, no fries this time."

"Hold the relish?"

I nodded sagely. "Yep, you know me well." I reached into my

pocket for my wallet and pulled out my Visa card. "Some extra napkins too, please."

"Oh, sorry, Dave, our card reader's down. Crapped out about an hour ago, and our repair guy's stuck in traffic." Marty inclined his head towards a handwritten sign on which someone had hastily scribbled CASH ONLY, SORRY.

"No problem," I said, reaching into the bottom of my pocket. "I usually don't have any cash, but I happen to have a few bills today."

"Twelve-fifty," Marty called over the counter as he stooped to unwrap a fresh pack of napkins.

I dug out the small wad of bills and thumbed two tens off the top. They were slightly sticky. I'd have to wash my—

KILL.

Again, those letters flashed by, and before I could register them, the top bill covered them up, but not entirely. A hint of red peeped out from around the edges, almost daring me to uncover the words—the words I still couldn't quite believe I'd read.

Before I knew it, my fists clenched of their own accord, and the backs of my eyes went hot. My mouth dried up in a flash, and my vision swam for an instant before becoming sharper and more focused, every pockmark and scratch of the counter before me outlined in precise lines. What was happening? I stumbled forward, almost landing on my knees in the gravel as my hands scrabbled at the edge of the counter for balance.

I'd never been a violent person. Never gave anyone the finger who brake-checked my car on the highway. Never ran my mouth when dealing with long wait times and unhelpful customer service representatives. I couldn't even watch medical dramas because the blood made me queasy. This feeling dredged up a memory that had been pushed into the back hallways of my mind until this very moment.

When I was eight years old, my dad used to watch boxing on Saturday afternoons, monopolizing the living room television with his sunflower seeds and six-pack of Schlitz. I wasn't allowed to sit and watch, but walking past the open doorway, I'd sometimes glimpse the fights on our grainy thirty-inch screen—and once, my timing was excellent.

I caught the very end of a round. A tall, hulking boxer with battered blue gloves dodged his opponent's jab then swung his gloved fist right into the man's jaw. Spittle spewed from the unlucky man's lips with an audible *thunk* of connection, like a steel-toe boot kicking a heavy grain sack. In that moment, my eight-year-old heart leapt with adrenaline and vicious glee, and my dad let out a crazed whoop. I'd stood in the hallway watching the slow-motion replay until the match cut to commercial, and my dad, noticing me, hollered at me to get the hell out.

Just like the fight I'd witnessed that day, those red letters on that bill ignited my rush of rage tenfold. I clenched my eyes shut, struggling to regain my balance. I was scared to open them—scared of what I'd do. My hands were itching to crush a soft throat, or snap an arm, with their steel grip.

"Dave, you okay?" Marty's voice cut into my consciousness. I didn't dare look up.

"Yeah, give me a second," I gasped.

"Geez, are you having a heart attack?" Marty's voice grew louder. "I think he's having a heart attack."

I opened my eyes just the slightest millimeter and stared at the gravel beneath my feet. As I took deep breaths, willing my thumping heart to slow down, a solitary ant wove its way slowly through and over the pebbles. Before I could think, my foot shot out of its own accord, my sneaker heel stomping downward. I ground the ant into the dirt.

My shoulders immediately relaxed. I was able to pry my fingers out of the tight fists where they had been starting to cramp. The sound of blood rushing in my ears began to subside.

A gentle hand touched my shoulder. "Sir, do you need an ambulance?"

I straightened up. I was flanked by two women with furrowed brows. All the people in the small outdoor eating area had turned to look at the weird guy crouched below the ordering window.

"No, thanks, I'm good," I wheezed. My face grew warm with

embarrassment. I hoped no bystanders would assume a flushed face was an additional heart attack symptom.

The women exchanged glances, and I could tell they didn't believe me. *Men,* I imagined them telling each other telepathically, *they never go to the doctor until it's too late.*

I stuffed the mess of bills and coins into my pocket, ignoring the few pennies that fell to the ground. Marty was staring at me.

"You know what, Marty, I'll pass on the hot dogs today. Maybe another time."

The women nodded, eyes soft with concern. *Like he needs a hot dog. Maybe this will be a wake-up call for him.* "Do you need us to call someone to take you home?" the shorter of the pair said. "Maybe you shouldn't be driving right now."

God, I knew these women were well-meaning, but a tide of crippling anxiety had rushed in to replace the rage. I just wanted them to go away and stop speaking to me.

"Really, I'm okay, but thanks," I mumbled as I turned away. They didn't respond, and I assumed they'd gotten the message. The background sounds of people eating and chatting resumed as I trudged back to my car.

Once behind the wheel, I locked all the doors before reaching into my pocket again. The sun shone hot through the windshield, and I could feel slick beads of sweat beginning to pool along my hairline. The heat was stifling, and I promised myself that I would start the car in just a moment. I couldn't deal with anything else before I faced the bill.

I pulled out the crumpled bunch of bills and began unfolding them one by one, slowly. I squinted my eyes until they were almost completely closed. Maybe if I shut them quickly enough, I wouldn't feel that wave, that urge of violence that came over me when I saw the red letters on the ten dollar bill.

First bill, nothing. I set it on the passenger seat.

Second bill, blank as well.

Third bill—

KILL.

The letters jumped at me, a crimson splattering across Hamilton's bland composure. A thirst for violence rose inside me like boiling oil before I remembered to squeeze my eyes all the way shut.

It didn't help.

I opened my eyes wide, keeping them focused on the steering wheel. My thoughts raced. *What if—oh God—what if someone were to knock on my car window, some concerned Samaritan from the hot dog stand asking yet again if I was okay, and what if I reached up, clutched their head in an iron grip, and forced my thumbs into their eye sockets—*

A slight shifting noise caught my attention, and I flicked my glance to the passenger seat before I could help myself. The water-filled plastic bag had slumped with the angelfish now moving around inside, wide awake. I looked right into its lidless, flat eyes and hated everything about it in that moment.

My hands, curled into claws, grabbed the bag and lifted it up. Now I knew what those horrified bystanders at Fatso's had felt like, powerless to do anything as they saw me keel over into the gravel. All I could do was watch. I dreaded and relished what was about to happen.

The poor fish began darting around the bag, fins flicking as it tried to find a place to hide, accustomed to the weeds and coral in an aquarium tank. My hands began to squeeze the bag slowly. Whereas the ant's death had been sudden, some twisted part of me wanted to draw this one out. Emotions that humanity had long ago resigned to the brain stem, through hundreds of years of social conditioning, were surging to the surface in a terrifying and thrilling rush. I was a predator to the fish but prey to this impulse of anger, rage, and violence.

Pressure built up inside the bag until the seams gave, and water began dribbling, then spurting out of holes torn in the stretched plastic, pouring between my fingers and wetting the seats and center console. A faint briny odor filled the car. The angelfish had run out of room and options and hung in the remaining space, which was getting smaller and smaller as more water gushed from the mangled bag. I had one last glimpse of silver and black scales, and that tiny, helpless eye, before I completely crushed the bag between my hands, pulverizing the poor creature within.

The entire ordeal took about thirty seconds—from nervous, to furious, to bliss. Relief crept in as I regained control of my body, followed by disgust and horror at the mess I'd made. I'd killed an innocent animal in the most brutal way possible! Angry tears sprung to my eyes, and I wiped them with my wet sleeve. I couldn't bring myself to look at the crumpled plastic bag discarded on the seat.

I wiped my soaked hands on the sides of my jeans, then, fixing my eyes on the dashboard, I blindly stuffed the mess of cash into my wallet—anything to hide those red letters burned into my memory. Seeing them would set me off again.

And I still didn't remember which exact bill contained the ominous word.

I started the car and slowly pulled out of the parking lot, flicking a guilty glance at the stand. No one paid attention as I cruised away, my shaking hands the only indication that anything cataclysmic had occurred only ten minutes before.

***

WHEN I PULLED OPEN the front door, the smell of fried onion and garlic smacked me in the nose. Martha was peeling carrots in the kitchen. "Hey, hon," she said, crossing the room to kiss me. "All done with errands?"

"Yeah," I responded, wrapping my arms around her waist and burying my face in her hair. I closed my eyes and inhaled deeply. "You smell so good."

"It's the garlic," she laughed, gently breaking my embrace. "Let me stir it before it burns." She glanced down at her apron, where I'd left a damp stain. Despite driving home with the windows down, my clothes and car interior had not completely dried. "Why're you wet?" she asked, dabbing at her apron with a dishtowel.

"Spilled some water in the car," I said in a rush. I'd thrown away the bag with the dead fish before coming inside. I quickly changed the subject. "You're making dinner already? It's not even three."

"Remember, we're going to Jodie's for dinner," Martha replied, taking up the knife and slicing the carrots. "It's potluck for Harry's graduation."

I snorted. "That's tacky."

Martha shrugged. "I don't care, I'll take any excuse to cook. I'm making black bean soup. Speaking of which, can you wash your hands and open those cans for me?" She nodded toward the counter where two cans of beans sat waiting.

"How was Fatso's?" she asked, picking up the knife and slicing the carrots into thin strips.

I shrugged, and after no response, remembered her back was to me. "I didn't go." *Should I tell her what happened?* I hardly believed it myself. Those letters were fading quickly from my mind.

"Huh," she said. "Were they closed?"

"No," I grumbled. "Didn't feel like hot dogs today."

The last thing I wanted was a million questions thrown my way. I could hear them now. *What exactly happened? Are you sure you're okay? Are you feeling dizzy? Does your chest hurt?* If I wanted all that, I would've just agreed to the ambulance in the first place.

By this time, my head was feeling clearer and my heartbeat was plodding along with its slower, familiar pace. For some reason, the afternoon's events already seemed like a hazy recollection, like the fragments of a dream right upon waking. The more I tried to grasp the urgency of that cursed bill in my wallet, and remember what I'd done to the angelfish, the further away the danger felt.

"If you want lunch, there are leftovers in the fridge," Martha said, breaking into my reverie. "Help yourself."

"Think I will," I said, opening the last can. I threw a container of last night's dinner in the microwave, and as it warmed up, dumped my wallet and keys on the table. I then ran back out to the car to fetch the shopping.

"Oh, did you get your new angelfish, like you were planning?"

Martha called as I stepped out the door, but I pretended not to hear her.

By the time I had my feet up on the ottoman, guzzling pesto pasta in the living room while watching a *Seinfeld* rerun, I was feeling almost completely normal, and had forgotten all about that ten-dollar bill.

"Beer?"

"Sure," I said, accepting the cold Coors can and cracking it open.

The graduation potluck was bustling. About thirty people were packed into a hundred square feet of Jodie's fenced-in backyard. Fairy lights dangled between bamboo poles, adding a warm glow to the slowly creeping darkness as the night set in. Solid shapes were a little fuzzy around the edges, but I couldn't tell if that was from the dim evening light or the beer I'd consumed. Probably both.

Martha's soup had been well received; on my fifth trip to the buffet table, I noticed a guest scraping the bottom of the serving bowl. The party guests had been ravenous. Only a few dishes sported remnants stuck to their sides. Just scattered crumbs remained on the dessert table. And everyone was guzzling the cheap beer like water.

"Dave," said a voice behind me. I turned and saw Chris with his wallet in his hand. "I'm making a beer run. You mind throwing in a few bucks? Didn't want Jodie and Brad to feel like they needed to pony up cash for the drunks."

I rolled my eyes. "Really? We guests brought all this food and they don't even have enough beer?"

Chris huffed sympathetically. "Yeah, I know, but I'd rather just get more to drink now—while I can still drive—than regret it later, when we actually *are* out of beer and I can't drive."

"Fair enough," I replied, reaching into my back pocket. The moment my fingers touched the leather, I froze. The afternoon's events rushed back into my mind, sending chills down my spine like cold lightning.

How could I have been so stupid, leaving the bill in my wallet? I couldn't open it up now. What if I saw the bill? Or gave it to Chris? What would I do to him? Or him to me? Maybe I was just being ridiculous.

Chris was watching my face drain of color. "You okay?"

"You know what?" I gasped through a dry mouth, "I don't have any cash on me. Just remembered."

"No worries," said Chris, turning away to pester someone else for beer money. "I'll cover you this time." As he walked away, he shot me a worried glance over his shoulder.

I stepped away from the crowd to think. Maybe when I got home, I'd pull out my cards, then throw the whole wallet away. It was a good wallet, though . . . no, I knew what to do. I'd close my eyes, pull out all the cash, throw it into the trash. Wait—what if I accidentally saw the red-splattered bill in the trash can? Okay, I'd close my eyes, pull out the cash, stuff it into an old sock, then throw the sock away. That sounded good. As soon as I got home.

I was mentally revising how much money I'd be out when Martha came over and slipped her arm around me. "How're you doing, hon?"

"Fine," I said, not paying attention to her. Most of the partygoers were milling over to one side of the backyard. Harry, who had just graduated from high school, was flanked by Jodie and Brad, his parents. He laughed as he sat down in a camping chair while Jodie turned to a side table with some wrapped gifts and a shallow wicker basket filled with graduation cards. She handed her son a gift bag while Brad took a photo. The other guests were chatting quietly, forming a loose circle around the family.

"People sure loved my soup. Did you see?"

"Uh-huh."

Harry reached into the gift bag and pulled out an envelope. He opened it up and took out a card, reading it aloud. It must have been funny—some people chuckled—but I couldn't hear what Harry had said. He spoke a few words and put the card aside.

"Oh, hey, don't worry about Chris. I gave him cash for beer, since you told him you were out. I forgot to tell you I'd taken some money from your wallet, but I didn't think I'd taken all of it."

"Yeah."

Harry was opening a new envelope. His fingers fumbled with the seal.

Then I processed what Martha had really said.

"What? You took money out of my wallet?" I stepped away from her, and my eyes must have been blazing with terror, which she interpreted as anger. She frowned at my reaction.

I was torn between concern and fear. Had Martha seen the bill and lashed out, like I did? Had she killed something . . . or someone? She hadn't left the house since I'd come home, and the place was spotless when we left.

Could she even read those four red letters? I thought of the young female cashier at PetSmart, counting out my cash with a cheerful smile. She hadn't clenched her fists or broken out in a cold sweat like I had when I saw the cursed bill. Perhaps women didn't fall under the money's spell? I had no way of knowing.

As I put the pieces together, Martha's voice, sharp now, cut into my stream of thought.

"Jesus, Dave, it was only fifty bucks. I could've sworn I left some in there—"

"What did you do with it?" I spat. My hands were starting to shake again. "Where is it?" My hand shot out towards the purse under her arm as she leaned back, eyes wide.

"I didn't rob you, for Chrissake. I needed some money for Harry's graduation card, so when you were in the shower, I took some out of your wallet. What's the big deal?"

Martha looked pissed.

A strangled scream tore my eyes from my wife, and I looked up just in time to see Harry springing out of his seat and lunging for his mother's throat.

LINDSEY RAGSDALE LIVES IN CHICAGO, writing grants for non-profit organizations by day and dreaming up horror stories by night. She loves to read, game, and cook in her free time. This is her first published story.

Illustration by Joe Radkins

ACKNOWLEDGMENTS

We the artists and writers of this anthology offer our love and gratitude to every member of HOWL Society for supporting both the development of this project and the growth of our community. Special thanks to Discord users Mantis Shrimp and Guolverain for bringing the hype, Anna, Asenath, Kips, Philippa, and The Left Reverend for beta-reading stories, Cheese Dance for developing our website, Mollyec for designing our graphics, and of course, The Sleeping Queen, for without her recruitment post on /r/HorrorLit and her ensuing creation of our Discord server, neither HOWL Society nor this anthology would have ever existed. And furthermore, we cannot forget Lord Mordi, a.k.a. THOT Father, who upon the hibernation of The Sleeping Queen dedicated his life to building and maintaining a place that we horror-lovers can call "home."

Furthermore, while the writers in *Howls From Hell* devoted countless hours to critiquing, copyediting, and proofreading one another's stories, we would like to acknowledge those specific individuals who volunteered further services toward the culmination of this project: Solomon Forse for overseeing the entire operation, Alex Wolfgang for formatting the book, Thea Maeve for managing our social media, Shane Hawk for championing our cause on Twitter and beyond, and both Joe Radkins and P.L. McMillan for taking on nearly all the artwork single-handedly.

Lastly, we would like to recognize those members of the greater horror community who have not only contributed to the success of this anthology but to the spirit of HOWL Society: Grady Hendrix, B.R. Yeager, Mercedes M. Yardley, Tim Waggoner, M.E. Bronstein, Thomas Tryon, Stephen Graham Jones, J.D. Horn, Laurel Hightower, Cina Pelayo, Ellen D. G., Surging Goremess, and Shane's grandma.

About the Horror-Obsessed Writing and Literature Society

HOWL Society, located on Discord, is the most active horror book club on the web. With hundreds of members, the club offers readers the chance to join a supportive community where they can enjoy books alongside other horror-lovers while engaging in meaningful discussions and forming long-lasting friendships. Aside from serving as an organized platform for discussing books, HOWL Society is also home to a tight-knit group of horror writers. Additionally, members can participate in tangential conversations about horror films, horror games, and much more. Because the club aims to provide equal access to all readers and writers around the world, membership is 100% free.

The Book Club

- No membership fees
- All club activity for HOWL Society takes place on Discord
- Each month, club members vote on the horror titles that will be read in the following month

About the Horror-Obsessed Writing and Literature Society

- The club reads one book per week, members obtaining copies of physical books, ebooks, or audiobooks according to their preferences
- Members are not expected to read every title
- Each book is separated into three sections and assigned to an individual channel
- Discussions for each section initiate on Mondays, Wednesdays, and Fridays at 12:00 p.m. EST
- During discussion, members use spoiler tags to ensure a safe discussion for those who choose to read at their own pace
- At the end of each discussion, members may participate in a survey to share a personal blurb which may later appear in the official HOWL Society review

Learn more at howlsociety.com.

Made in the USA
Las Vegas, NV
29 May 2021